VICTORIA BROWNE

I0685862

NOW
AND
THEN

Neville House Publishing

First published in United States in 2019
by Neville House Publishing

Paperback: 978-1-7335498-1-3
EBook ISBN: 978-1-7335498-0-6

Printed and distributed by
Createspace

instagram @VixBrowneAuthor
VixBrowneAuthor.com

NOW—LUCY

I never thought about living my life without her. The thought of being left behind pinches my soul every day, the "if only it had been me instead"—or at least "as well." Survivor's guilt, I'm told it's called. These quacks think they know it all, but they know nothing, none of them do.

I also dream. Sometimes she's there, sometimes she's not—but I always dream. Her voice is like mine. There are moments when I think I am actually crazy. Who wouldn't? Hearing voices in your head, hearing your own voice—yet it's not my voice. It's Laura's, isn't it? I'm so sure she's there.

THEN–LAURA

I'd never really thought about dying, not in the true sense of the word. My sister and I would joke about who'd die first: me, of course, because I was the oldest.

Lucy was my identical twin. We weren't much alike, but I liked that. Complications at birth meant that Lucy was born three hours after I was. She never liked the fact that I was older than her, and I was sure she had made it her life's mission to be better than me at everything because of it. But what happened to my little sister in the womb for those three hours without me? How did she, the younger sister, become so protective? Was it really medical complications that held her back?

Those were questions I eventually found the answers to, and then it was my turn to become the protective sister.

CHAPTER 1

THEN–LAURA

Cornwall, three years ago
May 21ˢᵗ

Leaving work, I headed east toward Union Street. I made my
way to the Union Tavern, where I was meeting Lucy and her
boyfriend, Ben. As I waited at the bar to be served, I did a quick
visual scan of the dark and dingy pub, but I didn't see either
of them. The old, cracked leather seat scratched the backs of
my bare legs as I perched on a bar stool, waiting. Eventually, I
ordered a beer from a boy I hadn't seen there before—he must
have been new.

Taking my drink, I found a table by the window. It was May,
and an early heat wave was sweeping the country. I was making
the most of the weather by wearing a light weight floral dress
and sandals. After all, it would no doubt be raining next week.
The door to the pub swung open, but it wasn't them.

"You waiting for Lucy, Laura?" Mike, the publican, called over.

I nodded and checked my watch—five forty-seven. We were
supposed to meet at five thirty.

The pub door swung open again, and in walked a few familiar faces, but not Lucy. Cornwall is where we lived, a town called Looe, in the south of England. We had moved there at the age of five from Torquay, on the English Riviera. I don't think my mum ever forgave my dad for making us move, even if it was for his work. She always said how she missed Torquay. I liked Looe. But then, I was only five when we moved, and I couldn't really remember much from Torquay. I did, however, remember my parents arguing a lot, so why my mum missed the place so much confused me.

I finally saw Lucy standing on the cobbled pavement opposite me, and I waved through the window. She hadn't seen me; she was looking at her phone, probably texting Ben. I admired my twin sister for a moment, wondering if I looked that pretty. Her blond, silky hair almost reached the top of her ripped jeans. She looked up, but not at me. She was watching for something down the street. Then I saw Ben reach her, and they embraced. I averted my eyes.

A moment later, they crashed through the door to the pub, laughing and touching each other like stupid schoolchildren.

I darted my hand into the air and waved. "Lucy," I called out. "Here—over here."

Seeing me, they approached speedily.

"Didn't you get me one?" Lucy pointed at my beer.

"No, I did not!" I said incredulously. "You earn more than me; get your own."

Lucy bent to kiss my cheek. "Want another?" she offered, and I shook my head.

Ben sat down on the other side of the table. "Hey, Laura."

He was wearing a small black t-shirt printed with the words "I WORK OUT—YOU CHECK ME OUT." I looked at his skinny arms and sharp, angled face, and wondered what girls saw in him. What did my *sister* see in him?

"Hey," I replied lightly, watching Lucy walk to the bar. "Letting Lucy get your drink again?" Ben's vacant stare made me wonder if he'd picked up on my obvious undertone.

Then he said, "You both look the same, but you're not the same, are you? You're fun, or so I've heard." He winked.

I didn't react. I knew his type, and I wished my sister wasn't with him. Even so, for Lucy's sake, I resisted the urge to smack his perverted face. Instead, I let the awkward silence linger for longer than most people could handle. Ben didn't seem fazed by this, and I was the one who started to fidget in my seat.

Finally, he got up. "Think I'll give Lucy a hand."

"Yeah, you do that." My tone felt slightly unnerved.

I scrolled through my Facebook feed, but nothing interesting jumped out at me. Marie, our best friend, was banging on about a holiday to Thailand, which we all knew would never happen—not on a McDonald's employee's salary, even if she *was* the manager.

Lucy's beer spilled as she set it on the table, making me look up. Ben threw down three packs of peanuts from behind her.

"You're not drinking and driving, are you, Lucy?" I gestured at her beer.

"One's fine," she said dismissively. "So how was work? Actually, don't answer that—I can't bear another story about Mrs. Adams and her psychic predictions."

I laughed.

"Has she ever gotten any right?" she asked.

"Well, she *did* say you would follow me to the ends of the earth." I placed my right hand over my heart and gave her an angelic smile.

Ben looked confused, but I wasn't going to explain.

Lucy rolled her eyes. "I, on the other hand, had my name put forward for a promotion at work. Exciting, huh? I need to apply for the position, but how good is that? It's like an extra £3k per year on top of my salary—if I get it."

"*When* you get it," I said encouragingly, trying to look excited. Let's face it, Lucy only worked in a sofa store.

But who was I to judge? At least my sister had a well-paying job with some sort of potential for a pay raise. I worked in Mystic

Journey Bookstore for the slightly insane. The latter wasn't part of the name, obviously—that was just what Lucy called Mystic Journey. I had worked there since finishing school and couldn't bring myself to leave. I practically ran the place with Ed, the owner, but there was no money for a pay raise. It baffled me how the store stayed open. I often joked that it was fate.

Lucy looked elated. "I'll get a company car as well. No more sharing Mum's beat-up Mini Cooper."

I nodded.

"Looking forward to tomorrow night, Laura?" Ben asked with his arm still draped around my sister's shoulder.

More so if you're not there.

"Yes," I said. Then I leaned in toward Lucy, and she toward me. Ben's arm fell away. "What if we wear the same outfit tomorrow?" I asked her. "What do you think?"

Lucy cocked her head.

"Oh, c'mon, Lulu," I whined. "We've not dressed the same since—"

"Since forever, Lulu," she butted in, repeating our twin nickname. Our dad had given it to us when we were five and wanted to have the same name. "It's our twentieth birthday, not our second."

I glared at her. "So you're fine with having the same nickname, just not the same dress?"

Lucy sat back into Ben's arm, and I watched him pull her close. "Come on, Lucy," he said, "do it for your big sis—look how happy she is."

I smiled sarcastically. The last thing I wanted was Ben coming to my aid, but it worked. Lucy's face morphed into a grin, and we were instantly sucked into our normal exchange of dialogue—talking fast, eye rolls, ums and ahs, face pulling, and inevitable sisterly bickering.

After a few minutes of ideas, Lucy held out her smart phone. "How about this one, then?" She had pulled up a picture of a size zero model wearing a tight black mini dress.

"Where's it from?" I asked, taking the phone.

"Topshop." She snatched the phone back. "Sorted. I'll get them on my lunch break tomorrow."

Ben stood. "Want another, Laura?" He pointed to my nearly empty pint glass.

Openly shocked, I said, "You're paying?"

"Do you want one or not?" His reply sounded more like a snarl than a question.

"OK, go on, then—a beer."

I knew Lucy would say something as soon as Ben was out of earshot. I didn't look at her.

"Laura, stop it, will you?" she whispered at me, checking over her shoulder. "Why are you being like this?" She pulled her sad face, which I absolutely hated. The corners of her mouth dragged down on either side of her chin, and she looked like a clown with no face paint.

"Sorry, Lucy."

"What is it about Ben that you don't like?" she asked. "Everyone else thinks he's great, and you know how much I like him. Are you jealous?"

The question made me recoil with laughter, much to Lucy's disgust. At school, it was no secret just which of the Whitcombe twins was the jealous one. My little sister had set that crown squarely on her own head.

"You're calling *me* jealous?" I replied. "You do remember the day you stole Matthew Kemp's ant farm and then emptied its contents into the bags of my three new school friends, don't you?"

Lucy glared at me. "You mean Jessie, Heather, and that dickhead Kitty Hollister? They plagued your life. They deserved it all."

"Yes, Lucy, but when six-year-old girls grow up to be the popular girls in high school, you're screwed—at least, I was. I'm not like you. I don't thrive on drama."

"What? I don't thrive on drama."

"Lucy, you locked Heather in a music room closet because she called me a dog in class. Then there was the time you put pepper in Jessie's water. I can't even remember why you did that."

"She pulled your hair in gym class. I was protecting you; you should be thanking me."

"You know, I'm sure they bullied me more because of your reactions."

"I doubt that."

We sat in silence for a moment.

"Lucy, come on now," I pleaded. "I'm not jealous of you and Ben."

"So why are you giving him such a hard time? Laura, I really like him. He makes me happy." She plunked her forehead down onto the wooden table.

"Lucy, stop acting strange." She didn't move. "Lucy! Stop—you're such a weirdo. Lift your head up." I was conscious people were looking, and I could see Ben picking up our drinks. "OK, OK—I'll be nice to Ben," I promised. I'd say anything to stop a scene. "There, now sit up and act like a normal human being."

She sat upright, smiling like a crazed person, and I couldn't help but laugh. My sister was completely nuts, and I loved her for it. She truly didn't care what people thought of her. Lucy only cared about Lucy—oh, and me. I was ninety-nine point nine percent sure that Lucy cared about me as much as herself, and that was why she was known as the jealous twin. In hindsight, "protective" would have been a more accurate word. No one—but *no one*—got to me without Lucy's approval first, so help them God.

"One beer for you," Ben said, handing me my drink, "and a Diet Coke for my princess."

I watched him kiss the crown of her head. Maybe I *was* being a little jealous. Sure, he was slow to get the drinks in and happy to let my sister pay for things, but what if that was the modern way? Equal rights and all that jazz. Not quite the perfect gent, but if he treated my sister well, wasn't that all that mattered? Anyway, Lucy had been with him longer than with any other boyfriend—five months. She hadn't even slept with him, and that was something for my sister. There was never a chance of my sister being used by a boy—more like her using *them*.

Rightly or wrongly, I decided to let up on Ben for Lucy's sake, give the guy one more chance. Maybe I had gotten him wrong; only time would tell.

We left the tavern relatively early. Lucy drove Ben home and then us. We were still talking animatedly about our pending party as we piled out of the car and through the front door. I heard the ten o'clock news playing from the TV in the front room. I could see the back of our dad's head through the crack in the nearly-closed door as he sat on the hideous faded blue leather sofa. He was alone—Mum must have been in bed already. Lucy and I both called out to our dad as we headed up the narrow stairs to bed, and he replied as he always did.

"Sleep tight, girls."

Lucy walked to her room, and I walked to mine.

Before we parted ways, she whispered, "Want to come read magazines in my room?"

Shaking my head, I asked her, "Do you want to take the car again tomorrow?" After all, she was sorting our outfits out.

"No, you take it." She found the keys in her bag and threw them across the hallway at me. "You need to get home fast to get ready; tomorrow's going to be so much fun." Her eyes were vibrant at the thought. "Night, Lulu."

I slipped quietly into my room.

Mindful that my mum was in the room next to me, I closed the door as softly as I could. It was pointless, really, because she had probably heard us coming up the stairs. I laughed to myself. We lived in a small, three-bedroom Edwardian house—or as our mum used to say, two bedrooms and one box room.

Lucy had moved into the box room not long after our eighteenth birthday. Luckily, she didn't turn out to be the collector in the family—that was me. My walls were decorated by shelves holding Enchantica dragons and fairies along with all kinds of crystals that Ed would let me take home from work. They also housed my collection of classic books, including full sets of *The Chronicles of Narnia* and the *Harry Potter* series, to name a few.

In the middle of the room, my clothes were still spread aimlessly across my floor where I had thrown them earlier, and I noticed a glass of juice that had started growing mold. I retched and moved the glass away from my bedside table.

After undressing and brushing my teeth, I got into bed and checked my phone. The brilliant white light illuminated the darkness and locked me into a familiar trance, and I started to scroll. Marie was still posting comments and asking questions about places to visit in Thailand. I found myself wondering if I would ever travel.

I often thought back to our family weekends away—to Wales, normally. Dad would drive, and Lucy and I would sing "She'll Be Coming 'round the Mountain," with Mum joining in if we sung the wrong words. Our family trips were fun when we all got along, when our dad's badly-timed jokes and comments that carried little to no context didn't irritate our mum, inciting one of her one-way screaming frenzies—or *flip-outs*, as we labeled them.

Still surfing social media, I clicked on the events icon. Forty-seven people had indicated "Going" in reply to the invite Marie set up for "The Whitcome Twins' 20th Birthday Bash." Nine had said "Maybe," and four "Can't Go." I looked through the "Going" list for people we might know. I knew it wouldn't be many, even if it was our party. The reason Marie had arranged the party in the first place was that we didn't have many friends.

In high school, we had made friends relatively easily at the start, Lucy with her loud personality and me being so agreeable, but they never lasted long. Lucy always managed to offend and argue with people, so little by little, no one spoke to Lucy. Of course, I stood by my sister—also ending up friendless. Our only friend was Marie, the one person who could tolerate Lucy. If there was one thing my sister and I did not share, it was her mean streak.

I recognized the majority of the people on the list, but they were Marie's friends—people we hung out with occasionally, people we had a good laugh with and even liked. Everyone knew people like that: acquaintances. Still, most people had acquaintances *and* friends. I—or Lucy and I—only had acquaintances. Did I care? To some extent, yes, but that was who we were. Me, Lucy, and Marie—it worked, and we were happy enough that way.

Even though the guests were all Marie's friends, excitement loomed inside my chest. All of her friends were so cool, and I loved hanging out with them. Lucy was right—tomorrow night was going to be so much fun.

A light knock on the door distracted me from my thoughts, and then the door opened.

"Thought you were sleeping," Lucy whispered, slipping into the room and closing the door behind her.

"I am." I sat up and switched on the bedside light.

Lucy jumped onto my bed, simultaneously crossing her legs. "How can you be asleep and liking things on Facebook?"

"I was about to go to sleep."

"Sure, sure."

"I was!"

She opened a copy of *Yo* magazine from my bedside table.

I snatched it from her and flipped through the pages. Shoes and makeup advertisements jumped off the glossy pages at us. I kept flicking.

"Oh, look." I jabbed a finger at an article. "Lizzy Inglewood— she's wearing the same dress we're getting."

Lizzy Inglewood had just won *America's Next Top Model* and was hot gossip for being blind, which Lucy thought was ridiculous and insulting to blind people, and that's what she told me with no uncertainty.

"How is it insulting?" I shook my head in disbelief.

"Because blind people, deaf people, and even dumb people should already be top models."

I giggled and repeated, "Dumb people."

"Dumb as in can't talk—you dummy." She pushed me off balance.

A noise outside indicated someone leaving the bathroom. Our eyes locked as my bedroom door opened.

"Girls." Our mum's head popped around my door, her voice measured. "Girls," she said, "I'm going to sleep now, so can you keep it down?"

"Sure, Mum," I replied. "Night."

She smiled and retreated.

"It's been well over a week," Lucy said quietly. "A flip-out is long overdue, and I'm betting it will be on our birthday."

"Lucy!" I scolded.

"What? You know it's true. Anyway, forget that. I see Marie invited Hollister to *our* birthday?"

I stared at her. "I told her to."

"What? Why? Laura, you're not still talking to her, are you? She tried to make you cry every day at school."

"And she's sorry." I gave Lucy a small kick from under the bedcovers that made her move away from me.

"Fine, whatever. It's your life."

"That's right."

Lucy smiled, edging back up the bed toward me. "Ben said Kitty asked him out, and he said no. She's so sad."

I found Lucy's statement hard to believe, knowing Kitty and the person she had become since leaving school, and I suspected Ben had just wanted to make Lucy jealous.

So insecure of him, I thought.

As if she could read my mind, Lucy asked, "Why don't you like him? He likes you; he told me he thinks you're really fun."

Fun! I wondered what type of fun he really meant by that statement.

"Oh, Lucy, it's not that I don't like him; it's just …" I searched for the right words. "He's very … confident. I just think sometimes people like that are hiding their own insecurities, you know? I just don't want to see you get hurt."

"And what if he isn't insecure? And so what if he is? Seriously, Laura, why don't you like him? For real? You said you would give him a break." She stood.

"Lucy, shh! Mum will hear."

"I don't care."

"You will—sit down," I hissed.

Lucy sat. I couldn't have answered her question if I had wanted to. I didn't know Ben Jones; no one did. He didn't go to our high school and seemed to have just popped into our lives one day and never left.

That day had been six months prior. Lucy, Marie, and I were all playing air hockey at the local cinema arcades, laughing and joking noisily. I hadn't noticed anyone at first, but then Marie nudged Lucy and pointed to a guy leaning against the slot machines. He was watching us play. Lucy, being Lucy, beckoned him over, and that was that. One month later, Lucy and Ben were exclusive. All we knew was that Ben Jones had apparently moved from London to Cornwall for work. However, he had no family here, and no friends—just a few lads he knew from the building site where he worked. He injected himself into Lucy's life a little too quickly for my liking, and I had never liked the way he became friendly with Marie's friends so readily. He knew some of them better than we did. There was something off about him, and it was like I was the only one who could see it.

"Look, Lulu, I'm sorry. You're right. I said I would give him a chance, and I will. I can't change my mind on him just like that, but I promise tomorrow I'll be on my nicest behavior." I smiled. "Maybe he will—"

"Show you what a perfect boyfriend he is?" Lucy finished.

"Yeah, something like that."

CHAPTER 2

NOW–LUCY

London, present day
May 21ˢᵗ

The guttering on the bedsit roof is broken, and I can hear rainwater pouring down into the unkempt back yard. I peer through the kitchen window into the night. I hear someone enter the kitchen behind me and turn quickly to see which resident it is, but I don't recognize him. I nod my head politely, and he nods back. I'm not in the mood for polite conversation; I never am these days. Especially not tonight, the night before our—my—birthday. I move quickly, retrieving my dinner from the stove and washing the pans I've used.

As I leave the kitchen, I hear the stranger wish me a good night, but I pretend not to hear. I make a mental note to buy more microwave dinners so that I don't need to use the communal kitchen as much. Plate in hand, I climb the old wooden stairs to Room 11—my room, and the place that I call home, at least for now. I can hear Priya and her loud, annoying friends in the room next to mine, music playing and girls giggling. I walk carefully. A pointless conversation with Priya's posse is the last thing I want right now. I've always been careful when choosing friends, and the gypsy girls that hang out with Priya definitely don't make the cut. I turn the key slowly in my door and slip inside my room, closing the door behind me—undetected.

My room is minimal, just a small wardrobe and chest of drawers that carries an older-than-legal microwave on top. I don't have any pictures hung, just the one that was on the wall when I moved in last year; it was left by the previous tenant to cover a large chip in the wall.

I eat sitting on my bed as I always do, staring at the badly painted vase of sunflowers; however, not even this hideous painting can top how ugly my life is right now. Maybe that's why I haven't thrown it out. Maybe the smudged oils remind me that not everything in life is perfect.

Memories dampen my appetite, so I swap my half-eaten plate of food for a bottle of vodka I have under my bed and take a long swig. The bitter taste doesn't affect me anymore. It feels smooth on my palate, and I like it. The liquid runs down the back of my throat and warms my chest. Closing my eyes, I lie down and think back to the day that Laura left me and the last time I heard her voice. My eyes are heavy, and I feel myself slipping in and out of consciousness. I try to keep her voice alive in my mind, frightened that I'll forget what it sounds like, but it's no good—I succumb to sleep.

"Lucy, over here—quick, look."

I turn. "What? What's wrong?"

Laura is pointing at a river that was hidden by some brambles at the bottom of our garden. I'd never noticed it before. I'm staring at her, staring at Laura—not the mysterious river. She is there, right in front of me. I reach out to hold her, and she giggles as we embrace. I hold her tight.

It's the same every time.

I feel myself turn toward the river and ask, "Where does it go?" I don't wait for her reply before climbing down the bank. Excitement now looms inside me, and I hold out my hand for Laura.

Ivy and other weeds strangle the flowers that creep along the bank. The water is dark and murky, and I feel it bubbling into my sneakers, but I don't care much. I start to walk. The river runs for what seems like miles behind little terraced houses standing at attention. I wonder if the river has an end, and if so, where. My mind dances with thoughts of a large reservoir and the possibility that if we keep walking, we might slip over the edge of a beautiful waterfall and plunge to our impending deaths.

"Lucy, wait." Laura's arm reaches out to stop me from stepping off the edge of the waterfall. "I'll find you. Don't go home ... Wait, I'll find you, Lucy ... Lucy ... Lucy ... Lucy?"

A loud bang on my door wakes me. I've slid off my bed and am collapsed in a heap on the floor next to my unfinished food. I reach for the bottle of vodka and take a gulp as another bang focuses my thoughts, accompanied by Priya's bellowing voice.

"Lucy!"

"Not tonight, Priya. I'm sleeping."

She bangs again. "Lucy, open up. It's just me—they've gone. Come on, let's have a drink together."

I check my watch—11:58 p.m. "Can't—got work tomorrow," I splutter.

I hear Priya laughing. "Bullshit. You told me they cut your hours yesterday. I know you're not working the morning shift. Open up!"

Against my better judgment, I open my door, and Priya stumbles in. She looks drunk.

"I only have this." I hold up my bottle of vodka, which barely has enough for one more glass.

In return, Priya holds up a bottle of wine. "Have some of mine, then." She smiles and sits on a wooden chair, the only chair in the room.

I watch as she pours wine into a pink mug and drinks it down as if it is soda. How did I get here? How did this type of girl become my friend? I take a swig of vodka and have a sobering thought. If Priya is "this type of girl," who am I?

"Cheers," she says, clinking the pink mug against my bottle.

Who am I to judge her? Who am I in general? A failure, that's who. Since coming to London, I've made bad decision after bad decision. When I arrived in South London a year ago, Priya was a stranger willing to help another stranger in her darkest hour, and for what? To sit in my room drinking wine with bitter old me.

"Cheers," I say back.

Whatever makes her happy.

My first two weeks in London were spent trying to find hostel accommodations or room shares, but that was harder than I naively thought. Most of the hostels had been expensive and full of backpackers suffocating me with happy adventure stories and eating through my cash, and the cheaper hostels were full of homeless thieves, as I found out on my third week.

With my backpack and all my belongings gone, I'd fallen to the floor of the hostel where I was staying, smashing at the concrete floor with the palms of my hands and sobbing like a mad woman. No one helped me; no one even looked at me. But then, my behavior wasn't actually that out of place there, so why would they? After all, I could have just as easily been another person tripping out on some bad drug.

After I'd stopped my antics, I looked up through damp eyes and saw Priya standing over me with her hands on her hips, frowning down at my sorry state. But I didn't want her help; I didn't want *anyone's* help. I was filled with spite.

"You finished making your noise?" she said.

I was angry. "Fuck off, you Packi," I retorted. Then I braced myself for a good kick, but it never came.

Instead, Priya retrieved something from the opposite bunk. She threw my backpack at me and left.

I rummaged through my bag. All my things were inside, minus my money, but that didn't seem as important to me at the time. I was still new to being on the streets, so I clung more tightly to pointless possessions like mascara or hand cream. I didn't realize then just how hard it would be to replace the stolen money.

"Hey." I got to my feet and hurried out of the hostel doors. "Hey!"

I found her sitting outside on the curb, smoking a cigarette. The ground was wet from rain.

"You're lucky I saw who took it," Priya said. "I'm not down with stealing from our own." She wasn't looking at me. "Don't leave your stuff alone again; it's not a hotel. People will take what they can."

I felt terrible for the racist comment I had shouted. I had been angry and just wanted to hurt someone.

"I'm sorry," I said feebly, hoisting my backpack onto my shoulder.

"Yeah, you are," she said, looking at me. "A sorry little bitch … What's up? Lost your fighting spirit now that we're outside?" She was now glaring up at me.

I took a step back, poised to run, but she laughed.

"I'm just messing with ya. Ha! Here." She patted the wet ground next to her and offered me a cigarette.

"I don't smoke."

"Of course you don't."

I sat. "What do you mean by that?" I asked, confused by her kind but hostile behavior.

She laughed again; she had a loud, piercing laugh. "If I thought you meant what you called me, I'd be happy to smash your face all over this pavement. But I don't—I was you once. Scared and pretending to be tough. You're lucky you said that to me. Someone else in this place would have cut you in the night for a comment like that." She nodded at me, and I nodded back. "Where you from, princess? Did ya have an argument with Mummy about pocket money?"

The mere mention of my mum enraged me. Hatred shook all my limbs, and I felt my face crumple into a nasty sneer. I can't recall what I said after that. Hot rage swept through my body, and my words polluted the air between me and Priya.

The next thing I remember is running across the road into a park. Priya must have caught up with me, because she held my shoulders and fixed her eyes on mine. I remember focusing on her lips and her muffled words.

"Breathe ... breathe."

To this day, she hasn't mentioned my mum again.

Sometimes I wonder how long it will last. Priya chose a life on the streets because it was better than living with a drunken, abusive father. But I didn't choose this life, I don't want this life, and I'll do anything to get out of it—anything.

"Pass me a mug with some of that nasty wine stuff," I say after finishing the last of my vodka.

Priya hands me a mug, spilling some on the trodden brown carpet. "So you going to tell me what's up?" she slurs.

"Nope."

"Is it because it's your birthday tomorrow?"

I swish the wine around in the mug Priya gave me. "Don't go there, Priya."

"Figured it wasn't that anyway," she says. "It's a good thing I know, then."

I look up at her.

"They're laying you off at the factory next week, yes? I know 'cause I heard that corporate bitch Jenkins talking in her office." She takes another sip of wine. "Said you didn't take it well. What did you do?"

"My mouth. You know what I'm like."

"What did you say, then?"

"I called her an inbreed, amongst other things." I suppress a laugh; Priya does not.

"Girl, you have a vicious tongue." Priya is now howling with unnecessary laughter, which grates against my soul. Tonight of all nights, I don't need this. I wait until she is finished.

"It's not like she can do much about it," I say. "Not unless she wants me to grass her up for employing immigrants—she's lucky I don't. And that's not because I care about her; I wouldn't do that to Paul or Hofstadt." I reach for my cigarettes and offer one to Priya. "Want to come downstairs with me for a smoke?"

We make our way outside. In the garden, I hold out a light for Priya.

"You smoke too much," Priya says, sucking on the white stick.

I nod. "And you're the one who got me hooked on the damn things."

It isn't raining hard anymore, but the gutter water is still overflowing, splashing at our legs as it falls onto the stone yard. We huddle close, swaying on the back doorstep under the awning.

"I can't go back on the streets, Priya. I can't."

"You won't. You'll figure something out; you always do."

I blow a cloud of frosty smoke into the night. "Not this time, Priya. I've applied for job after job and gotten nothing. The job market's flooded, and who wants me? I've not worked a sales job in over two years. I've been paid cash in hand for the last year, so according to them, I've been unemployed for a year. How do I explain that to a new employer? All I'm good for is factory work, and I'm not even getting callbacks for that. I'm fucked. And God knows where all the cash jobs have gone. I got rejected for a car-washing job last week! Priya, I'm going to lose my room if I don't find something fast. I need cash."

"You can stay in my room."

"Thanks," I say, "but you know the bedsit rules. If we get caught sharing, you'll be homeless too. No … this is my issue, not yours."

It's raining again. Priya jumps off the step, her arms stretched wide, and starts to spin on the spot.

"Priya, you're crazy." I laugh. "You're getting wet."

She stops spinning. "Don't matter anyway, bitch."

I look at her, waiting for her to talk crap about how we will win the lottery and buy a castle in Scotland like she normally does.

"Tell me, Priya, why doesn't it matter?"

"Because we don't really exist, do we?"

"Priya, what are you on about?"

"It's true—Hofstadt showed me an article about parallel universes. All the scientists are talking about it."

I shake my head. "About what?"

"About string theory. That's what it's called. Or is it the multiple universes?"

I know what she is talking about; physics was my strongest subject at school.

"Priya, you're talking crap."

She looks at me with conviction through the rain. "But what if heaven is the main universe, the one that makes all the other universes? And when we die, we just pop into another universe until we get it right. Then, when we get it right, we go to heaven."

I stare at her, motionless. She sounds just like her. This is the type of conversation I used to have with Laura—my measured arguments about the laws of the universe and her stupid notions about past lives and theories of the afterlife. I know Priya doesn't know what she is saying or the emotional impact her words are having on me, but she has unwittingly disturbed emotions that I'm trying desperately to keep at bay.

She moves in front of me. "Lucy? Lucy, what's wrong?"

"I'm going to bed. Don't follow me." I turn and walk inside. I hear her call my name, and I hope she doesn't follow. She knows me well enough to know when to stay away from me.

In my room, I rummage through my wardrobe, pulling out plastic bags filled with car radios, watches, phones, and other things that I've found or stolen, hoping to sell them for cash. I reach behind a bag of clothes and pull out an old cigar box.

Sitting on the floor, I open it. From inside, I retrieve a small, ripped piece of paper and read the words that I scribbled on it.

Wait. I'll find you. Be careful.
Don't go home.

I stare at my handwriting. It is written on a small, dirty piece of newspaper. I can't remember Laura's words that clearly anymore.

My mind drifts back to last year, when I started to drink more than normal with Priya. It was our way to forget our pasts. At first, it was fun. Even before the bedsit, when we lived in hostels and spent some nights on the streets, a small bottle of vodka got us through the night. It warmed our blood and made me laugh, and laughing is something I find hard to do without alcohol.

Priya's earlier words have shaken me because it has been so long since I've heard from Laura. And Priya sounded so much like her with ridiculous notions of afterlives. I'd written down Laura's instructions when her words started to become vague in my memory, no doubt from my increased alcohol consumption. How long does she want me to wait for her to explain why I can't go home? Not that I want to. I used to think I was better off without my family in my life, but now I think they are probably better off without me.

I place the paper back in the box. It has been three years since that dreadful day, and I miss my dad; maybe Laura was wrong. Maybe I should go back to Cornwall. As normal, I banish the thought. It is a foolish thought. I'll always miss my dad, but I can never go home now. I was a disgrace then; what the hell would he think of me now? No, home is never going to be an option, just a painful thought that will plague my birthday for the rest of my life. My dad is better off without me.

After replacing the cigar box in its hiding place, I lie on my bed, flipping my sister's driver's license around in my fingers. I stop and look at her face on the photo card, remembering the day we took our driving test. I slip the driver's licence back into my card holder. The time for reminiscing is over. I miss my sister, but she isn't here now. I wish I knew where she's gone, but the fact is, I don't, and right now, I need to figure out a way to get money for rent—and fast.

However, the thought of sleeping on the streets alone is eating away at any rational thoughts that pop into my head. My fear spikes. All I can think about is being alone again. Laura is gone, and now Priya.

My door vibrates under repeated pummelling from Priya's fists, pulling me from my self-pity.

"Open the door, blondie," she calls from the other side.

I hear Adewale from down the corridor. "Priya, shh," he hisses.

"What? She won't open the door."

"Maybe she doesn't want to." His level Nigerian accent disables Priya momentarily.

"Lucy," she whispers loudly.

I can imagine Adewale smiling at her like a naughty child trying to push his boundaries. Most people at the bedsit are scared of Adewale, and I can see why. Think Adewale Akinnuoye-Agbaje, the Hollywood actor, and you pretty much have the picture. Our Adewale shares the same name and physique, but he is a spiritual man with his own type of stardom—astrology, amongst other spiritual things.

There is another whisper. "Lucy, pleeease. Come on, I'm worried about you."

I open the door.

"Finally." Priya pushes past me.

I look out into the hall, and Adewale comes into view. "Are you OK, Lucy?"

"Yes, no. Probably will be." I shrug. "I suppose you want to come in too?"

"No." He shakes his head. "I just wanted to check on you."

"SHE'S FINE!" Priya shouts. "I'm here."

I glance over my shoulder to see Priya slouched on my bed.

Turning back to Adewale, I say, "I'm good; thanks for checking. It's nothing I can't handle—you know what it's like. I was planning on going to bed, but Priya is in one of her moods, so I'll probably be up all night talking about pointless crap instead." I laugh.

He doesn't move.

"Adewale? I'm good ... thanks," I repeat. He's not looking at me; he's looking beside me. "Adewale?" I say again.

Then he speaks. "I'm seeing double. There's two of you?" He looks directly at me. For a split second, I'm frozen. I know Adewale can see the fear in my eyes as chills run down my spine.

"Adewale, get out of here." Instinct takes over as I attempt damage control. "For a sober man, you're talking drunk, and I'm not doing this god shit with you tonight. Leave, go." I close the door in his face.

I turn to Priya with my best fake smile, ready to brush off Adewale's odd claims, but there's no need. She's asleep—passed out like a baby. I fall into the chair next to me, trying to regroup my thoughts. What the hell just happened? Is Adewale some kind of psychic as well? Can he see where Laura is? Does he know what has happened?

Impossible. I must have misunderstood; after all, Adewale does have a strange sense of humor. I then wonder if I misjudged his attempt at a joke. Had he been looking past me at Priya passed out and trying an attempt at a funny drunken reference? Seeing double is something drunk people say. I pull a weary hand over my face. Did I just shut the door in Adewale's face for no reason?

What a bitch, I think. *Damn.* I need to get a grip.

Some time passes, and I wake from a fragmented dream. Although my dreams have become clear and lifelike recently, they still never make much sense. However, they do unsettle me more often than not. I sit in the chair, watching Priya sleep and letting the strange feeling of my dream dissipate. Then I change into my bedclothes and squeeze beneath my sheets, tugging them out from below Priya's dead weight. I stare up at the ceiling, listening to the air bubbles popping in Priya's throat between her snores. An elbow jab to her side sends her rolling toward the wall.

Normally, I would kick her out to her own room, but not tonight. The thought of going back to the streets terrifies me, and I am about to hit rock bottom. It is like I can see it happening but can't stop it. My will to live is low, and with my birthday hanging over my head, my *want* to live is low. Tonight, I need someone close to me. I don't want to be alone. Although a part of me has given up on Laura coming back, I can't budge the feeling that if she is going to come back, she will tomorrow—on our birthday.

CHAPTER 3

THEN–LAURA

Cornwall, three years ago
May 22ⁿᵈ (twentieth birthday)

When I arrived home from work, Lucy was already there. Even from outside, I could hear her bellowing at the top of her voice—something about toast. I locked the car door and ventured inside, expecting to find Mum and Lucy in some kind of petty argument.

Sure enough, when I reached the kitchen doorway, I could see my mum was frantic and seething with anger. Lucy looked desperately at me.

"MUM!" Lucy shouted, "It wasn't me. I've got a muffin. Look!" She thrust a plate with a sliced, toasted muffin toward our mum. "I didn't eat the last of the damn bread."

"Where's Dad?" I asked my mum.

She turned sharply toward me. "Where do you think? Not here, as normal. He's never here when I need him."

"Need him for what?" Lucy retorted. "To be the wheat police?" She walked past me into the hall, whispering, "Happy fucking birthday, Lulu." She headed toward the living room.

"I heard that," Mum shouted, then turned to look at me for some kind of guidance. "She can be such a bitch."

"Mum, stop." I scowled.

She always did this. She flipped out over the smallest of things because she couldn't control her anger, not even on her daughters' birthday, and then she felt guilty. She would never admit that, though. She would just try to justify it, and she typically used me to do so.

"Laura," she started, "Laura, you know how routine is crucial for me? The new therapist said I needed routine for treatment to work."

I didn't reply. I knew this was a lie because my dad had told me that she was not in treatment; she never went back after the first session. She told Dad that the new therapist didn't know what she was talking about and was underqualified.

"Laura, look at me." She took my face in her hands. "I'm really trying here." Lying came easy to my mum. "I know it's your birthday, and I'm really trying to get through today. You're both getting so big, and … and, well, that scares me. My little girls are growing up."

She would have said anything to avoid admitting she was wrong or, God forbid, having to say the word sorry. I did wonder, though, if there was a little truth in her words. It must have been hard to see her babies growing up.

"It's OK, Mum," I said, not wanting to argue. "I'll text Dad and see if he can buy some more. Is he at work still?" I hoped this wouldn't send her into another frenzy. There was a good possibility they had already had an argument and Dad had stormed out.

"Yes. Some boy is playing up at school or something. I don't know; you know what he's like. He never tells me anything these days."

I found that hard to believe but didn't say it. "I'll text him now," I said and walked into the living room.

Lucy was sulking on our ugly blue sofa. Her hair and makeup looked freshly done, and she was wearing my bathrobe. I walked over and turned down the volume on the TV. Pepper Pig's irritating laugh turned to silence.

"I was watching that," Lucy said.

"Figures. It's about your intelligence level."

She pulled my hair and laughed.

"Ouch, Lu, you little bitch."

She rubbed my head better and smiled. "You going to text Dad, then?"

I ignored the fact that she didn't say sorry for pulling my hair. Just like our mum, Lucy didn't seem to have the word "sorry" in her vocabulary.

"I'll do it in a second," I said. "Won't tell him what happened, though, just to pick up more bread. She'll be fine by the time he's home, like nothing happened." I rolled my eyes to the ceiling.

"Come on, I'll do your eyelashes for you." Lucy stood and pulled on my arm.

"Go get me a muffin too, and I'll get ready."

"No way. Did you not just see schizo Mum just now?" She pulled on my arm again.

"Don't call Mum that; she's sick."

The front door slammed, and our dad walked into the kitchen. I hadn't texted him, so he wouldn't have the bread. I listened to see if he and Mum would argue, but they didn't. On the contrary, we heard hushed tones and then laughter. Lucy looked at me, and I looked back at her.

"Our family is messed up," she whispered.

I can't argue with that, I thought.

Moments later, Mum and Dad walked through the door, each holding a small blue box. Dad handed me a box, and Mum handed Lucy hers. I knew this was Mum's way of saying sorry; I could see it in her eyes when she handed the box to Lucy. I also knew that Lucy was not in tune with our mum's vague apology attempts, yet she looked happy enough about the gesture.

Mum kissed Lucy and then me on the cheek. "Happy birthday, girls," she said, looking pleased with herself.

"Happy birthday, Lulus," Dad echoed.

I opened my box with the reverence I thought it deserved. Inside my box was a silver necklace with half a heart. I glanced over at Lucy. Her heart pendulum was the right half, and mine the left. They were beautiful.

"Thanks, Mum; thanks, Dad." I beamed, delighted.

"Yeah, thanks," Lucy said. "We can wear them tonight. Speaking of which?" She nodded toward the door.

I grabbed Lucy by the hand and pulled her from the sofa. We ran up the stairs two at a time. Mum called out something about not using the last of her perfume, as if that would stop me. She never went anywhere to use her perfume, so if I didn't use it, Dad wouldn't have had anything to buy for her. I was doing her a favor.

I flew into my room, calling out to Lucy, "Get ready in my room."

"Um, I'm ready. You're the one that needs to get a wriggle on. Go shower." She dashed past me into her room. "We can put our dresses on when I've done your hair and makeup."

After the fastest shower known to man, I made a beeline for my bedroom, announcing loudly as I entered that I was ready for Lucy to beautify me. Then I stopped dead in my tracks. Ben Jones was sitting on my bed, grinning at me with an air of arrogance.

I pulled my bath towel tight. "You could have warned me."

"Hey, Laura," said Ben.

"Hey," I said.

"It's OK, Laura." Ben stood. "I'll wait outside; don't leave your room because of me."

He eyed my exposed shoulders as he left the room, and I quickly closed the door behind him.

"You should have warned me," I whispered.

"Sorry," Lucy mouthed back.

I couldn't stay mad at her; she looked so pleased that he was there. "I was just a bit shocked, that's all," I said.

I pulled on a t-shirt dress because Lucy was still in my bathrobe, and then I opened the door for Ben to come back in. Lucy set about my face, coating me with a thick layer of foundation. The music was too loud for anyone to talk at a normal level, and I could see Ben amusing himself with my book collection. He turned to me whenever he found one he liked, giving it a thumbs-up sign. I'll admit I had to giggle when he pulled out *Pride and Prejudice*, shaking his head. He seemed to like *Mocking Jay* from *The Hunger Games* series the best. He gave a little hip wiggle when he held that book up. Maybe I had gotten him wrong.

"I've got an idea." Ben raised his voice over the music. "We could start a book club, and you could read your books to me."

"How about you Google the definition of 'book club' and get back to me on that idea, Ben?" I shook my head.

"Harsh." He smiled and pulled out another book.

After my face had an adequate amount of war paint applied, Lucy started on my hair. I asked Ben to turn the music down, knowing we were pushing our luck playing it so loud for so long. The last thing I wanted was another argument between Lucy and Mum.

"Want some?" Ben had retrieved a small vodka bottle from his jacket. He took a swig and then extended it to me.

"I'll wait," I said.

"Wait for what?" Lucy grabbed the bottle and drank. "It's our birthday." She thrust it into my hand.

"What the hell," I said and necked it.

"Easy, tiger." Ben pulled the bottle out of my hand, laughing. "You should pace yourself, Laura."

"Why? Maybe tonight I don't want to pace myself; maybe tonight I want to get wasted," I lied. I had no intention of getting drunk. I just wanted to act like I was, and I was a master at that tactic. Down a few at the start of the night, and then swap out my vodka for Sprite or water while everyone else got drunk and made fools of themselves. There was something satisfying in doing that. Like a super power, I could see and judge situations that no one else could. It was also amusing to watch intoxicated people.

Lucy rolled the last piece of my hair around the tong and into a perfect glamor curl. "I love your hair, Laura."

"It's the same as yours," Ben said, pointing out the obvious.

"Can't I love my sister's hair?" Lucy retorted. She ran some serum through my hair. "There. Ready."

"Beautiful," Ben said. "Both of you."

Such a creep, I thought. Then I saw Lucy beaming at him.

"Here." I handed Lucy a black dress and looked at Ben.

"I'll wait outside." He left the room.

We squeezed into our matching dresses and then stood side by side in front of the mirror. The feeling I got when I saw Lucy by my side never failed to take my breath away, and I'm certain Lucy felt the same. She threw an arm around my shoulder, and in that moment, I knew nothing could come between us, not even Ben.

"You know what, Lucy? Take away our personalities, and we are literally the same—same embryo, same life, same person. We don't need anyone else—well, anyone other than Marie, that is," I added.

"Girl, please. I've been saying that forever."

I smiled back.

"Here." She retrieved both birthday boxes. "Our necklaces." She handed me mine.

The door opened slightly. "Can I come back in yet?" Ben called out.

"Sure." I pulled the door open.

"You can help me fasten my necklace," Lucy told him.

I watched Ben fumble with the clasp around Lucy's neck. He must have sensed me looking, and his eyes met mine. I smiled, and he held my stare for longer than I felt appropriate. I looked away fast.

"Just going to use Mum's perfume; meet me downstairs," I said and left the room.

Much to Lucy's annoyance, we agreed to take the bus to Marie's and not a cab. The bus stop was at the end of our road, down a steep, bendy hill. The sun had set, and it was dusk, my favorite time of day. As we neared the bottom of the hill, though, I wondered if we should have listened to Lucy. I didn't often wear high heels, and I could feel my toes being pressed tightly into the points of my pumps. I glanced at Lucy walking hand in hand with Ben. If her feet hurt, she wasn't showing it.

It didn't take long for the bus to come, and two stops later, we were there. As we approached the large Victorian house, I could hear the music, loud and aggressive. The neighbors were going to hate us.

It was dark, but the night air was still warm with a gentle breeze. It was early for summer weather, and I found myself hoping that when the summer months came, we would still get some nice weather.

The door was open.

"Marie," I called out over the music. "Hey!" Then I waved to a group of girls and boys in the front room. I recognized some of them. They were friends of Darren, one of Marie's housemates.

"Finally—you're here." Marie hurried down the hall toward us.

Ben told Lucy he was going to hang out with Darren, and we followed Marie into the kitchen.

"What's this?" There were blue plastic cups in a triangle on the kitchen table.

"Beer pong. Come on—play, Laura," Marie said.

So much for my not drinking. "OK—but I'll watch you first." Pleased with my avoidance tactics, I watched from afar as Marie and Lucy threw ping pong balls into cups. Alcohol splashed everywhere, mixed with screams of delight over the game. A girl I'd met before but whose name escaped me passed me a cup of vodka. When no one was looking, I poured a Sprite into a cup and left the vodka on the countertop. Then I slipped out of the kitchen before the game ended. Ben was still in the front room with Darren. I liked Darren and his friends. They were trendy but in an "I don't give a fuck" way. None of the girls were in heels; they all had ripped jeans and boots. I felt slightly awkward at first, but then Jen told me I looked sexy.

"Thanks," I said. "Lucy picked our outfits and did my hair."

"She did well," Jen said. "Happy birthday." The others echoed her birthday wishes.

The house was dark. All the lights were either off or dimmed. I enjoyed talking to Jen, but it was difficult to hear over the music, not that it seemed to matter after a while. She was drunk, and my mishearing made *me* appear drunk. More people filled the house, and the noise level inside became deafening, so I decided to slip out to allow my eardrums some recovery.

Outside, there were people scattered everywhere, laughing, drinking, kissing, and acting unruly. I stood away from them by the side of the house. It was strange to think that all these people were here for my birthday, yet they didn't even know me.

"Boo." Ben jumped out from the shadows.

"Shit, Ben, you scared me." I clutched my chest.

"Desired effect achieved, then. Why are you hiding out here? Marie is looking for you; I think she's made you guys a cake. But you didn't hear that from me—it's a surprise."

"Well, in that case, you'd better go find Lucy and tell her to hide."

Ben looked confused.

"You've not tasted Marie's baking before?" I asked. He shook his head. "Well then, trust me when I say we should hide here all night." I couldn't resist the smallest of smiles.

"Did we just have a moment?" Ben asked. "You know, you're cute when you laugh."

I looked awkwardly at him. I never knew if he was joking when he made comments like that, but I *did* know they made me feel uncomfortable.

"What? You are cute when you laugh. Jesus, Laura, you're so uptight. Have you ever had a man? I mean—"

"I know what you mean, Ben. Why do you always say stupid stuff and ruin it?"

"Ruin what? Laura, do you secretly like me?"

I'm not sure what he meant, and I felt a little intimidated, so I just looked at him. He did that a lot—said things with double meanings. Lucy and Marie couldn't see it, said I was sensitive to innocent innuendos. I wasn't, though. Sometimes, Ben's comments made my intuition scratch at my rationality. I knew his comments were anything but innocent, and standing by the side of a house in the dark with him was not putting me at ease.

"Come on, let's not ruin it," he said. "I'm sorry if I offended you—"

"You didn't."

"Well, I'm sorry for whatever stupid thing I said. Look, Laura, can we just be cool? I like your sister, and I like you too, but you just make me nervous, and I end up saying dumb stuff."

I refrained from my normal sarcastic retort and shrugged. I'd promised Lucy to give him a chance.

"Here you are." Lucy ran along the side of the house toward us. "Why are you out here?"

"Hiding." Ben winked at me.

I smiled.

"Why?" Lucy asked, intrigued.

"Ben says Marie has baked us a cake," I told her.

"Oh." She cringed. "Well, in that case, we should all jump in the bushes now."

We giggled.

"I'm up for a threesome if you two are," said Ben.

"For god's sake, Ben," I spat.

"He's joking, Laura." Lucy laughed. "Aren't you?"

"I am, unless you'll do it—joke, joke!" Ben held up his hands.

How my sister fell for that jerk, I would never know. I flashed a fake smile and walked back into the house to find Marie.

Marie's baking skills had improved over the last year, and she promised that there was no cannabis laced inside the sponge this time. We were halfway through the night, and I'd only consumed the gulp of vodka in my room and a shot of wine I couldn't get out of doing after losing a random game of "throw a bottle cap in the wastebasket." How I lost while sober, I don't know. Schoolgirl error. I decided to avoid all games, even the ones I thought I could win.

"Laura," Lucy called, running into the front room with Marie. "I love this song. Dance, dance!"

We danced, loudly singing the words to "Rhinestone Cowboy." People laughed at our antics, but I didn't care. It was our night, and we had our best friend to thank for it all. It was perfect, and I was having the time of my life. In that moment, I wasn't drunk, but I definitely looked it. I was lost in the song with my two best friends in the whole world.

"Ha-ha, I love you guys," I shouted.

My hand hit Lucy's hand, and my Sprite went flying. "Oh, no—sorry, Marie." I stood staring at the wet patch on the carpet.

"Keep dancing; don't worry." Marie grabbed both my hands.

I laughed so hard as we bounced together in time to the music, spilled drink soon forgotten. Our birthday was going so well.

Still more people filled the house, and before long, every room was filled with people dancing. Eighties and nineties music seemed to be the preference, and that pleased me. I loved seeing people doing the running man dance move badly, still thinking they looked good.

"Here." Ben took a sip from his cup and pushed a drink into my hand.

Without thinking, I took it, took a big swig, and then smashed the empty cup back into his hand.

"Laura, you sexy beast," Ben shouted at me over the music.

I glanced at Lucy, then back at Ben. "You can't say that to me."

"Why? Laura, it's all good. I'm just being friendly."

"Having fun, Lulu?" Lucy called over to me. "I'm going outside with Marie for a cigarette, coming?"

"Are you smoking?"

"No. Just mingling."

I followed Lucy and Marie out into the back garden, where we watched Marie smoke. Some boys joined us. They were cute, and I thought one was flirting with me. He made jokes about good girls who didn't smoke but still wanted to hang out with the bad boys who did. I liked him; he seemed nice.

"Want to try a vapor pipe instead?" another boy asked, holding out his vapor device.

I shook my head. My body felt hot, and my bowels had suddenly turned to water, but I couldn't say that.

"I need a pee." I did a dance like a little girl who needed a wee and then rushed off. I heard them laugh behind me. "Excuse me," I said, stepping sideways past people, quickly making my way along the hall to the toilet.

"Happy birthday," I heard a girl call out.

I recognized another one of Marie's housemates standing with her friends. "Emma. Hi, thanks!" I shouted back over the heads of a group of drunk boys that I hadn't met before. I wondered if she knew which twin she was talking to.

I kept edging down the busy, packed hallway to the end, but then I stumbled and reached out for the wall. My vision blurred. Was I drunk? I couldn't be; I hadn't had that much to drink.

As I fumbled for the handle on the toilet door, I heard Darren call out to me.

"You OK?" he seemed to say.

I nodded. I thought I could see other people with him, but my vision was hazy. Ben? Could I see Ben behind him? I strained to see.

"Had a bit too much to drink?" Darren asked.

I didn't answer and fell into the toilet. Pulling up my dress and down my panties, I sat. I heard Marie shouting for everyone to come into the garden, and something about a beer game. I retched, and my head felt light. I couldn't remember anything after that.

I felt sick. What time was it? I pressed my hands onto the cold concrete floor and stood. My surroundings were vague—the garage? How had I gotten here?

I heard voices. Lucy? Had I heard Lucy?

"Darren, have you seen Laura?" she said.

I turned in the direction of her voice, toward a door. I could hear music. My steps were clumsy, and I fell.

Darkness.

Something was wrong. Time felt like edgy fragments of reality. Where was I? Someone was pulling at my arm—I opened my eyes. It was a guy. "Get off," I said, pulling my arm back toward me. I was at the top of the stairs. *How did I get there?*

"Lucy," I heard the guy shout. It sounded like Tye, Jen's boyfriend. "Lucy, she's up here."

He was slapping my face, not hard, but I wanted him to stop. I shook my head and flapped my arms.

"Get off me, get off me," I screamed, but my voice was weak, and I barely made a noise. I stopped flapping. Tye was saying something. He was telling me to stay awake, and he started to slap my face again.

"Stop it." I tried to push him away.

"Laura?"

My eyes sprung open. *Lucy?* I wasn't sure if I had said her name or just thought it.

"Laura, where the hell have you been?"

I tried to stand. "I had to pee."

"That was an hour ago." Lucy helped me up. "How did you get this drunk, Lulu?"

I was now standing. I felt ill. "I'm not drunk," I said.

Lucy smiled at me. "Of course you're not. Ben, hold her up."

I felt Ben's hands slip under my armpits, and I just hung there like a dead weight. I wondered if I was paralytic drunk. Was this how it felt?

Then Marie ran up the stairs.

"Marie," I slurred.

"Wow, girlfriend, you are fully wasted. Lucy, the Uber will be here in three minutes, but I'm not sure it will take her in that state."

"Laura, can you try and walk?" I heard Lucy saying.

I nodded.

"Easy." Ben gripped me tightly. "Slowly," he said. "Let me carry her downstairs first.

I felt my legs lift as Ben picked me up into a cradle carry, carefully making his way down the steps. The house was still filled with people, and I caught sight of Kitty.

She came, I thought before it went black again.

"Just let her sleep," Ben was saying. Where was I? I wasn't in an Uber.

"We need to get home," Lucy said. I could tell by the tone of her voice that she was worried. "Just pick her up; we're nearly there. Look, she can't walk anymore. How the hell did she get this drunk?"

I opened my eyes. I was sitting at the bus stop at the bottom of our road. My head throbbed.

Odd. There were no night buses on that route. I felt Ben hoist me up, only this time, he wasn't giving me a cradle carry. I was hanging over his shoulder as if he had just rescued me from a fire.

More time passed, and the next thing I knew, Lucy was undressing me and tucking me into bed. I tried to push my hair away from my face, but it didn't help. Lucy laughed and tucked my hair behind my ears. What was going on here? I shouldn't be in this state. I hadn't drunk enough, surely. An unsettling feeling that something had happened at the party was churning inside me, but just *what* had happened?

"I didn't drink that much," I said, trying to keep my eyes open.

She tucked the duvet into my side like a child. "Sure, Lulu."

"Lucy, I'm being serious. I didn't drink."

"Laura, you downed a vodka here and a few at the party. You had a drink in your hand all night—I saw you." She laughed. "It's OK, you're allowed to let go and get drunk from time to time. It's actually nice to be the one looking after you for a change."

"No, Lucy." I tried to sit up, not wanting to fall asleep, but felt queasy again. I slumped back down. My guts gave a heave, pushing bile up into my throat. Swallowing the acid reflux, I went on. "Lucy, I was drinking Sprite. I swapped out my drinks when no one was looking."

"And the ones you downed? Were they Sprite?"

I looked away. "But they weren't large drinks. Not to be this drunk—I've never been this drunk on the amount I drank."

Lucy puzzled over this. "Laura, do you think someone swapped your Sprite for vodka or something?"

I tried hard to remember the night. Thinking back, I remembered Ben giving me his drink, but I saw him drink some first, so it couldn't be that. I sighed.

"I never put my drink down to have it swapped," I said.

"Laura, maybe you shouldn't down drinks again. You're not a big drinker and clearly get drunk easily. You should sleep it off. Mum will kill me if she sees her perfect princess like this."

"Lucy!" I snapped. "Take that back."

"Such a baby." She laughed. "You're funny when you're drunk."

My eyelids drooped, and I struggled to focus. "Maybe someone did just swap my drinks, then. But how would they know I was drinking Sprite? I didn't tell anyone."

Through half-opened eyes, I watched Lucy watching me, her instinctual desire to nurture and protect me. She stroked my hair, the same way she did when we were small, when I wouldn't stop crying over our parents' continuous arguing.

"Lucy," I quietly said, "I think something happened to me."

"What do you mean?"

I wriggled around, desperate not to fall asleep. "At the party. Something happened. Something doesn't feel right, you know?"

She didn't know. I could tell by her expression. But I had worried her; I could see this because she looked at me the same way our mum did if we were sick.

Her voice was beginning to sound low and muffled, as if my ears were blocked. "Like what, Laura?"

"I don't know. I just know something is off; bits of time are missing, and—" I stopped. I wanted to tell her that I felt dirty, but I didn't know how to say it.

"What, Lulu, what?" she pushed.

"Dirty ... or something, I don't know how else to say it. I think something happened at the party."

"Dirty?" she questioned, her nurture changing to definite concern. "What does that mean?"

I shrugged. "Don't know. I feel like something happened that shouldn't have."

"Oh—Laura!" Lucy sat back. "Did you have sex with someone? Is that what you're saying?"

"I don't think so. But maybe. Shit. I don't know—that's my point."

"You were upstairs with Tye when I found you ..." Stark realization washed over her expression. "Laura. Did you sleep with Jen's boyfriend?" Standing, she carried on. "The pig! How dare he do that to her with you, my sister! You didn't know what you were doing; you're drunk; look at you—you're out of it!" Lucy raged in her normal irrational fashion.

"No! Lucy, shh. Just listen to me."

We were both silent for a second.

"I don't know," I said finally. "I can't remember what I did. It's all so sketchy. I remember Darren talking to me by the toilet, and then hearing Darren's voice—" I stopped. Did I remember hearing Darren? I tried to recall the night in my mind before continuing. "Tye was pulling at my arm. I was upstairs."

"Shit, Laura." Lucy stared back at me in disbelief.

I didn't reply straight away. I was wondering if I had actually slept with Tye.

"Laura, do you think Tye swapped out your drinks for vodka?"

"When? I never saw him till the end of the night." My words had started to slur again.

"Laura, you look so drunk. OK, clutching at straws here, but you're sure you didn't just drink too much?"

I shrugged. "Maybe this is what being drunk feels like; I did down more drinks than normal."

Lucy nodded. "Also, would Tye really get you drunk just to have sex with you? And with his girlfriend there? Do you really think you had sex with someone? You said you were talking to Darren; you like him, and he is cute." She giggled. "Do you think you might have slept with Darren?"

A fresh wave of sickness flowed over me, and I started to feel sleepy. What had I done? Had I really slept with someone and failed to remember?

CHAPTER 4

NOW–LUCY

London, present day
May 22ⁿᵈ (twenty-third birthday)

I throw my coat onto the chair and let the door slam behind me—there's no point in being quiet. The room below is blasting 90s rave music through speakers that sound as old as the music they are strangling. I stomp hard on my floor. The music continues. Collapsing onto my bed, I glance at the clock on my microwave. It reads 9:59 p.m. My birthday is nearly over, and Laura hasn't come.

Falling back, I stare at the murky brown patch on the ceiling from a leaky pipe that's yet to be fixed. How has my life gotten here? I'm alone in this flea-riddled building full of drunks like my current self. I've gone from a happy little girl who only wanted to hang out with her sister and buy clothes to a bitter big girl who can't find her sister or afford clothes. My heart pinches. Where is she? Why hasn't she come back for me tonight? What am I supposed to do now, wait another year? I was so sure tonight was the night—so sure.

Music vibrates through my chest. Throwing my leg off the bed, I thump it on the floor over and over.

"SHUT THE FUCK UP!" I scream, though no one will care.

My phone rings. I sit up and answer—it's Priya.

"Drink in my room?" she asks.

I decline and hang up.

It's Monday night, yet the place is rocking like it's the weekend. I have to get out of here, to go somewhere and think. With swift movements, I gather up my coat from the chair again and dart out the door. I know Priya, and I know it's only a matter of minutes before she will knock on my door with a new drinking request. Now, don't get me wrong. I have every intention of drinking, just not here—or with Priya. Tonight, I want to wallow in the memory of what used to be. It's my new birthday tradition.

I head down the hall and out the communal front door. I pass Adewale outside walking his dog, a tiny Pekingese. It's an odd fit. I don't stop when he calls my name.

The air smells damp, but it's not cold. The roads are wet, and cars drive recklessly, their tires splashing as they pass me. West Croydon is a dreary place at the best of times, but tonight, it's just plain miserable. I make my way along the main road, toward Sadiq's off-license.

When I arrive, I'm greeted with the familiar smell of spices and herbs. A bell indicates I've entered, and Sadiq looks at me. The shop lights are dull like jaundice, and there's a low hum of foreign music playing. A man at the counter is paying for his goods, so I wander to the back aisle, stopping to look in each large fridge as I wait for the shop to empty.

I hear Sadiq wish his last customer goodnight. The coast is clear, so I head to the counter.

"You good, Lucy?" Sadiq asks. He reaches for a bottle of vodka. It's the cheapest bottle—Sadiq knows what I drink. I'm here most days.

"Yeah, you?" I reply.

He nods. "No Priya tonight?"

"No. And if she comes in looking for me, you haven't seen me, right?"

I hear a noise behind me and turn. It's Sadiq's uncle. He smiles, and I smile back.

"I just want to be on my own," I finish.

"I hear ya." Sadiq puts the bottle in a black bag.

"I'll take a pack of Marlboro lights, too," I tell him.

I take the bag and walk around the corner, then up the alley to the rear of Sadiq's shop. This is where I drink when I want to be alone. I feel safe here. There's a dim light above the back door to the shop, and they have CCTV cameras. I know Sadiq can see me; I've seen the screens under his counter. I wave at the camera like I normally do. Removing the vodka from the bag, I place the plastic on the step and sit on it.

There's an hour and a half left, I think, staring at the time on my phone.

Just then, a text from Priya comes in.

WHERE YOU AT, BLONDIE?

I don't reply, instead sliding the phone back into my pocket. I light a cigarette before making a start on my vodka. Laura isn't coming back. She probably can't find me here because this place is hell. Do I even *want* her to find me?

I do.

"Is this it, then?" I say aloud, spite now raging inside me. "Fuck you, Laura—where the *hell* are you?"

I hear a noise over by some dumpsters. "Laura?" I say, though I know it's not. It can't be.

A fox darts out of the shadows and through a gap in the fence.

"Crazy bitch," I whisper to myself.

Behind me, I hear the door being unlocked and soon see Sadiq's brown face peering out at me. I wonder if he saw me wave on his monitor after all.

"Hey," I say.

He steps out and sits next to me. "Got a light?" he asks.

I hand him my clipper. "You'll get piles."

Sadiq looks baffled.

"That's what my—" I stop. "What my mum used to say. She'd say that if we sat on wet ground, we'd get piles, and our bums would bleed." He looks perplexed. "Never mind," I say. "You'll get wet."

He shrugs, and we sit in silence. I like Sadiq. He's nice to me and lets me take goods from his shop on tick, which means on loan—like a ticking clock, I suppose. I normally do this the day before payday so my tick is never long, and he's never had to remind me of money I owe.

"So why are you on your own tonight, Lucy?" He rolls his cigarette between his short, stumpy thumb and index finger. "It's late—you not working tomorrow?"

I shake my head. "They cut my hours. But I do have a job interview." I take a large mouthful of vodka and offer the bottle to Sadiq.

"No, thanks."

"Not that there's much point in going," I continue. "Last week I went to five interviews and haven't heard from any of them. It's a fucking joke."

"What type of work you looking for?"

I shrug. "Anything now, but I was trying to get back into sales. I used to work at a big furniture store, and I was good. Had my own business card and everything. Sales executive." My smile is wide and genuine—and short-lived. "But I can't get a sales job now for love nor money."

"You come from Cornwall, right?" Sadiq enquires.

"That's right," I say, but I can't recall when I told him that. I must have been drunk one night. There have been many such nights. Or maybe I need to work harder on losing my Cornish accent.

"Is your family still in Cornwall?"

"Probably."

He looks taken aback by my answer. "You're not in contact with them?"

I shake my head.

"Do you have brothers or sisters?" he presses.

I hesitate. I like Sadiq but am not sure if I want to have this conversation.

"Sister," I say, then regret it. "But that was then. This is now."

He nods. "When did you leave Cornwall?"

"Last year. One year ago to the day, actually." I take a hasty gulp and splutter.

Sadiq pats my back until I've stopped coughing. "Makes sense."

I'm confused. "What makes sense?"

He gives a small knowing laugh. "Why you're drinking alone in an alley tonight."

"Yeah," I say. "That and the fact that I'm getting laid off at work. I need cash, and fast. I'm not going back on the streets again. You ever lived on the streets, Sadiq?"

"No."

"It's scary. Always scared of getting beaten up or raped. At least when I first came here I had Priya, but if I get kicked out of the bedsit, I'll be doing it on my own."

"You can't go home?"

"Can't. My sister told me not to."

Sadiq turns his head toward me. "Why?"

This is a question I also want answered. I shrug.

Taking the hint, he changes the subject. "So what's the job interview for?"

"Sales person. In a furniture store."

"You don't sound happy about it."

"I want to be excited, but what's the point? They will ask me what I've been doing for the last year, and what do I say? I can't tell them where I've been working because they will want a reference."

"Why can't you get a reference?"

"Because it's all off the books there. All cash in hand, and the company isn't exactly legal, I don't think. They normally only employ immigrants, but she must have thought Priya and I looked just as desperate. Anyway, she never gives references. If employers ring up, she says that she doesn't know who you are."

"You're joking," he says.

"Nope. She is some nasty piece of work. I hate her."

Sadiq flicks his cigarette butt across the alley and stands up, rubbing at his wet jeans. "Look, Lucy, sorry, but I've got to get back inside. I can't leave my uncle on his own for too long; you know what this area is like. I'll keep an eye out for you." He points to the camera. "You should go to that interview. What's the worst that can happen, hey?"

I nod, and he disappears through the door.

Alone again, I think and light another cigarette. The bottle, though not the largest, is half empty already. It's started to rain, so I stand close to the wall for shelter. It's too wet to stay out drinking, time to go home—*when the rain eases up*, I think. But the rain isn't letting up tonight, and before I know it, I've nearly finished the bottle.

Headlights illuminate the alley, and a slick black car pulls alongside me. It's an Audi. I know this because it's the car I was meant to get when I worked at the furniture store in Cornwall. But it's the more expensive one, bigger than our company cars. The windows are tinted, and I can't see in.

Then the window opens—not a lot, just enough to reveal a man in a suit. He looks jittery, and he is checking his rearview mirror.

I place the bottle into my coat pocket. "You lost?" I say.

"How much?"

I freeze. He thinks I'm a prostitute. "Get out of here." I laugh. But he persists. "Come on, how much? £20?"

"I'm not a prostitute." I spit the words.

Now he is looking me over. My coat is open, and I'm still wearing my factory work clothes, a set of ill-fitting navy overalls.

"Just a hand job?" He fully opens the window. "Come on, now—it's raining. Get in £30. Just a quick rub, that's all."

As if ignoring him, I look away to the CCTV camera. It's facing us, and I wonder if Sadiq can see me. I step from side to side with my hands in my pockets, trying to ward off the cold from the rainy night.

"You really aren't, are you?" His fat face squashes into a smile. "You're not a prostitute."

I open my coat wider and gesture to my uniform. "I've never seen a prostitute dress like this, have you?"

He glances down at my factory code boots. "I suppose not."

But instead of driving on, he's switched off the ignition.

"So what will it take?" he asks, now in a more confident voice.

I'm not sure exactly what he means, but I've got a good idea, and I know what he is insinuating is ludicrous. But I do need the money. I couldn't do that—could I? I think back to the hand jobs I used to give boys at parties for free. Is this not the same? It's not, I know, yet I don't walk away.

He carries on his advances. "It's no different than meeting a guy in a bar, is it?" It's like he's a mind reader. "I mean, if you're not a prostitute, then it's the same thing. I'll just pay you for what you would have drunk if I had taken you out. Think of it like that."

No. No, I can't do this. I turn to leave.

"£100." His voice sounds rushed. "Come on. £100, just a hand job."

I slowly turn back toward him.

"And kissing."

I turn away again.

"OK, OK! £100 and one kiss. Just one—it will feel more like a date then." His face is now hot red, as if the exchange is flustering him.

"£200, no kissing." I'm slurring the words, adrenaline making me feel even more drunk than I was before this crazy situation.

"£150."

"£200, one kiss, and we do it here," I say firmly. "Just a hand job, and I hold onto the car keys. That's final." After all, it's money. I know the risks, but they're no different from the risks of living on the street. At least this way, I have a choice.

Just this once. I'll just do it this once. It will give me a few more days to find work or sell some more of my stolen stock.

He checks his rearview mirror, considering my final offer. "Here?" he says. "Maybe we should go over there." He points to a parking space up the alley in the shadows.

"No, here. Right here. Keys." I hold my hand out.

"What if another car comes?"

My hand is still outstretched. "Keys," I repeat.

He gives a large sigh. "Get in."

"Keys first." He sighs again and mumbles something about a start button, then slaps the keys into my hand.

As I walk around the front of the car, I glance up at the CCTV camera. I don't know why it makes me feel better. There's every chance Sadiq will see this hideous act. Still, he knows my situation. He will understand if he sees, and I know him well enough to know he doesn't judge. Besides, if this fat prick tries to rape me, I'll smash the window, and Sadiq will see—or so my drunk self hopes. I get in.

The car smells brand new. It's clean. I wait until the interior light fades to turn and look at the man. Am I really doing this with this fat prick? He is saying something, but the vodka has saturated my blood. Its poisons are intoxicating every inch of my body, including my mind. I try to rationalize my predicament. I've dealt with men like him before. I've never been paid for it, but I *have* jacked a guy off because he had drink and I wanted some. It has never been quite as clinical as this, though. I'm about to cross a line here, a line that might mess me up in my head. I reach for the door handle.

"It's OK." His hand is on my knee.

"I feel dizzy." My thought comes out as sound.

He smiles at me. He looks kind now, not like before. The negotiations are over, I realize. He has no need to put the pressure on since I've already agreed. I'm in his car. All he wants now is what he's paid for.

"No rush," he says. "Let's talk?"

I nod.

"My name is Simon. What's yours?"

Should I give him my real name? Is that wise? "Laura," I lie.

"Well, Laura, it's nice to meet you."

I laugh. This situation is too fucked up to do anything else. Simon eyes me suspiciously before giving a little chuckle too.

"New car?" I ask. "Smells new."

"It is new. Got it last week."

"Why?" I ask because I don't know what else to say.

"Why not?" He shrugs. He unbuttons his suit jacket, and I take a deep breath.

£200, I think. *Do it fast and get the hell out of here.* "Is £200 the going rate?" I'm curious to know.

He howls with laughter. "Shit, no, I could get this for £20 down the road."

"Then why didn't you?"

He focuses on me, and I feel intimidated.

"Because you're not a prostitute. I like that."

His reply makes me feel a little less like a prostitute. If I do this, though, that's exactly what I am. It's not too late to back out, but it *is* too late to be finding money for rent. My rent is due the day after tomorrow.

"Right," I say. "Shall we just do it, then?" I need to do this before I lose my nerve. I need this money.

He unzips his trousers and fumbles inside the slot.

Oh, great, I think. *He's not hard yet.*

He must have read my mind because he's tugging on himself with quick, jerky fist thumps. This is one messed-up situation I'm in, but this guy is not as confident as he wants to be—should I not be getting him hard? The thought repulses me. If I don't take control of this, the longer it will take—or I won't even get the money.

The money, I think. In the movies, they take the money upfront.

"Wait," I say.

His red face looks at me. "What?" he asks, his hand motionless but still hidden in his zipper.

"The money? You need to give me the money first."

"Do I?"

"Yeah—you do."

"Why?" He starts to tug at himself again.

"Because that's what they do in the movies."

He stops. "What?" His hand retracts from his trousers. "You really haven't done this before."

"I thought we had established that already?"

He reaches inside his trouser pocket and pulls out a money clip. He counts out, "Twenty, forty, sixty, eighty, one hundred," and hands it to me.

"We agreed on two hundred."

A smarmy smile creeps across his face, and he counts out the rest. I snatch the notes. This exchange actually aroused him, I realize, looking down. Not wanting it to deflate and prolong this shit show, I grab it and start jostling it in my hand. I don't know if I'm meant to be doing it harder or softer; I'm just doing what I've done on boyfriends and lovers. But he isn't my lover. I can't think about it. I need to clear my mind, just do the act and get it over and done with.

He's groaning, and his hand is rubbing my knee feverishly. With my free hand, I move it off me. I don't want him getting carried away. This is a hand job, that's all.

54

"Kiss me," he breathes.

I can't. I feel repulsed. *I can't kiss this.*

"Fucking kiss me." His face is close to mine. "Please, Laura. You said one kiss. Just one. Come on, ahh yes." He bites his bottom lip. "Just one, it will get me there faster—do it."

Oh god, this is so fucked up. I lean forward slowly, not wanting to, and he grabs the back of my head with his hand. His fingers grip my hair tight, and he pushes his thick, wet tongue into my mouth. I freeze with terror. Is this it? Has he lost control of himself? Is he going to rape me?

Suddenly, it's over. I sit back in the seat.

Walking home in the rain, I don't care that my coat is open or that I'm soaking wet. I pass the West Croydon bus station and stop to sit on the stone-slabbed steps of the courthouse. I push my forehead hard against the railing and thump my head a few times. I'm not even heading the right way home. At the thought of home, I slam my forehead into the railing again, but harder.

What have I just done? I had no choice; I had to do it. I can't live on the streets again. My hand slips into my pocket and feels for the money. What am I doing walking the streets with all this cash? I shove the money down my bra and stand up.

I correct my direction and head quickly toward the East Croydon train station. From there, I can double back and walk down the side roads to West Croydon. It's 2:27 a.m. The streets are dead other than a few passing cars. The only sound is the rain pelting on my back. I'm nearly home, half mile tops.

A police car pulls alongside me. "Need a lift?" the policeman inside asks.

I shake my head, turning to fully face the car. I can make out a female constable next to him.

"It's late for a young girl to be wandering the streets," he says. "Where are you going?"

"Home."

"Where's home?" he asks.

"Er … St. James Place on St. James Street," I say honestly.

He nods. "The bedsits?"

"That's right," I say, knowing I've just put a target on my head. They will surely search me knowing that I live at the St. James Place bedsits. It's full of drug dealers and thieves.

"Where have you been?"

I don't know what to say, so I don't say anything. The car engine goes silent. *Oh, just great. I'm going to get searched.*

"Where have you come from?" He is getting out of the car, and so is the female officer.

I watch her walk around the car toward me. "At a friend's."

"Where?" she asks.

"West Croydon."

The man has his hand on his radio. "What's your name?" he asks.

"Lucy Whitcombe."

The lady continues her questioning. "Where in West Croydon?"

"Top of Darby Road."

She steps close. "What's your friend's name?"

"Sadiq."

"Got anything on you that you shouldn't have, Lucy? Drugs or paraphernalia?"

"No," I say, ready for her next instructions to turn out my pockets.

"You won't mind my looking in your pockets, then?" she says on cue, snapping on a pair of latex gloves.

I shake my head.

"Arms up, please."

I comply.

"Anything sharp that could cut me in your pockets, Lucy?" She is using my name like she knows me. The police do this a lot; it must be a tactic of some kind.

I feel stone-cold sober now. "No," I answer.

I hear the man calling in my details. I don't have a record—I've never been caught. The lady has searched my pockets and is now patting me down. She runs her fingers hard over the bone of my bra.

"What's that?" she asks, feeling the roll of money.

"It's money," I tell her. I retrieve it and pass it over.

She counts my money. I hear the male policeman getting the all-clear on my name.

"That's a lot," she says. "Why do you have this in your bra? Where's it from?"

I'm about to say that Sadiq owed me money, but I rethink my answer.

"My rent is due, and I don't want to leave it in my room. It's safer to have it on me. That's why I put it in my bra."

She tilts her head toward me. She doesn't believe me, I can tell, but what can she do? She hands my money back. "Get in. We will give you a lift home." Her request is not optional.

The bedsit is quiet. I creep up the stairs to my room and jump as I see Adewale standing in his doorway.

"Adewale, why are you still awake?" I whisper.

His demeanor is as stern as a head teacher. "She's looking for you," he says.

"You waited up to tell me that?" I keep moving down the hall. "She's always looking for me." I'm feeling a little guilty for not answering Priya's earlier text, but I don't want to talk. "Get some sleep, Adewale. I'm a big girl—you don't have to keep looking out for me." After I pass him, I take one a quick glance over my shoulder, but he's gone.

"Weirdo," I say and turn my key.

There must have been an outage because the green numbers on my microwave are flashing 12:00. I check my phone—3 a.m. on the dot.

I remember the interview tomorrow. "Damn," I say and pull off my wet clothes.

I want to punch myself, so I do it. I punch myself in the side of the head over and over and over again. Tears stream down my face, but not because it hurts. It doesn't hurt. What hurts is my soul. Deep down, I know I want to go to this interview tomorrow. I want to get out of this life—I *need* to get out of this life—and a respectable job is exactly what I need. And if I hadn't messed it up by selling myself for rent money, I would be in bed asleep by now.

But then I would be homeless in two days, I remind myself.

"Why is life doing this to me?" I cry and slam my face into my pillow.

CHAPTER 5

THEN–LAURA

Cornwall, three years ago
May 24th

"How are you feeling?" I heard Lucy's voice before she appeared in my bedroom doorway.

I reached for the near-empty glass of water on my bedside table and groaned.

"That good, hey?"

I couldn't speak; I needed water. My throat felt like sandpaper, and my brain felt twice the size it should be. Lucy bounced on my bed and apologized when I heaved, but I didn't throw up.

"Sorry, Laura. You're in a bad way." She looked somewhat more concerned than last night. "What can I do?" She touched my forehead like I was a sick child having my temperature taken. "How do you feel about last night? Remember anything?" She gave an ambiguous smile, which I found odd, given our conversation the night before.

"I don't know," I said. "Just need to drink water."

"I'll get you more water." She sped through my door, and I heard our mum shout to slow down.

Fragmented memories from our birthday party edged into my mind. I thought about seeing Darren by the toilet, and Tye pulling at my arm. Why was I upstairs with Tye?

My door opened slowly, distracting me from my thoughts. "Laura?" my mum said softly. "Laura, can I come in, honey?"

"Sure, Mum."

"Oh, Laura." She looked at my sorry state and approached curiously.

"I'm OK, Mum."

"What's wrong, honey?"

At that point, Lucy came thundering through the door. "It's all good, Mum. I've got this." She placed two of Dad's pint glasses filled with water next to me, looking triumphant. "Here you go."

Our mum, on the other hand, looked horrified. "Laura, how much did you drink? Oh my god, you didn't take drugs, did you?"

"No, Mum." I winced in pain.

"Mum," Lucy said, taking control, "leave this to me. She didn't take drugs. This is Laura we're talking about here, remember? She didn't even drink that much—according to her." She added the last bit under her breath, pushing our mum out the door.

Mum wasn't ready to give up. "Then why is she in such a bad state?"

"Mum, stop, will you?" Lucy's back was to me, having finally banished our mum into the hallway. "She's fine, just needs to drink water and sleep it off. Just like you told me the first time I came home drunk, remember?"

I heard Mum reluctantly retreat down the stairs. Lucy came back in and closed my door a little too loudly for my liking. She gently sat next to me.

"Laura, you're really hungover," she said. "You really shouldn't drink that much anymore."

I really didn't want to rehash my consumption of alcohol again, and anyway, that wasn't the issue. The issue was that something had happened last night. Had I really slept with a boy and not remembered?

"So," Lucy said, as if reading my mind, "What happened with you and Tye, or was it Darren?" She grinned.

Irritated, I shrugged. "I told you, I don't remember."

"But you said you'd done something you shouldn't have?" Lucy was grinning widely at me. "Laura, I'm all for you getting laid and all that, but you need to be safe about it. Do you remember if you used protection, or did you forget that too?"

"What do you mean, 'protection'?" I took another sip of water and a few level breaths to ease the sick feeling looming in the pit of my stomach. "I don't know if I did sleep with anyone. Bits of the night are missing. I told you this."

"Missing?" Lucy echoed.

I nodded.

"Convenient."

I thought Lucy understood. We'd gone over all this the night before. Something sinister had happened to me, and I thought she would be screaming and shouting with promises to find and kill the son of a bitch who interfered with her sister. But she wasn't. She just looked conflicted.

Eventually, she spoke. "OK, so you're saying you still don't remember, and—" She hesitated. "You're sure you didn't do anything willingly?"

To say I was taken aback by her question would be an understatement. "No." I pulled the duvet tight to my chest. "No. What? Why would you even say that?"

"Sorry. I'm sorry."

"Why did you say that? We went over this last night." A wave of nausea made my voice wobble. "Are you not concerned about last night?"

"I am," she said, though she didn't look like she was. "It's not that I don't want to believe you. It's just something Ben said this morning."

"Ben?" I hitched myself into an upright position. "What did Ben say?"

Lucy took a deep breath as if trying to prepare herself and then said, "Ben said he saw you in Darren's room with Tye last night."

"WHAT? No. No, I was never in Darren's room. And Tye? What's Ben insinuating? That I slept with both of them?" I slid back under the covers. The confrontation was too much to handle.

"He said just Tye," Lucy said awkwardly. "He said that Tye uses Darren's room if they have parties because it has a lock and Jen can't find him."

"No, Lucy, no. That's horrible. I'd never do that. Well, not willingly." My words were muffled by the blanket.

Lucy jumped up. "Willingly? Are you telling me that Tye raped you? Is that what you're saying?" She had that crazy look, the one she used to get at school. "I'll kill him if he did."

"No, Lucy, sit down. I'm not saying that."

She didn't sit. "Then what are you saying, Laura? I don't know who to believe—"

"Believe?" I snapped back.

"I don't mean 'believe' like that—"

"Then what, Lucy?"

She sat back down beside me. "After talking to Ben, I thought I'd figured out what had happened last night, but if you're saying you still don't remember, then I'm going straight over to Marie's to ask Tye myself, because if you didn't sleep with Tye, then what? Something happened last night. You either got shit-faced drunk and the nasty feeling is guilt, or it's more sinister."

I clutched my head. "I just know I don't remember and that I feel like something happened."

"Stay here."

"Lucy, don't go to Marie's. It's not fair to mess with Jen and Tye not knowing what really happened."

"I won't. Just stay here. Let me see what I can find out." She left the room.

My sleep was broken. Each time I woke up, I tried to call Lucy, and each time, she didn't answer. My mum came into my room a few times to check on me, and she brought me painkillers and a vitamin C drink. Around noon, she made me some chicken soup, and I reluctantly ate half.

Sitting on my bed, I thought about the night before, trying to edit it back together like a film. I remembered seeing Darren, but I wasn't in his room. I didn't even know which room was his. I remembered hearing Darren, and then—oh, no. Tye was pulling at my arm immediately after. No. That couldn't be right. I wasn't in a bedroom when I heard Darren's voice; I was in the garage. Wasn't I? I gave up thinking and slumped onto my dribble-stained pillow.

By 2:00 p.m., I was feeling a little better and showered. I was still in my bath towel when I heard Lucy crashing through the front door and up our stairs.

"You bitch. You fucking bitch—how could you do that? What was your plan?"

"What?" I asked, dumfounded.

Lucy's face was inches from mine. "He told me everything." She spat the words at me.

"Lucy, what the hell are you talking about? Who told you everything?" I stood, then sat again.

Lucy marched back and forth a few times before continuing her assault. "You and BEN!" she screamed into my face.

"Girls, be QUIET!" our mum shouted from downstairs.

Lucy lowered her tone but not her vengeance. "I went to Ben's to get Tye's phone number out of Ben's phone and found naked pictures of YOU!" she hissed.

I'd never seen Lucy so mad at me. I was actually scared. "No. Lucy, no way. I'd never. I don't even like Ben."

"Exactly," she snapped.

"What did he say?"

"That you were drunk, and it was dark, and you wanted to do a naked photo for him. He thought you were me?"

I laughed at his excuse but quickly realized that was not an appropriate reaction.

"Funny, is it?"

"No, Lucy. It's not—why would I do that? And why did he not tell you this last night?"

She stepped close. "Because he thought he had taken a naked picture of *me*, you bitch. How could you?"

"I didn't."

"I've seen the picture, Laura. It's you." She thrust her phone into my hand. I stared at the picture. It was me, all right, but I didn't remember it. When? And where?

Is that Marie's garage? Jaded memories snapped in and out of my mind.

Lucy stormed out of my room.

"Lucy, wait—Marie's garage!" I shouted and followed her. "Lucy, it's not what you think. Something happened in the garage. I remember now."

"Yeah, I know. You taking your clothes off is what happened. How COULD you?"

Mum had stormed out of the living room and was at the foot of the stairs, and I knew this wouldn't end well.

Mum accosted Lucy. "What's going on?"

"Ask her." She pointed up at me, pulling her arm free from our mum's grasp.

"Laura? She's been in bed all day. You're the one screaming—what's Laura done?"

"Mum, leave it," I said.

"No, I won't leave it. Lucy, why are you always so aggressive toward your sister?"

Our mum was making everything worse, as normal. I could see Lucy glaring at her, and I ran down the stairs.

"Mum, please leave it."

"Yeah, Mum, leave it." Lucy sneered. "I'll let your precious little goody two-shoes tell you the truth—if she can handle that." She left the house, slamming the front door on her exit.

I took the stairs two at a time, ignoring my mum calling my name as I headed back up to my room. I scooped up the floral dress I had worn the day before last and pulled it over my head.

Damn it. I threw clothes around my room, looking for my other shoe. A splitting pain cracked across my brow.

"Got ya." I shoved my foot into my Converse as soon as I found the second shoe and made for the stairs once again.

I had to find Lucy—I had to explain. I didn't know about the pictures. I hadn't consented to them. What the hell was Ben playing at?

"Laura," Mum said, blocking the front door, "what is going on?"

"Nothing, Mum, I'll tell you later—but it's not Lucy's fault, OK?" I dove nimbly past my mum, ignoring her cry of protest.

"Laura, where are you going? Do NOT drive. Laura, I'm warning you."

Too late. I had already swiped her Mini Cooper keys from the hook by the front door. Running as fast as my heavy legs let me, I unlocked the car, started the ignition, and was letting off the hand brake by the time she appeared behind me in the rearview mirror.

"Sorry, Mum!" I shouted, then floored it.

The ground was wet, and the car wheels spun off the drive.

"Shit," I cursed, gaining control of the car again.

Through the open window, I heard my mum shouting promises of car bans. I didn't care. I just wanted to find Lucy, and fast.

Marie's, I thought. *She'll be heading to Marie's for sure.* I wanted to get down the hill before she got on the bus. I felt sick. My head was burning, and I winced as a fresh wave of nausea overwhelmed me.

I stepped on the accelerator as hard as I could as I rounded the corner and flew over the crest of the hill. Sure enough, Lucy was there at the bottom, standing with her hand out. The bus was approaching but slowed by the hill.

I'll get there first. I held my foot down to the floor. I wasn't sure of my speed, but it was fast—too fast—and increasing. *I can do this,* I thought, determined to reach Lucy before she got onto the bus. She had to know I'd never do anything like that to her.

On the descent down the hill, I sounded my horn. At that moment, some sick pushed up into my throat. I heaved, then retched, and acidic vomit filled my mouth. One hand over my mouth, I tried to steer around what looked like a dog in the road, but I lost control instead.

"NOO!" I screamed. The car was on the wrong side of the road, and then in the air. I took both hands off the steering wheel and covered my head. It all happened so fast. There was glass smashing and metal scraping, and then nothing.

Was I OK? Everything was dark. *My eyes must be shut,* I thought. I mentally checked myself—no pain. I actually felt better than I did before, peaceful.

Lucy. I could hear Lucy. She was screaming—howling, even. I started to panic. Why couldn't I see her?

Open your eyes, I told myself. And I did.

I wasn't in my car. I was standing in the road. Had I been thrown free in the crash? Lucy was howling like our mum had when our grandma died. She was holding something and screaming my name.

I looked around and suddenly noticed fire engines and an ambulance. How had they gotten here so quickly? I saw medical packaging on the floor, and one paramedic was clearing the discarded plastics away. No one was rushing around shouting instructions. On the contrary, everyone was silent—apart from Lucy. I heard Lucy scream my name again.

"Lucy, I'm here." I reached for her shoulder, but then I saw my dress and legs.

I gasped. She was holding me. "No, no, no," I whispered. "This can't be!" My eyes darted about my surroundings again. "What is happening here? Lucy? Lucy, I'm here. I'm right here, Lucy." She carried on rocking my motionless body. "Lucy," I repeated.

This was a dream; it had to be a dream! I saw people from the bus standing at a distance, some crying and others with their backs to her. A medic approached and tried to touch Lucy, but she bellowed at him, her face venomous like a caged animal. Her eyes were crazy, crazier than I'd ever seen before. She continued to rock my body back and forth.

I heard a woman say my name; it was Mrs. Bacigal from next door. She was telling a policeman where we lived. I wondered how I could have heard her, as she was standing at least twenty feet away, too far away for me to hear that clearly.

Then it hit me, just like that. Was I … ? I lifted my hands up to my face. Nothing. I didn't have any hands, just an odd shimmer. I wanted to see my face but couldn't move from where I was.

I need to look in the car window, I thought. Immediately, I was next to the car. I stared at my face. It was me. I was there, all right—a faint image. I wouldn't call it a reflection, but it was definitely me. Lucy had stopped screaming and was weeping softly into the side of my head. I hadn't seen my face yet and wasn't sure I really wanted to, but I told myself to look, and I saw.

It was horrific. Blood from my head was smeared down Lucy's cheek and seeping into her beautiful blonde hair. Was that really me? My face was unrecognizable. My own hair sprawled across my face, glued there by coagulated blood. I averted my eyes for a moment.

A mellow peacefulness eased through me, and I felt like I was drifting away. Suddenly, Lucy's voice grounded me again, and I looked over to see her talking into my ear. I wanted to be with her. I pictured myself close to her, and then I was. I was practically lying on top of myself, staring directly into Lucy's tear-stained face. The pain in her eyes was too great.

I reached out to touch her. "I'll make it right," I said, though I didn't know how. "I'm sorry."

Lucy started to whisper again. "Don't leave me, Laura. I'm sorry, I don't care, I believe you, I don't care," she said over and over. "Please, Laura, please don't leave me."

Suddenly, I flew away from my body, though not by choice. Something propelled me.

I don't want to go. I want to stay. Lucy needs me. I fought. A burning desire to be with my sister stopped me from leaving.

A different medic approached Lucy but was hissed away like a scorned degenerate. Then new screams of terror rang out, and I turned to see my mum stumbling out of a police car and running toward us. She was running so fast it looked as if her legs would give way and buckle beneath her. It was an odd thought to have.

The peacefulness was drawing me in again, but I fought against it. I wanted to feel. I wanted to be scared, to cry and scream. To be with my family. I wasn't leaving them, especially Lucy. I couldn't leave my sister alone.

I reached Lucy at the same time as my mum fell to her knees, pulling my lifeless body out of Lucy's arms. I wanted to tell them I was there, to make them see me and know it was OK, that I was all right, but it wasn't—it was devastating.

And then I felt it again, a peacefulness radiating through my entirety. I couldn't fight it this time, and I didn't want to. I wanted to be—to be nothing. Nothing. I wanted nothing, felt nothing, just like the time I'd had my wisdom teeth taken out under general anesthetic, minus the lightheadedness.

Everything started to move away from me, moving into the distance. It was as if the fabric of life itself was shimmering and reforming right in front of me. My sight blurred.

"It was all my fault," I heard Lucy say in the distance.

"NO," I shout back. "Stop, wait!" I felt a renewed desire to stay with my sister; I couldn't let Lucy blame herself. "It's not your fault, Lucy."

But she couldn't hear me—no one could.

I was dead.

CHAPTER 6

NOW–LUCY

London, present day
May 24th

A distorted view makes it hard to see. Everything has a dull blue haze about it, and then I'm awake. I'm not sure of the time because the microwave clock is still flashing 12:00 from the power outage, but daylight fills my room. My head falls back to my pillow, and I drift back into the hazy dream I just left.

I'm at the bar of the Union Tavern, ordering a beer. It's dark inside. Laura and Marie are waiting for me in the beer garden, and as I walk outside, I squint in the ultra-bright sunlight.

Now I'm not holding my beer, nor are we in the beer garden anymore. We're walking to Marie's house. None of these facts give cause for concern. It all feels quite normal. I'm giggling with Marie about something the way we used to, and now I turn to Laura. Her features are slightly blurred at first.

Laura is talking about my new job promotion. I smile and tell her it's a done deal—why wouldn't I get the job? I'm their top sales executive.

"No, Lucy," she tells me. "It's not a done deal. You need to go for the interview and fight for it—don't give in."

I find myself laughing at her comments. I've already told her the interview is just a formality for HR purposes, and the promotion is mine for sure.

"Chill out, Laura," I say. "Why are you so bothered? I'll get it. And I'll get a new car, so you can use Mum's Mini whenever you want."

Marie disappears, and the haze lifts. Now it is just Laura and I. The brightness makes it hard for me to see anything but my sister. Her blue eyes are intense.

"Lucy, for once in your life, will you wake up and listen to me? I don't have long. Do you understand?" Her words are urgent. "Now wake up, Lucy, and fight." The light clears, and I can see we are standing on Marie's front lawn.

"Why are you saying that, Laura? Fight for what?" I don't understand her stern attempt at encouragement.

"The job, Lucy. You need to fight. This job is your way out—I don't have long."

"Wait—way out of what?" I blink as Laura starts to blur and fade away in front of me.

"Lucy," she's calling. "Lucy, wake up and listen to me. I'm back. Wake up."

My eyes jolt open. Adewale's small mutt is yapping outside my door. I pull the covers back over my head.

"Adewale, take it downstairs, will you?" I shout with difficulty, my head thick with dehydration.

The yapping fades as Adewale's heavy feet descend the stairs. I crawl out of bed, trying not to think about the night before. Once I'm at the sink, I plant my mouth around the tap, sucking up the running water eagerly. After I have my fill, I fall onto my bed with the remnants of my dream in my mind. Laura was so clear to me. My words were meaningless, but hers were poignant and deliberate.

I don't have long.

What did that mean?

Wake up and listen to me. I'm back.

I jump to my feet and shout the words. "I'M BACK!" A splitting pain grinds against my head.

"She's back. She actually came back," I say under my breath. "Laura?" I whisper in disbelief. "Are you here?" I'm quiet, waiting for a response.

I sit back down on my bed as I try to make sense of what is happening. The last time I spoke to Laura, she was just a voice in my head. People thought I was crazy, but I knew I wasn't. I knew it was Laura's voice in my head and not my own. When things fell from the walls, she was there. It was her. Laura had told me she would be back; that was the last thing she said to me. I'd started to doubt it. After all, it had been a year since she last spoke to me, and no one believed me.

I'm not crazy, though. This dream was not like my normal dreams; it wasn't a nightmare replaying the day she died, nor was it a memory. She was there, as real as could be, talking to me. I knew if she was coming back it would be on our birthday.

"I knew it," I say and punch the air.

I recall the dream again, trying to work out the clues. The Union Tavern—that didn't mean much. Marie had been there in my dream, but she didn't say anything I can remember. What else did Laura say? That's right—*fight.*

Fight for the job! It's your way out. My way out of what?

"The interview." I stand and glance at the clock. It still reads 12:00 a.m.

"Oh, no." I dive for my phone and look at the screen for the correct time. It's 2:55 p.m. The interview is at 3:30pm.

"I can still make it," I say. "Is this what you mean, Laura? You want me to go to the interview?"

Grabbing a spray can, I douse myself in deodorant and then squeeze toothpaste into my mouth before adding a piece of chewing gum. There's no time to brush my teeth.

"That should do the trick," I say and pull on an out-of-shape black cotton dress and heels. I grab my coat and rush out my door, down the stairs, and outside. I manage to avoid Adewale's attempt at a conversation and his Pekinese gremlin's attempts at biting my ankles and run toward the tram stop.

Ignoring my body's objections to my cardiovascular system working this hard, I press on to my stop. I jab my finger at the ticket machine and input my destination. A hard wind nips at my neck, and I pull my coat tight. It's still damp, and memories from last night try to sneak their way through my thoughts.

What I did. How I did it. His face—his fat, ugly face.

I have to put that out of my mind, though. Laura told me this interview is my way out—I have to focus on the interview. Does Laura know something I don't, or can she see the future where she is? She must be able to. That's why she is telling me to fight through my hangover and go to the interview—because I get the job. My steps feel lighter. Laura is looking out for me, and I'm getting out of this nightmare life.

"Come on, come on—work." I hit the side of the ticket machine. "Come on." The tram arrives while I wait for the ticket machine to flash the price. "How much?" I kick it.

The doors to the tram are already open. I pay, grab my ticket from the slot, and then sidestep through the doors as they close.

A short ride later, I arrive. Adequately confident and ready to change my life, I find my way along the busy highway. If I've followed the instructions in the email correctly, then the road I'm walking along is called Purley Way, or as the locals call it, *the* Purley Way. It looks like an industrial dumping ground for superstores and reminds me of Plymouth—dull. I check the email again. I've passed Next Home, and I can see the signs for PC World ahead. I just can't see Furniture Forever.

Finally, the faded sign comes into view.

"There," I say aloud and increase my pace.

Slowing as I approach, I feel butterflies in the pit of my stomach. Can I do this? Another interview, and with a hangover? Can I deal with yet another rejection email explaining that they have found another candidate and thanking me for my time—or worse, no email at all? I think about my dream, about Laura and her words to me.

Fight. I certainly am—I'm fighting a stinking hangover along with a world of regret.

Two automatic doors open, and I step inside. The store is large. There's a huge dinner table display directly in front of me, and fancy gold-trimmed plates and fantastic-looking wine glasses line the table perfectly. From behind the display, a girl with huge, round, gold-rimmed spectacles is smiling at me.

"Welcome," she says.

"Hi," I nervously reply.

She moves into view, giving my attire a quick glance. Her eyes are magnified by the thick glasses.

"Are you here for an interview, or—"

"Yes." I stop her.

"Great, follow me." She walks away.

I follow, and she leads me up a wide set of stairs to the side of the store.

Turning, she lowers her voice. "This is the bed section."

I nod and whisper, "Why the low voice? Is the bed section the quiet section?"

"Exactly!" the girl says, delighted that I understood. "Bed time, quiet time."

"Ha. Of course." I glance about, wondering if this girl is for real.

The bed section isn't very big. Behind it is what looks like a janitor closet; however, it actually opens into a corridor. She points to three plastic chairs that look as if they have been taken from a school classroom and tells me to sit and wait. Opposite the chairs is another door, and I can hear muffled voices coming from the other side.

"Mr. Stevenson won't be long. When you leave, you can use the fire exit." She points to the far end. "Good luck," she wishes me with wide eyes.

"Thanks," I say.

I watch her leave the way we came, and then I take a few deep, cleansing breaths. This hangover is not easing up anytime soon, and I have to stay focused.

You've got this, I tell myself.

Though I now know Laura is with me, I still feel alone, and after five job rejections last week, my confidence is shaky to say the least. My foot is rapidly tapping with nervous energy, and I urge myself to sit still. I think about the questions I might be asked and the lies I have practiced as suitable replies. Then I find myself wondering if I should just be truthful this time. Could that be where I've been going wrong? So what if I've been living on the streets? Is that not the sign of a committed hard worker? Yes, that's it. This time I will tell the truth. I will fight for this job. I'll make them see that I'm the only candidate that wants this job—no, that *needs* this job, and that I'm more motivated than any other person they will see today because I've lived on the streets.

Then the door opens, and a fresh wave of nerves hits me.

You're the best person for this job, I remind myself. I can't see inside, but I can see a young man in a suit, one hand on the door handle, laughing at something funny that had obviously been said prior to the door opening. He steps out, closing the door behind him and still grinning at the private exchange.

"He said you can go in."

"Thanks," I say and stand.

You can laugh, I think as the suited man walks toward the fire exit. *This job is mine; I have it from higher authority*. I allow myself a smug smile and push open the door to the interview room.

The door to the room slams behind me, making me jump a little. The meeting room is stark—only a desk and a sizable man in a blue suit who is seated but has his back to me. He seems to be looking for something in a filing cabinet. I stand there awkwardly, waiting for him to ask me to approach. My eyes trace the bare, paint-chipped walls. Should I wait, or is that too timid? Should I be bold and sit down in front of him like a confident salesperson would?

I'm still standing in the same spot when the man in the blue suit pulls out a file and swings his chair around to face me. I look at him properly for the first time. As our eyes lock, the color from his face drains as fast as I feel mine drain; however, he regains his composure faster than I do.

"Wh—what is this?" He looks behind me as if someone is hiding between me and the door. "Who let you in here?"

I freeze. I can't believe it's him—the hand job guy. What are the odds? I'm speechless, then confused—this is my job, my way out.

He lowers his voice. "What's the meaning of this?"

"The interview," is all I manage to say. I try to recall his name—Steve, Stuart? All I can think of is "Hand Job Guy"— Simon, that's it.

With a jolting motion, he opens the file and looks inside. "You're Laura?" He looks as nervous as I feel.

"I—I—I'm Lucy."

My legs have turned to jelly, and I can feel them shaking. Images from the night before flash intermittently through my mind. His fat tongue shoved down my throat, his hand twisted into my hair. I'm remembering the whole seedy event with him right in front of me.

I flinch as he slams the file shut. "You have to get out, get out now."

"Why?"

"Do you really think I can have you working here after what you did?" He glances over my shoulder again, then whispers, "You're a prostitute."

The name cuts deep. "Prostitute?" I ask, and by his expression, a little louder than he'd like. "You said you didn't think I was a prostitute!" I'm unsure why his opinion should matter, but it does. "I'm not a prostitute."

"Shh," he hisses at me. He stands, his shoulders now pushed back. "You weren't until you took my money. No. No, you need to leave, just leave!" His fat hand slams hard onto his desk.

I step back quickly, hitting the door.

"Now get out, you hooker!" he insists. "We have no need for your type here."

I turn and fumble for the door handle. I can hear him breathing. He's panicked, like an excited, overweight bulldog fighting to breathe. Why am I running away? He is just as guilty as I am. The handle finally jolts down, and I yank the door open, but before I leave, I turn to face him. I can't just run away and let him have the last word, to have power over me like that.

"I'm not a hooker," I say. "You convinced me to do it. You knew I needed that money, but you didn't offer me a job interview, did you? You're scum. You manipulated me with money. You're the whore, not me."

He's silent. His cheeks flush, yet his eyes narrow in on me. "Everyone has a price. Get out."

"Fucking die." I draw phlegm into my mouth and spit at him.

I run down the corridor, through the fire exit door, and out onto a steel set of external steps. The one-way door closes behind me, and I just stand there at the side of the building looking over what must be the staff parking lot. I take deep, long breaths through my nose.

"Shit," I say. "What the hell was that?"

Hesitantly, I make my way down the metal steps toward the tram stop. My eyes are burning, and I can't stop the tears from falling.

Prostitute. Is that really what I am now? I don't stop at the tram stop. I'm just walking, sobbing as I think about the night before. There are so many emotions I didn't want to feel, didn't *know* I would feel, but I'm feeling them now. My hands shake as I try to light a cigarette, the white stick bouncing between my quivering lips and my fingers unable to control it. I throw it to the ground in frustration.

My frustration is not only with myself but with Laura. She said this was my way out. How the hell was this my way out? I trusted her—people back home in Cornwall thought I was crazy, but I still trusted her, trusted that she was there, not just in my head. Now what? Did I literally dream up a dream because I wanted to hear her that badly? Am I a crazy two-bit hooker destined for a life with no family and only a friend like Priya? Immediately, I feel bad for thinking of Priya in that way—she is all I have right now.

Sadiq isn't at the till, thank goodness, because my eyes are red, and he would have asked why I've been crying. As normal, his uncle hands me the cheapest bottle of vodka they stock. I thank him and leave.

"Lucy!" I hear Sadiq call out to me as I exit.

I wipe my eyes dry, irritated with the delay. I just want to go home.

Sadiq follows me outside. "Hey, listen, I'm glad I caught you." Then he notices my face. "You OK?"

I just look at him. *Do I look OK?* "Fine," I say. "I'm just fine and dandy, Sadiq, can't you tell?"

"Lucy, you're not fine. Come inside."

"Sadiq, stop. I just want to go home." I resist a burning desire to vent.

"OK, look, Lucy, I just wanted to let you know …" He is fidgeting and won't keep still. "I—I saw you last night. On the camera. It's OK, I'm not judging you, I—I, um—"

Too late. Boiling point reached. "AHH!" I scream at the top of my lungs. "Why am I even ALIVE?"

Sadiq looks horrified at my outburst.

I start to run. Fast, faster, faster. Tears sting my eyes in the cold wind, and people move quickly out of my way as I pass them. In the distance, Sadiq cries for me to stop. Rounding the corner, I fall to my knees on a wet patch of grass outside an apartment block. I clutch the bottle of vodka tight, gasping for air between sobs.

Looking up, I see Sadiq panting next to me, bent over with his hands on his knees. He looks as if he is going to pass out. I can't help it—I just start laughing, then crying. It will never stop amazing me how the people you least expect to care for you do.

"Lucy, what's wrong?" He's fallen down next to me, and his short arms are holding me in a tight bear hug.

"I'm—I'll be OK," I sniff.

He pulls away from me, his breathing still heavy. "Lucy, please, don't say things like that. You're scaring me. You're alive because you're a good person. Life can be tough—tougher for some than others, granted, but you do what you have to do. It's not your fault. Listen, I saw the CCTV."

I move to leave—the embarrassment is too much—but he stops me.

"Lucy, stay, please. I didn't watch; I figured out what was happening. It's OK. I get it. I just want you to know it's not your fault. I've seen that car around here before. Listen to me, if you want to tell the police—"

"Police?" I scoot away from him along the grass.

"No, no, Lucy, listen—you don't have to. I'm just saying if you want to press charges, I have the video."

"No, the police would arrest me. And—no, I just want to forget about it." I get to my feet. Sadiq helps me over to a wall, where we both sit down.

He lights a cigarette for me then says, "It's OK if you don't want to report it, but if you do—" I try to speak, but he holds up a hand. "If you *do* want to report it, the police won't press charges on you. I know because they are in my shop all the time talking to me about scumbags like him. They want to clear the streets of dicks like that, and they need girls to come forward."

I don't answer.

"The video is there if you want it," he says. "And I'm here if you ever need me." I nod. "Can I walk you home?"

"I'll be OK."

"Sure?"

"I'm sure."

He throws an arm around my shoulder, and I lean into him for a closer hug.

The bedsit is quiet for a Tuesday evening, and I'm glad to slip into my room undetected. I purposefully leave the lights off; I don't want anyone to know I'm home. The only light I have is the glow from the yellow streetlight directly outside my window. I fill a cup with vodka and fall onto the wooden chair. I just stare at my feet, then at my muddy knees.

I think of last night, of the dream, and then of the interview. I still can't believe it happened; the coincidence is laughable. Crazy. But I don't *feel* crazy. I think about my sister's words again.

Fight. My way out. That's what she said.

"Fight for what, Laura?"

Nothing makes much sense. I sigh heavily. Could I have really dreamt Laura up?

In my dark room, I reach for the bottle of vodka. There is a sliding sound, and then the bottle slams to the floor.

"Shit." I stare at the puddle. My desire to scream is suppressed by the realization that I didn't touch the bottle, and definitely not enough to make it slide away from me and smash to the ground.

"Laura?" I look about the unlit room. "Laura, are you here?"

CHAPTER 7

THEN–LAURA

Cornwall, three years ago
July

When Grandma Betty died, people said she would be at peace in heaven. If this was true, I couldn't say. I'd not seen Grandma Betty, and "peace" was not a word that I would have used to describe my state. Perhaps "clarity" would be a better word—I understood I was dead, but I did not feel peaceful. I couldn't have told you how long it had been since the day I left my body. I couldn't have told you anything other than … nothing. That was my state: nothing. I suppose I could have said darkness, but then darkness would have implied something other than nothing.

That was my state until I heard them—faint whispers pushing through into my nothingness. Just like I'd done hundreds of times before, I told myself to open my eyes, but this time, they actually opened.

It was so bright I had to squint. Was I in a park, maybe? I saw grass, and it was vibrant—an ocean of tiny green blades shimmering about me. People stood in the distance, or so it seemed. The dark figures seemed familiar, so I moved toward them. I would have called it walking, but I'm not sure if walking was what I was actually doing. Glancing at my feet proved that they were striding—or perhaps even gliding—over the grass, which didn't squish beneath my feet. Amongst the crowd, I saw Auntie Cassy, her features oddly blurred, along with Kitty, Jen, and a man I was sure was Mr. Livingston from the corner shop.

Why is he here? I wondered. Next to him stood Marie and Ed, my boss. Eventually—and I mean eventually in the loose sense of the word because my comprehension of what was happening felt somewhat untrustworthy—my grasp on reality caught up with my blurred sight, and then I saw Lucy and the priest throwing dirt into a hole in the ground. The sound of the mud splattering down onto the casket confirmed what was going on—this was my own funeral.

It wasn't something I had ever given much thought to. I never considered the people who would attend and those who wouldn't, the people I hardly knew crying for me, and the people I loved numb. I couldn't watch. I thought myself away behind an oak tree. Why had I come back? What use was it to see my loved ones' grief? I couldn't help them. I didn't even know what I was. A ghost, or trapped in limbo?

From my vantage point, I snuck a peek. People were exchanging kind words and warm embraces. I could see family I'd not seen for a long time, friends I didn't know I had, and even people I didn't recognize—Dad's work colleagues, perhaps. I wanted to be close to Lucy, but not with so many people around. Things felt overwhelming, and suddenly it was as if I could hear all their thoughts. The silence had become deafeningly loud.

I waited for people to leave. The people I hadn't recognized left first, followed by the friends who hadn't bothered to talk to me since we left school. I noticed Kitty hovering near Lucy as if she were going to approach, but she didn't. I watched her walk away to catch the other non-family members. My dad led Lucy to a bench, where she sat with her head in her hands and Marie by her side. My mum was standing by the grave. People shook my dad's hand and kissed his cheeks. I could hear what they were saying. I tried not to listen, but all the chitter-chatter echoed relentlessly. I didn't want to hear people's sympathy for my dad's loss. It was my loss too—I had lost my whole family. What felt like an agonizing howl built inside me, yet all I released was a small whimper.

I moved to where Lucy sat on the bench. Being close to her felt right—I felt whole. It took us being parted for me to grasp how together we were. Her energy synergized with mine, giving me what I can only describe as life force. Noticing that she wasn't crying, just staring, I followed her gaze over to my grave, where our parents stood. Then I looked over at Marie, glad that Lucy was not alone.

Marie was holding a leaflet—the service program, I guessed, as it had a picture of me from the night of our birthday. I noticed the left side of my silver heart necklace hanging around my neck. Then I saw the date: July 28th. Was it really July? Had two months really passed, and why would they wait so long for my funeral?

I watched the last of the cars drive away through a grand set of old iron gates. My vision had an odd shimmer about it, and blinking wasn't clearing it. I reminded myself that I was dead, so comparing things to my old life wouldn't help. Was I there to help? The thought lingered. And how could I help? I was the one who had caused all this; if I hadn't driven, if I had—

My thoughts stopped. Something, the thing blurring my sight, had caught my eye. I moved closer to Lucy. Little vertical gold chains shimmered about her from head to toe. On closer inspection, I saw they were minute links of light, of energy. Somehow, I knew this for certain. I looked over at Marie, and she had the same shimmer. My sight wasn't distorted or blurred; I'd just been seeing it all wrong.

A deep sense of clarity filled my soul, and then, like a surge of electricity, I understood. I understood everything—the ground beneath me, the air, the trees and pollen blowing in the wind, my parents, Lucy, and Marie—even the bench they sat on. It was all connected, a collaboration of information. I had all the information I needed; anything I wanted to know was right there in the fabric of life. I just needed to let it in. To feel it.

As I slowly ran my fingers through the shimmering chains, I felt her—Lucy. I could feel her energy pulsating. Her heartbeat was in rhythm with my own.

Thud-thud, thud-thud, thud-thud.

I felt alive. And then I saw them—memories, not mine, but hers, accompanied by her emotions.

Through her eyes, I saw the Mini Cooper speeding toward her and then felt the stark realization that the car had lost control. I felt the soul-wrenching fear as Lucy screamed my name at the moment of the impact. It all happened so quickly. Lucy went running to the car. Parts of the car were bouncing and crashing to the ground, and glass was falling from the smashed window because she was yanking at the door handle. My body was slumped toward the passenger seat, and by the look of it, my head had smashed too. I could actually feel Lucy's adrenaline raging as she frantically unbuckled my seatbelt and pulled me free of the car.

Someone grabbed her from behind, a man who told her she shouldn't move me. I couldn't see his face. I was seeing everything my sister saw, and her eyes were fixed on me, my ragdoll limp body. She screamed at the stranger to let her go, but he held her tight. Someone else was assisting me on the ground. I was muttering and making noises, but my eyes were shut. Lucy yanked herself free from the grasp of the stranger, shouting my name and dropping to her knees next to me. Holding my hand to her tear-soaked cheek, she demanded I stay alive.

Quickly, I withdrew my hand from the chains. How was this possible? I'd just been inside my sister's mind, seen her deepest thoughts, and experienced her pain. She was still sitting in front of me just as before, but I wasn't the same. I'd never felt anything like this when I was alive. It felt like belonging, only on an organic level. The earth beneath me filled my being with information—it was literally talking to me.

I could hear the wind talking to the trees, and the birds as they sung to be free. My eyes darted from trees to flowers and into the mud housing the tiny blades of grass. I listened to the small bugs tapping and clicking to tell each other where to go, which direction the best pollenated flowers were in. There were thousands of them, all connected yet all individual. We belonged to each other—I belonged to *them*. How had I not seen this when I was alive? How had I not felt this profound sense of connection?

Lucy blew into a tissue, drawing my attention back. Now that I understood how I could connect, I hesitantly reached out. I wanted to connect again, to find out why. Why had I come back? Would swiping another chain give me answers as to why I was still there?

I swiped.

Was this a police station? Lucy was sitting on a hard plastic seat inside what I quickly identified as the Looe police station. Mum and Dad were there too. A young man with a police-issued tie over his shirt led them back to an office. From behind his desk, he started explaining something, but Lucy was not listening, so I couldn't make out what he was saying. All I could hear, see, and feel was Lucy. Overwhelming feelings of guilt drowned out everything. I could hear her thoughts as she wished it were her dead instead of me. She was mumbling in her head, pleading for the universe to slip away, begging God to take her.

Then my dad's hand brought her attention back to what the policeman was saying. Dad smiled at Lucy softly and nodded as if encouraging her—a silent exchange letting her know he was there. My dad didn't let go of her, and I could feel the warmth of his hand on top of hers. The policeman seemed to be confirming information that my family already knew.

"The results confirm our suspicions," he said. "Rohypnol was found in Laura's system."

My mum was quietly crying, and I could feel Lucy's thoughts drifting back to desires of dying. Another hand squeeze from my dad brought Lucy back to listening again.

"As you know," the policeman continued, "my team searched Darren Gibbin's room and found Rohypnol. He was taken into custody, and as for Tye Baker, he has been released without charge."

"Why?" Lucy shouted.

"I understand this is difficult to hear," he said, "but there is no evidence to suggest Tye had any involvement."

"No," Lucy objected. "Ben said he saw Laura in Darren's room with Tye."

The policeman appeared to consider his next words carefully. "Lucy, we've been over this already. Tye was with his girlfriend Jen all night."

"No, he was the one who found her. Jen wasn't there."

"Jen said he had gone upstairs to his room to get her a sweater, and that's when he found your sister. He was not away from Jen for more than a few minutes before she heard him call for you. Tye did not have anything to do with what happened to your sister, and if it's worth anything, I believe Jen and Tye. How long have you known your boyfriend Ben?"

"Ex," Lucy corrected. "Seven months. Why?"

The policeman didn't answer.

"Why?" Lucy persisted. "Do you think he had something to do with this? He didn't."

"I'm not saying that, Lucy, but what he is telling us and what the evidence show are two different things."

Silence fell, and Lucy slipped back into a pit of self-loathing. I wanted to stop her thoughts but couldn't. All I could do was observe as she asked herself why had she not done more to watch out for me at the party, not looked for me sooner.

Lucy thought back to her breakup with Ben. She was in Marie's car in a McDonald's parking lot, and Marie was urging her to eat. She pushed the nuggets away with a look of disgust. I could feel her stomach acid spitting, craving food, but her heart ached with guilt at the thought of eating to live. She'd dialed Ben's number, told him that she wasn't in the right state of mind to be in a relationship. He'd protested.

"Ben, please don't push me to stay with you. It's too much. The thought that you took those pictures of my sister when she was drugged—" Her own words choked her.

"No, Lucy, oh god, never. Never. The police believe me. You have to believe me."

"The police said there's no evidence. I—I just don't understand why Laura would do that. And she said she didn't remember."

"Lucy, I swear to you. She asked me—maybe she had taken the drug by then and didn't know what she was saying. But I swear I didn't know, baby."

Lucy ended the call, though there was a part of her that wanted to believe him. It was Ben, after all. She knew him, and he would never do anything to hurt anyone.

The next thing I saw was Lucy staring into the bathroom mirror as if I were staring into my own soul. Tears had swollen her eyes, and her emotions seemed numb. I saw the razor in her hands as it fell into the sink, and then it all went dark.

Standing at the top of our stairs, I heard raised voices. It wasn't shouting, more like raised whispers between our mum and dad. Lucy's wrists were bandaged. She didn't want to die—I could feel it. I felt her regret and remorse that she had frightened our dad by cutting herself.

He has enough to deal with, she was thinking. *Laura was his daughter, and he can't handle losing me too.* Lucy listened as our dad told our mum to let up on her, pleading with her to remember that Lucy was her child and was hurting at the loss just as much as she was.

"The loss?" Mum hissed back. "She is *dead*, not fucking lost. I told Lucy to stop giving her such a hard time. I knew something was wrong. I asked if she had taken drugs; I could see it in her eyes, my poor baby's eyes. I could see it, Robert. I could see it."

"I know, Kathrin, but Lucy didn't know."

"She should have known—*I* knew. I could tell Laura wasn't just hungover. Lucy must have known too, but she ran out of the house knowing Laura would run after her. She knew Laura would go after her, she knew it—she knew she would chase her. Why, Robert? Why did she have to do it?"

Lucy looked down at her wrists.

I withdrew my hands from Lucy's chains. What had happened to my family? And Rohypnol? I'd been roofied! Did that also mean I'd been—the thought repulsed me. Darren, no. I knew Darren, and he would never do something like that, surely. He always seemed so genuine.

So that's why my funeral has taken two months, I thought. *Because of the drugs they found in my system.* I looked at Lucy's wrists, which were still bandaged. What had she done? What had been going on? Why was our Mum blaming Lucy? It wasn't her fault—it was mine.

Marie had moved close to Lucy on the bench and pulled her under her arm. I watched them for a moment as they silently cried side by side. I questioned the reason I was there. I couldn't see other dead people, and I was in a graveyard. If I was dead, surely I'd see other spirits—or whatever I was. Then, in a moment of clarity, I knew. Heightened energy—they had drawn me back.

Of course, I thought. All of my friends and family were in the same place thinking of me at the same time; I was bound to be drawn back. But now what? What was my purpose now that I was back?

I looked over at our parents. They stood side by side, looking down at my casket. What was my mum thinking, blaming Lucy? And then I was there, right in front of her. Call it intuition, but somehow, I knew I could connect; her energy was so potent. I stood close but didn't reach out. Instead, I breathed in through my nose, just like I used to do when meditating. I breathed steadily, deep down into my belly. I focused on my breath, the rise of my stomach on my inhale and the fall on my exhale. Then I let it all go, everything I'd just seen and felt with Lucy.

It was easy to connect after that, and my mum's energy flowed with mine. I even thought she saw me at one point. Her head sprung up, and her eyes darted around as if looking for something. She knew I was there, I could feel it. I could feel my mum yearning to be with me again. She was gazing directly into my eyes, my soul. And then she was gone—just a shell looking right through me. The connection was lost, and all I felt from her then was spite.

"You OK, Kathrin?" my dad asked.

I softly whispered into her ear, "Mum." I felt her energy wrap itself around me again, but it was suffocating and toxic. I couldn't bear it and wriggled as if I could shake it off, but it stuck.

"Kathrin?" My dad placed his arm around her shoulder and thankfully broke the connection. I gasped, breathing in fresh air. My mum shrugged my dad's arm off her shoulder, which was not unusual. I'd never really seen them overly affectionate when I was alive. My dad's energy was stout. His chains shimmered bright compared to how dull my mum's were, and they appeared brilliant white.

Shifting in front of my dad, I felt an overwhelming urge to hug him and tell him it was all right. I could feel his love for me emanating into the space around him, and I could feel the sheer despair he held for my mum and his determination to protect Lucy.

"Kathrin," he said quietly, "it's nearly time to go. People will be waiting for us back at the house." He reached for her shoulder, but she moved to the opposite side of my grave. She didn't look at my dad, just stared into the hole in the ground.

"Dad," I whispered.

He couldn't sense me, not like my mum had—she had known I was there, but her sorrowful energy was blocking me. My dad just wasn't listening. I was sure I could get through to him if he would slow his energy down so I could get in. His energy was swirling around so fast there was no way I could connect the same way as I did with my mum. Not knowing what else to do, I reached out and swiped in the hope I would find some of the answers I was looking for.

I felt him immediately, and my heart raced. Then I saw memories, but I couldn't make sense of them all. My dad's mind was racing. It looked as if someone kept hitting the fast forward or rewind button.

Suddenly, I was in a living room. Lucy and I were just babies, and Mum was changing one of our nappies—mine, I felt. Dad was holding Lucy and rocking her in his arms. It must have been our home in Torquay, because there was nothing on the walls and just a few boxes in the corner. I remembered my dad telling me that they had moved into the cottage just after we were born.

Then it got all mixed up again. Images jumped in and out of view: our first day at school, sports day, our dad shouting up the stairs to turn the music down. Christmas dinner at Grandma Betty's. My mum shouting at him from the passenger car seat.

I urged my dad to slow his energy, and eventually, I was able to grasp another memory. It was an odd feeling, a feeling I'd never felt. He was in a prenatal unit lifting me out of a clear plastic crib and into his big, hairy arms. My mum was in bed with her knees up. Her hair was astray, and sweat had stuck it to the side of her face. She looked exhausted. My dad looked down at me in his arms, and I felt it again: a warm sensation, as if he could laugh and cry and scream all at the same time. Every inch of skin that was touching me tingled. He never wanted to let me go. It was a true love I'd never felt, a love only a parent could feel, and one that I knew I'd never get the chance to feel for myself.

I pulled my hand away so fast that I flew backward, narrowly missing a fall into my own grave. It was all too much to comprehend. Why was this happening to me? I thought myself away to behind another nearby tree where I could watch from afar again. What did all this mean? I had a new awareness, but what good was that to me if I didn't know why and what for?

The bird songs grew louder, the trees rustled and snapped above my head, and bugs with their teensy weensy wings and tiny feet tapped loudly. Even the grass being blown by the wind was deafening.

"Stop. Just STOP!" I pleaded. My hands spontaneously slammed over my ears, and I fell to my knees.

Silence. The noises had actually listened to me. It was all so quiet. I quickly got to my feet and checked to see if my family was still there. They were. My parents were walking toward my dad's car, his arm outstretched behind him and beckoning Marie to bring Lucy.

As I prepared to join them, I saw Ben. He was standing a ways off in the distance next to a bush. I went to him. Once I was in front of him, I could tell right away that his energy was strange and had a bad smell—it actually stank. I had to get away.

Suddenly, I was in the car, sitting between Lucy and Marie. No one was talking. We drove toward the old iron gates the other cars had left through. I felt Lucy's phone vibrate, and I sneaked a peek. It was Ben. The text simply read, I LOVE YOU.

I turned and looked through the rear window just in time to see it—a glimpse directly into his soul. This was the real Ben, and the reason I was back.

CHAPTER 8

NOW–LUCY

London, present day
July

My door vibrates, and Priya's voice stirs me from my sorry state on the floor. I guess I fell off my bed in the night. I rub my eyes.

"Lucy, open up!" I hear.

I don't answer, hoping that if I ignore her, she'll go away.

A second voice joins the unnecessary commotion outside my door. It's Adewale.

"Priya, what are you doing?"

"Adewale, she's not come out of her room in over a week," Priya says.

"I think you should leave her be," he replies.

Silently, I agree with him and pull the duvet over my head. This is the last thing I want to be dealing with right now. My sister is back, and although my life sucks and I'm heading in the general direction of utter hopelessness, I think I know what I have to do.

"And if she is dead in there?" Priya persists. "Then what?" She gives a more urgent knock, and I assume the fetal position.

"Lucy is not dead, Priya. Just leave her be. She will come out when she is ready."

"What are you saying, Adewale? That Lucy is avoiding me?"

"No—no, dat is not what I am saying. Priya, she does not want to see anyone. Let her come to you when she is ready."

"You think you're so wise—"

"No, Priya, I do not. I think you are stupid."

From under my duvet, I shout, "ENOUGH! Enough, you two."

I crawl to the door and open it to see two sets of brown eyes looking back at me in astonishment. I can only imagine what I must look like. I've not washed in a week. Without a word, I walk back into my room and fall onto my bare bed.

Priya hurries in behind me, picking up my duvet and the remnants of a midnight snack that fell from my mouth in the dark and is now scattered about the floor.

"Lucy, you'll get rats living like this," she scolds.

I don't answer. Adewale pulls up the chair in front of me and sits, his arms folded across his body and his head to one side. He looks inquisitively at me.

"What?" I say.

He moves his head to the other side as if observing a newfound breed of person. Silence doesn't make him uncomfortable.

"What's the date?" I ask.

"Wednesday," Priya answers incorrectly while stacking my dirty plates on the counter.

"Date. What's the date?"

"Da 28th," Adewale answers.

I slam my head into my mattress. Of all the days Priya knocks on my door, it's on the third anniversary of Laura's funeral. What are the odds? I would laugh at the irony if my face wasn't numb from sleeping pills. I don't think I can even cry right now.

"Lucy?" Adewale says. "We can go if you want."

My face still planted in my mattress, I shake my head. I don't want them to go; I just don't want to talk about it, any of it

—the day she left, the police telling us that roofies had been found in her blood, hearing that Darren had been arrested, and the feeling that I'd let her down. I should have protected her. My face is still buried, so I can't see the scars, but I know they are there: two long, faint, white bumps across my wrists. Priya and Adewale never ask about my scars. I thought one day they might ask questions like why, or how long ago, but they haven't, and I'm glad. I sit up and ask Adewale to pass me the bottle of water next to him.

"Thanks," I say when he does.

Priya sits gently next to me, and I'm quietly grateful, as any kind of bouncing will most definitely end with me vomiting. She strokes my hair, and I wonder if she learned that from her own mum. I have good people around me; why I can't I let them in? I can't answer my own question, and I don't have the emotional real estate for that. Everyone I get close to leaves anyway.

"Lucy." Priya disturbs my thoughts. "What's been going on with you? Is it about—?" She looks over at Adewale. "You know," she says, trying but failing to keep her question vague.

"It's OK, Priya. Adewale knows. I told him."

Priya is referring to Hand Job Guy and the interview. Over the past two months, I've confided in Adewale a lot—not about Laura, although sometimes, with the strange things he says, I wonder if he knows. He also managed to get me a temporary job at the car wash down the road. It's not a lot of money. The pay covers my rent, and that is it. To eat, I either beg or scrounge off Priya, but at least I'm not homeless.

"Is it working?" Adewale points to the dream catcher above my bed. He gave it to me last month. It's comments like those that make me wonder.

"Well, it's not caught me a dream job, so no," I say.

Adewale smiles his regular smile, the all-knowing wide grin. Priya is right—Adewale *does* give off the impression that he thinks he's wiser than everyone.

"So what's up, Lucy?" Priya asks, starting to tidy up again.

"Well, I'm fresh out of cash, and I don't have anything more to sell other than myself." A look of sheer horror streaks across Adewale's face. "It's OK, I'm not going to do that again. I've learned my lesson. I've still got that laptop to sell." I gesture toward my cupboard. "But I'm holding off till I really need to, which is probably now." I try a chuckle.

Priya holds up a toothbrush that she retrieved from under a shoe.

I shrug.

"Look, you guys don't need to worry about me—I have a plan." This is not exactly true, but close enough.

It's not like I can tell them that the reason I've been locked in my room not making any noise isn't because I'm depressed but because I've been taking sleeping pills to keep me asleep so that I can communicate with my dead sister. I've been branded crazy once before after confiding in someone I thought I could trust, and look where that got me. No, telling them about Laura is not an option.

In my dreams, I appear as my former self, from before the accident, but Laura is different. She is stoutly—mature, even—and persistent. The night after the mortifying interview incident, she appeared in my dream as just an image, saying nothing. Then there was nothing for a few weeks. The second time she came back, I was taking a nap, and that's when I thought of it: sleeping pills. If I could keep myself asleep, then I'd be optimizing her chances of getting through to me. I asked Adewale if he knew anyone who could get me some pills to help me sleep, and that's when he gave me his dreamcatcher and a few wise words about sleep meditation or something. He did, however, come good on the pills last week. I've been hibernating ever since, waiting in vain for another sign.

That was until yesterday. I was starting to think the pills might be blocking her, but yesterday, she appeared again. At first I was in a regular dream, stitched together with memories of real places we used to go. Then I was back in the same dream I'd had many times, walking along the river with her. This time, we reached the end of it. Laura stood at the edge, a massive waterfall behind her, and held out her hand. I slipped my hand neatly into hers, and she jumped. We didn't hit the water; we didn't hit anything.

As I faced her, there was nothing, and yet it felt like everything. My eyes locked on her, scared to lose sight of her, although I felt that if I'd looked into the darkness, I would have seen so much more. A vodka bottle appeared in her hand, and she poured out its contents. I nodded. I know she wants me to stop drinking. Her hand drifted silently through the dark until it came to rest over my eyes. Images of the interview flickered in and out of view, and then I saw Sadiq telling me he kept the CCTV footage. There was one final image of Hand Job Guy—Simon. He looked remorseful. That's when I woke. Am I meant to confront him?

I've not taken another sleeping pill. I've run out, and Adewale made it very clear he would not get me more, not that it matters. In the last week, Laura has only come to me once, and I won't find a job if I'm asleep all day.

I've heard of sleep deprivation, but what's the opposite, and what are the effects? Are they what I'm feeling now? I spent the best part of last night trying to stay awake and not to let the pills pull me back into slumber as I replayed the dream over and over in my head, thinking about how Laura felt familiar and yet not. Has she changed in three years like I have? Has her reality, whatever that is, weathered her the same way my reality has shaped me into who I am today? And the nothingness I saw, the nothing that felt like everything, is that her reality? Where is she?

"Is this part of your plan, Laura?" Priya asks, pulling me back into the present.

She is holding up Laura's driver's licence, which she must have found on the floor.

I snatch it out of her hand. "Give that to me."

"Lucy, where did you get that? Why d'you have a fake ID? Tell me this plan of yours isn't dangerous?"

"It's not," I say, holding my sister's driver's licence tight. I glare at Adewale, who is giving me another of his knowing stares. "Adewale, stop looking at me like that," I snap.

"Like what?"

"Like that—like you can read my mind or something."

"Lucy, if I could read your mind, I would not be sitting in your room wondering if you have gone crazy and need professional help. I would also be able to help you, but how can we help if you won't tell us what is going on?"

I sigh. "I'm sorry; you're right. That job thing properly messed me up. But I'm back, and I know what I need to do. Or I think I know, anyway. I've got half a plan, and I'll wing the rest."

Priya reaches for Laura's ID. "Going to tell us the plan, then?"

"I'm not sure if I can." I push the driver's licence under my mattress. "I mean, I only thought of it last night—or was it today? What's the time?"

Adewale's heavyset chest has risen, and he lets out a deliberate sigh.

"I know I sound crazy, Adewale," I say.

Priya hands me my toothbrush. "Go brush your teeth. Then you are telling us whatever you're planning, and that's not an option."

"All right," I say and snatch the toothbrush.

I stand in the bathroom, hurriedly shoving my small toothbrush around my mouth. There's no harm in telling Priya and Adewale some of what I'm going to do, but I'm certainly going to leave out the part with the dreams. I look in the mirror, and I see that I look like crap. My eyes are yellow and bloodshot.

Jesus. I've always been skinny, but even I know I'm wasting away. I pull up my dirty T-shirt, revealing two pronounced hip bones, and run my hand across my concaved belly, thinking how sick I must look to people. Pulling at the skin below my eyes, I know what I have to do. Stop drinking is the first thing, and the second, get that job. I should have seen this sooner. Laura told me to do this on my birthday, the night before the interview.

Fight, she had said, yet it's taken me till now to get it. Hand Job Guy *will* employ me; he'll have no other option after I've finished with him. I smirk at my reflection.

"Right, OK, if you want to know," I say, walking back into the room, "I've decided to follow Hand Job Guy and find out where he lives."

"Then what?" Priya asks.

"Then … then I'm not sure. But," I say quickly, before anyone can interrupt, "I have options. I could confront him, report him to the police, or get him beaten up."

I decide not to tell them about my plan to get the job—not yet, anyway. Not until I actually know how I'm going to do it. Blackmail is my current line of thought, but I need to see where he lives, if he has a family. I need to find out what I'm working with, what leverage I have. Then I'll tell them the truth.

"Lucy." Adewale is not hiding his disappointment. "No. You cannot do this. I will help you if you want to talk to da police, but you do not want to go down the violence route, do you? Where will dis get you? You have bigger things to concentrate on than revenge. Revenge will not pay your bills."

"Adewale, you have to trust me on this. I have to follow him, and when I see him, I'll know the plan. I know I sound crazy, and I told you I only had some of the plan, but—"

Priya jumps in. "I'm coming with you."

"I will go too," Adewale says.

"Absolutely not. Look, it will be much better if I do this on my own."

"And how will you follow him?" Adewale asks. "You do not have a car. And what if he turns violent on you? Who will protect you?"

I consider this. "You're right." *Damn.* My head is still thick from the sleeping pills and not working quite as fast as I'd like it to. I look down at the carpet as if the answers are woven into the brown threads.

"So you need me to drive," Adewale is saying.

"I do, but I'd rather do this alone. Can I borrow your car?" I ask, but I already know the answer.

"No. Like I said, it is not safe."

"Fine. Let's do it tonight?"

Adewale and Priya both agree. Like it or not, I'm not doing this alone.

Three hours later, we are all piling into Adewale's car. I climb into the back and instantly regret my choice of seat when I find an old Burger King box with its leftovers trying to colonize the limp cardboard. We head toward the Purley way and then hit rush hour traffic.

"Bloody hell," I say. "This queue goes on forever."

Slowly, we edge around Reeves Corner's one-way system and into the Jubilee bypass. From there, things start to flow a bit faster—that is, until we take the exit ramp onto Stafford Road and hit a gridlock.

I check my phone for the time. "I hope he doesn't leave before closing."

"You do not know when he leaves?" Adewale asks.

"No. How would I know that? I don't even know if he will be here."

Adewale bounces his eyebrows at me. I don't react; he was the one who wanted to help me. We travel the rest of the way with just the radio for entertainment, as no one speaks.

As we turn left toward PC World and then take a right into Furniture Forever's parking lot, my heart pumps a little more blood through my veins than feels comfortable. I tell Adewale to reverse into a corner spot furthest from the store but with a clear view of the entrance and the fire escape on the side of the building. I hope there's not a back entrance. Then we wait and wait—and wait.

It's hot, and Adewale's car has no air conditioning, so I manually wind a window down. Then our waiting pays off.

"There." I point. "There, coming out the front, that's him—that's him."

"Yuck, he's big," Priya observes. "Fat."

Adewale's top lip pushes up toward his nose. He follows Simon out of the parking lot.

"The traffic is still slow-moving," I say, "which should make it easy to follow him. Stay a few cars back."

Adewale does what I say and sits two cars behind the black Audi. It's easy to follow him, too easy, and my nerves spike. What if he has seen us? Adewale smiles at me in the rear-view mirror.

"It is OK," he says. "He does not know we are here."

"How d'you know that?" I ask.

"He has been on his phone, and I can see him laughing and talking. Trust me, he has no idea what is going on."

I nod, hoping Adewale is right.

We are heading toward Coulsdon and into Chipstead Village. The traffic is still thick, and we are now four cars behind, since I was getting worried that we were too close and asked Adewale to drop back. Simon lives further out than I had anticipated, and the farther we follow him, the less traffic there is. I didn't think it would take us this far out of town; we've been driving for over thirty minutes now.

His Audi takes a right down a narrow country road, and now we're only two cars behind him. Adewale holds back, losing sight of him when we coast around the bends in the road. Then the car in front of us turns off, and I'm worried Simon will notice our car behind him.

"Guys, this is a bit close for comfort," I say.

The Audi slows, and its indicator flashes for a right turn. We are coming up even closer, so I duck out of view. Thankfully, we turn back onto a busy road and are soon hidden among other cars. We stay on the A217 until I see a sign for Lower Kingswood. Not long after that, the Audi makes a left turn, and we follow with two other cars between ours. Then he pulls up onto a large, open driveway. Bingo. Adewale continues driving and then doubles back at the bottom of the road so we can we sit opposite. The house sits high on its patch of land, making it easy to see over the low, manicured hedge. The thatched roof weighs heavily on the wide, one-story home, and it looks like something straight out of a country living magazine. Then I panic—Adewale's car will stick out like a sore thumb in a quaint upper-class village.

"He has a wife, then," Priya says.

A slight young woman with ringlet-curled, mousy brown hair has appeared in the doorway. She is holding a baby. I take my phone out and start snapping pictures. Hand Job Guy points his key toward the car, and the lights flash in unison. He strides toward the woman, kisses her on the mouth, and kisses the baby on the head.

"Looks that way," I reply to Priya.

How sad, I think. That poor woman has no idea what her man did—or does—with women. And they have a child. I want to hang my head in shame at my part in all of this. The door closes, and then he's gone.

"Now what?" Priya asks.

I pass her my phone. "Now I have pictures of his perfect little family." I can't help but feel bad for the woman as Priya looks at the images. I take my phone back. I can't think about the woman. She chose her life with him, and now I am choosing my life.

"Lucy," Adewale says, "why do you need pictures of his family? What are you planning?"

"To get a job."

"How will you get a job?" Adewale asks.

"Blackmail," I say simply.

Priya looks at me. "Ha, that's my girl. When? How? I'm fully in—what do you need me to do?"

I knew Priya would be on board, but it's not her help I need—it's Adewale's.

"I need to get back to Sadiq's shop to get the footage and then drive back here. Adewale, is that OK?"

Adewale is massaging his temples.

"Ha, ha." Priya pulls his hand away, and I can now see his smile. "It's not that bad," Priya says.

I add, "All you have to do is drive."

"And who is paying for my petrol?" Adewale asks. "My car will not run on its own."

"We can all chip in," Priya volunteers on my behalf. "I'll pay for Lucy's part." She smiles at me.

Adewale shakes his head. "Oh my god. Lucy, you are always roping me into things. You are a bad influence on me. But ... I suppose it's safer if I am wid you."

I lean though the seats and plant a kiss on Adewale's cheek.

CHAPTER 9

THEN–LAURA

Cornwall, three years ago

My house was the same as I remembered—well, other than the fact that it was full of guests dressed in dark clothes. People were packed into the cozy living room, seated on garden chairs that had been squeezed into a semi-circle and carefully positioned around our hideous blue sofa. I watched as they politely ate finger foods off paper plates balanced precariously on their knees, making small talk. My funeral was so sad. Weren't people meant to laugh and remember the good times?

Seconds later, my mum walked into the room, and my dad guided her to the sofa. People I vaguely remembered from Torquay edged over to make room, and the lady closest to my mum rubbed her back while the other reached across to pat her knee. That was why no one was laughing and remembering the good times they shared with me—my mum's grief was suffocating. No wonder the energy in the house was so stagnant. She wasn't coping, and why would she? She couldn't cope when I was alive, so what hope did she have now? I was her rock, her voice of reason, and now I was gone.

I rushed over to her. I wanted to push away these women I hardly knew—where had they been all these years when she needed them? She needed *me* now, not them. I knelt in front of her. I needed to remind her to breathe, to remember the day we were born. That always recentered her.

"My firstborn," she muttered to no one in particular. "She was my firstborn."

Remember Lucy, I urged.

The woman next to her said, "You still have Lucy, Kathrin."

My mum didn't reply, and my dad left the room.

"Dad," I said, and went after him. His face was all screwed up. "Dad?" I knew he couldn't hear me, but I wanted him to. "Dad, stop, what's wrong?"

When he saw Lucy, his face softened. She was standing with Marie just outside the back door.

"How you holding up, girls?" he asked, stepping outside with them. Lucy smiled in response, and my dad pulled her under his arm.

"It was a lovely service," Marie said.

My dad ruffled Lucy's hair like he used to when we were kids.

"Oh, Dad, don't." She batted his hand away and fixed her hair.

"Well, I'd best get back inside to your mum; just wanted to see where you were," he said. "Look after yourself, Marie."

"Thanks, Mr. Whitcombe," Marie called after him as he headed back indoors.

I stayed with Lucy and Marie, hoping to find out what else had happened since my passing, if you could call it that. I hadn't passed anywhere; I'd been in a place of nothingness.

Once Dad was gone, Lucy turned to Marie. "Have you heard anything more about Darren?"

Marie shook her head and wandered away from the back door. Lucy and I followed her over the long grass to the end of the garden, where she sat on an upside-down flower pot. As Marie smoked a cigarette, Lucy stood quietly behind her, braiding her long, brown hair the way she always did mine.

"You're not pulling it tight enough," Marie said, mimicking the words I used to say when Lucy would braid my hair.

Lucy tugged at Marie's hair, jolting her head back the same way she always did to me, and we all laughed. I wished they could see me. I wished they knew I was still in on their jokes, laughing along with them.

"I'm moving out of the house share," Marie said.

Lucy stopped playing with her hair. "Where are you going to move to? You're not leaving, are you?"

"No—no, god, no. I'd not move away from you. I just can't live in that house. You won't come over, which I totally understand. It just feels all fucked up living there, knowing what happened there to—"

"Yeah," Lucy said.

"Tye is moving out as well."

Lucy sat in the overgrown grass in front of Marie. "Do you believe he didn't have anything to do with it?"

"I don't think he did."

"And what Ben said about Laura being in Darren's room with Tye?" Lucy prodded, picking at a patch of straw grass. "Do you believe Ben? And the pictures? Sorry to keep going over this, but—"

"It's OK," Marie reassured her. "I don't know—I think I do. He could have gotten them mixed up; they were dressed similar, and the police let Tye go. Let's not talk about it today."

"He keeps texting me," Lucy admitted.

I'd seen Ben's soul back at the cemetery, and he was not who Lucy thought he was, who everyone else thought he was. Even my doubts hadn't come close to the truth. With a soul as ugly as his, I was certain that it ran deeper than taking indecent pictures of me, and I was not going to rest until I found out.

"It's too soon, Lucy. You've got me and your dad; you don't need him right now. Give it time."

No, don't give him any time, I thought.

Lucy pulled out a chunk of grass and sprinkled it over her legs. I watch the dead grass fall between her tiny energy chains, which were shimmering in the sun.

"Think I'll get a small place of my own," Marie said. "Maybe a two bed, and you can stay over anytime."

"I'd like that—I'd *love* that," Lucy said. "This place is intense at the moment."

"Your mum?"

"Yep, her daughter killed her favorite daughter."

"No," I said. "No, Lucy, that's not true."

"Has she said that to you?" Marie asked the question I would have if I could have.

Lucy shook her head.

"Why do you think that, then?"

Before Lucy could answer, our Auntie Cassy shouted through the back door that she was leaving, and Lucy waved.

"The night I came back from the hospital after this"—she held up her bandaged wrists—"I heard her telling my dad that she thought it was my fault—"

"Fuck, Lucy, no, it's not." Marie moved down to the grass next to Lucy.

"I made her chase me out of the house. That's what she thinks."

Marie pulled Lucy into an embrace. I watched them clinging to each other like lost children, and there was nothing I could do. I wanted to hold them and ease their pain. If they knew I was there, maybe they'd be at peace a little more. But there was nothing I could do to help, so instead, I knelt on the grass beside them, willing their energy to settle and hoping it would sooth the pain just a little.

Without warning, everything got loud, and I covered my ears. It all started to move. The fabric of life was stretching them away from me, the way it did the day I left.

"NO!" I shouted. It didn't stop. I breathed in as deep as I could and sunk all my energy into the earth. "NOOO," I bellowed into the sky, and it stopped. I stopped. I was back in front of Lucy again.

"Did you hear that?" Lucy asked, pulling away from Marie. "Sounds like thunder's coming." They looked up at the clear sky.

"I didn't hear a thing," Marie replied.

Lucy heard me, I thought. I had connected, and she felt it. Time was running out—whatever that was would be back for me, and I needed to find out more. Leaving Lucy with Marie, I headed back to the living room. My mum was talking to people and looking somewhat better, and my dad was talking to Douglas, a teacher. Douglas was leaning against the doorframe with his arms folded, and by the sound of their conversation, they weren't talking about school. Hearing my name, I moved closer. My dad stood partly in the hall and far enough away for my mum not to hear though she was still in his line of sight. The other man was asking my dad really personal details—he must know my dad well.

In a low voice, Douglas asked about the coroner's report. "You're saying they found Rohypnol but no evidence of ..." The man didn't finish his sentence.

My dad raised his chin in reply. "Yep, the police think he got disturbed."

My dad and Douglas stopped talking as John from number seven walked out of the living room toward the kitchen and straight through me. It felt like a gush of wind or a dizzying sensation that threw me off balance. There were no memories or emotions from him; I just felt a bit giddy, and it took me a while to refocus myself.

"Are you going to the court hearing?"

"No." My dad shook his head and glanced over at my mum. "No, I can't trust myself—you know what I'm saying?"

Douglas nodded in agreement.

"I've thought about it," my dad continued. I wondered what he was talking about. "If it wasn't for Lucy and Kathrin, I'd do a life stretch."

Douglas nodded again. "You're right to stay away, Robert. Lucy and Kathrin need you. I can't begin to imagine what you're going through, though—always here for you, buddy. Just don't do anything stupid."

"Thanks, Doug, I won't."

I realized that my dad was talking about revenge, and that was not a conversation I could listen to. I went to my room. It was exactly how I had left it—clothes still spread about the floor, and even the two pint glasses Lucy had fetched for my so-called hangover still resting on the bedside table. I went over to my bookshelves and gazed at all my beloved books that I'd never read again, tracing a transparent finger along their spines. I wanted to feel their bumpy textures and the time-weathered covers, but I couldn't. All I felt was me, my energy mixed with the stories inside.

Looking down, I saw myself sitting on the floor with my mum. I hopped back, not wanting to step on us. I was ten, and it was the day my dad fitted the bookshelves for me. I'd come home from school so excited to see all my books lined up in their new home. That was the day my mum gave me her childhood box set of *The Lion, The Witch, and The Wardrobe*. I'd been so excited that day, and even though I'd read them all many times over before, we sat at the foot of the new mahogany bookshelf as my mum read to me until dinnertime.

I watched the images playing out in front of me for a long moment. Then, bending close to my mum's face, I tried to touch her. It was no good; my hand swept through the projection like air. She looked so real. Around the corners of her eyes, I noted faint smile lines that I'd never paid much attention to in life. Her soft golden hair was looped up on top of her head in an effortless mess, and a few strands had escaped and hung about her freckled neck.

Suddenly, I understood why my room had not been touched. I was gone. I had disappeared from their lives, and all they had was memories. Presumably, my mum would come into my room to be close to me, just like I was close to her now. The image vanished.

By my bedroom window, I let my thoughts wander as I watched some more guests leave. Why was I here? Was I meant to atone for something? Was that why I'd not crossed over? Before I'd had time to process this thought, though, my eye caught sight of Ben. He was at least two hundred yards up the street, but I saw him as clear as day, as if he were right outside. Then I remembered—Ben, that's why I had not crossed over, I was sure of it. Watching him, I got a sense I'd not experienced when I was alive. It settled my thoughts and quieted the outside noise enough for me to focus.

I willed myself to leave my room and approach him. Once I was directly in front of him, I leaned into his face, looking deep into his eyes. The stench of his soul had not lessened, and it caught in the back of my throat. I stepped back a few paces to give him some room. He was looking straight through me, with his hands firmly shoved into his jean pockets and his shoulders hunched up to his ears as if he were cold. I followed his gaze up the street to my house. Without taking his eyes off our house, he retrieved a cigarette out of a box in his pocket and lit it. I watched as dirty smoke wove between the murky energy chains that hung around him.

Does he really hold the answers? I wondered. If I touched his chains, what would I see? Breathing in his energy meant breathing in his stench. Back at the cemetery, I had seen a darkness inside him, and now I was apprehensive about how or what his memories would make me feel. No one knew where he'd come from or what kind of life he'd led before moving to Looe, but it was time for me to find out just who the real Ben was.

Gingerly, I approached and then flinched as he flicked his unfinished cigarette through me. He was leaving. If I was going to find out who he was, I needed to do it right now. As Ben pivoted away from me, I extended my arm and swiped his chains. When I did, a dark, gas-like cloud of pollution escaped and surrounded me. I was trapped. Ben was walking away while potent black gas snaked about my soul as if taunting me. Instinctively, I breathed in sharply, sucking the energy in. I felt my head throw itself back, and my chest rose toward the heavens before settling, and then there was nothing but black.

At first, I thought I'd been taken back to the place I'd come from, the place where there had been nothing. But this was different. Here there was darkness, but there was *something*. I could feel it—I'd just not seen it yet. I wondered if I'd swiped the wrong part of Ben's chains, or if maybe there was nothing to Ben. I'd always wondered about his lack of genuine empathy; had I been right all along? Was Ben so shallow even his energy had nothing to offer? Then the "something" caught up with me, and I saw that Ben was far from shallow. An intense feeling of depression settled onto me as I opened my eyes into his soul.

It was the night of our party, and Ben was in my room. I could see through his eyes—his fingers were fumbling with the fiddly silver clasp on Lucy's necklace. Then he looked at me, and I smiled. I felt him as he became aroused, and I saw myself quickly drop his stare. He liked that, enjoyed that he made me feel uncomfortable—vulnerable, even. He was still standing close behind Lucy and looked back at her as she fixed her necklace. He gently touched the back of her hair, so gently she couldn't feel it, yet he wasn't actually focused on her but on me. I was across the hall in my mum's room, and Ben watched me through the reflection in my mum's mirror. He saw me pump fragrance into the air and twirl around as it fell on me. He thought I was pretty. He was also apprehensive, though I could not yet tell why.

After a dull flash, I saw we were at the party, in Marie's kitchen. Lucy was playing beer pong, and Ben was standing by the door. Why had I not seen him standing there that night? I thought he had stayed in the living room with Darren. He was watching Lucy, the way she flicked her hair, her laugh. He really cared for her, wanted her, yet it didn't feel right to me. I searched my own soul for what Ben was feeling, connecting both of us.

He wanted absolutism. She must want him and him alone, believe in whatever he told her. Lucy caught his eye, and they held a smile for a second before she looked away. He loved her. His attention turned to thoughts of what the night might hold for them—would Lucy enjoy their first time sleeping together? She was kind, unlike him. He was nervous. His thoughts turned back to the reality of the night ahead—what if she rejected him or didn't like it? I felt an overwhelming sense of panic as inadequacy compressed Ben's self-esteem. My chest felt tight, and it was hard to breathe. Then Ben saw me by the sink, my back to the door. I remembered what I had been doing—I was swapping out my vodka for soda. Ben's anxieties subsided, and he felt in his pocket, rubbing a plastic bag between his fingers and feeling the small pills inside.

Wait, what? I tried to make sense of his thoughts. Ben had the Rohypnol. He looked back at Lucy, and I heard his thoughts. If Lucy didn't agree to have sex with him tonight, he would slip her just a little, maybe a quarter pill, to get her relaxed and willing.

Now it was later in the night, and Lucy, Marie, and I were dancing. Ben was standing with Darren, Tye, and Jen watching us—watching *me*. My hand hit Lucy's, and my cup of Sprite tumbled to the floor, but we kept dancing. Instinctively and without a word, Ben left the room and headed along the packed hallway, fist bumping another boy before sidestepping into the kitchen. He found a red plastic cup and filled it with a small amount of neat vodka.

Ben checked over his shoulder before retrieving the small plastic bag from his pocket. He wanted nothing more than to sleep with Lucy; she was beautiful. Trepidation that Lucy might reject him plagued his consciousness. With no one looking, he dropped the tablet into the cup and returned to the living room. His next thought horrified me. If he could get me on my own, he thought, he could practice, practice being kind and gentle the way Lucy would expect.

You're crazy, I thought, terrified to stay connected, to see what really happened to me.

"Here." Ben sniffed the cup and then pushed the drink into my hand.

I watched myself take a big swig and then crash the empty cup back into his hand.

He smiled. He was actually enjoying it, knowing the power he was going to exert over me.

I remembered this moment. I thought Ben had taken a swig when he was really checking for a scent. His confidence kept growing until all his anxieties about having sex had disappeared, replaced with belligerence and adrenaline. This was not the first time Ben had done this, I realized. He felt an uncontrollable urge, one he'd felt before.

Ben didn't take his eyes off me from that moment on. He trailed me as I followed Lucy and Marie into the garden for a smoke, stopping at the end of the hallway to watch us through the back doors. At that moment, he wasn't thinking about what he might want to do; he already *knew* exactly what he was going to do. Still, this was causing him a bit of discomfort as his craving started to wrestle with his conscience. I was his friend.

I saw intermittent flashes of Ben's memories from when he was a child. I couldn't work out where he was—a trailer of some kind, or maybe a World War II bomb shelter? The walls looked as if they were made out of corrugated iron. There was a woman there, and a man. It was dark. The man was on top of the woman, and they were both groaning.

Ben wanted to protect her. I saw him pulling at the man, but the man backhanded him, knocking him to the wet ground.

"Mum!" he cried.

The woman kicked him. "Stay under the fucking blanket next time."

Ben was asking a well-dressed woman for money. He glanced briefly at a passing double-decker bus that displayed a sign for Oxford Street on the front. The well-dressed woman pulled her hand away from him as if she might catch some kind of disease, and Ben dropped eye contact with her and scurried away, ashamed—and worse, empty-handed. Soon, he was scolded by a woman he knew, but not the one he called Mum.

All Ben's concerns about being my friend and his girlfriend's sister vanished. They were replaced by utter disgust for me, for all women. Ben wanted to humiliate me, disgrace me, and inflict shame. He no longer desired to have kind sex with me; he wanted to make me feel helpless—hopeless, even—to control me. All he concerned himself with now was making sure the drugs took effect. Ben watched as the cute boy offered me his vape, and he pressed his brows together, resisting the compulsion to attack him. Ben sidestepped out of sight as I approached the back door, and I walked straight past him down the hall. Traversing the shadows, he followed me. I was all over the place, stumbling and rebalancing myself on the walls and other people. Darren stopped me as I scrambled around for the toilet door handle.

"You OK?" Darren asked. My eyes briefly met Ben's, and he retreated back into the shadows. He watched as I closed the toilet door.

Marie shouted from the back door, "Beer pong! Everyone in the garden now." She saw him. "Come on, Ben." She beckoned, and he followed her with swarms of others. But he didn't participate; he loitered just outside the back door with one eye on the toilet. The majority of the guests were in the garden thanks to Marie's beer game announcement, and this pleased Ben. His adrenaline was still rising, knowing what his intentions were, but the element of fear was now fueling him. He saw the toilet door open and darted toward me.

"Hey, Laura," he said, slipping my arm around his neck as if helping me. "Everyone is in here." He opened the internal door to the garage.

Inside, he turned the lock. The lights were off. The music from the house was still blaring through the walls, and loud whoops were rattling from just behind the steel garage door. Ben looked around. There was no car in the garage; it had been converted by the housemates into their poker room. A round table was in the center, and to the side stood a beer fridge, washer, and dryer next to shelves holding garden chemicals, all sorts of detergents, watering cans, and other tools. I was having trouble standing and was slouched over the table on my stomach as if presenting myself to Ben, and that is exactly what he thought.

Unzipping his fly, Ben stood close behind me and rubbed at his penis vigorously while groping feverishly at one of my butt cheeks. One hand bounced inside his jeans, and the other kneaded my flesh in his palm. All thoughts of being kind were quickly forgotten, and I felt his rage and growing urge to humiliate me. He kicked my legs apart and moved to press himself inside of me, but I groaned and twisted, violently falling to the floor.

I didn't immediately move, and he wasn't sure if I had hit my head. He knelt beside me, watching my eyes as they flicked open then shut and watching my head fall from side to side with each groan. My inability to move my limbs or defend myself was pleasing. Straddling me on the floor, he slipped the straps of my dress off my shoulders and pulled them down. My small breast sprung free. Ben was about to rape me, but then he stood instead, turning on the light and pulling out his phone. The flicking of the broken light filament must have aroused me, because I opened my eyes and tried to stand. My hands were behind me, and I rested on my palms.

I tried to speak, and then looked down at my bare chest and up at Ben.

Ben snapped a picture. "Shh, shh, shh." He was smiling, enjoying it.

I moved to stand, and he straddled me again. I fell backward onto the floor like a rag doll. Ben's jeans were still unzipped, and he removed his penis, but he still didn't enter me with it. Instead, he moved up over my face and eased himself into my mouth.

I couldn't believe what I was seeing but couldn't stop the memories. His dark energy had taken over my thoughts. There was nothing I could do but watch as he rammed himself into my mouth, my arms flailing from under his legs as I tried to push him off. He was laughing. My choking noises stopped his attack, and he sat back on my belly. He pulled my dress strap back onto my shoulders and started to stroke the side of my face to calm my noises. My eyes were shut, and I'd stopped moving. I just lay there, no clue as to what was happening to me.

Ben watched my chest as it rose and fell with each breath. He'd never taken this long with a girl before and knew he needed to hurry. There was something about how completely the drug had taken over me that made him want to push his own boundaries. Then he reached for my neck. I thought he was going to rip away my silver heart necklace. He didn't. He slipped his hand around my throat and lightly squeezed at it. His penis twitched, and he squeezed harder. I started to struggle and flap my arms, and he released his grip. I stopped moving, and he laid his body down on top of me, moving my legs apart with his knee. I watched through his eyes as he replaced one hand around my neck. I was repulsed at what he was about to do and braced my soul.

Squeals from the garden echoed into the garage, followed by a deafening crash as someone must have fallen into the garage door. Ben sprung to his feet. Heart pounding, he fled the garage, leaving me alone on the cold floor.

As Ben was talking to Lucy, she asked him if he had seen me. He shook his head, but he was lying, because at that very moment I was dragging myself up the stairs behind her. Ben pulled Lucy close into a long, passionate kiss as I disappeared.

My eyes opened, and I was back on my street in the present. Ben was gone. I had to warn Lucy. Then the sky brightened, and it all started to move away again as before. I grounded my thoughts, my energy, into the earth. Whatever this was didn't want me to stay. I wasn't meant to be here, but I couldn't let it take me back. I had to warn my sister about Ben.

Everything went white.

CHAPTER 10

NOW–LUCY

London, present day

We are back to Sadiq's shop in less than twenty minutes, and I know that driving back to Hand Job Guy's house will take the same amount of time now that rush hour is over. My plan will be executed by the end of the night, and I'll have the job, my ticket out of this hellhole life. Adewale pulls the car around the back of the shop, and I jump out.

"Wait here." I poke my head through Priya's window. "Won't be long—oh, and I'll need to go back to the bedsit. I've got a laptop there that I can play the recording on."

Adewale doesn't look pleased at this extra request. "Give me your keys. I will go get it."

"No."

"Lucy, dis is me. You can trust me."

"And me." Priya pushes my shoulder. "Come on, don't be like that—give me your keys. It will be quicker if we go while you're in there." She juts her head toward the shop.

I trust them, and it's not like I have anything to steal, as I've sold it all anyway.

Passing the lone key and single flimsy ring into Priya's hand, I say, "Be careful with it—I still have to sell it at some point."

"Not if you get your job," she says, nodding her head.

"Just be careful, and quick."

I watch Adewale speed up the alley. Then I walk around to the front of the shop and enter through the front door. West Croydon High Street is busy with people, and Sadiq's shop is close to the train station, making it a hub for travelers killing time before their train. I dodge two young boys as they bound out of his shop, nearly knocking into me.

Sadiq is serving two men at the counter. From their perfectly timed exchanges, I guess they are a couple. It's obvious from their headshakes and smiles after reaching an agreement on which chocolate bar they want to buy.

To share, I think. *How sweet*. I still wish they would hurry up. It is eight thirty, which gives us about another two hours before dark. The last thing I want to do is confront Hand Job Guy in the dark.

"Hi," I say, stepping up to Sadiq once they've left. "People are choosey over chocolate, hey?"

"How you been, Lucy? I've been worried, not seen you in ages." Sadiq lengthens his neck and looks over the display like a meerkat and calls out to someone in his language.

Then he turns back to me as his uncle comes into view. "Let's go out the back."

I follow him to the back of the shop, though I'm not sure where he is taking me. He unlocks a door and holds it open for me to walk through. Stacks of boxes line the walls, and in the corner is a bench with a computer. It smells of dampness. I see the back door that leads into the alley.

"Are we going for a cigarette?" I gesture to the door.

"No. You're here for the CCTV recording, aren't you?"

I tilt my head. "And how do you know that?"

"I didn't. But you didn't ask for vodka or cigarettes, which is all you ever want from me. But it's OK—I don't take it personally. Part and parcel of being a shopkeeper, I suppose." He gives a small laugh. "I just thought it would be the recording you wanted."

"You still have it, then?" I ask.

"Of course. I said I'd keep it for you."

He moves over to the makeshift office space and rummages about before swinging back around and holding up a small black USB drive.

"Oh, wow, you put it on a memory stick?"

"Yeah, didn't want to leave it on the system just in case it got wiped by mistake. It's been a while." He frowns, handing me the drive, and I interpret his expression as a question.

"I know. I got pretty messed up over it all. But I'm OK now, honestly—I know you worry about me. I should have let you know I was OK, just didn't think."

"It's OK. I asked Priya, and she told me you were safe and hiding in your room."

We laugh.

"Yeah, I've been a bit off the radar lately. Sorry."

Sadiq unlocks the rear door. "Cigarette?" He offers his pack to me.

"Sure." I move through the door and outside.

He holds out a lighter, and I bend to light the tobacco. "Thanks."

"Are you going to the police with it?"

I don't want to lie to Sadiq, but what option do I have? What if he doesn't agree with my blackmail plan? Then what? I don't have time to try to convince him to get on board.

"Not sure. I—"

"I'll go with you to the station if you want." His response is sincere.

I smile. "That's kind, but I've got this. Just wanted to have it so that when I'm ready, I can go through with it."

I see Adewale's car round the corner.

Priya hangs out the window. "Hi, Sadiq."

I open the back door and slide in. "Thanks again, Sadiq," I say.

"Be safe. You know where I am, Lucy."

Adewale pulls away.

"Did you tell him?" Priya asks, and I shake my head. "Here." She hands me the laptop. "Did you get the video?"

I hold up the USB drive.

Just off the main road, Adewale pulls into a petrol station, and we all chip in together. I have £4.78 in change, but Priya rejects it and hands him a ten-pound note.

As we sit in silence, I think about my sister and the dreams. I'm not questioning what I saw, but my skeptical mind is poking at the meaning of all this craziness. However, right now, this is actually the best idea I've had. If Laura is right, then I will get this job. It may not be in the proper way, but at least I'll have a credible job, giving me options and opportunities. I look at Priya. She's rolling a joint. I'll be sorry to leave her behind, but I will if I have to. We were never going to be forever, or so I keep telling myself.

Apprehensive, I stay quiet. I can't have any fear, not if I'm going to get this job and then work for Simon. He is the one in the wrong, not me. I did what I did out of necessity; he is the one with a loving family, the one who doesn't know what he has—doesn't *care* what he has. I want a job, and his feelings don't count for anything other than being scared enough to believe that I will tell his family exactly what he did to me.

We make good time along the twists and turns of the country roads. In the backseat, I flick through the footage. It's hard to watch and going to be even harder to show him. We arrive just before dusk. The house is completely lit, and I can see into every window, right into his life. The woman is upstairs bouncing the baby in her arms in what looks like a nursery. He is there too. I watch him as he watches his family from the doorway. Then he moves out of sight and reappears downstairs in the living room. He sits on the sofa, and I see the TV come on and display the evening news.

Adewale speaks. "Are you ready?"

Am I?

"We will be right here." He leans his cumbersome body through the seats and pats my knee. "Nothing bad will happen to you with me here." He holds up his hand and squeezes it into a fist. "I would crush his head."

I laugh.

"D'you know what you're going to say to him?" Priya asks.

"Not yet." I take a deep breath. "Here I go."

I make my way up the steep driveway quickly so as to not be seen by the woman in the upstairs room. Her back is to the window—she looks so small. Standing in front of the door, I have an attack of doubt. What if he laughs at me again, calls me a whore, and calls the police? What if the woman knows what he is like and comes to defend her man? I look over my shoulder. I can just about see Priya and Adewale in the car. It is getting darker, so I should hurry. I pull down the hood of my black sweater and rap my knuckles on the wooden door. Through the living room window, I see his face peer out to see who's outside. He looks visibly shocked. I hear the woman call out, asking who is at the door.

I hear him reply, "No one, sweetie, just an employee. I'll just have a quick chat with them outside. Don't want to wake Catalina."

That's a fitting excuse, I think.

"It's fine, they can come in," the woman shouts back.

The door opens as he shouts back another reply. "It's fine, sweetie, back in five minutes."

He looks furious, and it is clearly taking all he has not to slam the door and scream at me. Instead, he closes the door softly and grips my arm as if to march me off the doorstep.

I yank my arm away and shove my face up to his. Through clenched teeth, I snarl at him, "Don't fucking touch me."

The sound of a car door opening from across the street pulls his attention off me and toward Adewale, who doesn't look best pleased.

"Who the hell is that?" he hisses. He politely gestures his hand for me to walk away from the house and over to his car.

"That is a friend who will crush your head if you touch me the way you just did," I tell him. "Do you understand—Simon?" All my fear is gone, and seeing Adewale has given me the support I need.

Simon glances up to the bedroom window. "Well, tell him to get back in the car before he's seen."

I sign over to Adewale, who understands my hand flaps and lowers his large frame back into his small car, making him appear even bigger than he already is.

"Your wife?" I ask Simon, nodding toward the house.

"None of your business. What the hell are you doing here?"

Folding my arms across my chest, I look him up and down. His top button is undone after a hard day's work, his crisp white shirt is untucked from his perfectly pressed black trousers, and his shoeless feet sport black socks.

"What, what do you want from me, Lucy? That's your name, right?"

"My name is whatever I tell you it is." I lean against his car.

"Don't do that." He moves as if to pull me off the car, then thinks against it.

"That's right, you're learning fast." I grin.

His movements become erratic and he glances again at the upper window. "Just tell me why you're here. How do you know where I live?"

Shit, I think. I left the laptop in the car. "Wait here. I've got something you might like to see." I try to sound confident, like it's all part of the plan.

"And what if I don't?"

"Oh, that's OK—if you can't wait, I'll just give it to your wife," I say, then stride away before he can answer.

I shove my head into the car. "Forgot the damn laptop, didn't I?" I say.

"How's it going?" Priya whispers.

"I think he literally shit his pants when he saw Adewale."

"Good," Adewale says. "I will crush his head."

I laugh. "Not today, Adewale."

As I walk back toward Simon, I notice the woman looking out of the window, baby still in her arms. I wave, and Simon looks horrified.

"Lucy, if you don't tell me why you're here right now, I'm calling the police."

"Ha, of course you are. And you can call me Laura." I open the laptop and set it on the hood of his car.

Flinching, he says, "Careful, the paint."

"Simon," I say, "this will go a lot quicker if you stop trying to control the situation. I don't care about your car's expensive paintwork, and you are not in control. I am."

His jittery movements stop immediately. I'm not sure if he's angry or just at a loss for words, so I continue.

"I don't want to ruin your life; I just want to make mine better. I can see you're happy; you have a loving woman, and your daughter, Catalina—"

He steps close to me, and his breath smells of stale smoke. "Don't threaten my daughter."

Placing one hand on his fat chest, I slowly but firmly push him back to his original spot. "Let's not be dramatic now, Simon. No one is threatening a baby—yours or otherwise. So melodramatic." I laugh. "All I want is a job."

Then it is his turn to laugh.

"Find something funny?" I say.

"Yeah, you. What makes you think I'd ever employ you?" He laughs even louder and even smiles up at the window as if we are having a fun chit-chat, but the woman is not there anymore. "I thought you had some nerve coming here, but never thought you would want a job." He is still laughing at me, but I let him continue. "What on God's earth gave you the bright idea that you had a hope in hell of getting a job with me? Are you completely bonkers?" He smiles smugly.

"Exactly." I flash my best cheerleader smile at him. "I'm certified insane—well, I would have been if I hadn't run away from the mental hospital they wanted to lock me away in." Now it is my turn to smile at him. He has no idea if I am telling the truth or not.

I hit the play button. I've already prepared the recording to play at the precise time I want it to. Simon's face straightens, and he leans towards the screen, a look of disbelief etching itself into his small, round eyes.

"What? How?"

I don't answer at first. He keeps watching, and I zoom into the shot.

"Looks like we are kissing—oh, look, you're biting my lip. How sexual you are, Simon. Do you do that to your wife?"

"Leave her out of this," he hisses into my face.

"Then you had better give me a job, Simon."

He pulls away from me, thrusting his hands through his hair. "Why do you want a job with me? Go work anywhere."

"Oh, Simple Simon. If it was that easy, I would—I really, really fucking would. Don't flatter yourself. I don't want to work for you. I just need a job, and badly. So you see, I don't have much choice. Look, give me a job, and as soon as I can get another job elsewhere, I'll leave. I don't care about screwing up your life." I step close to him. "I just can't let you screw up mine."

His eyes narrow down onto mine. "The job is gone."

"You're the boss; make another one."

"I can't just—"

"Everything OK, honey?" The front door has opened, and the now baby-less woman is standing in the doorway.

"Yes, sweetie. Go back inside."

I wave from behind Simon, and she gives a small hand raise in return. *She knows something is off,* I think.

"Bring her in if you'd like?" Her voice sounds unsure about her offer.

"I'll be two minutes, sweetie." He looks back at me and sees the laptop open on the hood of the car. He makes a small sideways step in front of it. "Just two minutes, promise."

"My fault," I chip in. "We are just finalizing my start date. Sorry."

A faint smile ghosts her face. "OK then, if you're sure." She gives one last look at Simon, me, and the laptop, which is thankfully too far away for her to see, then retreats back inside.

Simon swings around to face me. "Are you crazy? What if she had seen?" He slams the lid of my laptop closed.

"I don't want her to see either, Simon," I retort spitefully, "And she won't if you give me a job."

"It's not that straight forward, Lucy."

"Laura, I told you it's Laura."

"Laura? Whatever your bloody name is. I can't just give you a job; it's no longer there."

I shrug and pick up my laptop. "Not my problem, that's your issue. You have a week; I'll see you ready for work next Wednesday, nine a.m. sharp—I won't be late," I add, moving to leave.

"And if I say no?"

I hold up the laptop. "You won't. Think of it as atonement for being a pervert. Whatever helps you sleep at night." I start to walk down the driveway, still talking. "You are the last person I want to work for; trust me when I say it's a temporary arrangement." I stop at the bottom. "Do this, and it will all go away."

I sling open the car door, still fired up from my final threat. As I crawl in, Adewale pulls away, spinning his rear wheels, and I fly back in my seat.

"Wow, easy," I say, hurriedly fishing around for my seatbelt.

Priya hands me half her smoked cigarette. "How'd it go?

Think it worked?"

I shrug. "I gave him a week—I just hope he believes me, and I don't turn up to work next week to be arrested for blackmail." With that thought in mind, I pull the USB drive out of the side of the laptop and push it into Priya's hand.

"What's this?" Her brow furrows.

"If he calls the police, then there's no evidence of blackmail if you have it, is there?"

Priya considers this. "What if they question me?" She hands me back the USB. "No—I can't get in trouble again."

"You won't. Just say you were holding it for me because I asked you to. It's not a gun. They can't search your room just because they want to."

Adewale chuckles to himself.

"What's up with you?" I say.

"You two—you are talking as if you are holding a list of covert operatives."

I lean as far forward as my seatbelt will let me. "Well, you take the USB for me, then."

"If it will make you feel better, Lucy."

"It will," I say and slap the drive into his open hand. "Don't lose it." I sit back. "So now it's a waiting game. He's seen the footage, and I think he can tell that I'm a little desperate, which is good, because if I've got nothing to lose, then I'm a loose cannon aimed directly at his perfect little life. I really don't have any other options. If there isn't a job at the end of this, then going to the police makes sense."

Priya pokes her head back at me. "How so?"

"Selling this laptop is the last bit of money I can get my hands on. I'm thinking if I go to the police, then they might help me out with a shelter or something."

"I think this will work," Adewale says. "From what I saw, you did good."

Adewale manages to find a parking space in record time and only a block away from the bedsit, and we all stroll home in silence. I see Dereck from the room below mine walking out of the entrance and presume he is going to the corner shop. He has a walk that I know well, the walk that says, "I have accepted my place in life." He has no more desire to strive for a better life.

But I do. For the first time in over a year, I have a purpose—I'm going to make Laura proud of me. I feel for my sister's driver's license in my sweater pocket. I'm getting out of this place, going to start a new life as Laura. I'll live the rest of my life for her—*as* her—and make her proud of me.

"Want a drink?" Priya asks. "My room?"

I shake my head. "Not tonight."

For the first time ever, she doesn't protest.

Opening my door, I switch on the light and take in my bleak living arrangements. The room's carpet is a dirty brown, and its dusty window blinds are cracked. My bed sheets are thrown to one end of the bed, and I start to straighten them out. Hopefully, I'll get a good night's sleep tonight now that the pills have worn off. I might even get a clear dream, something to tell me to stop worrying. I finish making my bed and close the blinds. As I do this, I catch sight of an unfinished vodka bottle on the counter. I think about my dream and consider tipping it down the sink. Then I reach for a pink mug that Priya must have washed up for me earlier. The liquid fills the mug halfway. For a second, I look down at it in my hand.

Last one, I tell myself, though really, I'm telling Laura.

Happy with my internal confession, I raise the mug, but at the same time, the streetlight outside my window flickers. As I glance over, I hear a crack. The mug crashes down into the sink while the handle remains in my hand.

"Wow!" I jump back, still gripping the mug's handle.

OK, Lulu, I hear ya, big sis. I hear ya.

CHAPTER 11

THEN–LAURA

Cornwall, three years ago
January (six months later)

I knew where she was, Grandma Betty. I just didn't want to go there—not yet, anyway. Unlike before, when I felt nothing, this time I felt *everything*, and so much more. Trying to describe where I was would be like trying to describe to someone how they felt on Christmas Day as a child or when their first child was born—or for the lucky few, maybe even the day they won the lottery. It was indescribable happiness, and white—lots and lots of whiteness. I didn't know you could get so many shades of white, but that is where I was: in a happy white place with everything.

However, with my *everything* came a small fragment of *nothing* shading a corner of my bright world. People talk about a bright light when they die, but this didn't feel quite the same. It was more than just light; it was as if this light held pure clarity about everything, all the answers to any question, and all I needed to do was let it in.

Then why didn't I? Simple—Ben was that small shadow smudging my perfect world, and although the feeling of *everything*, the clarity of life, was what anyone would want, I somehow knew that meant leaving Lucy behind forever—and I was not ready for that. Lucy was in danger. And then I heard them, faint whispers pushing through into my *everything*, telling me that Lucy needed me. I couldn't stay, not until I was ready to fully process my life and also ready to leave it behind.

The whiteness subsided, and it was dark. Not dark as in nothingness, though. It was nighttime, and cold—very cold. I did a quick review of my location. There were cobbled stones beneath my feet, perhaps an alley between buildings. It felt familiar. I moved, then immediately recognized the small road. I was standing on Looe Street outside the Minerva Inn. Wondering why I was there, I moved to the front of the building just in time to see Lucy stumble out of the pub doors. I was confused as to why Lucy would be in this particular pub, as it wasn't a place we'd ever drunk in, and I followed her. Moments later, I saw Marie—and to my horror, Ben—hurrying down the lane toward her.

That's it, that's why I'm back, I thought. *Ben. I have to get her away from him.*

"Lucy," Ben was calling. "Lucy, wait, I'll drive you home."

Lucy was laughing and stumbling away, so Ben and Marie had to practically carry her to Ben's car. Something about her persona felt lost. Even though she was laughing, she wasn't happy. Her energy was stagnated. I sat next to her in the back seat of Ben's car, watching her head vibrate against the closed window as we drove along the dark roads. What was going on? I wanted to know, but I didn't reach for her chains. Lucy was so intoxicated I didn't know what I would see or feel. Marie, though drunk, was nowhere near as drunk as Lucy. Why was it so cold when it had been a beautiful midsummer's day what felt like moments earlier, and why were they out with Ben? I'd left him outside our house on the day of my funeral, and Lucy was not on speaking terms with him at that point. How long had it been?

Ben and Marie were talking about an event that had presumably happened earlier in the night, and they were laughing loudly. His mere presence disabled me, and then I started to vibrate. I'd have called it shaking, but when you don't have a human body, physical sensations are somewhat different. My energy shuddered, and understandably. The last time I had seen Ben, he was attacking me. I'd been shocked, but then I was gone, and now I was sitting in the back of his car, terrified by his presence.

He twisted his head over his shoulder to check on Lucy, and our eyes met—instinctively, I jumped.

He can't see you; he can't see you, I coached myself.

We rounded the corner to Union Street, drove around the Crescent, and left on Hartwell Street. A few turns later, Ben stopped outside a small terrace house. Under the streetlights, the houses all looked the same color, though I knew my home town, so I knew the houses on this street would be different shades of yellows and pale blues. Still, I didn't know anyone who lived on this street, and it wasn't where Ben lived. This was confirmed when he stayed seated in the car as Marie helped Lucy out of the back seat.

Seriously, what is happening here? I followed them through the doors to the unfamiliar house, glad to be as far away from Ben as possible.

Lucy climbed the steep stairs unassisted. "Are you working tomorrow?" she called over her shoulder to Marie.

"Late shift."

"I'll cook and save you some, then," Lucy said. She headed into one of the bedrooms.

I was halfway up the stairs after Lucy, but when I didn't hear a reply from Marie, I turned back toward her just in time to see her brow furrow. She shook her head and shouted up the stairs loud enough to be heard through Lucy's closed bedroom door, "I told you, *I have a date!*"

Marie paused as if considering something and then took the stairs two at a time. I followed quickly behind. Without knocking, Marie swung open the door Lucy had just shut.

"Lucy, don't you go messing this up for me." She stood in the doorway with her arms folded firmly across her body. "I mean it. I love you and all, but don't try any tricks."

Lucy, who was sitting on her bed unbuckling her boots with some difficulty, stopped. "And what's that supposed to mean?"

"It means exactly what it means. Don't try any of your little tricks to scare him off like you always do."

Lucy kicked off her now-loosened boot and started unbuckling the other. "I don't—"

Marie cut her off. "You do, and it is not happening with this guy, OK? Don't be ringing me in tears saying you forgot I had a date, all panicked and guilt-tripping me into coming home. It won't work this time. I know your games."

Lucy kicked her second boot toward Marie, who stepped sideways, letting the boot fall outside her door. "Fine. I won't leave you any dinner if you don't want. That's … all you had to … say." Lucy slurred the last few words.

Marie didn't move from the doorway. "Lucy, babe, you need help. Your drinking is getting out of hand. Maybe your dad is right—maybe you should see someone, a therapist."

Wait, what? I thought.

"Marie, I'm fine." Lucy stood, stumbling slightly, and then gave her cute little laugh, the one she always used to disarm our parents when she was getting told off. "I won't ruin your date; I just want you to find a good guy, that's all. And I'll lay off the booze. Promise." She smiled.

I knew that smile—Lucy wasn't promising a thing. Marie didn't know that, though; I could tell by the smile she gave Lucy in return before hugging her good night.

I watched as Marie shut the door on her exit, and Lucy crawled into bed, switching off the bedside lamp. It was her bedside lamp from home. What had been going on here? Where was I? It looked like Lucy was living here. I noticed her pictures from her room hanging on the walls. The small chest of drawers that Dad had made her sat in the far corner, and even her old lightshade, the one with pineapple prints, hung from the ceiling. Had Lucy moved in with Marie?

Deciding I needed to find out the date, I nosed about the living room. I found a small, light brown leather sofa that had seen better days, but it looked trendy that way. Three crocheted, mustard-colored footstools doubled as seats, or so I guessed, considering there wasn't any other furniture to sit on. A low table scattered by ash from an overfilled ashtray sat in the middle of the room.

Bingo. On top of the table was a magazine. I was moving closer to take a look when I heard a noise, presumably from the kitchen. I took a quick glance down at the glossy magazine cover for the date. *January 4th.* Had it really been six months? Had I been away that long? What if that wasn't even the date? After all, I didn't know how old the magazine was. So why had I come back today? January was not a month I was aware of, no one's birthday that I knew of. Then my intuition kicked in—Lucy. She was spiraling, and Ben—well, I had an unshakable fear that his threat to my sister was paramount. The sound of water running in the kitchen distracted me, and I moved to see who it was.

Marie stood by the sink with a glass of water, happily engrossed in something on her phone. I thought myself next to her and peered over her shoulder, hoping to determine the date and possibly learn something more—anything. Marie was texting someone called Dylan. I figured out from the messages that Dylan was her date tomorrow night. He seemed nice—polite.

She replied good night and closed the phone. I didn't get to see the date. Then I noticed she was wearing an Apple watch, but the screen was black. I needed her to look at her watch, so I blew in her face, hoping to make her rotate her wrist. It didn't work. Marie retired to her room with me in toe. Her room was a lot bigger than Lucy's, and I immediately felt bad for my sister—she always got landed with the small room.

I watched as Marie got her work uniform ready for the next day; she obviously still worked at McDonald's. Finally, she angled her wrist at her face, and the screen on her watch lit up. It was January—not the fourth but the twenty-eighth. I had to find out what had happened in that time, and not just from Lucy. As Marie pulled her nightshirt over her head, I reached out and swiped her chains, almost without thinking, and was sucked into a whirlwind of images, thoughts and feelings.

I knew touching chains from drunk people wasn't such a good idea. Marie walked past me, throwing me off balance. Then the room went dark, but only because she had switched off the light. Her energy flowed like wind in a wind tunnel between buildings. I was thrown off balance again as she passed on her way back to bed. Like a spinning top, I spun on the spot—round and round I went. My hand stretched for something to hold onto, anything, but I kept spinning faster and faster. I reached up for the light cord hanging above my head—it was in reach. I looked like a ballerina as I tiptoed upward, my fingers splayed to grasp the cord. But it was no good; my hand passed right through it. I fell to the ground.

My idea might not have worked how I'd hoped, but at least I wasn't spinning anymore. I was also not really on the floor, more like between floors. My hands hovered somewhere between Marie's bedroom and the ceiling of the living room. I knew this because I was looking down at the messy living room table I'd seen earlier, its ash still spilled un-hygienically about it, and the magazine was still sitting to the side. I could also see Marie's bedroom carpet. How very odd. If I adjusted my vision to far or near, like a pair of spectacles, I could see what I wanted. Getting to my feet, I looked about at things.

Just like last time, I saw energy chains, yet this time, there was more. I saw what everything was made of: the fibers, minerals, and chemicals mixed together. I could feel the whole room talking to me, and it was truly amazing. I spun on the spot, but this time, it was because I wanted to see everything, not block it out. I wanted to hear their stories, know what country all the microscopic particles came from. The room was alive on so many levels. The furnishings were actually talking to me—this was madness. I giggled at the dust mites bumping into each other and sending each other off in different paths; it was really quite cute to watch. My time in the white place had clearly advanced my perception. Perhaps that's what the white whispers had meant by telling me to not be long. Was I meant to also learn something by being here? And who would be waiting?

Marie shifted beneath her sheets. I'd been so caught up in my abilities I'd not realized that I had lost my connection with her. Crossing the room, I stood next to her bed and hesitantly extended a hand down onto her forehead. Immediately, I was thrown through the air. An intrinsic reaction grounded me before I flew out of Marie's room and into Lucy's.

Drunk people are difficult, I thought. Quickly, I pressed my feet hard down to the ground, breathing through my nose and into my abdomen before releasing air out my mouth like breath on a cold day. I was never that good at meditation in the living world, but I had sure nailed it in death. My time at the white place was certainly paying dividends. I was quickly realizing that death was far more complex than the living realm. Eventually, Marie's thoughts slowed and started to order themselves and line up with the right emotions. When they were ready for me to understand, I set my intention to only see relevant memories. I didn't want to be viewing my best friend sitting on the toilet seat or something.

Vibrant sunshine reached out to touch the rows of flowers that spread along the pavement. There were bouquets of roses, tulips, arum-lily, and lots of sweet pea, one of my favorites. Between bouquets and squished by the plastic cellophane wrappers, small teddy bears peered out at me with their little round black eyes. Some had my name stitched on their paws, and others were holding notes. I wondered what the notes said and who'd left them. Marie was holding a bunch of hand-picked wildflowers, possibly from the park behind her house. That's why Marie was my best friend, even in death—she knew me, knew my soul, and what I liked most.

Marie set down the small bunch of wildflowers, which were tied together with a straw bow and more beautiful than any rose or tulip. There was wild jack-in-the-pulpit, trillium, some meadow rue, and even butterfly weed. I saw a ragged old sunflower wedged between them, drooping to one side. She stood back. She wasn't looking at the colorful display of flowers on the ground; her gaze had fallen to the base of the lamppost. The authorities hadn't replaced it yet. Tears rolled down her face, and I could feel them wet against her skin. She didn't try to wipe them away.

She read a card that peeked out of a bouquet: *In life we love; in heaven you wait.*

"Are you?" she said to no one. "In heaven?" Marie didn't believe in God, but I supposed it was comforting for her to think I might be in heaven. I'd never known just how much I'd meant to my best friend—why would I? Being inside her thoughts and feeling what she felt for me brought it all home.

Marie's thoughts jumped to the day we'd met. She'd been dropped off at the local youth center by her new foster family. I hadn't noticed her at first, but now I was seeing this through her eyes. Marie strolled through the center doors, stopped, and looked at the cool kids in the corner. She decided immediately, just by the fact they held what looked to be acting scripts, that this was not the group she wanted to befriend. Then her gaze fell on me and Lucy. I giggled at her first thoughts of us.

Eek, who are those two weirdos? I already knew that's what she had thought because she'd repeatedly told us over the years, but it was different to hear it from her and feel it for myself. It was funny—funny because we became such good friends, best friends.

"Three weirdos forever, Laura," Marie said from next to the lamppost.

"Always will be," I whispered back.

I was in a toilet cubical, and music played loudly from the other side of the wall. Marie held back Lucy's hair, and I watched my sister's back heave with each retch, followed by a splatter into the water below.

Shouting, people were shouting. Marie was standing between Lucy and a group of people outside the Union Tavern. Marie's hand pushed against Lucy's chest, holding her back, while Lucy swore profundities at the group over Marie's shoulder. Then Mike, the publican, stepped into view.

"You're barred, Lucy. Don't come back."

"Good, I hated this place anyway—Laura hated this place. Told me it stinks. She's right."

"*Was* right." Someone I didn't recognize corrects her.

Lucy lunged at them, and Marie wrapped both arms around Lucy, pushing her up the road. "Leave it, Lucy, leave it," she was saying.

"Didn't you hear what that prick said, Marie? Let me fucking go. I'll kill 'em."

"No, you won't." Marie's grip tightened, and she shoved Lucy. "Walk on, Lucy. I mean it this time."

My dad took a box out of Marie's arms and loaded it into his car, which was packed with her belongings. She followed him down the driveway of her old house share, her scarf close to her neck. She peered at the boxes through the car windows—her whole life packed into one car. And the only person helping her was her best friend's dad, who looked as if he wanted to crawl into one of the boxes and pack himself away forever. Marie's mind wandered to thoughts about who her parents might be, if they knew or cared how long she'd spent in foster care, how many families she'd had to fit in with. Always trying to fit in, though never quite feeling as if she did.

Marie watched as my dad tackled the box into the car. She was pleased Lucy had such a loving dad; he would never leave her. Even during his darkest hour, his thoughts were consumed by Lucy and seeing that she was safe.

A true parent, she thought. *Shit, he is even looking out for me. Such an amazing man.*

My dad gave the box a sharp ram with his shoulder and then closed the trunk of the car.

"All in," he said, clapping his hands against each other as if removing dust. Maybe he was just cold. "Are you ready to go?"

As my dad turned to Marie, I got a good look into his face. It was weathered, and tiny white whiskers teased the edge of what might have been the start of a mustache. A dozen more smile lines traced his face, though I doubt they came from smiling too much.

Marie nodded and gave a quick look back at the house. She waved to Tye, who stood in the doorway, and I thought I caught sight of Jen over his shoulder.

"Mr. Whitcombe?"

"Robert, please."

"Robert. Lucy, she—well, she—"

My dad held up a hand as if to stop her. "I know," he said. "She's not coping." My dad gestured with his head for Marie to get in the car. Closing his door and reversing off the driveway, he said, "Thanks for letting Lucy house share with you, Marie; you're a good pal to her. Listen, don't ask her for the rent. I'll pay it each month."

"Sure, but why? I thought Lucy was going to go back to work."

My dad didn't answer immediately. He indicated and then changed lanes before drawing in a long breath. "She went back yesterday." There was another pause. "She got fired," he said, turning left onto the main road.

"Really?"

My dad's brow furrowed. "Apparently, a customer's children were squabbling about bunk beds or separate beds—"

"Oh."

"She told the kids to shut up and be grateful one of them wasn't dead."

"Oh dear."

"As you can imagine, that didn't go down too well with the parent."

"No," Marie agreed, "but did they have to sack her for it? Surely the manager knows what's going on?"

My dad drew in another long breath. "They didn't sack her for that; they sacked her because she called the manager a—" He hesitated. "She called him the C-word, then told him to go eff himself."

"Ah."

"Yes, 'ah.'" My dad pulled the car up outside Sydney Street, which I now knew to be Lucy and Marie's home. "I want her to see a therapist," he said, turning off the ignition.

"Hm." Marie winced. "Does Lucy know that?"

My dad nodded.

"Right, I get it. Lucy is not so keen on the idea, and you want me to talk her round?"

Getting out of the car and popping the trunk, my dad continued. My focus was intense as I took it all in. "Going to see a therapist isn't the issue." He handed a small box to Marie. "I want her to go with Kathrin—joint therapy."

"Jeez, now you're asking for a huge favor—that rent just doubled." She smiled. Walking toward the narrow house, she continued, "Does Lucy's mum want to go?" She dropped the box on the doorstep in time to look back and catch Robert's expression. "That's a no, then."

"Triple rent?" My dad grimaced.

"Jeez, it's a tough ask. I'll do my best, but Lucy isn't stupid. She knows her mum blames her, and it's fucked her up pretty bad. She's so possessive with me now, I can't even talk to a guy in a bar these days without her giving him the third degree or worse. And her mum is not helping with that. I think she has abandonment issues, you know?" Marie didn't wait for a reply before turning to open the front door.

I shook my head, shaking Marie's memories away. She was lying in bed looking at her phone in the dark. I couldn't believe what was going on with my family; my death wasn't Lucy's fault. Why was Mum blaming her? I stole the car keys and drove too fast, believing I was hungover. Lucy wasn't to blame for that. Ben was, and now he was back in their lives—and for what?

I hovered over by the window. The blinds were closed, but this didn't actually matter; I could see clearly through them. The garden was small, with waist-high fences. All the neighbors could see into each other's back yards.

They must hate this house, I thought. The garden was overgrown, and in some places, the weeds were as high as the fence. Lucy was like this garden—overgrown with weeds, hiding her beautiful soul beneath ugliness and noticeable problems. I was troubled by what I'd seen in Marie's memories, but not as troubled as by seeing Ben with my sister tonight.

Through the adjacent wall, I saw Lucy. She lay in bed, and there was no sign of movement. I decided to let her sleep. It had been six months; a few more hours wouldn't hurt. I hoped by morning her thoughts would be less muddled—I didn't want a repeat of riding drunken energies. I moved effortlessly through the wall, stopping next to my sister. She looked so peaceful. I watched how her eyelids twitched under the spell of sleep, and how her lips parted ever-so-slightly with each outward breath before sticking back together again. Her hair was effortlessly displaced over her pillow.

I though back to Ben and wondered how anyone could want to hurt such a beautiful soul. What was his end game by raping me? Then I was filled with a dreadful and sickening thought. Ben hadn't raped me, not in the true sense of the word—he never actually had sex with me. I thought of how he had grasped my neck—what if he was evolving? I thought about all the nights I'd sat on the sofa with Mum, Dad, and Lucy watching *Criminal Minds*. Rapists and murderers evolved, didn't they? Each time they became more confident, figured out what they liked, pushed boundaries—that's what the show said. What if Ben saw Lucy as a second chance with me?

"Oh, no." I fell to the floor, but I didn't stop there. I fell right through Lucy's bedroom floor and into the kitchen. On my hands and knees, I heaved as if to vomit on the cold tiles, but of course, nothing came up. I didn't notice any energy from the stones. I was too consumed by my own revelations. Was that really Ben's end game? To rape and strangle Lucy? Had I really gotten this right, or had I just watched too much TV? Composing myself, I went to my sister again, though this time I took the long way around and walked up the stairs.

By Lucy's bedside is where I stayed all night, through the witching hour and until the sun rose. Its glorious light filled the room through what looked to be brand new white Ikea curtains, the ones with large silver loops for curtain runners. It had started to snow. At about eight thirty, Lucy stirred. She opened her eyes, and if I wasn't very much mistaken, she smiled at me before falling back asleep.

Not quite knowing what I was doing, I blew in her face the same way I had with Marie in the kitchen the night before. Nothing happened. For a moment, I thought that maybe if I whispered a message, she would hear subconsciously. But what?

After thinking for a moment, I had it—something connected only to me. If she understood, I was sure she'd know I was there. Bending, I whispered the words "cuckoo family" in her ear. I repeated it over and over: *"Cuckoo family. Cuckoo family. Cuckoo family. Cuckoo family. Cuckoo family."*

I wasn't trying to make my twin sister crazy. "Cuckoo family" was a story that Lucy made up when we were very young, around six or seven years old. She would sneak into my bed and tell me stories about a family of cuckoos. They lived in a cuckoo clock in a human's house, but they had normal lives: the kids went to school, and one even got bullied by bad kids. The mum and dad had jobs, and they all sat down for dinner each night like any normal, loving family would. Now that I think of it, Lucy was probably playing out a perfect life—one our family didn't have.

The cuckoos ran normal lives, but every hour, one of them had to be back inside the clock to cuckoo. I laughed so hard when she told me stories of how the daddy bird would speed and beep at people to get out the way so he'd make it home in time, and how the mummy bird would pay for a coffee but leave it on the counter and rush out of the shop, the barista shouting after her, "Madam, you forgot your coffee!" I loved those cuckoo stories. If I could get her to hear my message, maybe I could send her a more poignant one about Ben. I didn't want to scare her; from Marie's memories, I knew she was vulnerable. I decided the cuckoo message was the safest way to test my theory.

Lucy didn't wake for another hour. She stretched her body, her hands making their way over her head, and then she winced in pain.

"*Yep, you're hungover,*" I said.

"Oh, shit," she said to herself.

Lucy stepped out of bed naked and looked down at herself as if trying to work out why she had no clothes on.

"Must have been a big night," she said, pushing hair back off her face.

I followed her downstairs and through the kitchen to the bathroom. She was still naked. Marie looked up from a little table that looked like it should be in a primary school, not a house. The table and Marie were somehow squeezed into a space at the end of the galley kitchen.

"Morning, cave girl." Marie shook her head.

Lucy didn't answer.

I didn't follow her into her bathroom; there are some things sisters don't need to share. Instead, I took a look over Marie's shoulder. She was flicking through a travel guide—Thailand.

So she still wants to go to Thailand, I thought. *Good for her.* Marie closed the magazine and fetched a glass, filling it with water.

The bathroom door opened, and Lucy walked out. Marie held out the glass of water, and Lucy took it without a word, not stopping her stride.

"Lucy," Marie called after her, "you have tissue paper stuck to your butt."

Lucy didn't stop walking or turn around. She held her middle finger up over her shoulder.

Marie laughed. "I'm going to McDonalds. Want a breakfast meal?"

"Sausage McMuffin, please," she shouted back.

I was glad to see Marie and Lucy were still on talking terms after last night. Quickly, I flew up through the ceiling so I was waiting for my sister as she opened her bedroom door.

"No time like the present," I said. "Let's find out what's really been going on." I swiped her chains.

There was no wind tunnel of energy this time, nor did I get thrown through the air. It was easy, but then, why wouldn't it have been? She was my twin. I flicked past images, lifting my arms to move the memories as if swiping them on my iPad, plucking one chain and then another. Setting my intention first really helped me view the important things, though with Lucy, there were many more memories relevant to me. My funeral was one of them, but it was hard to watch through her eyes. Seeing as I had been there anyway, I skipped over it.

The day Lucy lost her job was intense. Lucy didn't just swear at the manager; she ripped off her name badge from her shirt and threw it at him, told him to effing die, and then called him the C word. The memories only got worse from there.

I searched back in time to before Lucy lost her job. She and Mum argued a lot at first, but later Mum seemed to be out whenever Lucy was in. Lucy knew what Mum thought, and she told Marie one night in the Union Tavern that our mum avoided her because she killed me. This wasn't new information to Marie, so it didn't appear to shock her, not in the same way it had the day Lucy confided in her back at our house after the funeral. However, it did help explain why my sister was drinking so often and so excessively.

It was Christmas Day. Marie was there, and so was my mum. *That's good*, I thought. Christmas was only a month ago; had Lucy and Mum figured it out? They all sat watching TV. Dad, Lucy, and Marie were on the ever-hideous blue sofa, and Mum sat in the armchair. No one spoke. Lucy shifted in her seat; she felt awkward in her own skin. No one really wanted to be there, and it felt as if they were all doing what they thought they should: celebrating Christmas in memory of me. In reality, Lucy wanted to be as far away from our house as possible.

I looked on. I needed to find out how Ben was back in Lucy's life. *There*. I stopped and moved the memories back a few days.

Lucy found Ben sitting by the flowers. The lamppost had been replaced, and only a few bouquets remained. They were fresh, though, perhaps left by my mum and dad. She hesitated at first.

"Ben?" she said, approaching him.

Ben stood. "Lucy, hi. Sorry—sorry, I'll go."

"No, it's fine," she said. "You don't have to." She stood silently next to him.

He felt familiar and safe to her, someone who knew and cared for me as much as she did. She'd stayed away from him for so long because the police liked him for something, but the sergeant couldn't even say what. It was unfair, she thought—Ben hadn't hurt me. He'd helped carry me home that night and was devastated to think he had taken pictures of me and not her. He was even more upset to think I had been on drugs when I asked, and that he hadn't noticed.

That had also upset Lucy at first. If Ben had realized I was on drugs, she reasoned, then I would be alive today. But she didn't feel like that now. She felt remorse for him—he must blame himself for my death like she blamed herself. Lucy thought Ben was the only person in her life that shared the guilt she had for my death. She reached her fingers for Ben's, and their hands slipped together.

"*No!*" I shouted and withdrew my hand.

On my knees, I panted, trying to regain my composure. So that's how he did it—he made her think that he knew how she was feeling, that *he* felt the same. I heard Marie shout out to Lucy that her food was in the kitchen. Still giddy at the thought that Lucy had not only let Ben back in but had sympathized with him, I stood just in time to bump into Lucy as she passed me on her way out of the room.

Blurred, fast-moving, and muffled images propelled me back into the room. Holding my hands out as if to hold onto an invisible rope, I stopped myself from flying out of the house and onto the snowy street below. And then I saw it—well, more like heard it: the cuckoo family memory. As images and sounds flashed before my eyes like countryside views on a fast-moving train, it was there, imbedded between jumbled thoughts of the night before. I balanced precariously on the window ledge, still inside the room, thank goodness. An impact with tarmac was not an experience I wanted again, not even in death.

Jumping down from the window, I called out, "Lucy."

She had heard me. I had touched her thoughts with the cuckoos, and what she had was not a childhood memory but the memory I had given her. My voice, my words. She obviously hadn't registered it, but that didn't matter. What mattered was the fact I'd connected with her in the real world. My sister had heard me; my idea had worked.

CHAPTER 12

NOW–LUCY

London, present day
January (six months later)

Furniture Forever's "Bed time, quiet time" motto is no longer in effect. A mere eight weeks is all it took for me to terrify the life out of Emily—Glasses Girl, the one I met at my interview six months ago. She swiftly put in a transfer request, and they shipped her to the Wimbledon branch. I've heard through the grapevine that Emily has requested to be move back to Croydon now that I've been promoted and am moving to the Wimbledon branch.

"Hey, Laura."

The name makes my thoughts yield, but I don't answer.

"Hey. Laura?" Malik's heavy hand taps my shoulder.

I flinch. "Huh?

"Didn't you hear me call you?"

"Sorry. I was in another world."

Malik takes one end of the fitted bedsheet I've been struggling with and tucks it over the opposite corner of the mattress.

It's been six months using my sister's name, but I still forget sometimes. Once I move into my new apartment and away from people who still call me Lucy, it will become easier. I hope it will, anyway.

"You sad to be leaving us? No, don't answer that," Malik says as I open my mouth. He covers his heart. "You go, girl. I wish you all the best, and you will need that attitude over there for sure. There's people at that store who've been there for years, and you get promoted in six months. You're a bad-ass bitch, so they are going to hate you."

"There's a compliment in there somewhere, Malik. Now get out of here." I flick my wrist at him. "I've got a meeting with Simon in ten minutes."

Walking quickly, I head through the door that looks like a janitor's room, then into the corridor. I've been in the interview office multiple times since that dreadful day—it's actually where we have our regular store meetings—and the mere thought of it doesn't paralyze my limbs anymore. The first time was tough, but James, my floor manager, is normally the guy sitting behind the desk. Simon is the regional manager, based out of the store, yet our interaction is sporadic. The first few months were tense, to say the least, though once Simon could see I had no interest in making trouble for him, he let up on me, even started to be nice. I think he is secretly relieved that I turned out to be a star employee. After all, it makes him look good. I'd bet money that he sits in his bigwig meetings droning on about how he can spot real sales talent. If only they knew.

I knock and enter.

"Laura, hello."

"Simon." I nod.

"Sit, please." He gestures with his hand.

He is still fat and just as repulsive as the day I first saw him hanging out his car window at the back of Sadiq's shop, yet it pleases me that we have found a way to get over that. We've moved on professionally, though he still irritates me on personal level— but then, most people do nowadays. I'm not a threat to him, and he is not to me. I pull out the chair in front of the desk and do as he requests. He is flicking through a buff file—mine, I presume.

"I brought this month's figures if you want to see them."

He shakes his head. "I know your figures." He closes the file. "No, I just wanted to have a meeting with you to congratulate you on your excellent performance. You said you would be my hardest worker, and you really are. I know—I mean, I can imagine—how hard it must have been to—to, well, you know." His awkwardness around me has lessened over the months, but I still enjoy watching him squirm, though it's normally only if we are alone. "To start working here. But you have kept to your word and proven yourself."

I just stare at him for a moment. *Proven myself? I didn't prove myself to you—I just wanted to get promoted and get paid more. You're just something I have to endure occasionally, and unfortunately, someone I have to impress professionally. But call it what you must.* Obviously, I don't say that out loud. Instead, I smile.

Simon is stumbling over his words. I think he is trying to apologize without having to say the words, *I'm sorry for using you as a prostitute and then being a dick after I gave you a job.* Not that I would expect an apology—he was a pervert, but I'm the one that blackmailed him. In my eyes, we were even on my first day.

"I'm glad you did so well here," he continues. "And I know you will make a brilliant senior sales person over at Wimbledon."

"Thanks," I say simply. *What the hell does he want?*

Then as if reading my mind, he says, "Laura? Look, I know how we met was a bit—"

"Don't, Simon." My voice rises, and I fight to keep an even tone. "Don't, let's just leave it. This situation has been working nicely for both of us; don't mess it up." I smile and hope it is as empathetic as possible.

Just let sleeping dogs lie, I think.

He looked defeated. "OK, but—"

"But nothing." I fake a smile. "There's no need. We are even, all dues paid. Let's just make money and live the good life, yeah?"

He nods, stands, and extends a hand. "Well, good luck for your first day in Wimbledon—tomorrow?" He glances at the file as if to check the date, January 28th. We shake hands. "You know where I am if you ever need me."

"Thanks," I say and leave the room.

Outside, I head straight for the fire escape, taking the external route out of the building. *Great.* Hand Job Guy has found a conscience. Just what I need, Simon being nice. I'd rather he kept avoiding me, but something tells me that Simon thinks that we just had a moment in there, buried the hatchet and all that. The wind bites. I pull up the zipper on my coat in one swift action. I just hope he doesn't want to be friends. Still, having Simon on my side might not be such a bad thing—it could actually work to my benefit. I glance at my watch. I need to get home—it's time to start my new life, yet also time to leave even more loved ones behind.

★   ★   ★

Looking up at the new ornate apartment block, I swallow back my tears. The building looks creepy, clearly built in the seventies, with its square design and wood beams mimicking the Tudor era. In the dark, those imitation wood beams merge into the shadows of the creeping ivy. But it's affordable for a studio apartment in Wimbledon, even if it *is* closer to Morden and not the exclusive SW19 post code of Wimbledon's elite. But it will do for now.

All my belongings are shoved into two bags, and I'll be sleeping on the floor until I can afford a bed, but I have my own bathroom and kitchenette, and the landlord agreed to leave an old rocking chair in there for me.

New start. A completely new start—on my own.

"Shit, I'm going to miss you guys," I say to myself.

And then I see it. As I bend down to pick up my duffle bag, there is Adewale's dreamcatcher poking out the top of the bag. He must have tucked it inside without me seeing. I feel guilty for not saying goodbye to Priya; I just couldn't bring myself to do it—to leave her the way everyone leaves me.

★ ★ ★

Whoever said that sleeping on the floor is good for your back needs to be shot, I think as I try to rotate my hips discreetly during the staff meeting. I've been in the store thirty minutes, and Malik is right. They all hate me, or so it appears. After a quick motivational speech from Bryan, the store manager, and an even quicker nod to my arrival, we all make our way to our individual sections. I follow Bryan, a seriously tall man with sharp, narrow shoulders, up to my section. He is the only person who has been slightly pleasant thus far. Not the best start to my new life, but if I'm honest, I don't really care.

I'll be working in the bed section, which is at the top of a sweeping set of navy-blue carpeted stairs. When we get there, I do a quick check to make sure Emily is not hiding somewhere. She's not, thank goodness. The floor is vast, bigger than I'd imagined. There's a mezzanine which overlooks the first part of the floor below.

"Wow," I say to Bryan, who ignores me.

He is looking over the mezzanine at a girl who waves and runs up the stairs.

"Sorry, my car wouldn't start again," she says. "It's the cold mornings—takes longer to warm up. It's snowing out there now; have you seen it?" The pasty-skinned brunette girl is still panting.

"We can see the snow, Sarah. Get up earlier tomorrow," Bryan scolds her. "Sarah, this is Laura."

"Hi," she says and gives me her hand to shake.

So not everyone here is a complete dick, I think, shaking her hand.

"Good, I'll leave you with Sarah," Bryan says. "Come find me if you need anything, Laura. Sarah, Joe is at the dentist till ten, so get Laura settled in."

We both watch him descend the stairs.

Sarah's skin is pale but smooth, and I guess she is about my age. She has a sweet face. She's nice, maybe a bit *too* nice. *Priya would eat her for breakfast*, I think, then feel a pang of sadness. Priya is gone.

"Do you have a boyfriend?" Sarah asks.

I shake my head.

"I do. Dan."

I smile.

"You don't remember me, do you?" she asks.

I angle my head, trying to understand her question.

"I sat next to you on introduction day—we started at the same time."

"Did you? I don't recall." I look about the floor for some kind of escape.

"I'm glad you're a girl."

I cast a curious look over at her. This conversation keeps getting stranger. "OK … ?"

"Because I'm the only girl in the store now that Emily has gone," she explains.

I smile, not quite knowing what to say.

"Nice to have you on board," she concludes. "Come find me at lunch?"

I don't answer.

Sarah spends most of the morning skulked over the sign-up desk texting on her phone, and I do my best to avoid her. This is tough because either Sarah didn't pick up on my stand-offish attitude or it doesn't bother her. After I meet Joe, I settle for the latter—she is clearly used to working with temperamental characters.

As I walk the floor, I observe Joe's interaction with Sarah, and it's brutal. No wonder she is glad to have another girl in store. By the end of the day, after seeing Sarah finish every customer contract for Joe, I'm confident that Joe will not be on the leaderboard much longer, not if I can help it.

I watch Joe hand another form over the desk to Sarah and rush toward a new customer at the top of the stairs.

Not this time, buddy, I think, and stride toward the young couple. Joe is leading them into the middle of the section.

"Joe," I say with a well-practiced angelic smile. "It's OK, I can deal with this lady and gentleman. I know you have paperwork to finish."

He looks genuinely confused. "No, I don't."

"You do." I point at Sarah scribbling away. "I can take it from here," I continue. "You don't want to lose a deal over late paperwork, do you?"

I can't tell what Joe is thinking. He seems to only have one mode, and that is frustration—and it's about to get a whole lot worse now that I'm here.

The customers didn't stay long and were only browsing. I wave them off down the stairs and see Bryan waiting for them to leave before locking the main doors.

Turning, I see Joe right behind me. "Joe, did you not get the company memo on personal space?" I sidestep, retreating toward the sign-up desk where Sarah is sitting.

"We don't do that here," he says, catching up with me.

"Do what?"

"Try to steal clients from each other?"

"Sarah, stop," I say, and she looks up at me through frightened eyes. "Joe, fill out your own contracts from now on. Sarah, if Joe asks you to do his paperwork again, do it, but submit it as a deal split. The company rules are clear. You are only credited with a deal if you submit the paperwork yourself. If you want Sarah to do your paperwork, then a commission split should be made.

Now, before you both leave, make sure you adjust and submit your end-of-day figures correctly, with split commission."

"What? No! You're not my boss—you don't tell me what to do." Joe flaps his arms high.

"This is not open for debate," I tell him coolly. "It's company policy. Do it, and if you have an issue, go talk to Bryan. I'm going home."

I don't leave immediately; I loiter to make sure Joe submits his figures correctly. I notice that Sarah looks visibly petrified but is doing as I say. After today, I wonder if Sarah will start to climb the leaderboard. It's not that I'm a nice person, but if Simon sees an improvement in her figures, it will only make me look good. I do like her, though. It's been a good day.

"Laura?" As I revel in my thoughts, I spin to see Sarah pacing toward me. "That was so brave. Thank you so much—look, I'm meeting some friends in the wine bar across the road. You should come."

"Thanks, maybe."

"No, seriously, I think you would really like them," she persists. "No one from work—just my friends."

I nod noncommittally.

"OK, well, if you change your mind, we'll be over there. See ya!" She takes off toward the stairs.

Delayed, the bus schedule reads. I shiver as I wait alongside a handful of other commuters.

Maybe I should go for that drink with Sarah, I think, looking over at the bar. From where I stand, I can see clearly through the window. The bar is filled with merry people who look somewhat happier and warmer than me. They laugh and chat like normal people with normal lives, and I expect they also all have beds to sleep in.

A bus pulls to a slow halt. It's not my bus, and I check the board again. I've been waiting over twenty minutes now—surely my bus is next. I breathe into my hands and rub them together, hoping for even the smallest amount of warmth. I look back at the bar. Sarah and another brown-haired girl jump excitedly to greet a friend. Their jovial smiles touch me with memories of times long forgotten, times I'd do anything to live again, to cherish, and to remember each and every detail. I find myself wandering toward the window. They look so civilized drinking from slender wine glasses, a far cry from my pink mug. And if I do go inside, what is it that I'm looking for?

Friends. The word pops into my head the way thoughts used to years before, and I shake it out just as quickly. I don't need a friend; they get in the way. Two men have now joined Sarah and her friends, and I wonder which one is Dan, Sarah's boyfriend. Then one kisses her.

So that's Dan, I think. He looks clean-cut and handsome, as my gran would say. They all look clean-cut. *What if they don't like me? Why do you even care?* I ask myself and shrug.

The bus hydraulics hiss as the doors open—it's my bus, but for a split second I hesitate. Then, as I give one last glance back at the window, I feel a thud on my back like someone has thrown a snowball at me. I turn. *Odd,* I think. I run to make the bus before the doors close, not that I need to—the line of people before me is still hustling their way on board. I reach a hand over my shoulder and down my back, then under and up my back. My coat is dry; no one has thrown a snowball at me. I tap my bus pass and find a seat on the lower deck to the rear and watch Sarah laughing like she hasn't a care in the world. The bus pulls away, and I close my eyes.

Day one is over, I think.

I wait until a little past ten at night before I make my way down to the bins on the lower level of my apartment block. Earlier, I'd taken down a pizza box and seen that someone had thrown out what looked to be cushions, perhaps from some outdoor furniture. I'd not taken a proper look at the time. People were coming home from work, and the last thing I needed was for my neighbors to see me dumpster diving.

I walk up to the large blue metal bin, where I can still see the top of the cushions poking out. Peering over the top, I'm delighted and disgusted at the same time: delighted because three quarters of the cushions are tucked nicely into a bin bag, and disgusted because someone has emptied what looks like the contents of their garbage disposal on top of the bag. Swiftly but carefully, I pull the cushions free from the smelly bin. Thankfully, they're unsoiled. I retreat quickly to my apartment.

To say that I'm ecstatic with my new makeshift bed would be an understatement. After shaking out the dust and what I hope is just normal debris from outdoor furniture, I drop my old blanket down on the cushions and then stand back to admire my work. It's perfect, even if my feet will poke off the end. I'm sure my back will thank me tomorrow.

Before I get into bed, I hang Adewale's dreamcatcher on the back of the rocking chair. "What do you think, Lulu?" I say. "My find should tide me over nicely till payday. After that, I'll take out a contract on a mattress from my work. I get a staff discount and paid commission on the sale. How good is that?"

Keeping on my clothes from that day, I slip into bed. It's cold in my apartment because I've not put on the heating—my plan is to keep costs as low as possible for as long as possible. I shiver beneath the blanket. The laminate floor is not as warm as carpet would be, but I remind myself that I've dealt with worse.

Just be thankful you're not on the streets.

Looking up at the shadowed ceiling, I think back to what happened earlier by the bus stop. "Was that you?" I ask aloud. "Did you shove me, Laura?"

Silence.

"I'm going to be honest with you, Lulu. I still wonder if you're real or if I'm just getting crazier each day. Did you want me to go into the bar? Why? I don't know what to do. It was easy when I met Priya—I needed her, and she protected me. But I don't need protecting now, and I don't need friends."

I think about this for a second before reiterating. "I don't. I'll just get hurt when they disappoint me or if I have to leave them. And anyway, I shouldn't mix work with pleasure. I didn't do that at the Croydon store—and yes, yes, I didn't need to. I know I had Priya and Adewale. But Laura, I don't need another friend … . Oh, I don't know. Sarah is sweet. Reminds me a little of you—she's kind. But she's been letting that dick Joe walk all over her. I'm hoping that having Sarah on my side will set me up for the floor manager position, if there even is one. But if there is and I *do* get it, then I'll make Sarah my star seller." I grin before relaxing my face and giving a sigh.

My eyes fall over the dreamcatcher. "Tell me, Laura, tell me what to do. I'm here, right where I planned to be—away from that bloody bedsit. But I don't know what to do now. I want to live my life for you. I want to make you proud; I just don't know how. Tell me, Lulu—show me what to do next."

Silence.

As I lie there with my blanket tight under my chin, I feel my eyes suddenly dampen. I quickly blink back the tears and swallow away the lump that rises in my throat. I'm out of that poisonous life, so I should be happy—my fight is over. I sniff. So why do I feel so empty? I roll onto my side and curl into the fetal position for some extra warmth.

The soft glow of streetlights has turned the darkness in my room to a gentle ginger. The dreamcatcher that hangs on the rocking chair looks as lonely as I feel.

My fight's not over, I think. On the contrary, the life I want to live for Laura has only just begun.

CHAPTER 13

THEN–LAURA

Cornwall, three years ago
February

"Lucy," Marie called up the stairs, "your dad's here."

Lucy had openly detested the therapy sessions ever since agreeing to them. I knew Marie and my dad thought it was all due to their gentle persuasion that she even went, and I was grateful to them for that. They had unwittingly reinforced my nightly messages. Lucy agreeing to joint therapy with our mum, was, I would say, more of a group effort. And that's if you can even call it joint therapy—Mum lied most of the way through the first session, which frustrated me endlessly, and Lucy somehow evaded nearly all questions directed at her. But it was a start, and a distraction from my current predicament.

Life, or whatever I was living, weighed heavily on my mind. I still didn't know where I was or what eternity had in store for me next. All I knew was that I missed my family and would never hold them in my arms again. And so, night after night, I did what I could to keep them safe with warnings of Ben—none of which had worked. If only Marie could see, then she could reinforce this message for me. Lucy still thought of him all the time. He'd only texted her once in the last month, but that was one time too many in my view. Nothing I did to communicate was working, and by the end of each night, my energy felt drained. I was too low on energy to even think about trying to connect during the day.

There had been a few times that Lucy repeated what I'd said in conversation to Marie. This, however, was quickly passed off as her inner thoughts, and they just talked them away. Marie agreed that being careful with Lucy's feelings was a good thing, but they both still thought Ben was innocent. Frustrated but not defeated, I dropped the nightly "Ben beware" messages to turn my attention to joint therapy for a time.

My hope was to rebuild my family. If Lucy felt loved by our mum, maybe she wouldn't need to look for love from Ben—or Marie, for that matter. I'd become overly concerned with my sister's apparent dependence on Marie emotionally, and I could see how much time it was taking away from Marie and her new boyfriend Dylan, which was definitely a bone of contention between Lucy and Marie. Dylan was not letting Lucy's antics come between them, but my worry was that it would soon come between my sister and Marie. I needed to keep Marie and Lucy strong as friends, and Lucy and our mum strong as a family—but that was easier said than done.

Lucy's head poked out from behind her bedroom door. "Why? Marie, you're driving me there, aren't you?"

"Lucy?" I heard my dad's voice call up to her, and I whizzed down the stairs to see him. "I just want to see you before you go, honey."

"OK—give me a second," she called back from her room.

My dad stood at the bottom of the stairs looking up, and I stood midway looking down. I tilted my head slowly from side to side, trying to work out if he knew I was there or not. All I saw was indignation in his face, though it was hidden well. He didn't know I was there; he was truly invested in Lucy, and Lucy alone. I move closer. I knew my dad loved me, and I was so heartbroken that my sister couldn't see that our dad had enough love for her, that she didn't even need our mum's love. Having said that, I frowned. Of course she did—everyone needs, or at least wants, their mum's love. Sadly, Lucy never really got that much of it. I just hoped that my dad was right—that therapy could, at the very least, make our mum love Lucy the way she had before. Parents aren't meant to have favorites, and most of the ones that do hide it better than our mum had. The best I hoped for was for our mum to stop blaming Lucy and at least love her the way she had before I left.

My dad pressed his fingers hard against his temples with small circular motions. He looked tired, beaten, and like he'd aged even more. All I wanted to do in that moment was hold him and tell him I was all right. Closing myself off mentally but opening up emotionally, I opened my arms and did just that: hugged him. My arms slipped around his chest like silk. With every bit of positive energy I could muster, I projected deep into his soul. I thought it would be difficult—draining, even—but it wasn't that way at all. Instead, it was as if his soul reached out and hugged me right back. I felt safe. I'd been loved and still was.

Suddenly, I was no longer at the bottom of the stairs hugging my dad. His soul was with mine, holding me tight as we flew through the astral plane deep between the folds of the fabric of life. In the blink of an eye, we danced with Jupiter as a backdrop, my feet on top of his, like we used to when I was a child.

I certainly felt like a child again. We danced to the echoes of life, a song more beautiful than anything. I was elated, and I laughed as my dad's soul twirled me effortlessly between the stars. He looked so happy, young, and full of energy, as if he didn't have a care in the world. It was the way he used to look when I was alive. Our steps were vast, effortless strides across the cosmos, one last waltz with my father, as beautiful as the song. He pulled me close, lifting my feet off the ground, and spun me round and round on the spot. The more I laughed, the happier he looked.

Oh, how I wished Lucy could be here dancing with us, and our mum watching the way she always did, from a distance.

Two left feet, she always claimed. *You three dance for me.*

"Dad?" Lucy's voice drew us back.

Our dad's smile was vibrant and easy. He might not have seen the star-crossed dance with me, but I was sure he'd felt it. "Lucy, honey." He held his arms open.

I stood next to them as they hugged, hoping Lucy's energy didn't drain away what I'd just given him. He needed it.

"How are you feeling?" he asked, stepping back. His hands gripped her shoulders. "You know how proud I am of you for going with your mum, don't you?"

Lucy grimaced, then pulled away. "Don't get all soppy. And you? Are you OK?"

He thought for a second. "Yes," he said finally. "I think coming here to see you has really cheered me up."

"Well, glad to see I'm good for something."

"Lucy, don't say that; come on, now." He pulled her into his chest. "You are so brave. I know how much you miss her; we all do, and talking about it is hard. But you're strong. You're my daughter, so I know that. I need you to know that too. I love you, Lulu." Lucy slipped her arms around his waist. "We will all get through this, I promise." He kissed the top of her head. "Lucy," he said, looking slightly more serious than before.

"Yeah?"

"Give it a chance. Tell the lady how you really feel."

"I have."

"I mean *really* feel. Lucy, I'm your dad, I know you, remember?"

"You should tell that to Mum—I swear she believes her own lies half the time." Lucy pulled her coat from the coat stand, shoving her arm inside.

"Then call her out. If she tells a lie, call her out on it."

"What, and make her hate me more? Why aren't *you* there? If you came, you could call her bloody out—she's fucking psycho."

"Lucy, don't swear." My dad scowled.

"Sorry. But why don't you come?"

Dropping his chin, my dad spoke to the floor. "Mum didn't want me to. And if me not being there means that you two can fix things, then that's how it's to be."

"Fuck, she—"

"Lucy."

"Sorry—sorry. She is so manipulative, Dad."

"Lucy, just give it a go. Open up, please—for me?"

Marie appeared from the kitchen. "Ready to go?" she asked.

Lucy reached up and kissed our dad on the cheek. "I will, Dad. For you."

He nodded at Lucy and gave her one last vibrant smile. "You better go."

I was glad I'd hugged him. I'd never felt like hugging anyone like that before. It seemed to revitalize him—and me. I felt like my own energy had been given a kick start, and I was going to need it for this session. My mum and sister might have been apprehensive about reliving the events of my death, but if they had to, I'd also have to, and possibly even listen to how they felt about it.

Maybe the therapist won't go there today, I thought.

"Come on, then. Let's get this over with." Lucy's smiley persona had vanished with my dad's exit, and so had mine.

"Here." Marie handed her a scarf. "It's cold out there."

★ ★ ★

Marie pulled up outside the doctor's building, and I left the car immediately. She and Lucy had argued the whole way, draining me further. With me outside the car and them inside, I hoped to escape their bitchy snipes at each other, though that would have been near impossible for me. Even if they'd been whispering, I'd still have heard them. My hearing was like a super power, one I'd like to be able to turn off at times.

"Fine." Lucy grabbed her bag from the back seat. "But he did."

"He did *not* hit on you, Lucy. Shit, how do I put up with you and your lies?"

I could tell Marie was getting fed up with the same argument, and I wished I could talk to Lucy, or at least explain my sister's fears to Marie. If they each knew what the other felt, it could all be fixed.

Maybe the two of them should be in therapy, I thought.

"Whatever. Just don't say I didn't warn you what he's like," Lucy said, leaning back to the car.

Marie rolled her eyes. "OK, I've been warned."

Lucy hesitated, infuriation etching her face. She slammed the car door.

"Remember what your dad said," Marie called out her open window.

★　★　★

I stood next to Lucy in the elevator on her way to the sixth floor.

You're not alone, I whispered the way I had before. *I'm here.*

This was their second session, and I knew she was frightened. I also knew what about. Since she had heard my cuckoo message, Lucy had started to talk to me when she was on her own. At first, it was just a few words—she asked if I could hear her or if I was there. At first, I thought she actually knew I was there, but she didn't, at least not with the clarity that I thought. Maybe she was sensing me, but if she was, she didn't know it. Lucy was just doing what most people do when they lose a loved one. I just wished she knew that I really could hear her. I wished I could tell her that I knew she was frightened, and talk to her about the crash, her feelings, and our mum. I wished I could tell her that Dad was right. She was strong. I moved to tuck a stray hair behind her ear, but my hand floated right through her. She shivered.

The elevator doors sprung open. Our mum sat at the far end of the corridor, cross-legged, with her small red leather handbag balancing neatly on her knee. Her calf-length pleated skirt made her look as if she were dressed for church. Lucy sat down in the seat next to her, but they didn't say a word, not even a pleasant glance to acknowledge each other's arrival. What Lucy said to me last night was right—the sessions were a waste of time and money if Mum was going to be like this. Why was she being so childish? This was a pointless thought, though, because I knew full well how pretentious and petty our mum could be.

Before too long, the door opened, and Hellen, the therapist, beckoned them in. I followed behind. Hellen was a pretty middle-aged lady with short brown hair. She had a cute, round face and elevated cheekbones.

"Hello, Lucy," she said, gesturing inside toward the comfortable-looking couch. "Kathrin, good to see you again." Lucy and our mum entered the room.

The door closed, and we all settled into our seats, not that I was sitting. I chose to float between the two-seater sofa and Hellen's leather armchair. The office looked just like it sounded— an office, with a desk in one corner, overlooked by a bookcase. It was perfectly arranged, and I noticed no personal pictures as I moved about the room. Modern art filled the walls—prints, mainly—but not one photo of Hellen or her family, and I wondered if other therapists also used this room. After all, it did look very staged.

No one spoke. I wanted the session to go well, so I spoke into my sister's ear and reminded her what our dad had said about opening up. I thought about doing the same for my mum, but that would have been pointless—we didn't have a connection in the same way.

"I'm glad you came back this week," Hellen started. "I can imagine how hard last week must have been for you both, and it's good that you both want to continue to work through this."

I wondered if Hellen caught my sister's looked of indignation before Lucy let a smile wash over her face. My mum politely nodded, then contradicted herself with a shrug.

"OK—Kathrin, why don't you tell me about your week?"

Hellen scribbled notes as my mum talked, and Lucy watched the walls as if they were about to close in on her.

My mum's weeks had fallen into day after day of sleeping or crying. "I know what I said," my mum said. "I said last week that I'd get washed and dressed, even if I wasn't going to leave the house, but …" Mum fiddled with the strap on her bag. She hesitated, but Hellen waited patiently for her to continue. "All I want to do is sit in bed and look at pictures of her."

Hellen's chin rested gently on the top of her fist. "There's nothing wrong with looking at pictures," she said. How do you feel when you're looking at them?"

"Sad. Happy sometimes, I suppose … then sad when I feel happy."

I moved to my mum's side and stroked her face. It was heartbreaking to hear them talk this way about me, but there was nothing I could do to ease their pain.

I noticed Hellen scribbling notes. Under my mum's name she had circled "acceptance." Next to that read, "Depression but self-managing," and beside that, she had scribbled, "Kathrin is looping back to anger."

Once our mum had finished, Hellen turned to Lucy. "And what did you do?"

"Not much. Nothing, really. Went to the pub and got drunk—" Lucy looked up to one side as if trying to recall more information. "Yeah, that's about it. Oh, saw my dad. He likes to pop over to make sure I've not tried to top myself again."

"Lucy!" Mum berated her.

"What? It's true," she said.

Silence.

I asked Lucy to stop being defensive, but there was nothing in her eyes. She couldn't feel me—she was too consumed with resentment for our mum. I needed this session to go well if our family was going to repair itself.

"And how do you feel about that, Lucy?"

She shrugged. "Shit."

"Shit why?" Hellen probed.

Lucy shrugged again. "Because I know how much I frightened my dad trying to—well, you know."

"Is that the only reason you feel shit about it?" the therapist asked.

"Well, I'm not going to do it again, if that's what you mean."

"And what made you feel like you wanted to hurt yourself?" Hellen asked. She scribbled the word "guilt" next to the word "undoing." I hoped that Hellen's notes made sense to her, because I couldn't figure out what she was thinking about my sister right now.

Undoing what? I thought.

When Lucy didn't answer, I watched Hellen write the words "complicated grief" and circle them.

"Lucy," Hellen said, "I know it's hard, but can you think back to that time and tell me what you were feeling?"

There was a long silence before she answered. My mum's eyes looked as if they would burn a hole in the side of her face.

"I blamed myself, didn't I?" Lucy shrugged in defense. "Like everyone else blames me."

My mum stopped looking at her.

"Why do you say that, Lucy?" Hellen pressed.

My sister stood and walked over to the bookshelf.

"Sit down, Lucy," our mum instructed.

"It's OK, Kathrin." Hellen held up a hand. "Go on, Lucy. Why do you think that?"

Lucy spun to face them. "Because it's true. I know you blame me, Mum." She turned her back to look out the window. "I heard you the night we came home from the hospital." Restless, she turned toward them again. "You asked Dad why I had to start an argument knowing Laura would follow me."

There was a pause before my mum answered. I was glad Lucy was opening up, just apprehensive about how this particular wound would heal itself, especially with so much depending on our mum's response.

"Why did you, then?" Mum replied curtly.

Desperation filled my being. I could tell where this conversation was about to end up. Mum didn't need Hellen; she needed me. I was her voice of reason, but I was gone. What hope did Lucy have now? All those years I thought I'd been doing the right thing by getting involved and keeping the peace, but I hadn't been helping. I saw that now—I had made it worse. I should have let them argue and figure it out for themselves.

"Because I thought she had hit on my boyfriend," Lucy said.

"What, Ben?" my mum shouted back. "That scumbag! Laura didn't even like him."

Hellen had a hint of unease on her face, and so she should. I knew the look in my mum's eyes; she was mad, really mad. If Lucy wanted Mum to tell the truth, she was about to hear it, and Hellen was about to see the other side of our mum's personality. I braced myself.

"Yes, she *did* like him, she was just being protective," Lucy retorted.

"And the pictures on his phone? How did he get them?" Our mum was now on her feet, striding toward Lucy.

Lucy stepped out from behind the desk to meet our mum face on. "He said Laura asked him to take them."

"What? And you believe him?"

Hellen quickly maneuvered herself between them but didn't

say anything. She gestured for some space. Mum didn't move, but Lucy took a step away.

"I don't know, Mum," she said. "I don't know who to believe—"

Mum started to speak, then shook her head in apparent disgust.

"Lucy," Hellen said. "Tell me what you're thinking. Why don't you know who to believe, and how does that make you feel?"

Lucy looked down to the street below. "Ben, my ex. He told me that he thought Laura was me, that she must have been"—Lucy hesitated—"already drugged when she asked him to take the pictures of her." Hearing Lucy defend Ben's lies riled me. She went on. "The police don't like him, but no evidence was found to suggest he had anything to do with it. And right now, he's the only one who gets me, who knows how I feel."

"What?" Our mum's hands flew into the air, and then she lunged toward Lucy. "You stupid girl!" she shouted in her face.

"Kathrin, please," Hellen said, frantically pulling her away.

"How *you* feel?" our mum continued. "Do you know how *I* feel?"

"No, Mum, I don't—that's why we are here. But I have no doubt that you're about to tell me."

"No!" I shouted desperately.

"That's right, Lucy, you show off with your smart mouth. Make it all about you, like you always do. Well, not this time."

Panicked and not knowing what to do, I reached out and tried to cover my mum's mouth with my palm. When that didn't work, I flung my arms around her the way I had with my dad earlier, but nothing worked. It just made me feel sick. My mum's anger raged, poisoning every inch of her soul. This session was not panning out the way it needed to.

Hellen's kind smile had turned to one of pure terror, and her eyes darted from Lucy to my mum and then the door. "Please, Kathrin, Lucy, let's sit. Take a moment. Please."

"Go on, then," Lucy egged. "Tell me, Mum. Tell me what you really think. I mean, that's why we are here, isn't it?"

"I didn't want to come," our mum spat.

"Well, that makes two of us then."

"You know what, Lucy? You're right—I do blame you."

Hellen let out the breath she had been holding. The poor woman looked as defeated as I felt. "OK, let's sit down," she managed. "If we calm down, then maybe Lucy can respond. We can take a break."

My mum stared viciously across the room at Lucy.

"I know you do, Mum," Lucy said. She turned back to the window. "I also know you wish it had been me and not her."

"That's right," our mum whispered. "I do."

As I stood between my mum and Lucy and next to Hellen, anger suddenly empowered my entire being. I wasn't sure if our mum had projected her emotions across the room and onto me, but I felt rage like never before.

"*STOP!*" I screamed toward the heavens.

I looked at my mum. She was still seething, poised to spit more hurtful words if Lucy pushed it. Then I looked at Lucy. She looked confused. Her eyes bounced around the room as if looking for something.

"Please, ladies," Hellen asked again. "Let's take a break."

No one moved.

"Lucy," I whispered. *"Lucy, did you hear that?"*

"Lucy? Are you OK?" Hellen asked.

"Fine." Lucy made for the door. "I'm leaving."

"Oh, no. No, don't leave," Hellen pleaded.

"Let her go," our mum snapped as Lucy passed her without even a glance. "This is what she does—she runs away from everything."

Infuriated, I screamed, *"NO, Mum!"*

Lucy froze. Her hand was on the door handle, but she didn't open the door. Instead, she turned to look at the room—

not at our mum or Hellen, though. She angled her head as if listening.

"Lucy?" Hellen approached.

"I've got to go." Tugging the handle, she left.

★　★　★

I didn't follow my sister. I needed time to myself to think. This life, my world, whatever I was— it was soul-destroying. I had to see the ones I loved most tearing each other down, and all because of me. If only they could see and feel what I did. If only they could know how precious life is. All my efforts to connect with my sister and yet I still couldn't help. There was surely no way Lucy would go back to counseling with our mum now.

I floated about the town aimlessly, occasionally bumping into people, which provided a nice distraction as I read their thoughts. Eventually, I thought myself back to my sister. She was not in a good way, sitting in the Union Tavern. Mike, the publican, had refused her alcohol and given her a black coffee instead. We were sitting at a small table in the far corner of the pub, my sister's head in her arms. A newspaper on the table showed the day's date: February 28th.

The pub doors opened, and Marie stepped in, sorrow displayed across her face. She stood in the middle of the almost-empty pub just staring at Lucy for a moment. I wanted to know what she was thinking, but she moved forward just as I reached out. I quickly retracted my hand, and she passed me and stepped up to the table. Her tiny energy chains fell about her, glittering.

"Lucy?" Marie put a hand softly on her shoulder, then sat down across from her. "How you doing, sweetie?"

Lucy raised her head, her eyes red and puffy.

"I thought you might be here when you didn't come home,"

Marie continued. "What happened?"

Mike approached, placing two fresh coffees down. Lucy turned her head toward the wall until he was gone.

Marie reached across the table, resting her hand on Lucy's. "Tell me, what happened?"

"Where do I start?" Lucy sniffed.

"Did the session not go well?"

Lucy raised her eyebrows. "You could say that. But nothing I didn't expect. My mum admitted that she blames me for Laura dying—oh, and she wishes it had been me and not Laura."

"What?" Marie sat back in shock. "She actually said that?"

"Yep."

Marie didn't look convinced. "Those exact words?"

"Yes. Well, basically. I told her she wished it had been me instead of Laura, and she said yes. I mean, I knew that, but it hurt to hear it anyway." Lucy picked up a paper napkin from the table and blew her nose with it.

"That's bullshit. I don't know what to say—listen, you know your mum can be a bitch; she's just lashing out because she's hurting. Not that I'm condoning it."

"Whatever. That's not really what I'm worried about."

"What is it?"

Lucy played with the napkin, ripping the tissue apart in her fingers. I leaned in, hoping she was going to say what I thought she was.

"Lucy, what is it?" Marie urged.

"I'm hearing voices." She stopped ripping the tissue and looked seriously at Marie. "And not just any voice—Laura's voice."

I settled down in the chair next to my sister. I was elated. She *did* hear me, and now that Marie knew, they could figure out together why I was here with them. I couldn't help but beam.

Marie looked back at her blankly. "OK," she said eventually. "When do you hear the voices?"

"No, not 'voices.' *Her* voice. Today in the session was the first time I'd actually heard her voice properly—like an actual voice. It was as clear as me and you now, but faint."

"What did you hear?" Marie asked.

"She was shouting at my mum, telling her to stop when she said nasty stuff."

"And you don't think it's just in your mind, like a protection thing or something?"

Lucy shook her head.

"So today was the first time you heard it?" Marie asked.

"Yes, but I think she's been talking to me in other ways—like at night." Lucy lowered her voice as a man and a woman sat near them. "I have thoughts, but they're not my thoughts," she whispered. "I can't explain it exactly. Until I heard her voice today, I didn't give it much thought. But now I think she really is trying to talk to me—the thoughts I get aren't like mine. There are thoughts from a conversation I've had, but I never actually have the conversation. Does that make any sense?" Marie shook her head, so Lucy continued. "It's as if I'm remembering something from a conversation I've not had. I think she's been talking to me for ages."

I searched Marie's face for some kind of understanding. This was not good—Marie had to believe her.

"Lucy, you're worrying me now." Marie reached for her hand. "Tell the therapist. Quit the joint session if your mum is being nasty, and go on your own."

Lucy shrugged. "I'm worried that I'm going crazy, Marie." Her eyes welled up again, and fresh tears streamed down her face. "Or what if Laura is still out there? What if she is stuck and can't cross over or something?"

"No, Lucy," I said but no one could hear me this time.

"I don't think you're going crazy, Lucy. It's just stress. And Laura isn't stuck—you can't think like that. I don't think you should stop the therapy."

Lucy nodded in agreement.

Just great, why is Marie not intrigued? They both think I'm not real. Now what? I agonized.

"Ben texted," Lucy announced abruptly. "He wants to meet me."

"Are you going to?" Marie asked.

Lucy shrugged again. "Don't know. I feel like he might understand me; I think he has the same guilt as I do."

To my horror, Marie nodded. "Maybe talking to him about it might help. Even if you don't stay in contact, it might be good for you to talk it out with him. I know your parents don't like him, but maybe they just need someone to blame. I never thought he had anything to do with it; he was with us all night from what I remember."

"That's what I thought," Lucy said.

"NO. NO, LUCY!" Why she couldn't hear me now? No matter how loudly I shouted, they just kept talking. Had my sister not understood my Ben warnings? Things were not going as planned, and I had to find another way to warn her.

CHAPTER 14

NOW–LUCY

London, present day
February

"Yes, on the floor," I tell the thickset delivery man. "Just there is fine. Thank you." He lets the heavy mattress fall to the bare floor, and it hits down with a thud.

"No bedframe? Is coming after?" The man's English is broken. Romanian, maybe.

"Yes, it's coming soon," I lie.

He nods to a smaller man, who hands me some papers to sign. I fill in my name, followed by the date—February 28th—and hand it back to him.

"Thanks again," I call out before closing my front door.

It's late—I must have been the last delivery of the day. I pull at the mattress's plastic covering. My one Saturday off, and I had to waste it by sitting in all day for a delivery. I quickly dress the mattress with a dark red sheet and a thick black duvet set to finish. Then I undress, though not for bed. I need to shower and get ready for a night out.

I'm meeting Sarah at seven thirty for a drink—nothing fancy, just a quiet one at a bar near work. I'm trying not to overthink things, but I can't forget that this will be the first time I've sat in a private establishment drinking alcohol since I left Cornwall. The thought is laughable, given the fact that I'm a borderline alcoholic. My thoughts bounce back to Priya, as they do now and then, but I swiftly banish them. I can't let myself miss someone I left behind.

Priya is another life, I tell myself.

I turn the shower knob, and cold water jets frantically hurl themselves at my naked chest. It's shocking. I wait for the water to warm up before soaking my hair and start talking to Laura.

"I won't stay long," I tell her. "I couldn't say no to her again. The girl's relentless—she must have asked me out nearly every day since I started there. I'm not sure if she has some kind of ulterior motive or if she is just being nice to me. Who knows why she would be nice to me? I go out of my way to ignore everyone at work, her included. It makes me wonder if she is up to something. Why would she want to be my friend?"

I squeeze a blob of shampoo into my hands. "I mean, I know I came to her rescue with Joe and all that, but that was over a month ago. She *is* doing a lot better with sales now, and she told me her pay will be better next month with all the split commissions that she is making Joe put through with her. I actually overheard her telling the store manager, Bryan, that since I started she feels more motivated ... Again, I don't know how I motivate her. Like I said, I ignore everyone unless they are customers." I think about my words for a minute as I wash. "Maybe she thinks I'm just being professional—focused or something like that."

After my shower, I consider my wardrobe. My clothing options are limited, but I do have a cute black sweater with sparkly bits on the shoulders—I bought it from a charity shop a few months back.

Couple that with a pair of jeans, and I'll look fine, I think.

"It's still bloody freezing outside, so a fancy sweater will work well." I pull said sweater over my head and turn on the spot in front of the mirror. "What do you think, Lulu?"

Silence.

A familiar thought nuzzles its way into my mind. *I'm talking to myself.* There hasn't been a dream or moving objects for over a month. Has she gone? Or am I just batshit crazy?

"Lulu, can you even see this?" I ask, trying to suppress my frustration.

Silence.

"Oh, Laura." I sigh. "Just let me know I'm doing the right thing here? This is your life I'm trying to live for you, so the least you can do is give me some regular input."

Silence.

I arrive at the bar early. I walk through the glass doors, thankful to be out of the blustery wind and inside in the warm. The lights are dim, giving the long, and narrow bar a welcoming glow. I find a seat at the bar and perch myself high on one of the empty square stools. Somehow, sitting at the bar makes me feel less committed than a table. Ridiculous, but this is my life now: thinking, then overthinking.

You would think having a dead sister sending you messages might be comforting, but it's not. It might be if I was sure my sister was really communicating with me; however, I'm not. I mean, I am some days, but then other days, I wonder if it's all in my head. The voices I used to hear, the dreams, objects falling—was it all in my mind? And let's be honest, my lifestyle since leaving Cornwall hasn't lent itself well to that of a well-adjusted sane person.

A tall bar man leans toward me. "What can I get you, gorgeous?" I notice a dark tooth that sits front and center of his mouth.

"Shanty-top," I say, trying not to stare at it. He serves my drink and flirts unnecessarily with me, and I pay.

I wish Sarah would hurry up. I check my watch. The bar is quiet, and this bar man might be good at his job, but he hasn't mastered reading his audience. And this audience wants to be left alone.

"Not been stood up, have ya?" He smiles, and I catch a glimpse of his bad tooth again. "He'd be nuts to stand up such a pretty girl like you."

A gust of wind from the glass door reveals Sarah, much to my appreciation. She waltzes up to the bar like she owns the joint.

I stand. "Hey," I say and allow her to give me an awkward hug before she peels her coat off.

"Hi, Terry," Sarah greets the bar man.

"Oh ... so you're this lovely lady's date, then." He glances over at me and winks.

Sarah might not pick up on my cold shoulder cues at work, but she definitely sees through my fake smile at the bar man.

"Ah, sorry, Terry, Laura has a boyfriend," she lies. "He's away ... in the army."

My expression is neutral. "Iraq," I say.

She turns to face me as the bar man skulks away.

"He's harmless." She leans in, and for some reason, I lean in to meet her. "My friend went on a date with him last week. She's not into him, though."

"Oh, right." I sit back.

"Beth. She's a teacher, not that her occupation has anything to do with it." Sarah turns back to the bar. "Terry," she calls. "Dry white when you're ready." He nods, and Sarah continues. "She's fun. You will love Beth. We went to university together— me, Beth, and Jess. All studied English, though Beth is the only one who used her English degree. Jess is a hairdresser, and I—well, I work with you." She smiles. "Sorry, I talk a lot when I'm nervous."

"That's fine. I don't talk when I'm nervous."

Sarah snorts a laugh. "You're not the most talkative at the best of times."

I grin. "You've noticed."

She smiles back. If I didn't know better, I would say it seems a bit patronizing.

Terry, the bar man, places her drink on the bar, and I watch her as she pays. Maybe I've gotten her wrong after all. She seems nice enough. I'm safe; it's not as if Sarah is like the people I knew on the street. They were jittery, and for other reasons. I don't think I need to watch Sarah for blades or needles.

"So what did you study at school?" She fires the question into my face and then smiles at me from over the top of her glass.

I'm stumped for words. "Um, well …" *Don't panic,* I counsel myself. *It's a normal question. Just lie if you can't answer it.* "I didn't go to university. Parents couldn't afford it."

"What did you do, then? Work?"

I nod.

"Where?" she asks. She's waiting for my reply patiently, and her eyes widen as if encouraging me to answer.

"In sales. An office supply store."

Now she looks confused. "What, like pens and stuff?"

I shake my head and can't resist a laugh. "No, I sold desks, filing cabinets—the furniture side of things."

This delighted Sarah. "So you have always sold furniture, and that's why you're so good."

I give a coy shrug.

"Come on, Laura—you know you're the best the company has."

This is a good conversation, I think. I don't mind talking about work.

Sarah keeps talking. "I was up two places this month thanks to you, Laura. I'm picking up so much just watching you with customers. It's madness how we both started at the same time but how much better you are than me. But now that I know how long you've been doing sales work, it's not so mad, I suppose. This is my first real job."

I nod.

"I reckon you'll make floor manager in no time."

Smiling, I nod again.

This time, there is an awkward lull in the questioning. I wonder if I should ask her something, but what? It feels like I am on a date.

Holding up my glass to the bar man, Terry, I smile, and he pours me another. Sarah's moving her head to the low music playing. She's nothing like Priya, yet being with her feels strangely familiar. Sitting at the bar with her feels good—normal. I feel it's only right that I should at least try and talk to her.

"Did you meet your boyfriend at university?" I ask.

"Dan? No. I met him just after I started working at Furniture Forever—I sold him a bed. He's an architect."

I take a large gulp. "So he makes good money, then?"

Now I find myself wondering what we will have in common, as she went to university and has a rich boyfriend. I, on the other hand—well, my life was different.

"Not sure." She shrugs. "I don't care about money."

I can feel confusion spread across my face. "Why are you doing a sales job, then?"

"First job I could get. I need to pay the bills."

Maybe we do have stuff in common. I laugh to myself. "So you live on your own?"

"Not exactly."

My eyes narrow. "You don't live with Dan already, do you?"

"Stop that." She slaps my leg playfully, which kind of makes me want to slap her face. I know she's only playing; I just hope she doesn't touch me like this too often. Then her smile fades. "I live at home. My mum and dad make me pay rent. They say it's my way of paying them back for my university fees."

"Tough gig," I say, hoping I hid my sarcasm.

"It is. I'm saving up to move out. The only reason I went to university was to get away from my mum, and now I'm stuck back there again."

I note Sarah's deflated slouch. "Why?"

Straightening again, and with a seemingly practiced smile, she says, "My mum's an alcoholic. But it's OK—I'm really open about it all. Never known any different; she's been a raving alcoholic all my life."

My blank response is clearly not what she was expecting.

"Oh no, have I offended you?" she asks quickly. "Sorry, do you have alcoholism in your family or something?" Her hands cross her chest in defense.

I shake my head. Her intimacy felt too soon; I barely know her. "No—nothing like that," I say, wondering why her words about her mum sound so confident when her body language screams the opposite. I feel a little sorry for her.

"Most people have loads of questions." Sarah continues her charades.

Before taking a sip of my drink, I say simply, "I don't like to pry."

"Right." She smiles. "I'm an open book. I basically left home for university to get away from my mum but didn't think about lining up a job in my last year to save money. Having too much fun," she blurts out. "And you?"

"Me? What about me?" I think about the cover story that I've gone over in my mind most nights since moving to Wimbledon. One thing I do miss about my street friends—they didn't want to know my life story.

"Do you still live at home?" Sarah asks.

"No. I rent a small studio apartment not far from here."

"So does your family live in Wimbledon?"

I take a huge gulp of my shanty-top. "My mum's dead. Cancer. My dad lives in Kent. No siblings." I reel off the list.

Sarah shifts on her bar stool. "I'm so sorry. When did your mum—?"

Wow, this girl is nosy. "Um, a few years ago, but I don't really like to talk about it."

"Sure. Yes, of course—sorry."

Silence settles. I feel oddly sympathetic to her as we sit side by side sipping our drinks.

She talks far too much for my liking and is way too happy about life—and a crappy life, from what I can infer—yet she is genuinely interested in getting to know me.

Suddenly, Terry slams both palms down onto the bar in front of us. "So, Sarah—when are you bringing Beth back in here to see me?"

Sarah looks just as taken aback as I do by his abrupt entrance to the conversation.

"Terry," she squeals at him, "you scared me. I don't know, call her—you have her number, don't you?"

"I've tried. She's not replying to me."

"There's your answer, then," I can't resist saying.

He turns his head slowly and looks as if he's about to say something to me, but then decides against it.

Good choice, I think. He moves down the bar to serve another customer.

"Well said." Sarah smiles. "Shall we get out of here? If you want to go dance, there's a small club down the road—it's only a bus ride away."

I almost decline this offer—I wasn't expecting a big night out—but I stop myself. If I'm going to be friends with Sarah and live a life my sister would enjoy, I should at least give it a go. Maybe just an hour—then I can leave, and loud music with dancing equals less questioning.

"Sure," I say.

★ ★ ★

At first, I am reluctant to dance as I stand next to our pedestal table in the corner of the cozy club. Sarah's been happily dancing feet away from me on her own for a while now. She keeps dancing over in a weird silly way and then dancing back again. The last time she danced up to me and beckoned for me to follow, I nearly did. She looks so carefree, like no shits are given, like there's no one else in the club. It reminds me of how Laura and I used to be. Sarah wasn't wrong when she said the club was small. It reminds me of a dungeon. The walls are bare stone, and chain shackles hang from them. At each end of the bar stand imitation fire torches, which are the main source of light for the entire room. The music is loud against my chest, but I've adjusted to the heavy vibrations shaking every bone.

A slower tempo R&B tune comes on, and Sarah slides toward me.

"I can't dance to the slow, sexy ones," she calls over the music. "I've not got enough rhythm." She takes a swig of her wine.

Sarah downs the last of the drink and reaches quickly for my hand, a bit too quickly for my liking. I yank my arm away and stand my ground.

Sarah withdraws. "Come get a drink," she shouts and walks toward the bar.

Looking down, I see my fists are clenched tight, and I'm not sure if Sarah noticed. I remind myself that I need to relax. We move through the sea of bouncing butts and waving arms to the bar.

After ordering, she hands me a bottle of beer and clinks hers on mine.

"Beer?" I ask.

"Two for one," she answers. "You get the next round in. Come on."

I follow her into the middle of the dance floor. I'm still not sure if Sarah is naïve, oblivious, or just a bit of an airhead. I think about this as the sea of bodies, including Sarah's, bounces around me. She seems genuine, and it's not as if I need to worry that she wants to steal my wristwatch or that the only reason she wants to go out with me is because she wants me to buy her drinks. After all, it was my turn to get the last drinks in, but she did it. I need to chill out and stop thinking as if I'm living at the bedsit. I have a normal life now, and there is a normal twenty-three-year-old girl who wants to be friends with another normal twenty-three-year-old girl. That's all.

"You got it, girl." Sarah sways in front of me from side to side.

I suddenly realize that I have been bopping my head and shoulders in time with the music without even knowing it. I give an awkward laugh and stop dancing. Sarah motions for me to keep moving, giving me encouraging head nods while thrusting her hips. It's not that I don't know how to dance—on the contrary, I know I'm good at it. I just haven't danced in such a long time.

I can feel the beer sloshing in my stomach as I move a little. I think about the life I want for Laura and what she would do. I think about my standoffish behavior and what Laura would say to me if she were here, what she would do, and how she would dance and laugh with us. Before I know it, I am dancing with Sarah and laughing in the moment. I'd forgotten how it felt to let myself go, to dance with a girlfriend, to giggle and act silly. For the first time since leaving Cornwall, I am acting my age, doing what other girls my age do: hanging out with a friend on a Saturday night. Things are different now. I have a safe home and a warm bed to return to. I even have money in my bank account.

A giddy feeling fizzes about my belly. I'm not sure if it is the alcohol numbing my inhibitions, but I snatch up Sarah's hand and start to dance with her. She's enthusiastic and dances back. I've not had fun like this in years. Laura would be so proud of me. The thought saddens me, but I push through the cruel pinch on my heart. I'm Laura now, so I need to feel and experience life for her. I keep dancing, keep laughing—keep living my life for Laura. She deserves for me to live her life, a good life.

Still laughing, I slam into the bar and wave my money in the air at the bar man. It's nearing closing time, and I've only just started to really enjoy myself.

I pass Sarah her beer and head outside into the smoking area. It's cold, but the alcohol numbs the harsh bite.

"Here." Sarah offers me her cigarette box.

Taking one, I resist taking another, an old habit I picked up from Priya whenever we took cigarettes from strangers.

"Thanks," I say, holding out a lighter for Sarah, my hand shaking.

"You can dance," Sarah says.

I shrug. "Been a while."

"Why? You're a good dancer. All the guys were checking you out, didn't you notice?"

I shake my head.

Sarah blows smoke up into the sky. She looks so at ease with life. I watch her take long drags of her cigarette while chatting away at me about utterly pointless stuff. She has a weird view of the world—it's as if she has accepted her place, be it good or bad. Her family is less than perfect, yet she smiles through it all. She stumbles off balance, and I move fast to catch her.

Her tolerance for alcohol is a work in progress, I think.

"It's late. Want to share a cab home?" Sarah's words chop the smoke as it leaves her mouth and mixes with the frosty air.

I shake my head. "I'll be OK taking the bus," I say.

"What? No way." She looks at her phone for the time. "It's nearly two in the morning."

Walking the streets doesn't bother me like most people. "I'll be fine," I try to reassure her. "I get the bus everywhere."

"Laura, you can't get the bus on your own; it's not safe." Her eyes narrow.

I know she is right, and it would be safer to get a cab, but I still don't agree to it. I might have a job and an apartment, but I don't really want to waste money on a cab home when a bus is cheaper. I am about to object again when a wine glass on a neighboring table flies over and smashes at my feet.

Sarah jumps about three feet in the air. "Where did that come from?" she asks, panicked.

I shrug and start to laugh as a group of people turn to look at the commotion.

"Why are you laughing?" Sarah laughs back at me.

I'm laughing because I'm pretty confident that I just upset my big sister, and if I don't want a glass landing on my head, I'll be sharing a cab home with Sarah. But I don't say that.

"I'm laughing at your reaction," I say instead. "You squeal like a little girl."

"Damn right, that glass came out of nowhere." She kicks the broken glass to one side. "So, you sharing a cab with me, then? Please don't get a bus on your own. I'd worry about you."

I hesitate, not because I want to get a bus but because I want to see if my sister will react again.

"Laura?" Sarah says.

I'm about to answer when out of the corner of my eye I see a plastic bag blowing around. Ordinarily, this wouldn't mean a thing—it's a cold and windy night, after all. However, the bag is the only thing moving. The leaves beneath it are still, yet the bag effortlessly floats in the air.

I smile. "Yes, I think sharing a cab is the sensible thing to do."

The bag drops back down onto the bed of brown leaves and stays there, motionless. We leave the club and head to the taxi rank.

I shout goodbye over my shoulder, but the night swallows up my words, and the cab roars off down the road with Sarah waving at me through the rear window. I move as fast as I can up the stairs to my apartment, where I instantly regret my decision to not put the central heating on before I left. After making a beeline for the thermostat, I try to reassure myself that seventeen degrees Celsius in winter is a modest temperature as I begin to get ready for bed. Thoughts of the smashed glass are on my mind.

"Why?" I ask my reflection in the bathroom mirror.

The question makes me feel a little guilty. I question my sanity regularly, but this time is different. This time, I think I actually want to know the answer.

"If you're here, Laura, if you're real, I need to know why. I need to know if you're trying to warn me about something, watch over me—what? What is it? Just tell me why!" I keep speaking into the air above the sink. "I got the job, I did what you told me to, and I'm out of that bedsit, so what is it now? What am I meant to do? Why are you still here giving me signs? Are you stuck, or are you trying to tell me something? Oh, Lulu, I wish you would talk to me like you did before."

I leave the bathroom and slide into bed under the duvet, thinking about all the Laura things that I've experienced. First, there was the odd feeling that she was still with me. When I lived at Marie's, I could have sworn Laura was right there next to me as I lay in bed at night. I had heard the words, *her* words. The first time in the therapist office, I hadn't been completely sure of it, but after that, there was no mistake. It was Laura's voice, as clear as day. The therapist had said otherwise, but she was wrong. I just wish I'd not been on the pesky pills; they had numbed my senses. If only I'd been free from their effects, I might have been able to have a proper conversation with my sister. The moving or smashing objects, now that I'm thinking about it, seem to only happen in high energy situations, times of anger or fear. The dreams are the most consistent form of contact.

But what does it all mean? And more to the point, why? Am I just mad? It *was* voices in my head, and let's face it—Laura and I have the same voice. Did I imagine my own voice into my head? After all, it was a highly stressful time. As for the moving objects, have I just put meaning into a meaningless situation? And the dreams … I sigh. Have I dreamt up my own dreams all these years? I think back to the days and weeks after the crash. The nightmares came thick and fast. Cold sweats woke me from my sleep in the middle of the night with a barrage of images and sounds: the screeching of brakes, glass smashing, and Laura's blood-splattered legs poking out from her floral dress. I always woke just as I looked down at her face.

I turn onto my side, facing the window. The blinds are open, and I have a clear view of the moon. Its fullness gives my room extra light, and its presence should amaze me, but it doesn't. And it doesn't because it's always there. I don't question the moon's presence; half the time, I don't even think about it. It just is. Maybe I'm not mad; maybe I just need another approach. Maybe Laura has become my moon, always there. She's my comfort. But what if she's not meant to be—what if I'm meant to question her?

Then I have another thought. What if I question her and find out it is all in my head—that it always has been? A spider scurries down the window pane and through a crack in the frame. Like the spider, I need to look in the cracks. I need to stop waiting for Laura to contact me and contact her. Not with dreams, though. I've tried that, and that wasn't something I would do again. No, I need definite communication. I must be sure Laura is real. I just hope I can accept the answer, whatever it maybe.

"Lulu, if you can hear me, we need to talk."

CHAPTER 15

THEN–LAURA

Cornwall, three years ago
March

Another month passed. Before I knew it, it was March 28th, and I had made little to no progress with my abilities. I'd not experienced any more pulling sensations, and nothing profound had happened—just day after day of watching my family falling apart. I wasn't even sure if I was making a difference in Lucy's life anymore. Occasionally, she heard a word I spoke, but I now worried I was driving my sister crazy. Then, to add insult to injury, Ben had convinced Lucy that somehow his grief was as deep as hers, and I'd been too frightened to touch his chains. His aura was black—not even differing shades, just black like thick, choking smoke. It snaked about him as if it knew I was there, with small fragments licking out at me if I got close, like toxins protecting their source.

Lucy was falling apart, and I was failing her. It was as if I had all this clarity about who we are, *what* we are, but none of it made any sense. I could see the very fabric of life breathing, yet

I couldn't help my sister, the one person I loved the most. I just didn't understand. Was that it for me, a lifetime of shadowing my sister, unable to help her? And when she died, then what? The thought petrified me. I could be walking the earth forever as a soul with no matter, alone.

"Three weeks, Lucy. Three bloody weeks." Marie's screaming drew me into the present as she followed my sister from the kitchen and into the living room. "Lucy, you can't keep getting fired like this." Lucy was sitting cross-legged on the sofa, stuffing her face with a bacon sandwich. "You'll end up unemployable. What happened this time?"

"Why do you care? My dad pays my rent." Lucy swallowed a bite of her sandwich. "The job was a joke anyway. All I did was copy shit into a computer all day, every day. Anyone can do it; they'll find someone else."

"That's what data entry is, and I got you that job. I vouched for you to my boss, remember? You could have worked your way up the ladder."

"The McDonalds ladder, woohoo—star burger flipper." Lucy fist-punched the air, reinforcing her mockery.

I hovered in the middle of the room, cross-legged like Lucy, though floating. I knew where the argument was heading. Give it a few more minutes, and Marie would storm out. I wanted to help, and I'd tried, but they never heard me. I had tried shouting at them, blowing in their faces, and even pushing objects, but they were always so wrapped up in their anger. It was such a pointless emotion; if only they knew how much energy they were wasting.

Through gritted teeth, Marie spat, "You don't flip burgers, Lucy. You didn't even need to leave the house. Do you know how many people would kill for a job where they work from home? You ungrateful little bitch." Marie left the room.

Lucy jumped off the sofa, dropping her sandwich on the coffee table. I followed after them. "Wait, Marie, I'm sorry."

She hurried out into the hallway, where Marie was shoving an arm into her denim jacket. "Don't go."

"I've had just about as much as I can take of you, Lucy."

"Please, Marie, don't storm out—I'm really sorry. I was being defensive. I shouldn't have; you know how I get."

Marie stared at Lucy. Her willingness to forgive people was indicative of her nature, but even I could see that Lucy was pushing her boundaries.

"Why, Lucy? What was it this time?"

Lucy shifted awkwardly on her feet.

"Tell me, Lucy, or I'm out that door and won't come home until you're gone." She glared at her. "I mean it."

"OK—OK. But I'm warning you, this might sound messed up."

"Go on." Marie nodded.

"Laura told me to."

I what? I moved toward my sister and stared into her eyes.

Marie shoved her other arm into the jacket and hoisted it onto her shoulders. "That's low, Lucy, even for you."

"No—no, Marie, it's true."

"It is not," I protested, but no one could hear me.

"Marie, stop. Please come back into the living room with me, and I'll tell you everything. Please. I've been dealing with this all on my own. I need to talk to someone. I think I'm losing my mind."

Marie's expression immediately softened, and she gestured for Lucy to lead the way.

In the living room, they both sat on the sofa. Lucy fidgeted with her hands as Marie listened. She explained that the voices at the therapist's office hadn't been a one-off, and although they hadn't been as clear or in any kind of sentence, they had been plaguing her thoughts.

I shuddered at her words. *"Plague? Lucy, I'm not plaguing your thoughts,"* I whispered, wishing that she might hear me. *"I'm trying to help you."*

"Why didn't you say something?" Marie asked.

"I didn't think you believed me when I told you the first time."

"Of course I believed you—I just didn't know what to make of it. Have you told the therapist?"

Lucy shook her head.

"What about the job? What happened there with the voices?"

Lucy covered her face.

"Don't cry." Marie coaxed her hands away from her face. And then I knew what was going on.

"Yeah, Lucy—don't cry," I mocked. This was the fake crying act she would pull when we were kids. I stared dumfounded at my sister, hands on my hips as I waited to hear what she was about to say. What was she up to?

Lucy sniffed. "I don't know; they didn't make any sense. I just couldn't focus. It was as if someone had turned the volume up on my thoughts, and I couldn't do my work."

"She's lying!" I protested to the room.

Lucy dove for Marie. "You can't tell anyone, Marie, please." Her hands gripped Marie's shoulders. "You can't. I'll tell Hellen. Just don't tell my dad. I can't have him thinking I'm—you know, crazy." She let go of Marie.

"All right, just calm down, Lucy. But only if you promise to talk to the therapist. You need to tell Hellen. She can give you meds."

Lucy nodded.

"But why haven't you told me any of this? Don't you trust me?"

I wasn't sure why she had blamed me for losing her job. I never spoke to her when she was at work; I'd never intrude like that. But I did know why she hadn't confided in Marie about me—I just wondered if she would tell the truth, tell Marie that she was frightened of losing her to him. I waited with baited breath for what Lucy would say.

"I thought that if I told you, Dylan would tell you not to let me live here anymore."

I slowly shook my head.

"Why?" Marie asked. "Why would Dylan say that?"

Lucy shrugged. "It's just the way he looks at me."

"Lucy, we've been here before. Dylan is not the enemy here. He likes you."

Lucy's eyebrows rose to the heavens.

"Not like that." Marie pointed at her. "What goes on in your head?"

"He did touch my leg, though."

"Don't start that again, Lucy. Dylan never touched you. If we are going down this route again then I'm—"

"OK." Lucy stopped her. "Want a bite?" She offered the bacon sandwich with a crooked grin.

"No." Marie pushed it away. "Listen, I'm concerned about you. You don't visit your parents, and yes, I know you don't want to see your mum, but your dad misses you. You shut yourself up in your room."

Lucy didn't answer. She was always good at awkward silences.

"Look, I've got to go post this letter," Marie said, trying again to engage my sister. "Come with me?"

"No, thanks."

Marie stood. "Back soon."

"I'm sorry, Marie, I'll try harder."

"You don't need to try harder. Just talk to the therapist. There are drugs they can give you for that sort of thing. You just need to trust people—trust me."

"I know—I will."

"All right, well, I'll see you soon, then. Won't be long." Marie kissed Lucy on the cheek and left.

The front door slammed, and Marie walked past the window up the road.

"Lucy," I said.

I followed her out to the kitchen, where she threw away the unfinished sandwich and then filled the kettle. A text beeped on her phone, and I peered over her shoulder to read it.

YOU ABOUT?
WANT TO HANG AT MINE?
Bx

Ben! What the hell did he want? I clenched my teeth, watching Lucy's reply. This was not the first time he had texted, but it was the first time he had asked to meet, and in such a friendly way. He had laid the groundwork, and now he was moving in.

GOING TO WASH MY HAIR.
I'LL COME OVER SOON.

The kettle whistle drowned out my banshee screams. I had to find a way to connect with Lucy—she had to believe in what I was telling her. She had to hear my message properly. Ben was dangerous; he was the real enemy.

My sister poured boiling water on top of the tea bag and moved upstairs, mug in hand. She set the mug down on the bedside table and left to shower. I didn't follow. Instead, I looked at the steam rising off the top of the deep beige liquid as it cooled. How was I going to connect with Lucy to show her I was really there? The last thing I wanted was for my sister to think she was insane. I stared at the mug of tea with determination. Maybe I could make the liquid cold, really cold, as cold as ice. Surely that would make her think. I focused my eyes on the mug as if I were Superman.

Nothing.

I tried again, but all I got was shaky vision. I could hear the shower running; Lucy wouldn't be much longer. I tried harder, but it was hopeless. What made me think I could freeze liquids? I wasn't a superhero. The shower stopped running, and I heard the shower curtain slide over the rail. She would be back soon; I had to do something. What was Ben up to? I looked down at the mug—I had to do something quick.

Behind me, the bedroom door opened. I could hear Lucy moving about her room, plugging in her hair dryer. My intentions stayed fixed on the mug, but nothing was changing, not until I saw the antiperspirant can behind the mug tipping over slightly. I refocused my intentions, and the spray wobbled more and more until *whoosh*—it fell off the bedside unit to the floor. I did it—I moved it. Elated, I turned to Lucy, half expecting to see her looking at the antiperspirant in astonishment. Yet again, that was not the case. Instead, Lucy walked over and returned the spray can to the table, then picking up her mug of tea.

Damn it.

The front door slammed. "Lucy," Marie called out. "Are you up there, Lucy? I'm back."

"In my room!" Lucy opened her bedroom door to call out. "Kettle's not long boiled—"

Marie was already at the door. "Thanks, I'll just have some of yours."

Marie came in and walked about the room, touching things like necklaces and books, repositioning a candle on the windowsill. I followed her. "So, how are you feeling now that you've had a shower?"

"Fine." Lucy gave Marie her mug of tea and then turned to blast the hair dryer.

"Where you going?" Marie shouted over the noise.

"Ben's."

Marie nodded as if she approved. "Dylan is coming over later!"

Lucy stopped the hair dryer. "OK," she said, raking a comb through her hair before hitting it with hot air again.

"Why don't you ask Ben to come over for dinner?"

"I'll ask," Lucy replied, turning her back to the mirror.

"OK, let me know." When Lucy didn't reply, Marie raised her voice over the blow dryer. "I said let me know!"

"Sure thing."

Marie edged slowly out of the room, presumably still confused about my sister's earlier confession about hearing voices. I mean, who seriously drops that bombshell on someone and then acts like nothing is wrong? I know my sister's ability to lie and manipulate, and she learned from the best—our mum. Not that Lucy would ever admit that. My sister would say pretty much anything that came to mind if she thought there was a chance someone would believe it. Somehow, Marie never got that about her, even after all those years of being friends. Strange, really—Marie was so rock and roll, yet so naively trusting. Lucy just didn't like her job, and when Marie called her out on it, she said the first dramatic thing that came into her mind to stop Marie from leaving—I was sure of this.

I walked out after Marie, who went down the stairs, through the kitchen, and out into the garden for a smoke. I didn't like touching people when they were smoking; it always felt so chemical. The nicotine particles ran a riot through her lungs, obliterating thousands upon thousands of cells in seconds, and when I was in her thoughts, they sickened me. But I didn't have the time to wait. I wanted to find out just what Marie was thinking before Lucy left for Ben's.

Trembling, I stepped in front of her and reached out. Marie blew smoke into the air, and I sidestepped, avoiding as much as I could. She was easy to read. Her thoughts flowed freely, like flipping through pictures on social media, there for the world to access. I flicked them about, swiping from moments of bliss when she was with Dylan to profound sadness. Her feelings for Dylan were clear—she might not have told him yet, but she was falling in love with him, and she was fairly certain he felt the same. I jumped past the lovemaking, and there was a *lot* of that. They talked a lot about traveling to Thailand or India, although thoughts of leaving Lucy halted this conversation the majority of the time, giving rise to contention between Dylan and her.

It saddened me a little—on the one hand, it was lovely seeing how much Marie cared for my sister, but on the other, I wanted her to go traveling, live her life. Moving about her, I swiped and flicked, looking for thoughts of Lucy. I wanted to know how Marie was feeling about my sister, how she saw Ben and her relationship. I swiped fast past images, soundbites, emotions, and—*there*. I stopped. I swiped back a few times and honed in.

There it was: the smallest fragment of doubt about Ben's involvement. It was buried deep under some heavy feelings, but it was there, all right. I could feel it. At some point, Marie had doubted Ben. It must have only been a fleeting thought, but it was still there in her mind. She had just forgotten it. I tried to push around in her emotions, but it was no good. They were too heavy and draining. Marie wasn't over what had happened; it was just all one big act. She gave the impression to the world that she was coping, and she even believed it herself, and in a way, I suppose this was true. We all bury our feelings, hope that if we don't dwell on them, then somehow, they will ease away. Who was I to judge?

This method was clearly working for her, but it was also keeping that fragment of doubt beneath it all. If Marie could feel that doubt again, maybe she would plant the same doubt in Lucy's mind. Reaching inside her mind with what I'd come to think of as my third eye, I pushed and pulled. Her grief for my death was tangled up with so many memories. Deflated, I sunk in the ground. Knee deep, I looked up at Marie puffing away at her cancer stick.

"*I miss you*," my soul whimpered.

Then I felt guilt from Marie. No pictures or memories, just a sensation. She wanted to be happy, I could sense that, but she had this huge weight of guilt pushing all her memories into a tight ball inside her soul. *Why?* I sprung out of the soil, trying to make sense of this feeling.

Lucy. She felt responsible for Lucy. Thailand. Dylan. That was it—Marie wanted to travel—no, Marie was *going* to travel, and with Dylan. She'd been putting off leaving until Lucy was stronger, not wanting to leave her, but she also didn't want to lose Dylan. Her worry was that if Lucy and Dylan couldn't get along, she might have to choose between them. She wondered if I would be looking down, angry at her.

"No, Marie, I'd never be mad at you," I say, watching Marie flick her cigarette to the ground. *"I want you to go. Go to Thailand and be happy. I can look after Lucy."*

Marie returned to the kitchen, and I followed her, feeling drained. I watched her through new eyes as she herself a cup of coffee. How had I not found these emotions sooner? As Marie waited for the kettle to boil, she looked out along the hall to the front door, directly through me. The kettle finished boiling, and Marie reached for the coffee.

Two scoops, I thought. I watched her heap two coffee scoops into a cup. *One sugar.* Sure enough, she stirred in one sugar.

I slumped down on top of the bin like Casper the friendly ghost. This was pointless. Two of the people I loved most were hurting, and I couldn't help either. I knew their deepest fears and desires, yet I was stumped on what to do next, forever a spectator in their lives.

Whoosh—the bin lid spun under me as Lucy threw an old Starbucks fruit cup inside.

"Oh, yuck, Lulu." I jumped, feeling a gloopy feeling slosh about me. *"How old was that?"*

"Ooh, it's cold in here." Lucy rubbed her arms.

"That's what you get for throwing moldy fruit through me."

"What time is Dylan coming over?" Lucy asked. Marie didn't immediately answer.

"Oh, you can't hear me now? Convenient," I said.

"I'm heading over to Ben's," Lucy said. "Feels a bit odd."

"How so?" Marie asked.

Lucy shrugged. "Because I've not been to his place since we were together; just feels a bit odd—you know."

"Do you want him back?"

"No," Lucy admitted. "I'm not ready—I don't think I want to—"

"It's fine. Don't overthink it. Is Ben in a new apartment now?"

Lucy nodded slowly, "He couldn't stay in the last place. Said it reminded him of what happened—couldn't settle after everything, what with Tye being wrongly accused."

"Did he think the police would come after him like they did Tye?"

"I think so. They really put the pressure on poor Tye when all along it was Darren. Can't blame him—that detective hates him. I can see it in his face every time his name is mentioned." Lucy stopped as if to think. "I feel bad that I thought the same for a while."

"Me too," Marie whispered.

Stay with it, Marie. Hold that thought, feel it. Feel it, I urged.

"But they were wrong about Tye, and look at him now." Lucy sighed. "He's a mess. I saw Jen last week, and she told me Tye is taking Xanax."

"No, really?"

"Yeah, he's in a bad way, so I can see why Ben was so spooked out by it. Who wants to be wrongly accused?"

"Ben's lucky to have you on his side." Marie's words snaked around my soul like poison ivy.

"Thanks." Lucy stepped over and hugged her tight.

And then I saw it—Marie's guilt. She hesitated ever so slightly before hugging her back. She was struggling with being there for my sister and wanting to live her own life traveling. I desperately wanted Marie to be happy; I just hoped it didn't cost them a friendship. Lucy wasn't generous with her feelings. The apple hadn't fallen far from the tree—our mum had disowned her, and Lucy would disown Marie if she hurt her badly enough.

She had lost me, so losing Marie to Dylan and to the other side of the world would wreak havoc. I knew it. I just didn't know how I was going to keep my two best friends together—and keep Ben away.

★ ★ ★

Lucy stood at the edge of a small green. On the other side, two tall, rectangular tower blocks shadowed the concrete jungle below them. She walked toward the east tower block with conviction in her steps. This area was unsafe—our parents had warned us plenty of times not to take the short cut through there. Apprehensive, I followed her.

There was a notice on the elevator that looked as old as the property, with grime smudged about its black and yellow words: OUT OF ORDER. I stayed behind Lucy as she made her way up the filthy staircase to the eleventh floor. The corridors were narrow, and the cream paint was barely visible beneath the dirt and graffiti. Large dogs barked outside from the green below. Music from an apartment echoed through the halls, and smaller dogs yapped as they sensed me passing their door. Lucy found Ben's door, knocked, and then waited.

A tag had been scratched into Ben's front door in large letters. "Risk!" she read under her breath.

A latch clanked on the other side, and the door opened with a squeak.

"Hi." Ben smiled at her from his darkened doorway.

Lucy shrugged. "I made it here alive."

Ben laughed, stepping aside to let her through. "It looks worse than it is."

He gestured her up the hall and into the kitchen.

The apartment was large, with rooms leading off a long hallway, and the kitchen was at the far end. As we passed the living room, I looked inside. An old sofa covered by a tie-dye throw was the only thing in there. There was no carpet, just wooden floorboards that were clearly meant to have carpet on top of them. To the side of the sofa was a guitar.

Since when did Ben play the guitar? In the far corner was a sleeping bag, pillows, and a duvet that looked like it would be white in color if washed.

My investigation was interrupted by a noise in the hallway behind me.

"Dude, I'm going out," a bearded man shouted. He didn't wait for an answer, and the front door slammed behind him.

I immediately moved to join Lucy in the kitchen, which was cozy in size.

"Who was that?" Lucy asked.

"Russ, it's his place. Beer?"

She shook her head. "Water, please."

"I have coffee," Ben offered, and Lucy smiled in agreement.

Ben pointed down the hall. "Russ gave me his room, and now he sleeps in the living room. That way he can charge me top whack for a room. He gets money off me, and money for government-assisted housing benefits. Don't let that dirty beard fool you; he's got a plan." Ben smiled.

"Right." Lucy didn't look as impressed. "So anyway, how are you?"

Ben handed her a hot cup and walked out of the kitchen. Carefully jumping down, she followed him down the hall, sneaking a peek into the living room as she passed, and then on to Ben's room. It had carpet that looked as if it was vacuumed regularly. The bed was made, and his clothes hung neatly in a wardrobe with no doors. Still, the room had the same dull, lightless feel as the rest of the apartment.

"Still doing the therapy?" Ben asked.

I wandered about the room looking for drugs, knifes, guns, or anything dangerous—poking my head through drawers, looking under the bed. *Clean.*

Lucy sat on his bed. "I still go. Not that it helps—well, I don't think so, but it keeps my dad happy, and he has enough on his plate with my mum and all."

"Is she still bad?" Ben sat next to my sister.

Keep your hands off her, you shit, I snarled into his face.

"It's all an act—she lost her temper with me in front of Hellen and can't admit when she's wrong, so she does what she does best and makes a massive fucking drama out of it. My dad is too bloody stupid to see what she is doing. She's always manipulated him like this. She goes crazy for a few weeks and then gets him all worried that she might kill herself or something." Lucy slurped her coffee.

"But why?"

"Deflection. By the time she calms down and my dad is off suicide watch, he's forgotten what the original issue was. She's done it all our lives; it's just on a bigger scale now."

I remembered my dad giving me some advice in life. He told me that the characteristics that you don't like in others are often a reflection of the characteristics that you don't like about yourself. I smiled at how wise my dad was.

"That's shitty," Ben said.

"Sure is."

"Want to listen to some music?" To my relief, he moved away from Lucy and over to his phone sitting in the dock. "Killers?"

My soul shook hearing the word.

"Sure." Lucy smiled, and Ben hit play.

He sat back down. The atmosphere was different—I felt it, and I was sure Lucy had too. However, I didn't think Lucy was feeling what I was. I was frightened. He couldn't hurt me physically, but he could hurt Lucy. Her nervous little laughs and quick side glances at him told the whole story. She trusted this asshole, and she was falling for his flirting. They chatted for ages about nothing—music, old friends, and places—and a few times, Ben touched her knee if she said something to make him laugh, a gesture he made look so innocent.

Listening to them chat about nothing in particular got me thinking about myself. I had thoughts that I didn't let linger, and fear I might be right. Was this what they meant by life after death? I couldn't help but deflate, sinking through the floor and into the apartment below. A cat hissed and jumped off an old lady's lap. I pushed myself up and back into Ben's room. Lying with my back to Ben's ceiling, I dissected my need to protect Lucy. It was intrinsic, something I had to do. If I accomplished this, if I got her out of harm's way, would I then cross over?

The afternoon pressed on. It would soon be getting dark, and Lucy needed to leave. Walking through this estate at dark was not wise for anyone, so I spent the next thirty minutes whispering into her ear, *"Time to leave."* I looked inside Ben's playlist and played any song with the words danger, leave, get out, bad man—anything to warn her.

"It's getting late," Lucy eventually said, standing and moving toward the bedroom door.

"Finally!" I breathed.

Ben followed her. "Stay."

"Back off, Ben." I dropped beside him.

"I should go."

"No!" he said with a harsh bite.

Lucy looked at him, puzzled. I stayed very still, worried that if she did or said the wrong thing, he might get nasty. He'd never shown her this side of him before. I waited with baited breath.

"I—I mean, don't go yet," he said hurriedly. "I can fix you another coffee. We still need to debate the state of the government."

Lucy gave a small laugh. "Thanks, but I should really go. It's getting dark."

"Sure," Ben said, opening the door. His arm brushed against her, and their eyes met. He stood close, too close. Their noses practically touched.

I shouted for her to step away. *"Leave the room, run!"* But she stared back into his eyes. Slowly, he edged forward, and his lips met hers. To my sheer horror, Lucy didn't move. Instead, she let his tongue search out hers.

"*NOOO!*" I screamed.

My hands tremored as if electricity was flowing through them. Glancing down, I realized that I was holding my hands in the shape of a ball. Nothing was visible, yet I could feel the energy like a compact snowball. I threw the ball with all my might.

Crack. A crack snaked its way from the top of Ben's window almost to the bottom.

"Shit." Ben pulled away and started for the window. A look of horror washed over his face.

"How did that happen?" Lucy followed him over to the window.

Ben looked out and down. "Bird, maybe. That scared me." He gave a nervous laugh and pulled Lucy into an embrace.

"*NOO ...*"

As my agitation grew, swirls of air or energy spun about them. The louder I shouted, the faster the clouds of white particles spun, rushing in and around the room. I spread my arm wide as if controlling the air and willed it to part them.

"Agh!" Lucy stepped back, clasping her head.

"What? What's wrong?" Ben looked genuinely concerned.

Just then, there was the sound of a key in the lock.

"I'd better go," Lucy said.

"Hey, Ben, you in there?" Russ knocked on the door. "I got some beers."

"Out in a minute, mate," Ben called back.

Ben turned back to Lucy. "Are you OK?"

"I'm fine. Think I've got a migraine starting."

Ben kissed her gently on the cheek.

Crack. I split the crack to the bottom of the window pane.

Lucy didn't hang about. She walked fast through the darkening estate toward the main road. At the bus stop, she seemed to be thinking over what had just happened. Touching her lips with her fingers, she didn't look as if she was reminiscing about it. On the contrary, she looked pale. I would swipe her chains if I could, but whatever I had just done had taken all my energy, and I was using every last bit of me to move. It was becoming abundantly clear that I could only do these radical things when I was angry, but why? I needed to harness this strength all the time. If I could control it, I could talk to Lucy and move things to confirm I was real.

The bus came, and Lucy watched the passengers alight, but she didn't get on. Instead, she started to walk back the way she had just come.

"Lulu, where are you going?" I asked, moving at a distance behind her. *"Stop, it's getting dark. Go home."*

Her strides became more aggressive with each step, and I was losing her. My energy was too low, and she was too fast for me to keep up. Where was she going? She seemed to be heading back to Ben's, but why? I was sure his kiss had given her second thoughts, so why was she walking toward his apartment? Stopping, I watched as she rounded the corner back toward the tower blocks. I might not have enough energy to follow her, but what if I had enough to meet her there? I decided to do exactly that.

I *did* have enough energy to get there, just not quite far enough. I was outside the tower block and not on the 11th floor like I'd wanted. I could see Lucy walking over the green. Any second now she would be walking straight past me. I hoped by the time she got to me that I might have regained just a little energy while I waited for her, but that's not what happened. Without warning, she turned off to the left and headed out of sight around the side of the building.

"What's she doing?" I asked myself.

With all the strength I had, I moved ever-so-slightly, giving me a clear line of sight. Lucy was standing below Ben's window looking up and then back down at the ground.

"She knows," I rejoiced.

There was no bird.

CHAPTER 16

NOW–LUCY

London, present day
March

Maybe a cat ran off with it, I think, looking down at the pavement below my apartment window.

"Morning!" A chirpy voice startles me.

Mr. Clifton from the apartment below mine is standing a little too close beside me. I smile awkwardly. I've found it best not to get into a conversation with Mr. Clifton. He is what you would call an over-sharer, and there's a likely chance he will tell me things I wish I could un-hear.

"You're up early," he comments. His dog, which is not much bigger than a rat, jumps at my shin, its tail moving like a metronome.

Bending to fuss the small dog's ears, I catch myself remembering Adewale's little dog. "What's its name?" I ask, forcing myself back to the present.

"Cat."

I stand. "You're joking."

He looks perplexed. Of course he isn't joking—what other name would crazy man Clifton give to a dog?

Ignoring my seemingly normal question, he steers our conversation back to his original line of inquiry. "What are you doing out here, then?"

Think quick, I tell myself. I need to say something that will get me out of this encounter quickly. "Um ..." My hands fidget in my coat pockets.

"Off to work?" he offers.

"Um, yes, but I just remembered that I forgot something up in my apartment."

He didn't look convinced. "So is that why you have been staring up at your window for the last five minutes?"

"Yes," I insisted. "I knew I'd forgotten something but couldn't for the life of me remember what—I've just remembered, so I'd best go and get it."

"Before you forget again, you mean?" he says with a scowl.

"Right."

His eyes move up to my window. "Your window is smashed?"

"That's ... correct," I say carefully. "A bird flew into it."

I really hope he isn't about to lecture me on how to deal with the management company. It's no secret how much he despises them.

He jumps into a story instead. "That happened to me once. I wasn't living here, mind. Was a place in Berlin, and a raven flew right into my window. I was in bed with a prostitute—"

I interrupt him right there. "OK." I edge toward the building's entrance. "Best run, Mr. Clifton. Don't want to forget what I was getting, do I, now?"

I make for the entrance of our block at speed, and a *lot* of speed. Behind me on the pavement, Mr. Clifton is telling the rest of the story to his dog.

Back in the safety of my apartment, I stand in front of my window, tracing the crack with my eyes. *Just like before,* I think.

No bird—or prostitute, for that matter. I giggle to myself.

"I don't get it, Lulu. What are you trying to tell me? Have you done this before? Smashing windows, I mean?" I think back to the time I was in Ben's apartment and his window broke.

There is no answer, not that I expected one. I scribble a message on a Post-it Note. It reads,

I smashed Ben's window.

"You know I'm trying to save money on heating, don't you?" I say, spinning on the spot as if trying to see her. "That crack is really not going to help my situation, and now Clifton saw it. I guarantee he will be knocking on my door every day to see if the bloody management company has fixed it. People will start to talk." I laugh. "And look at the place—I can't exactly let people in."

I fall onto my new—or should I say secondhand—sofa. I found it in a skip outside. That's how I met crazy man Clifton. He helped me lift it out and up to my apartment. After spending an afternoon with him, I realized he was eccentric but harmless, and I've met crazier people than him anyway. We cleaned up the white leather sofa, covering the ink marks with a hideous orange and brown knitted throw that he gave me.

"A housewarming present," he had offered.

Not that there was too much to warm. My bed and sofa barely filled the spacious studio, and with the lack of furniture, the place echoed. I was keeping an eye out for a rug, one that didn't look like it had been soiled, or even a cheap new rug. That would be perfect, though near impossible. Who knew rugs were so expensive? My rent took up most of my cash, leaving barely enough to eat.

A Post-it Note falls to the floor from the wall next to my cooker. I didn't even buy the Post-it Notes—they were stolen from work, one of the few perks of the job. Moving with haste,

I retrieve the yellow piece of paper from the kitchen floor to see what it says.

Become a cat lady LOL.

I'd written the note when I was drunk last week.

"Very funny," I say and furrow my brow.

It has been about six weeks since I decided to write messages on Post-it Notes and stick them all around my apartment. My room looks like an amateur detective wall, or maybe just like the home of a really, really forgetful person who writes bizarre messages to themselves.

Not many Post-it Notes have fallen, which surprises me. I wondered how I'd distinguish between my sister pulling them off and them just falling. Who knows? But I believe it's Laura. The first one that fell was the first one I'd written.

It simply said,

It's Laura.

After that, I knew this way of communication was working, and I kicked myself for not doing this years ago. It was hard to know what to write at first. I wanted to write messages about home, about Mum and Dad, but Laura always wanted me to see Mum's side when she was alive, so why would it be any different now? I didn't really want to fall out with my sister after I'd only just figured out how to talk to her, so I wrote messages like these:

I'm in heaven.

I'm safe.

I'm stuck.

You're in danger. (I'm glad that one has not fallen.)

I miss you.

I can see you.

I come to you in dreams.

Dad misses you.

There are more, many more, mainly around the kitchen area because that's where I sit most nights, nursing a bottle of cheap box wine or vodka. The second note fell about two weeks ago:

I can see you.

Since then, I've been writing anything that pops into my head. I have even started a two-part message system, with messages like:

Yes, Priya hates you.

No, Priya misses you and won't smash your face in if you go back.

Also,

I like Sarah.

I don't like Sarah.

Last night, one of them fell.

I like Sarah, it read.

This is a relief because I'm going out with her tonight after work. She has been bugging me to meet her friends, Beth and Jess. Sarah's all right; she reminds me of Marie. Beth and Jess, on the other hand, sound—well, to be frank, they sound loud, obnoxious, and not at all my type of people. According to Sarah, Beth is a man-eater, and Jess is the embodiment of anarchy. I don't see how either could be true. From the stories Sarah tells me, they both sound like stuck-up bitches to me.

A thud on my door tells me I've stayed too long. Sure enough, I see Mr. Clifton when I peek through the spyhole. I don't answer, waiting instead for him to leave. Then, gathering up my belongings, I quietly lock my door and creep down the corridor to the elevator. The doors pop open, and to my astonishment, Mr. Clifton is inside the lift.

"Hey," I say with a high strangle in my voice. *Was he waiting in the elevator for me?*

"Duct tape?" He holds up a roll of heavy duty tape.

I swallow hard. "What's that for?"

"Your window. But it's OK, I can come over later and tape you up if you like."

"No, ha." I smirk at his comment. "No, it's fine, really. I can do it myself—my apartment's a mess. Thanks for the offer, though." I snatch the tape before he can object. "Anyway, I'm out tonight." I shove the roll into my bag.

The doors pop open on the ground floor, and out I fly, faster than a bat out of hell.

★ ★ ★

March is an odd time of year. Winter is losing its grip, but summer's still so far. People aren't sure how to dress, though one thing is always certain—everyone carries an umbrella. Stepping off the bus, I look in my bag for mine.

"Oh, just great," I say under my breath as I pick up my pace.

It's not raining hard, but as they say up north, it's "that fine rain that soaks you through and through." As I approach the store, my steps slow. Ahead of me, in the parking lot, I notice one car in particular: a black Audi. It's Simon's black Audi, to be precise. The smart-looking car looks out of place against the dated, unkept backdrop of the store.

All things considered, we get on OK. He isn't so bad, but the fact that we have managed to put our unorthodox relationship behind us doesn't stop Simon from being an arrogant prick, nor the contrast of his being overly nice to me—guilt, I presume.

I stroll past his car, glancing in through the window. It might look like every other Audi, but it still brings back memories. I'm not ashamed of what I did with him, not anymore. Sleepless nights back at the bedsit, shadowed by searching for Laura in my dreams, put my shame into perspective. I did what I had to do, and if I'm honest, I'd do it again if needed. Still, it has changed me. This life is changing me every day.

Most nights I lie in bed thinking of my childhood—what I miss, what I don't—of Laura, Marie, my dad, and even my mum. I often wonder if things would have been different if I had been born sooner. Would my personality have been more tentative like Laura's? Did the stress of childbirth, of me getting stuck in my mum's womb, make our mum mentally sick—did I do that? Did I bring this life upon myself and Laura? Could I have saved my sister just by being born sooner? It's a ludicrous thought, I know, but lonely nights and vodka will do that to you.

As I step through the heavy glass doors and over the threshold into the store, I hear Simon's bellowing voice ricochet about the walls. Bryan laughs in reply to his loud, pointless jokes.

"Just what I need today," I huff.

Last night, I was up late snooping about the Internet—a pastime I do now and then. This time, I stumbled on some disturbing information. Ben is living in Croydon, and it's unsettled me. I have a new life now, and I never thought Cornwall would catch up with me.

Another cackle focuses my mind. Simon and Bryan are at the rear—in the table section, by the sound of it. Taking the steps two at a time, I make my way through the bed section and over to the sign-up desk, where Joe is bossing Sarah about as normal. He shuts up when he sees me.

"Laura!" Sarah says. She looks overjoyed at my arrival.

I greet her. "What's up, Sarah? Hey, Joe."

I watch as Joe skulks off without a word. "What's his problem?" I ask, looking back at Sarah. She is sitting behind the desk with her shoulders slumped forward, looking pathetic. "Sarah, sit up straight. I've told you about this. Look confident, and people will want to deal with you."

"Sorry," she says immediately, pushing her shoulders back.

I nod. "So what's up with Joe?"

"Oh, nothing. Just wanted me to put through some paperwork for him. He's having a tough time of it at the moment. His figures are down, and I think his girlfriend just dumped him." Sarah's shoulders slump forward again.

"Shoulders," I correct. "I hope you said no? We all have tough sales months. I've told you, he's a bully, and the best way to stop a bully is stand up to them. Anyway, if I was his girlfriend, I'd dump his sorry ass too." As I lecture her, I throw my bag into the bottom drawer and lock it. "Want a coffee?" I ask.

"Sure."

"Good, you can make mine." My smile is angelic. "Simon is down there. It's too early to deal with him."

Sarah drops her shoulders, and I don't correct her.

"I don't get it," she says, standing. "You get on so well with him."

"What?" I pull my hair into a high ponytail. "I definitely do not." With a few wrist flicks, I style it into a messy bun on top of my head and then sit in the warm office chair that Sarah just vacated.

"Other than the store managers—oh, and his boss—you're the only other person he talks to," she insists.

"That's not true. He talks to you."

"Yes, it is—he talks to *you* like a friend; he talks to *me* about work."

I laugh at the notion of me and Simon as friends. "Coffee—now." With a stern face, I point in the direction of the stairs.

Does Simon talk to me differently? I wonder, watching Sarah walking away. I suppose he does a bit, now that I think about it.

"Hey," Joe interrupts my thoughts. "Laura, can I ask a favor?"

"You can ask."

He looks uncomfortable. "I need to leave work early—can you help me put some contracts through?"

"Um, that would be a no. Joe, if you can't handle the paperwork, don't close so many customers." I stand. "Leave it to the pros, like me." I smile. "Here, the desk is free now, and there aren't any customers." I walk away.

Heading for the stairs, I look back. Joe is sitting at the desk staring into space. Sarah is too soft for her own good, but I'm not. I reach the top of the stairs and peer over from the mezzanine to see Sarah approaching with a mug in one hand and a Starbucks cup in the other. She climbs the steps, and on seeing me, she suddenly develops a ridiculous smile on her face.

"I told you," she says, reaching me and pushing the Starbucks cup in my direction.

"Told me what? Why are you smiling at me like that? And what's this?" I take the cup from her.

"Mr. Stevenson, or *Simon* to you, got you a coffee. So, still think he doesn't treat you any different?"

I take a sip of the coffee. "Whatever."

"What's up with you this morning?" Sarah asks. "You're always snappy, but this morning, you are excelling yourself."

"I'm not."

Sarah doesn't say anything for a minute. She just looks at me. "Laura, what's up?" she finally asks. "Has something happened?"

I shrug.

"Come on, you can tell me."

I hesitate. I like Sarah, and she is the only friend I have. But do I really want to share with her? I think of the Post-it Note, and the message that fell. *I like Sarah.*

"It's nothing, just that an old boyfriend is in town."

"Oh? Is that a bad thing?" she asks innocently. "Was he a dick?"

"Not really." I take a sip of my coffee. "I just didn't know he was living this way."

"Did you bump into him?"

"No." I consider how much and what to tell her before continuing. "I looked him up on Facebook—"

Sarah interrupts me. "I didn't know you were on Facebook! Add me?"

"It's not in my real name, and no, I'm not adding you. I just set it up to snoop. Don't know why, really—just want to see what the old gang is up to—where they're living, if they are even in the country. It turns out my ex is living not far from here."

I've been snooping on Marie and Ben for the last few weeks. Oddly enough, both of them have filled their timelines with public posts, making it easy to see into their lives. It makes me think that they purposely lightened their privacy settings, perhaps in the hope I'd do exactly what I'm doing. The notion has weighed on me heavily over the last few weeks, but I'm not going back. My life is here now, for my sister.

"Do you want to contact him?"

I shrug. "No, that ship has sailed. Way too much past between us."

Sarah has an annoyingly sympathetic look on her face. She could never understand what I've been through with Ben, and this is why I haven't told her. She's probably imagining an unfaithful relationship, or at worst, a terminated or lost pregnancy.

"Oh no, don't look now, but Mr. Stevenson is on his way up," she says in a low voice.

I have also seen Simon climbing the stairs. My eyes roll back in my head. "Just what I need," I reply a little less quietly.

"Laura," he shouts from the top of the stairs. The fat under his chin wobbles as he walks. "I see you got the coffee? Cheers." He knocks his cup into mine.

I smile that perfect fake smile of mine, the one with a hint of sarcasm—or "bitchiness," as Sarah tells me. Simon can't tell it's fake, but I can see Sarah in my peripheral vision, and she is literally squirming on the spot.

"My star seller," he tells Sarah, nodding at me. "If you make me as much money as her, I'll bring you coffee too."

Wow, what a great incentive, I think. My smile doesn't falter.

"Joe, how are you?" Simon's voice is loud enough to summon Joe over to us.

Deciding I want out of this ass-kissing meeting, I excuse myself. "Thanks for the coffee, Simon, but I've got some paperwork to put through. Don't want head office on my back, do I?"

He smiles back. "That's my gal."

I hate it when he calls me that. "See ya, then." I can't stop my smile from falling into a grimace.

Seeking refuge behind the photocopier, I slump my back against the wall. My whole life is truly fucked up beyond belief, and I sigh. I'm talking to my dead sister, working for a man I gave a hand job to, and drinking his poor attempt at a suck-up gesture in the form of coffee—which tastes too good to throw away. Furthermore, my only friend is the epitome of high school cheerleader meets *Wizard of Oz.* I want to like her, but I think she is too perfect to be my friend. It's only a matter of time before she sees through me and finds out I'm a fake—or before I bolt and leave her.

And then there's Ben. What the hell is he doing in South London? I thud the back of my head a few times against the wall.

"Fuck, what am I doing here?" I mumble.

"He's gone." Sarah's voice startles me. "It still astonishes me how you get away with being so rude to him. It's as if he likes you more for it."

Composing myself quickly, I say, "Like I said, stand up to bullies." I jab some buttons on the copier.

"You can coach me on that tonight. Drinks after work? You've not forgotten again, have you?" Her eyes plead with me.

"Of course not. Looking forward to it," I lie.

"Good, because you'll love my friends, and they will love you."

I doubt that, I think before seeing a customer come into view. I turn toward them wearing my friendly, approachable smile. "Watch and learn," I whisper.

The rest of the day rolls by much the same as normal after Simon leaves the store. I avoid Joe as best as possible, and Sarah follows me about the store like my shadow, which I appreciate—it gives me less time to dwell on my sorry situation.

So much for living my life for Laura, I think. Then I make a decision. *That's it.* Laura's note said she likes Sarah. I'm living my life for her, so if she likes her, then I need to get on board. Sarah is like Marie in so many ways, and I can see why Laura likes her. I should feel lucky to have met another kind and selfless person, yet my sister never went through what I did with Marie, and that puts my guard up. I don't want to get hurt like that again.

"Right, I'm ready to go now." Sarah appears beside me in the parking lot and immediately strides off. "Come on, then," she calls back to me from under the inky blue sky.

Reluctantly, I follow Sarah across the street and through the doors to the bar that we first met in. Terry nods as we pass him on our way to the far end, where two girls are sitting at a table. One is waving. She has her hair styled half up, with victory rolls on top of her head. Her curvy figure and rouge lips suit the look.

Beth, I think. She looks just how Sarah described her to me. Next to her sits a tiny girl whose hair is more like Tinker Bell on acid: short and blonde with flecks of pink and blue. This is Jess, presumably. She is slumped in her chair, arms folded across her body. I note the leather jacket and Dr. Martens boots, and I remember the anarchist description Sarah gave of her. If you just added some gum chewing, she would rather be the picture of teenage attitude.

Play nice, I remind myself. *These are Sarah's friends.*

"Hello, girls," the brunette says.

"Beth, hi, this is Laura," Sarah replies hastily. "Laura, this is Jess." She points to Tinker Bell.

"Hey," I say, trying my very best to look excited.

After getting a drink, we sit, and they chat for a while about boys and other things that don't include me. Tinker Bell—Jess—is texting, cementing my judgment of her teenage attitude. They all seem fairly two-dimensional to me so far, even Sarah. The conversation they are having is so … airy. Damn, can't we talk about something other than makeup and men, or just drink? Conversation is always better once you're shitfaced—people are honest then, or in my case, at least honestly shitfaced.

Jess perks up at the mention of a round of drinks, slipping her phone away and heading to the bar. Her mannerisms remind me of Kitty Hollister from school. It's something about the way her nose wrinkles if she doesn't like something and how she dismisses Sarah with a glance of the eye before changing the subject.

I sigh. *Tonight is going to be a long night.*

"You all right, Laura?" Sarah asks, and I wonder if she heard me.

"Yeah. Having fun," I say.

"Don't lie." Jess is standing behind me. "These two bore the crap out of me when they start talking about boys. Here, one each." She places four small glasses on the table. "Shot that back, and let's get this night going."

I look at her, unsure how to react to her new, inclusive self. I take the shot glass without saying anything, our eyes still locked on each other. We neck the drink at the same time and gasp, then slam down the empty tumblers.

"Brandy shots," I say. "That's different."

"Sarah said you like a drink, so I thought tequila would be too normal."

I nod.

Sarah is eyeing her drink with disgust, as is Beth. "Normal for you two, but not us."

Jess laughs. "Oh, come on now. It's just a small drink."

"Well, not exactly," Beth says. "If you think of it, it's a neat glass of brandy that we are going to down in one to make it even stronger. In fact, I'd argue the point that it is a rather large drink, one that will get me quite drunk and give me a stinking hangover tomorrow."

"And your point is?" I reply. I hope my blunt tone doesn't offend, as it so often does.

Beth nods slowly. "OK—OK, but I warn you, new girl, I am not taking responsibility for any embarrassing dancing or insulting conversations I will no doubt try to have with complete strangers, and if I misplace my favorite pair of panties that I'm wearing, it's all your fault. Oh, and I apologize in advance for trying to kiss you."

I frown. "Sounds like a good night ahead, then." I push the shot glass closer to her. "Down the hatch."

"Wait." Sarah raises a hand in objection.

We all look at her.

"Just the one," she persists. "I thought tonight was going to be a quick after-work drink, not getting out-of-our-faces drunk. It's Friday—we have work tomorrow." She gestures at me.

I shrug.

"Oh, come on," Jess wails, sounding a little like that teenage attitude again.

"It will be fine," Beth says.

Sarah's shoulders droop.

Stand up for yourself, I silently encourage her.

"I just thought we could sit and chat," she says. "A few glasses of wine, you know, then home."

Jess sits down with a sulky thud but nods in agreement.

"How about we do this shot and see how you feel in an hour," Beth suggests. "Maybe you'll fancy a bit of a dance once you get some booze in you, ha-ha. What do you say?" Beth gestures for Sarah to drink the shot.

Sarah looks at the brown liquid. She's not convinced. *Say no*, I will her. *Say no.* She shrugs, and Beth beams at her with delight.

Before Sarah downs the drink, I decide to object. I've been looking out for her at work, and why stop now? Also, I can't stop thinking about the Post-it Note that fell. If Laura likes her, then I owe it to my sister to stand up for her.

"Sarah's right, Beth," I interject. "I've got work tomorrow and wasn't planning on staying late."

They all look at me.

Jess sits up and slams her hands on the table. "Come on, then." She looks to Sarah then Beth. "Down it goes. We can move on to a good bottle of wine and have a chilled night. I'm cool with that."

After that, the conversation moves back to Beth's love life, which to be fair is quite entertaining. Besides, it's fun to watch Terry try so desperately to gain her attention. Jess shares the same candid humor as I do, meaning I don't end up offending people all night. It's nice, actually, and I'm enjoying myself. Being with Sarah feels easy and comfortable. Jess is a lot like Priya in some ways, so I get to be brutally honest, which I appreciate. All in all, the night is going well—until they decide to be polite and ask about my life, that is.

"You said earlier that you wanted to see what your old gang was up to," Sarah says. "Don't you keep in contact with them anymore? You grew up in Kent, right?"

"Kent? What part?" Beth adds.

Kent was the first place I thought of when Sarah asked where I came from. I didn't realize then just how big Kent is.

I need a deflection, I think. *Come on, come on, Lucy. You're good at deflecting—think, think.*

"I lost contact with them when my mum died," I say. "Just moved away; it was too painful for me to stay. I—I don't like to talk about it, really." I look back at their blank faces.

There's a moment of silence before Beth asks in a soft tone, "Do you have any siblings?"

The pause seems to go on forever. I can't do this. "No," I say. "It's late. I think I might head off."

Standing, I see the shock in their faces. Immediately, they all stammer, their words falling over each other as they try to convince me not to leave. I know they felt the awkwardness and probably feel responsible for my sharp exit.

"Honestly—I better go," I tell them. "I can feel a headache coming on, and I don't want it turning into a migraine. Look, I've had a great time, thank you. Was nice meeting you all."

I turn to Sarah.

She nods, standing to embrace me awkwardly, and we giggle as I go for a simple hug and she moves to kiss my cheek.

"Are you OK?" she whispers into my ear. Her genuine concern touches me, and I smile and look at the others.

Is this it? I think. *Is this my new world? Laura's new life? And are these my girls?*

"Yes," I say. "I'm fine—really, fine."

And I mean it. Laura has told me she approves of Sarah, and after seeing all their compassion for me moments ago, I realize this is normal. This is the life Laura would want—she would want to be a part of a group of close friends. And so do I—I just need to ease into it a little slower than most. I'm also aware that the easiest way to lose a bunch of friends is for them to find out you're a completely different person than the one you say you are.

CHAPTER 17

THEN–LAURA

Cornwall, three years ago
April

Thankful to be out of the rain, I sidestepped as Lucy shook her umbrella. You would be surprised how noisy rain flooding your soul sounds. Dropping it on the doormat, she hurried along the hall and into the kitchen after Marie, where Marie proceeded to slam cupboards, cups, and anything else she laid her hands on. I knew that look she was wearing. Lucy used to make me feel the same way—infuriated. I stood back and watched, arms folded.

Marie slammed the drawer shut. "No already!" she said, pointing the teaspoon at Lucy.

"Why?"

"Because he's my boyfriend. I need to spend time alone with him—you're not the only person in my life, believe it or not. Now stop flipping going on at me. Tea or coffee?"

"Coffee. But Marie, please, I get so lonely, and we never do anything just us two anymore. It's always the three of us." Lucy's voice was full of indignation.

"Oh my god, girl. Can you not hear how messed up that sounds? 'The three of us!' Dylan is *my* boyfriend, and it is *always* the three of us. I should be the one upset, not you."

Another month had passed by the time of this conversation. I had followed my sister about, trying desperately to make some kind of meaningful connection again, yet she was so consumed with jealousy over Marie and Dylan—and guilt over my death—I feared my attempts were becoming arbitrary.

"I just want to spend some me and you time," Lucy whined. "Why are you making me feel so bad for that? You make me sound pathetic for wanting a friend." Lucy moved to leave.

"Wait," Marie said.

Slowly, Lucy turned to face her, and instantly I felt the same sympathy that Marie obviously did. "Sorry," Lucy muttered with drooped shoulders and red eyes.

Marie pulled her into a bear hug. "Oh, Lucy," she said, "you'll always be my friend. Just because I'm spending more time with Dylan doesn't mean I'd leave you." Marie looked into Lucy's face, pushing her fine blond hair behind her ears. "Is this why you're upset? I thought you were working through this with Hellen in therapy."

Lucy gave a small bounce of her shoulders.

"I really am sorry I can't come to the movies with you," Marie said gently. "You know I would, but he has booked a table. It's unfair to just cancel on him last minute—you must be able to understand that. Why don't we go tomorrow?" Marie's smile was broad.

My sister wiped her nose with her sweater cuff. "It's all right," she said, then quit the room without waiting for a reply.

"Lucy," Marie called up the hall after her. "Lucy—" She watched her disappear upstairs. "Damn it." Marie slammed the cup on the counter.

Heading directly upwards, I met Lucy in her room just as she came through her bedroom door. Seeing her face still tear-soaked wrenched at my heart. All I wanted to do was talk to her, tell her she was loved. I knew exactly how she felt, not because I was her twin but because when she was in therapy, I held her hand. I felt what she felt, and I couldn't help but feel guilty. All she wanted was to be like me when we were growing up, for our mum to love her like she loved me. All she wanted was for someone—anyone—to love her more than anyone else in their lives. Lucy had that in me; she rightly believed that she was the most important person in my life, but now I was gone.

She finished texting somebody and threw her phone onto the bed. I'd been so enthralled by her emotions I hadn't seen who she had texted. Then there was a tap at the bedroom door, and Marie's head poked around the corner.

"Lucy?" she said, still tapping as she opened the door. "You OK? Can I come in?"

"Sure."

"I made you a coffee. It's in the kitchen with a doughnut—I warmed them up."

"The stale ones?" Lucy managed a small laugh. "I know your trick. Warming them up doesn't stop them from being stale, Marie. The kids in Ethiopia won't hate you for throwing out old doughnuts."

"You got me." Marie held her hands up. "You OK now? Friends again? I hate arguing with you." Marie swung open the door. "Come on, then—you can drink the coffee, and I'll eat the donuts."

"Can't." Lucy shook her head. "Got to leave now; don't want to be late for the film." She started toward the door, pushing Marie out with her.

"You're going alone?"

"No. I texted Ben."

I froze.

"Oh, that's good," I heard Marie say. Her voice was muffled, like I was listening through a wall. "Have fun, then."

The door closed, and I just stared at my sister, who was applying the final touches to her makeup. She was oblivious, unaware of just who Ben was. I thought she had been starting to pick up my signs. I knew she thought the bird flying into Ben's window was off—I just couldn't seem to get her to commit herself to distrusting him.

I paced the upper floor, walking effortlessly through Lucy's room to Marie's and back. My sister's desire to be loved was so great it was overshadowing logic itself. I stopped at the top of the stairs. I could smell the warm doughnuts and heard Marie stirring sugar into her mug, oblivious to the danger. How was I going to protect my sister this time?

★ ★ ★

Ben smiled when he saw my sister. "Hey, Lucy. You look nice."

She wasn't overdressed, just wearing jeans and a little black leather jacket with a wooly scarf looped around her neck. She looked like she was about to throw up.

"What's wrong?" he asked when he noticed her expression, then reached for her.

"A little carsick from the taxi ride here, that's all. I'm fine." She waved him off, yet involuntary jolts in the pit of her stomach said differently as she retched. "Just need to sit down for a second."

Ben followed, his hands hovering about her arms as if wanting to hold her up. Finally, he decided to let her walk to the wall unassisted and stood watching her awkwardly with his hands in his pockets. Eventually, he sat next to her and placed a hand lightly on her shoulder.

Lucy didn't move away. "The guy drove so fast and jerky. I think he thought the accelerator was a pump."

They both laughed a little.

This was a disaster. Ben was looking after my sister and coming across as the good guy, and there was nothing I could do. I looked about my surroundings for something light to throw at him. No luck.

"I'll get the popcorn," Ben said after a moment or two, and Lucy started to move, but he told her to rest. "There's no rush," he insisted.

She rested back down against the concrete wall, placing her head in her hands.

"I'll be good soon, just need a few more seconds."

She didn't feel it, but I saw Ben ever-so-softly touch the back of her hair with a shaky palm, making my blood run icy cold.

"Take all the time you need," he said, reaching for her hair again. "I'll wait."

Lucy sat up, pushing her head into his hand. He didn't flinch.

"Better?" he asked, now openly stroking her hair.

Lucy nodded. "Thank you." She reached for his hand and pulled it onto her cheek.

"What for?"

She kissed his palm. "For being here with me."

Fury burned inside my soul as I watched Ben lean in for a kiss. Frantically, I tried to coax energy into my hands while considering what I could do with it. My eyes fell over our surroundings, but there was nothing I could push or throw. Finally, Ben and Lucy broke apart and moved toward the entrance of the theater. Frustrated, I pulled my hands apart, and a sudden gust of wind hit the ground in front of me.

Lucy's hair blew up and over her head. "Oh my god," she said, holding down her hair until the wind was gone. "That came out of nowhere."

Ben laughed and pulled her under his arm. "Must be a wind trap."

How on earth was I meant to handle this situation? It just felt as if I was following my sister about, waiting for this creep to snake his way into her life, and there was nothing I could do. I didn't know how to use my energy properly; I didn't even know what I was meant to be doing. And then a new, saddening thought struck me. Was this punishment? Was I sent to follow my sister to atone for not protecting her in life?

Stop it. I shake the thought. *Stay focused. I'm not the victim here; Lucy needs me.*

Being the perfect gent, Ben opened the entrance door, holding her gaze as she walked through it. The door slammed right through me as it closed. He paid for the tickets and popcorn as promised. As I followed them through the foyer to the screening room, he playfully threw a piece of popcorn at her. She laughed and lightly slapped his arm. It sickened me to see my sister falling for his feeble attempts at flirting.

"Shh, quick." Lucy giggled. "It's already started."

Ben took her hand and led her to their seats. They shared a drink, which pleased me immensely—at least I didn't need to worry about it being drugged. What didn't please me was Lucy's apparent change of heart. Only the night before, I'd been in her thoughts, and Ben hadn't been there—well, not in this capacity, anyway. I knew she missed him. She was lonely, but not ready for a relationship. I'd heard her tell herself that she needed more time to be sure what she wanted.

I floated aimlessly in the alcoves of the ceiling, looking down at them shoveling popcorn into each other's mouths. I thought back through the events of the day and landed on the argument with Marie.

"Bingo," I said. I flew down and into Ben's face, poking my own face between two chains. I was so close our noses were almost touching. *"She doesn't want you; she's just confused."* My words seemed to irritate his nose, and he raised his hand to rub his face, inadvertently swinging an array of chains through my head and sending me into a backspin across the room. I landed in front of the screen, looking out at a half-empty theater as if I was the show. Sitting up on my elbow, I thought for a moment that I'd gotten away with it, that I hadn't picked up any memories from him.

I was so, so wrong.

A bar. Music. Loud music. Ben had a short tumbler in one hand, holding what looked like spirits of some kind. I smelled it—whisky. He sat at the bar looking out over an extremely packed dance floor. A group of girls was dancing, and one kept looking back over her shoulder at him. He smiled back.

Another memory flicked into vision. It was Lucy. She was walking through the town and didn't know he was behind her. Stupidly, I shouted, *"Lucy!"*

Ben was no longer at the bar—he was standing over in a corner, and the music was even louder. He was standing near a speaker. The group of girls was still in his line of sight, but there were only three of them now—two had left earlier. He watched them all hug and say goodbye, giggling like silly school girls. Ben knew that the girl that kept looking back at him was a smoker, and the only other smoker in the group had just left.

The girl tried to search him out at the bar. He watched the disappointment when she couldn't find him. She was the largest of all the friends. He noted her flat shoes—presumably, she wore them because she was also the tallest, and if she wore heels, she would feel even more out of place amongst her peers with their perfect skin and manicured nails.

I was behind Lucy again. The memories must have gotten tangled when he moved. He was still following her. She had just left the Boots pharmacy—were we on Fore Street? He could see a box of tampons poking out the top of the small bag. Walking on, she headed into Co-op Food, and Ben waited just out of sight.

It was strange—it felt as if he was numb inside. However, when Lucy emerged, I definitely felt something from him—desire? No, that wasn't strong enough for this feeling. Obsession? Fixation?

He watched her soft blonde hair blowing gently behind her as she walked away from him, and he was momentarily unable to move. *Infatuation.*

The girl motioned to the exit, already holding a cigarette. Her friends nodded as she moved away from the group alone.

After that, the memories seemed to fly at me from random cross-sections of Ben's life. They came at me so fast—I tried to slow them down, but I couldn't. An intense squeezing cut over my forehead, and I screamed, yet the memories persisted.

A small box. No, a closet—there were clothes hanging above. The door opened, and Ben received a slap across his face from a woman with tight curly hair that made him recoil in fear. Tears stung his eyes, and he clutched his knees tighter into his chest. He flinched as the woman kissed his burning cheek, alcohol rife on her breath. "You know you deserved that. I didn't want to; you made me. Just stay quiet when I have friends over."

Then he was at a school canteen. He jolted forward from a shoulder barge, and his lunch tray smashed to the ground.

Ben was in a fight. His feet were quick, like a boxer. Swing, duck, swing. *Smash.* Blood splattered across the other boy's face. A teacher yanked at Ben's arm, demanding he step back. Ben didn't resist. The other boy glared at him in apparent shock. I felt good—*Ben* felt good—his veins were vibrant with adrenaline.

The girl from the bar was unsteady on her feet. Ben helped her, holding her up by her arms as she stumbled along, bent over as if to be sick. I could feel his heart beating fast. *Thud-thud, thud-thud.* He stole a look over his shoulder. The bar was out of sight now, and the beer garden had been almost empty.

None of her friends had seen them talking out there. No one was looking for her, not yet.

He saw an alleyway and guided her into it. The girl was finding it increasingly hard to walk and stumbled, crashing to her knees. Ben tried to help her back up. She was too close to the entrance, and if a car drove past, they'd be seen, he worried. But the girl was heavy and complaining about her grazed knees. Her hands brushed at her legs. I felt him reconsidering what he was about to do, and then a fleeting flash of my face in his mind startled me.

My face disappeared, and his memories were back in the alleyway. The girl wasn't moving; she was propped up behind a dumpster. I felt bilious as his hand slipped up her skirt. She was so out of it she hardly reacted when he jabbed two fingers inside her. I closed my eyes, not wanting to watch, yet it was no good. I was in his thoughts, so closing my eyes wouldn't work.

In an agitated movement, he tugged up her skirt and placed her hand down her own panties. She gave a groan and fidgeted.

"Stop it," he hissed in her ear. "Shh, now hush." He stroked her hair, and the girl let him place her hand back where it was. He was getting panicked that it was taking longer than he thought, and I could feel the thuds from his heart vibrating against his chest—it felt like my own. He quickly snapped a few pictures on his phone and then moved back to the girl to finish. It didn't take long.

Inside my own mind, I cried uncontrollably as I felt every thrust, every primal bit of satisfaction that he felt. I didn't think it could get any worse than not only witnessing but also feeling his actions—and then it did. Ben reached up and gripped her throat the way he had mine. I was finally able to establish a timeline as his thoughts flitted back to the night with me, and I saw myself on the floor of Marie's garage. I felt his erection softening. Ben quickly squeezed the girl's neck harder, shaking thoughts of me out of his mind. The girl gave some bubbled gasps and shifted beneath him—and then it was over. He released his grip, and she gasped for air.

It was still the same night, and he was in his room, trembling. Had he been seen? In his mind, he was retracing his steps, sure he had taken a route with no cameras. I felt nauseated, but it wasn't really me. It was Ben—he was feeling physically sick, which meant I was too.

He pulled a picture of Lucy out of a drawer. She was wearing her favorite pair of ripped jeans and a white T-shirt. I remember that day because I took the photo. She was trying to stand up from her bed, but Ben kept pulling her back down again. We all thought it was so funny. I had snapped a shot with my new Polaroid. She looked so pretty, her face full of laughter as she reached her hand out toward me in a mock plea for help.

"I'm so sorry." Ben addressed the Polaroid and sniffed back snot that now slid down his throat.

He meant it. The son of a bitch actually felt remorse for what he had done. But he also carried urges he didn't know how to control, and that scared him. A tear hit the picture, and he dabbed at it with his sleeve, careful not to ruin it further. He loved Lucy; he wanted her. Not like that, though—he wanted her to want him and was terrified that she would reject him either before or after he slept with her. Even so, something compelled him to want her in a way he'd not wanted other girls. She was easy—she didn't judge him and never asked questions about his past. Lucy's downfall was that she accepted him at face value.

My breathing was labored, but Ben's thoughts were finally free from mine. It was over. I saw that the theater was now dark and empty.

They'd gone.

Frantic, I tried to move but only managed to float a few inches forward before freezing, suspended in time. How long had I been there? Where had they gone? Fear and desperation gripped me. I didn't know how long it would take for me to regain my energy or how I would find Lucy.

Suddenly, I felt myself move. It hadn't taken long to energize, if you can call it that. It was definitely faster than the last time I used up all my energy, the time at Ben's apartment.

That's it, I thought. Ben's apartment—he didn't earn a lot of money and had just paid for the movies. He would take Lucy back to his place because he wanted to be close to her—that, or they had gone back to Lucy's since Marie was out.

Which one? I forced myself to make a choice.

★ ★ ★

She was sitting on Ben's bed, and he was looking for something in a drawer. Inside Ben's room, the light was dimmed low, and it was dark outside. I shifted quickly as Ben passed—I did not want to touch him again. I watched in horror as he sat next to my sister on the bed, holding what he had just retrieved from the drawer between his index finger and forefinger.

"Are you sure?" he asked, tapping the square packet on her nose.

Slowly, she nodded.

"*No, no, no. Lucy, what are you doing?*" I flew close to her, clapping in her face, blowing and shouting, yet nothing. I couldn't let her make the biggest mistake of her life, not now, not here, not with him. Coaxing the space around me, I tried with every inch of my being to pull another energy ball into my hands, but it was pointless. I had nothing left and needed to rest. It was like being in a box with limited air—the more you move, the more oxygen you use. I knew my box would refill if I gave it enough time, so I closed my eyes and waited.

Sloppy sounds of lips slapping against each other and Ben's distinct and disgusting sound of excitement grated at my soul.

The kissing stopped, and fabric rustled. With this warning that clothes were being removed, my eyes jolted open. He was on top of her, one hand up her T-shirt and the other tugging frantically at her belt. Surely she would have second thoughts? Instead, her clothed hips thrust into his. I saw him reach for the zipper of her jeans, and with asking eyes, he slowly pulled it down. I was about to try to coax something out to interrupt them when Lucy clasped her hand on her jeans, stopping him.

"Wait," she said breathlessly.

I could see the fear flood Ben's face. "What? What's wrong?" As much as I didn't want Lucy to sleep with Ben, I feared what he'd do if she rejected him.

"I'm not sure if I should do this anymore." She shifted away slightly, propping herself up on one elbow.

I knew my sister, and I pleaded with her to be tactful.

Ben swallowed his fear and laughed off her hesitations, pulling her off her elbow back down on the bed. "Shh, it will be all right." She let him kiss her for a second but then wriggled. Ben gripped her body against his. "Shh, Lucy, shh."

"No, Ben," she said, muffled with her lips still against his. "Stop."

"Lucy, don't do this to me—I want you so badly," he whispered in her ear, pushing his heavy weight down on top of her.

"Um—all right, then," I heard her whisper back feebly. She stopped moving.

I panicked. I suspected Ben hadn't been with a girl willingly, so just lying there might anger him. Why was she just lying there? A pain like I'd never felt before hurled its way from the pit of my stomach as I let out an almighty wail.

There was immediately a scraping noise, which seemed to disturb them, followed by a loud crash as the mirror next to the bed slid to the floor. It lay there unbroken.

Ben jumped up and Lucy quickly stood behind him, zipping up her jeans and reaching for her jacket.

After bending to pick up the fallen object, he saw Lucy by the door. "You're not leaving, are you?"

She shrugged. "It's late."

Ben's knuckles whitened as he tightened them around the mirror frame, and I willed her to see the warning signs, to run, leave.

"No, stay." He threw the mirror onto the bed. "I'm sorry if I got carried away. It's just—" He took her face in both his hands. "You're just so damn sexy, and you're the only person I want in my life. It's you, it's always been you—I love you."

My fist slammed down onto the mirror. *Smash.*

"What the fuck?" Ben rushed to his bed.

Lucy walked up behind him. "How did that happen?"

"Ouch!" Ben held up his hand, blood running from his little finger.

"Oh, Ben, be careful."

He lowered his hand. "It's all right, I'll live. Stay—don't go."

She shook her head softly.

"OK," he finally conceded, "but you heard what I said?"

"Ben—"

Placing a finger to her lips, he shushed her. "You don't need to answer. Just know I mean it." A drop of blood slowly slid down the outer edge of his hand. "I love you."

Lucy pressed her lips to his and kissed him. "I just need a bit more time," she whispered softly.

I watched Lucy leave but stayed riveted to the spot in front of Ben. His expression turned from soft to tense as soon as he heard the front door close. Pushing his hand hard thought his hair, he paced the room. This was bad. She had rejected him. From everything I'd seen, I was confident he loved my sister, and I was also confident that he couldn't control his obsessive, unbalanced desires toward her much longer. I had to find a way to either stop Ben or actually communicate effectively with my sister.

CHAPTER 18

NOW–LUCY

London, present day
April

Sarah reaches across her small coffee table in the house she now shares with Dan. "Swap," she says, taking the satay chicken out of my hand while passing me the sticky rice.

"Oh, did I tell you I'm not in the store Monday?" I ask.

Sarah shakes her head.

"I'm covering the Croydon store—yep, it's crap," I say, seeing her deflation. "But it's only one day," I add, though I don't tell her just how much I'm not looking forward to doing it. Being back in my old neighborhood was never the ideal situation. I quickly change the subject. "Has Dan texted you back to say where he is?" I ask, shoveling a mound of rice onto my plate from the box.

Sarah's shoulders rise with the sigh she gives me in reply. "Nope—not yet, and doubt he will."

"Why's that?" I ask. "It's a bit rude. I thought he was the perfect boyfriend."

"Was," she says. "No, that's harsh of me. He still is …" She trails off.

"So why the long face then?"

Sarah picks up the remote and hits play on the Netflix movie we'd been watching before the take-out delivery arrived.

"It's nothing; I'm probably just being needy."

"What? Wait." I take the remote from her and pause the movie again. "Where's this coming from? Needy? What's that supposed to mean?"

"I know, I know—be a strong woman and all that. But I'm not like you." She sees my confusion. "Laura, you're so strong and don't take any bullshit. I wish I could be more like you." I try to reply, but she holds up a hand. "No, wait. I've always been this way: needy. I think it has something to do with my mum not mentally being there for me or something like that. I'm like that with everyone; it's just who I am."

"Not with me, you're not," I say. Her pale cheeks are now flushed by the wine we have drunk.

"I am. You just don't see it because you're so un-needy. Half the time I don't even think you listen to me talking to you." She laughs, and I try to decipher the laugh's meaning. Then she continues. "Not that I'm putting you down for it—goodness, no, I know I can drone on and on."

"Who told you that?" I pass her back the rice. "You don't drone on, and don't take it personally if it looks like I'm not listening. I do that to everyone—it's just who I am." I wink. "Looks like both our mums messed us up good and proper."

I watch as she smiles. I've eased her concerns a little, but not fully. I can tell by the way she sips her wine to avoid answering or agreeing.

Holding up the empty wine bottle, I ask, "Is there another in the kitchen?"

Sarah nods, standing. "I'll get it."

I listen to her moving about in the kitchen. Sarah has always struck me as comfortable with who she is, yet now I'm not so sure. I feel a hankering to protect her, and it reminds me of how I felt for Laura at school. I hear bottles clanking, and then her phone vibrates opposite me. I see Dan's name and lean over to see what it says. I tilt my head so it's not fully upside-down and read:

WTF! I TOLD YOU I WAS WORKING LATE BECAUSE YOU HAVE YOUR FRIEND OVER!

Sarah's footsteps make me withdraw back to my side of the table.

"Rosè OK?" She holds up the bottle.

"Sure," I say, taking it from her. "Oh, your phone just vibrated."

I watch in astonishment as Sarah snatches up the phone, nearly dropping it in the process. Her fingers frantically fumble with the device. *No wonder why Dan sounded short over text. I would too if I'd told my girlfriend I was working late and she was asking where I was.*

"Everything OK, Sarah?" I ask. "Is it Dan?"

She doesn't answer.

"Sarah?"

She frowns. "He said he is working late and that he told me."

"Right?" I say in way of a question.

"He didn't tell me, though." She thuds back down onto the carpet opposite me.

I top up her glass. "Drink," I say. "What's going on? Talk to me. Are you sure you didn't just forget that he told you—do you think he's cheating?"

Sarah takes her time to think about my question. It's like I can see the cogs in her brain working as her eyes dart about the space in front of her. Normally this sort of dilemma would bore me, but it's Sarah—she accepts me, so I want to try to accept her.

"He does this all the time—stays out late and then says that he told me."

"So do you do think he's cheating?" I wait for an answer as Sarah sips her wine. "Do you?"

"No, he's not cheating," she says.

"Are you sure?"

"I think I am. Women have a sixth sense for that. But I do think he's out drinking with the boys and blaming it on work. He got a promotion, and to be honest, it's gone to his bloody head. He thinks he's a big shot now. All he wants to do is work late and then take "the boys" for a drink after. Over the last month, he's been out most nights and coming home drunk, saying that he told me he would be late."

I twist my mouth into a sympathetic smile, not knowing what to say.

"He's trying to climb the ladder at work," she adds.

"That's good in a way," I say, my encouragement falling short.

"Maybe, but not if I see him less and less. I'm secretly hoping they don't promote him again. Is that bad?"

I furrow my brow. "You need to stop worrying about what other people think, girl." I top up her glass again. "Come on, screw Dan—let's watch this damn movie." I smile, sitting back up on the sofa, and she follows suit.

Almost right away, Sarah seems to forget our prior discussion, along with Dan's behavior. She looks totally engrossed, giggling away and occasionally looking over at me from the opposing end of the sofa while picking at the leftover food from the boxes. I, on the other hand, have lost the plot of the movie and don't care to catch up, either. It's all fake: the actors, the story, everything.

It's annoying me, this situation with Sarah and Dan, and I don't know why. How dare Dan treat my friend like that? Who the hell does he think he is? Sarah is one of the nicest people I've met, and I'll be damned if a man is going to hurt her. Drunk Lucy is not the most pleasant of personas at times, and I feel one of those times could be now.

The end credits roll over the screen, but I'm so absorbed by my thoughts I don't even notice. It's not until the timer is counting down to play a trailer for another movie that I come back to reality. Looking over, I see Sarah is asleep, her head perfectly resting on her hand, which in turn rests on the arm of the sofa. I wonder how anyone could take such a sweet person like her for granted, and instantly, I'm taken over by fear. This happens now and then when I forget who I am. I swiftly pull myself back into reality. I am Lucy, and I'm lying to my friends, people who are not like my old friends. They don't live shady lives, and after spending time with them, I know they take things personally. In my opinion, they are way too sensitive, but they are all I have. Sarah is all I have.

The sound of a key unlocking the front door startles Sarah, and now she's awake. We lock eyes. I can tell she is not fully back to her senses yet, but by the time the living room door is open, she is on her feet.

Quickly I whisper, "Play it cool."

She takes my advice, dropping her hands from her hips and pushing her snarl into something that might resemble a smile if you are drunk enough.

Dan is.

"Babe …" He stumbles toward her.

She bends to clear the table, avoiding his grasp. "There's leftovers if you're hungry," she says.

"Indian?" he slurs and adds, "Hi, Sarah's friend."

"No, Thai," Sarah says.

I wave.

Dan turns his nose up at the food. "Nah, I've eaten anyway." He falls into the armchair. "Babe, I'm sorry."

"It's fine, Dan. Just leave it."

"No, Sarah-bear, I am. I might have forgotten to tell you I was staying out. I am sorry. The boys told me I was a jerk."

"They're right," she says simply. She picks up a handful of boxes and leaves the room.

I make to follow.

"So you're Laura, then?" Dan's question stops me.

Standing next to the armchair, I look down at him. "So you're Dan, then?"

He smirks, nodding his head as if my reply pleases him in some way. "I've heard lots about you."

"All good, I hope."

"Oh, yes." His gaze briefly washes over my legs. "All good."

I exit the room but hesitate just outside the door. The guy's a dick for sure, and if he is not cheating on her, I doubt it's through lack of trying. But that's not what concerns me. What concerns me is the enjoyment I got when he looked at me—his blatant desire, then my power to ignore his advances. I liked it, his desire and my power over him. I liked it more than I should have. I walk into the kitchen.

Sarah looks livid.

"Are you OK?" I approach cautiously.

She grits her teeth. "I hate it when he's this drunk, his eyes all dopey and slurring his words—it's pathetic."

"Sarah?" I step closer, checking over my shoulder, and whisper, "He doesn't hit you, does he?"

The question makes her recoil in laughter, "Oh god, no," she says. "If we go back in there now, he will be passed out cold. I'll put money on it. He's not like that."

I move over to where Sarah is throwing the uneaten food into the bin. "Why are you with him?"

She doesn't answer straight away, and at first I think she is ignoring the question.

"He never used to go out with the boys this much." She scrapes out the rice before tossing the box into the recycling. "I think I'm going to have to talk to him, aren't I?" she asks, facing me. "That's what you would do, isn't it?"

"It is," I agree. "Sarah, you need to tell him because you have to be happy too, and it's not like he can't see it. He is shitfaced, but at least he admitted that he didn't tell you he was staying out after work."

She nods.

"Leave it till tomorrow; don't hash it out tonight," I say, and then I do something that shocks even me. I embrace her. I'm a little awkward, but it is affection nonetheless.

★　★　★

As I stand staring out of my taped-up window, I have an overwhelming urge to smash it through. The management company is being slow to fix it, and they have billed me for the cost because of the lack of evidence of a bird strike, but this is not the thing that irks me. My apartment is covered in Post-it Notes, and not one has fallen for the last month. It feels as if whatever I try never lasts, which in turn is pushing me to question the reality of it all. My devoted desire for it to be true is making me wonder if I only see what I want to see.

Seeing Mr. Clifton on the pavement below, I step back out of sight and continue to gather my things for work. The sun is out, and it looks like a nice day ahead, though I place an umbrella in my bag anyway—April showers are no joke. Just before leaving, I stop and take a look at my oddly decorated room. For some reason, maybe because of seeing Sarah's perfect life for what it really is, I've realized nothing in life is true. I drop my bag. With frustrated swings, I grab at the Post-it Notes, dropping them to the floor.

It doesn't take long to clear the walls, not at the speed I'm moving at. After I finish these walls, I hurry to the bathroom to do the same. My fingers are millimeters away from snatching the last one off the mirror when it unsticks on its own. I watch it flutter down into the washbasin below. The note is laying face up, and the word I've looked at every day is prominent on the yellow square now resting motionless in the white ceramic bowl.

On the tram to the Croydon store, I allow myself to think back to before I left Cornwall, something I try not to do often. I also think about the word on the Post-it Note:

Danger.

Was that why Laura wanted me to leave and not come back? And if I was in danger, who from? Marie, Ben, Mum, Dad? I laugh at the thought of my dad being a danger. I miss him. I quickly stop myself going down that thought path. I gave up missing my dad a long time ago, and it looks like I was right to. *Danger.* I bounce the word about in my head. I wasn't in any danger back then, not that I know of. If anything, people were in danger because of me—even the therapist alluded to that.

I reach my stop and step off gingerly. *Danger.* I know I'm not that close to the bedsit, yet I am close enough. Am I in danger being back here in Croydon? Priya trusted me, and I betrayed her. I don't think she would stop to listen if she ever saw me, and I don't really want to find out, either. The Post-it Note must have just come unstuck—a coincidence, yet unnerving nonetheless. Walking fast, I make my way along the Purley Way, occasionally glancing over my shoulder.

Much to my dismay, when I arrive at my old familiar store, I see Simon. He's talking to Collin and hasn't seen me yet, so I quickly move toward the bed section. I've not gotten more than three steps when that changes.

"Laura!" Simon's obnoxious voice grates on my soul.

I spin on the spot and wave.

"You're late," he says, coming toward me with Collin close behind.

"Sorry." I shrug. "I didn't anticipate the right amount of travel time."

Collin's eyes widen, but he doesn't say anything.

"Well, you're here now." Simon puts a fat hand on my shoulder and guides us away. "Let's get you upstairs."

I steal a glance at Simon, and he smiles back at me. *Oh god, was that an innuendo?* I think.

"It's OK," I tell him. "I know my way around, remember?"

Thankfully, he agrees and wanders back with Collin the way they came. I climb the stairs.

Seeing Malik sitting at the desk makes me feel better about agreeing to come back here, not that the request was optional—but all the same.

"Oh god, you're working today," I call out.

Malik jumps to his feet. "Well, look at you," he says and pulls me into a warm embrace. "I didn't know you were here today."

I look about the floor to see if anything has changed. It hasn't.

"So why am I here?" I ask, turning to face him again. "If you're here, why do they need me too? Can't you cover the floor alone?"

Malik's eyebrows dart upward. "I don't know, no one tells me anything. I didn't even know you were coming today, unlike you."

"What's that supposed to mean?"

"I've seen you on managers' emails. Big shot now." His tone is clipped.

I frown. "What?"

Malik walks off over to the Sleeptight range at the back of the section, and I follow.

"Malik?"

Tossing me a pillow then a pillowcase, he says in a low voice, "You and Mr. Stevenson?"

I look at him, bewildered.

"People—not me, other people—have been saying that you and Mr. Stevenson are sleeping—"

"Stop!" I say, not wanting to hear it.

"Is it true?" he asks.

"Who's saying this? And no, it's not true. Now spill." I scowl.

"I didn't think it would be, but I did enjoy watching your face sober at the thought of it. Hannah from the Bromley store was here last week. She told me."

I ram the pillow inside the pillowcase, trying to think why anyone would think Simon and I were sleeping together. The idea is just repulsive.

"I don't get it. What gave her that idea?"

Malik shrugs. "Don't know, though it is obvious you're his favorite. And if it's not true—"

"It's not."

"If it's not true," he continues, "then calling him by his first name hasn't done you any favors to stop the gossip mill, not when he won't allow anyone else to call him Simon—not even Collin."

Malik has a point, yet I'll be damned if I will ever call him Mr. Stevenson like he is some authority figure over me. I think back to Sarah's observation about Simon favoring me and the coffees he buys. Maybe he does fancy me. Maybe I'm reading it wrong and it's not guilt. The sad prick might actually like me, and that might play to my favor.

"What are you smiling at?" Malik asks.

"Nothing that concerns you."

"Laura … what are you plotting? I know that look." I turn and walk away, and he calls after me, "Laura, where are you going?"

"To get coffee," I say. "Cover for me?"

"Capitano, please," Malik says.

"Just cover for me."

I head across the road for two coffees: one for me and one for Simon. Malik will forgive me, and I really don't have the cash to spare. If Simon likes me, there might be a way I can use this to my advantage, I think, pressing the button and waiting impatiently for the signal to walk. My mind jostles with manipulation. I know I'm in line for the floor manager position, yet I also know that the head office has requested all promotions be done at the end of the year. That is far too long to wait—I have bills to pay.

Walking into Sainsbury's supermarket, I head toward the coffee counter. Suddenly, something—or *someone*—catches my eye. I glance, and then glance again. He's gone. I stop and quickly scan the store, looking over at the vegetable area, and then beyond through the bodies of shoppers filling their baskets. Was it him? I'm sure, or I *think* I'm sure. I shrug and continue on.

The barista making my coffees is slow. I think she's new, and I want to offer advice—I mean, it's not rocket science, is it? After painfully watching her make both my orders for a second time after failing miserably the first, I flash a fake smile at her and pay. My thoughts turn back to Simon and how this coffee is about to get me an early promotion. I haven't worked out the finer details yet, but it's a start. The automatic doors open, and I exit the supermarket to an onset of rain.

"Oh, just great." Frustration looms as I edge back inside the doors until the rain eases up. The main road is too large to cross in this weather. My hair will frizz, and that won't improve my chance for any kind of promotion. *But being away too long getting coffee won't either,* my thoughts quickly add.

I'm about to make a run for it when I see him. It *is* him: Ben. He's put on some weight and grown a small beard, yet it's definitely him. He's not seen me. Fast thumps hit inside my chest. He's walking out to the parking lot, so I follow. Rain pounds the lids on the coffee cups. I walk faster to catch up. Should I even talk to him? I slow my pace. What if he knows something? I quicken my pace. A ludicrous notion slows my speed again, rain spoiling my hair. I wonder if he understands why I felt the way I did, how I must have made him feel—how I felt back then. Surely he knew I had no choice.

He's getting into a car. If I am going to do something, now's the time. A thought flicks into mind: *Laura.* Maybe she orchestrated this meeting. I'm approaching, nearly there, yet still I don't call out. He starts to close his door, so picking up the courage, I open my mouth to call out. Suddenly, something hits my shin. It's fast. The coffees fly from my hands, smashing to the ground along with me. A passing shopper comes to my aid, abandoning her shopping cart to help.

"I'm fine," I say, standing and brushing the wet dirt from my clothes.

I look up just in time to see Ben drive away.

"Did you slip?" she asks.

I think about her question. "No, I didn't slip," I say, bending to rub the bottom of my shin where I felt the impact, "I tripped." Getting to my feet, I scan the vicinity, yet I see nothing that could have tripped me.

Laura.

Did Laura really trip me? It all happened so fast. I think about following Ben, about the fall, and then the woman—she came out of nowhere to help me. I don't remember seeing her before. Is it happening again? Am I making things up in my mind? I think back to what Hellen my therapist once alluded to. *No.* I shake my head vigorously. A light buzz comes from my pocket. Pulling out my phone, I see I've cracked my screen in the fall.

"Damn," I say. Then I see Simon's name under the crack. "Shit, shit." Taking a breath, I answer, "Hello?"

"Where the hell are you?"

Oh, just great, I think. *It's going to take a lot more than a coffee to get what I want from him now.*

CHAPTER 19

THEN–LAURA

Cornwall, three years earlier
May (twenty-first birthday)

Saddened again by my sister's defensive response to people trying to help, I hurried behind her.

Lucy stormed from the kitchen and along the hallway, arms swinging like a soldier. "So you want me to move out, then?"

"No, Lucy, that's not what I said!" Marie insisted as she and I followed Lucy into the living room. "Will you stop being so melodramatic? All I'm doing is agreeing with your dad." Though they couldn't see me, I nodded in agreement. "If he thinks it might help you mend things between you and your mum, then you should move back home."

Lucy had her back to Marie and was watching a cat on the wall outside the window. My hands hovered over her heart, trying desperately to radiate inner peace, anything to stop the rage she harbored.

"Lucy, we're all trying to help you."

The cat jumped from the wall and out of sight, but Lucy continued to face the window. "Is that so?"

"Yes. Your dad misses you."

"What?" She spun to face Marie, eyes glazed by tears. I frantically pushed good chi into the space about her. "Didn't miss me enough to tell that bitch I call Mum to fuck off years ago."

"Lucy!" The astonishment in Marie's voice was prominent.

"What? It's true. I'm second best to everyone; I know that." She turned back to the window.

Her words cut into my soul. Willing Marie to leave it alone, I reached out with both hands as if stopping a boulder from hitting her. It was our birthday month, and I knew the smallest of things could set my sister back. The last thing I wanted was for Lucy and Marie to fall out. I just wanted them to stop with their bickering for one day. Maybe if they'd stopped fighting each other, my sister would have connected with me easier. I slumped to the floor. All the energy in the world wasn't stopping this argument.

Marie didn't leave it alone. "Don't be stupid."

Spinning on the spot, Lucy scowled at Marie. "Oh, no? So my mum didn't favor my twin all our lives, then? I made that up, did I?"

"You know that's—"

"That's what, Marie? That's messed up, that's what that is. What else is messed up is that my so-called mum openly blames me for my sister's death, and my dad lets it happen. I'm the one who moved out, not her."

To my relief, Marie didn't reply.

"And then there's you." Lucy pointed at her.

"Me?"

I looked up. *"Marie?"* I said.

"You and Dylan." She turned back to the window again. "I'm second best yet again."

Marie edged closer. "That's not how it is at all. You would never be second best to me. You and Dylan don't compare."

"Save it!" Lucy snapped as I heard a car pull up outside. "My cab's here."

"Lucy, wait, don't go like this."

Lucy retrieved a large bag packed with her belongings that was waiting by the door. "I'll be back for the rest of my stuff soon."

"No, you won't."

Lucy looked back at Marie as blankly as I did.

"Leave your stuff here; this is not a forever move." She stepped into my sister's personal space. "Do you hear me? I know what you're doing, and it won't work. You won't push me away. You can come back tomorrow if it doesn't work out; I'm just asking you to give it one last try. Do it for Laura."

With that, Lucy let go of her bag, dropping it to the ground in order to hug Marie.

"Oh, Lucy," Marie said, hugging her back, "you are always number one to me. I'll never let any man come between that. D'you understand?"

I watched Lucy nod, but she didn't understand. I knew what she was thinking because I had taken her hand in mine. Well-practiced and in tune with my twin, I could tell you that what she *did* understand was that Dylan had to go.

May was always an odd month. Sometimes it was hot like the middle of summer, and other times, it felt like a cold spring day. As we sat at the traffic lights in town, wind howled about the car, huge gusts blowing dead, dirty leaves along the street as if they were walking along in a procession. Sitting next to my sister on the back seat, I watched tear after tear roll silently down her cheeks. I looked away to the foot well, unable to help her.

I didn't understand why I was still here, and as the days, then months, passed, I was growing even more frustrated. It wasn't that I wanted to leave—on the contrary. I just wanted to understand what I was meant to do there. It was as if with each passing day I had been getting wiser, though not in the true sense of the word. No, I felt wiser as in more connected, universally. I understood things like objects; I could hear the quietest of sounds and then realize everything was vibrating. The wind, the light, and even solid objects like the car we were traveling in vibrated. Solid things vibrated low, and light and wind were loud and fast like an orchestra playing for the Queen at the Royal Abbot Hall. Every last teensy weensy element had its part to play in the orchestra of life, and yet I still didn't really know mine.

Our dad was waiting outside the house for us to arrive. Behind him, the net curtain twitched, presumably our mum. This was not going to be easy. Our dad wanted nothing more than to have Lucy back home, and he looked like a big kid waiting to see his best friend at school after summer break. His cheeks were reddened by the wind, and I wondered how long he had been standing there. He rushed to open Lucy's door, practically dragging her out and into a bear hug that she quickly wiggled out from. He paid the driver and ushered her inside, where I knew she wouldn't find our mum. I knew this because the sound of the back gate closing was carried over the top of the house by the wind.

"Kathrin," our dad called out, closing the door behind them once they were inside, "Lucy's home."

Silence.

Lucy gave her best I-told-you-so smile while our dad tried to justify our mum's absence.

"Oh, she did say she needed to nip out. I'm sure she'll be back soon. Come on, let's get the kettle on."

I couldn't tell you what our mum was thinking. Her energy was so suppressive I had stopped connecting with her about three weeks earlier. She took so much of my energy I didn't have enough time with anyone else, and there were a lot of people, a lot of thoughts to pick. My dad's, Marie's, Hellen's, Kitty's—I even saw Heather and Jessie from school. A few times, I visited

Tye and Jess, and once Darren. Poor Darren—he had taken the fall for it all. His whole life had been stolen from him. I didn't touch him; I just couldn't bring myself to do it. Instead I'd sat next to him all night, pushing as much energy as I had to give, working it into a protective white ball that surrounded him in the hope that it might protect him in prison—though I'd not had the heart to go back and check.

Mum came home as twilight made the gray sky dark. Lucy was in her room, door shut with her headphones on. She couldn't hear Dad calling to her from the bottom of the stair, so I lent a hand and interfered with the music, sending crackles into her ears. It had the desired effect. After fiddling with the wire running out of her phone, she pulled it out completely. Just as she was about to reconnect it, our dad shouted again.

"Lucy, dinner's here."

Discarding the headphones on her bed, she dove for her door. "What did you say, Dad? Dinner? I'm starving."

"Mum's brought us fish and chips home."

She hesitated, but our dad nodded his head quickly and sharply to one side. Lucy understood and reluctantly descended the steep stairs.

On the kitchen table sat one large opened bag of chips and three plates of battered cod. The chair scraped over the floor when Lucy pulled it out and took a seat next to Dad and opposite Mum. Our mum pushed a can of Coke across the table to Lucy.

They ate in silence.

Afterwards, Lucy washed and our dad dried. Mum had a headache, so she left to lie down in bed.

"See?" Dad whispered as he took a wet plate off the draining board. "Wasn't so bad, was it?"

Lucy didn't reply.

"Was nice of Mum to bring us back dinner," he tried again.

"If you say so."

"Come on, Lucy, give it a chance. For me?"

She plunged her hands into the soapy water to retrieve a fork. "Sure thing, Dad," she said, placing the washed fork firmly into his hand.

Once the kitchen was clean, Lucy sat next to Dad on the sofa and watched TV. Squeezing between them, I settled in for the night. I missed moments like this the most. Normality. Not the big celebrations, not the parties we went to, just this. Being normal. Being alive. Most people would have probably wanted to see both parents enjoying a family night by the TV, but that was never our family's normal. Mum spent most nights in her room alone, while Lucy, Dad, and I watched TV. For the first time since being dead, I felt alive.

That night and the ones that followed, I whispered kind messages into my sister's ears in the hope that it would sink in and help the situation, and I did the same for our mum. It didn't help. Our mum was cordial to Lucy, and Lucy to her—when Dad was around. As the days passed, however, our mum and Lucy still ignored each other in private.

When Hellen asked Lucy how it was living back at home, she lied and told her it wasn't as bad as she thought. Hellen didn't seem to believe her, though nothing she asked Lucy could coax the reality of it out. Week by week, Lucy withdrew more and more from therapy. She didn't trust that Hellen could help her with what she needed. How could anyone? But I could—I could keep her safe. Day by day, my abilities were growing. An unexplainable feeling told me I'd understand it all soon. And once I understood, I could truly protect my sister.

★ ★ ★

May twenty-second came around fast. I lay next to Lucy on her bed as she flipped her half of the heart necklace over the top of her fingers. About three hours ago, our dad had knocked on the door, but she didn't answer. We'd heard our mum crying in the morning, followed by her normal onset of rage. All day long, she would order Dad out of their bedroom before howling as if in pain, at which he would run back in to comfort her. Lucy's eyes were fixed on the ceiling, and she didn't flinch at any of it, even when I heard our mum ask our dad, over and over again, why Lucy had to argue with me that day.

I didn't need to touch my sister to know what she was thinking or feeling. The what-ifs looped in my own thoughts as well, and I felt that stomach-cramping wrench of knowing there was nothing I could do. I thought about the dark place I'd visited, and then the white place. Nothing made sense, though something inside felt as if I already knew the answer. It was like the type of thoughts you get just before falling asleep, when they all make complete sense in the moment of near sleep, but if you open your eyes, they appear to all be a mess of random thoughts. I told myself to be patient—I needed to preserve my energy. Today, of all days, I half expected to be ripped from this world again. Yet time pushed on: 6:00 p.m., 7:00 p.m., 8:00 p.m. At 9:00 p.m., after our mum and dad had brought their shouts down to a low growl, we heard the sentence I knew must have crushed our dad's heart.

"I'm leaving." Our mum's utterly selfish words desolated all of our souls in union.

My dad tried to reason with her, and if I'd thought it would have made the slightest bit of difference, I would have helped. Truth be told, though, I'd seen—or felt—this coming ever since Lucy had come home. It's not wrong for a parent to have favorites—some people bond differently with others—but since knowing my mum in this new way, I knew it wasn't normal. Lucy shouldn't be the one in therapy; Mum should. She was selfish, and as much as it hurt, I had finally started to resent her for it. All my life, Lucy had tried to protect our family against our mum's spiteful words. She stood in front of them like bullets aimed at our dad, and for what? It pushed Lucy and our mum apart, and then our mum decided to go and leave anyway.

Squeezing my eyes tight, I tried pressing my hands over my ears to drown out Mum's voice and my dad's pathetic pleas. Lucy, on the other hand, looked numb to it all. I suppose she'd had more years coming to terms with who our mum really was.

At 10:58 p.m., the front door slammed, and the house was silent.

★ ★ ★

I stood with my back against the front door, arms stretched, pleading with Lucy not to open it, but she did, right through me.

"I told you I'm not celebrating my birthday." She eyed the large gift-wrapped box that Ben held. "You can come in, but leave that on the doorstep."

As Ben placed the box down, his eyes narrowed. He then strolled down the hall after her, and I moved in front of him. I could tell Lucy rejecting his gift had not gone how he'd hoped.

It had been five days since our mum left, and Lucy had managed to convince our dad to go to work. At times, I wasn't sure who was looking after whom, and as painful as it was, there was also something poetic in the way Lucy and our dad were now propping each other up.

"It's only a hair dryer," Ben said. "I'll unwrap it, and I'll even take it out of the box and use it first. Take it, Lucy—you said you needed a new one."

She didn't answer.

"Screw you, Ben," I hissed into his pathetic face. I was seething. *"It's our twenty-second birthday, and you're the reason for all of this. YOU!"* I screamed.

Ben took the hint and dropped the topic. I actually kind of wanted him to keep on about it. Maybe that way, he would piss Lucy off, and she would throw his disgusting self out.

Lucy opened the fridge, retrieving two cans of Diet Coke. She slid one over the table to him and then cracked hers open before slumping into the chair. "So she left us," she said.

"Sorry, I couldn't believe it when you texted me." He placed his hand on hers.

My soul flushed hot. I wanted to slam his face into the table, pull his hair out—anything to get him off my sister.

"Ouch." Ben retracted his hand.

"What?" Lucy asked.

"Just a painful itch," he said, rubbing the back of his hand. "So you're not moving back to Marie's, then?"

I stopped listening to their conversation. Ben had felt me, felt my intention on his hand. I focused and jabbed a fingernail into the back of his hand and watched as he itched it again.

Finally, I thought. I could now set my intention to touch a person so they could feel me. I felt triumphant. Not only could I move objects, I could potentially move people.

"No," Lucy eventually answered. "I can't at the moment. Dad's a right mess. But I managed to convince him to go to work today, so maybe that will help. The sad thing is, I think she will be back."

"You think?"

"I do. She used to threaten to leave all the time, but Laura always managed to calm her down. She'll be back. I told my dad this, but he's not as convinced." She took a swig of Coke.

"And you? How are you holding up?" Ben asked.

"I have my dad."

He nodded as if he understood.

"Scum, you don't know anything about how she's feeling," I hissed. *"You did this. You."*

Rubbing his hands together, he said, "It's cold in here."

Lucy stood.

"What's wrong?" he asked, rising out of his chair as well.

"I shouldn't have texted you, Ben. I'm sorry, I can't do this. It's too soon. I've got too much going on right now. It just feels wrong." She made for the front door.

Ben followed at pace. "Lucy," he called out, "wait."

On the one hand, I was pleased, though also confused at this sharp turn of events. On the other hand, though, I was more worried. Ben was unbalanced, and if Lucy made him feel worthless, it might trigger him.

At the door, she stopped and just stared at him for a moment.

"What is it, Lucy? Tell me, please."

Stealing a quick breath, she said, "You scared me the other night."

I saw all the color drain from his face and couldn't help but feel an overwhelming sense of satisfaction, though I also felt uneasy because he looked wounded.

He tried to speak. "B—but—"

"I said no, Ben."

"Lucy." He swept her hand into his. "I am so, so, so sorry—you have to believe me. I'd never do anything you didn't want me to. Please, I love you. You know that—I don't want to lose you. I need you." He kissed the palm of her hand.

I sank instantly to the floor; he had said the exact thing she craved.

She pulled her hand away slowly. "I just need some time to get my head straight."

"It's OK," he said. "Take all the time you need. I'm not going anywhere without you."

He turned to open the door, and I gave him a helping hand.

Slam.

"Oh, Ben!" Lucy cried out as the door cracked his nose.

I knew instantly something was wrong. Lucy's voice was fading. I could see her trying to stop the blood with her sleeve, but their voices were becoming muffled.

I meaningfully harmed someone. The thought shook my soul. My anger was great enough to harm another, which we are all taught from childhood is wrong. Was this it? Was I going to be ripped away from my sister forever as punishment? Trepidation made me scream. I was scared that this would be the last time

I'd see Lucy, and that I'd just sent her back into the arms of the person I was meant to be protecting her from. Now I was drifting, my soul lethargic, even peaceful. I stretched a feeble hand back toward my sister, my beautiful sister.

This couldn't be the end, could it?

CHAPTER 20

NOW–LUCY

London, present day
May (twenty-fourth birthday)

I can hear my phone ringing—I think it's my phone, anyway. The lids of my eyes are heavy from the remnants of last night. The noise stops. A moment later, I hear a beep indicating a message. The phone rings again, and I slam a lazy hand about next to me, searching out the irritation.

Found it. I fumble, pop open my eyes, close them, and reluctantly open them again. I swipe and answer.

"What?" I slur.

"You called in sick?" Sarah says. "Or are you hungover?" She actually sounds annoyed with me.

I grunt. "What's your point?"

"Where was my invite?" she asks. "Morning, Eddie," she adds, and I hear Eddie from tables and chairs reply happily to her.

With a heavy heart, I manage to reply, "Oh god, everyone is way too bright for me right now. What do you want, Sarah?"

"Er, for you to be in work with me, but more to the point, why didn't I get invited out last night?"

I wonder who she thinks I went out with, Mr. Clifton? She must have figured out that I don't talk about other friends, and surely she can't be that naïve. I consider what I should tell her. The truth? That I was sitting in on my own drinking a bottle of neat vodka and eating a bag of chips for dinner? I'm about to lose my apartment if I don't get a pay raise—that or I can go back on the streets to give another fat twat a hand job. My dead twin stopped talking to me—oh, and it's my twenty-fourth birthday today.

"Mr. Clifton came over, and we got talking." A lie it is. "Sorry I'm not in—one too many glasses of wine."

There's a pause, and I wonder if she bought it. "Clifton the weirdo neighbor?" She sniggers. "You didn't?"

"Yuck, no, Sarah. What's wrong with you? I'd never. No, he just popped over to check that the window was fixed."

"Is it?"

"Yep, management replaced it a few days ago," I say a little easier now that the subject has changed. My splitting headache is no different.

I throw back the duvet with my free arm and try to heave myself out of bed. This is surprisingly difficult when you're hungover and on the phone and when your bed doesn't have a bedframe. I place Sarah on loudspeaker before running the cold tap in the kitchen and gulping back water. Sarah is droning on about the teambuilding event this weekend, which I normally wouldn't give two hoots about. However, this event is going to be different. This event is going to get me promoted.

"You're coming this weekend, aren't you?" Sarah inquires.

Leaving the kitchen, I fall back onto my bed, nausea looming. "Of course."

"Good. It's going to be so much fun."

"If you say so," I breathe.

"Come on, Laura, you know you'll enjoy it once you're there."

As sweet as Sarah is, there's only so much of her unwavering enthusiasm I can take when hungover.

"Good chat, Sarah. Enjoy work, and I'll see you Sunday. Pick me up?" I wait for her agreement.

"Sunday?" she asks. "You're not coming into work tomorrow?"

I roll my eyes in bewilderment. "If I come in tomorrow, they will know I wasn't sick."

"Ohh, I see. Smart," she says. "OK, see ya Sunday, 8:30 a.m. I'll beep when I'm outside."

I end the call.

Rolling over, I pull my knees into the fetal position and hug them tight. The dull ache in the pit of my stomach is joined by a wave of sadness that flutters about in my chest. I wait, hoping and praying it eases off soon. Sometimes, the sadness stays with me all day, but if this cramping pain in the stomach lets up a bit, then I'll be able to get up and function—even with a stinking hangover. Another wave hits me, and I brace for the onslaught of thoughts, the whys and ifs that have bullied me ever since that day. Tears warm my eyes. I never thought she would drive after me. There is a fresh cramp and a dull ache from my heart.

I try to think about Hellen's advice from when I was in this place before, yet I can't. I think I remember something about projection or guilt; I just don't know what to do with it. After removing the Post-it Notes, I've not had any dreams, and I thought I would. I replaced some of the more important Post-it Notes, but nothing has fallen. Now I'm wondering if I blew my chance to communicate with the other side, and last night I came to the conclusion that I'm just not worthy of love. Yet another person has left me. First Laura, then Mum, Marie, everyone—they all leave sooner or later.

The sadness doesn't wear off, and by midday Saturday, I wonder if I'll be able to pull off the teambuilding event the way I've planned.

★ ★ ★

The teambuilding event is a poorly-organized scavenger hunt around Wimbledon Village, one which I have no intention of participating in. There's really no need because Sarah is happily finding and working all the clues out for both of us. As we approach what must be the final clue, I see Malik and Eddie high-fiving each other.

"Too late, girls," Malik says, flapping an envelope about in front of us with vehemence.

I laugh, heading past him and toward the Dog & Fox pub garden, where I can see Simon chatting with an elderly lady who I'm sure works in the human resource department.

"Runner up, Laura? That's unlike you," Simon jokes.

"What can I say?" I hold my hands up. "I'm a solo kind of gal; others slow me down."

Sarah pushes my shoulder. "Hey." She frowns at me before heading inside.

I'm about to follow when Simon moves toward me. "*Hands solo*, you mean?" he breathes in my ear.

A whiff of beer floods my nose, but I know what I have to do. The groundwork I've laid has been leading up to this day, and there's no going back now. I wink, then give him a quick alluring smile.

Inside, Sarah is waiting for me at the bar, and she doesn't look amused.

"What was that all about?" she grumbles.

I order a vodka Red Bull, and then I turn to face her. I consider telling her what I'm up to—after all, my last real communication with my sister was about me trusting Sarah. That's if Laura is real. Sarah's eyes have widened, and I wonder how long it will be before she puts her hands on her hips the way she always does when she's pissed at Dan—or me. One, two, three, four, and there it is. Hands on hips.

I laugh.

"What's funny?"

"You," I say. "You're funny when you're mad."

"Whatever, Laura. You know you're a bitch sometimes."

"I've been told that once or twice."

"Why did you say I slowed you down? I did all the work, and then you make out I'm the issue. What are you playing at?"

"OK," I say, grabbing my drink with one hand and Sarah's arm with the other. "I'm going to tell you something." I walk her over to the fireplace away from the others. "Listen, I'm struggling with my rent, have been for a few months now." The warmth of the fire is hot on the side of my leg.

"Laura, I had no idea."

"It's fine; just shut up and listen. I have a plan." I shift closer to her, angling my mouth to her ear. "You gave me the idea."

"Me?"

"Sarah, shh! Listen, I need to get this out before the others get here. I got the idea when you pointed out that Simon likes me." I continue. "Turns out you were right, so I thought I'd play on that, use it to get me an early promotion." She pulls away and stares at me. I'm unsure if I should have said anything. "Sarah, you can't screw this up for me. Oh shit, I shouldn't have told you."

"No, no, it's fine. I'm just shocked—you never tell me anything, that's all."

The joy in her face at the fact that I've confided in her actually warms my soul.

"What's the plan, then?" she asks. "How are you going to do this? Promotions aren't till the end of the year."

We stop talking as Becky from accounts walks past.

"Not entirely sure yet," I admit, "but I think he thinks I'm going to give him a happy ending, if you get my drift?"

She screws up her face. "Laura, no, you're not going to—?"

"What choice do I have?"

"Hey, where are the toilets?" some guy interrupts.

I point. "That way."

"Can't you get a roomie?" Sarah offers.

"In a studio apartment?" I say.

"Good point." She nods.

I'm glad she isn't pushing the matter because I'm not about to tell her what I did to Marie, my last roomie. She would never be my friend, that's for sure, and I can't risk losing her as well.

"Look, Sarah, I'm telling you this because you're my friend." I register the delight in her eyes. "I don't need you to do anything, OK? Just let me deal with this my way."

"Sure thing," she whispers. "Just be careful."

"Be careful about what?" Simon appears out of nowhere.

I look at Sarah, and I'm sure she has just wet herself a little. I silently will her to hold it together.

"Sarah knows how cray-cray I get on vodka," I say and hold up my glass. I stare furiously at Sarah, trying to urge her to stop nodding her head like a pigeon on acid.

"Excuse me," she says after a moment, her words all in a rush. "Need to use the loo."

Thank god for that, I think, and turn to Simon, who is looking slightly less obnoxious in his everyday clothes. Dressing in jeans and a white long-sleeved sweater makes him look more like a normal human being than a boss I blackmailed and am about to exploit, if you can call it that—maybe he thinks he is exploiting me. Not that I particularly care. After all, he didn't care about me that night in the alley. There's only one person I need to focus on in life, and that's me.

I fish about in my brain for something work-related to say, yet drew a blank.

"How are you getting to the park?" he asks. "The coach?"

He is talking about the second half of the teambuilding day, the part where he thinks we are going to hook up. And he is correct—however, this hook-up comes with strings now.

"Looks that way," I answer, taking a few steps away from the raging fire. "Why do they have the fire on? It's like a midsummer's day out there."

He shrugs and moves next to me. "We could always sneak off, make our own way there."

I pretend to give his offer careful consideration before declining.

"Why?" he asks.

"Oh, come on, nothing is ever that easy with me, Simon—you know that," I turn my back to him.

He steps directly behind me, his belly against my back. I think he is about to say something when he walks away. I breathe a sigh of relief, though I'm not sure if I've done enough.

Sarah reappears. "Where's he gone?" she asks.

I nod at the bar. "Right where I need him to stay." He lifts a beer and takes a swig, and I smile.

"Why?"

I shake my head. "Come on—let's get out of here. I need a cigarette."

The coach that takes us a few miles up the road to the common is noisy with well-oiled staff members conversing joyously. I sit with Sarah and Malik, the only people I care to socialize with. Of course, I laugh and insult them both in my normal manner, keeping up appearances and all. When we arrive, the swarms of alcohol-intoxicated employees exit the coach with Sarah and me close behind them. The hydraulic doors close, and I examine my surroundings. There's a large blue-and-white-striped tent to the far right with clouds of smoke coming from a grill. At the table next to that, Simon seems to be making the most of what looks like a free makeshift bar.

"Come on, then—let's go play." Sarah tugs at my arm.

I don't move.

"Laura, come on, will you? You're here now, so just bloody enjoy yourself. Look, there's a giant Connect Four over there."

Reluctantly, I follow.

As we near the large plastic game, Sarah turns to me. "I know you said I'm to stay out of this, but Laura, you're missing a trick."

I eye her suspiciously.

She takes a small glance over my shoulder toward the bar table. "He is watching you—don't look!" She stops me from turning around. "Just give him something to look at. You're wearing a short skirt, so stretch high to put the coins in the slot, and bend low to pick them up. Get it?" She winks.

I nod slowly. "So you don't think I'm wrong for doing this, then?" I reach up high with a coin.

"If I'm honest, I wouldn't do it. But I have a boyfriend, and my rent isn't late."

A genuine smile fills my face. "Thank you," I say, feeling a whole lot better about the situation.

After taking Sarah's advice and seeing the desired effects on Simon's face, I start to suss out where and when this could happen.

"I can't leave with him—it needs to happen here, because the threat of rape charges will be far more powerful if I haven't gone off willingly first," I say, lying next to Sarah on the grass. The sky has now blackened and is lit by the full moon above. "I need to lure him to somewhere we won't be seen, and where he feels comfortable enough to let me seduce him." She giggles, and I jab her side in jest. "And then, afterwards, if he doesn't agree to my demands, I land him with the threat of rape charges. Promote me by next month or else. But I'm hoping it won't come to that, obviously." I take a drag from my cigarette. "The best situation for all of us," I continue, "is if he sees this for what it is—a working relationship. We have fun together occasionally, and I get something I want as well. Promotion now, the odd extra weekend off here and there—"

"And for me," Sarah adds.

"And for you." I laugh. "And maybe a bigger bonus at Christmas—that sort of thing, you know?"

Sarah sits up and looks down at me. "You like him, don't you?"

"What? No." I sit bolt upright.

"You do—you just don't want to admit it. Look, it's OK, you shouldn't be embarrassed. Is it because he's fat?"

I watch the whites of her eyes sparkle at me in the dark. She is being deadly serious. Now it makes sense why she is so willing to help. She thinks I actually like him.

"Quick, look." She points.

Simon is heading away toward the dark part of the common where the shrubs and brambles are. He looks back over his shoulder and then continues into the shadows.

"D'you think he's going for a piss, or does he want me to follow?" I ask, my heart thudding about in my chest.

"Go, find out. Who cares? Go get your man." She pushes me to my feet.

I walk fast around the outside, hoping to stay out of sight from others. I glance back at Sarah, but she's too far away for me to make out any features in the dark. I continue in the direction I saw Simon going. My chest is tight, and my thoughts are racing.

You can do this, you can do this, I repeat like a mantra. What if he's figured out it's a setup? Or worse, what if he isn't frightened by my threats and does what he wants with me anyway? *You can do this,* I repeat. Then quickly, and without warning, an arm reaches out and pulls me behind a bush.

CHAPTER 21

NOW & THEN–LAURA

The Lake of Reflection

I didn't know what was happening. All I knew was Lucy was getting further away. I couldn't leave her, not now, not knowing what Ben was capable of. And then I was here, here where it all finally made sense, where consciousness has meaning and life becomes complex beyond the realm of believable.

Shivering, I sat on the edge of a lake that stretched as far as the eye could see, my knees tucked close to my chest and gripped by my arms. The ground I was sitting on looked like black marble and felt just as cold. The lake itself was something that resembled liquid mercury—not that I'd ever seen a lake of liquid mercury, but that was my best description of my surroundings. Other than a gentle glow of purple which bounced off the lake, everything was dark. Feeling stiff as I stood, I silently asked myself how long I had been sitting there.

"A little under a human year," a voice said.

I thrashed my body around, looking for the owner. "Who said that?"

I waited for a reply, and when nothing came, I felt a new sensation—fear mixed with confusion. Over the lake was an angelic horizon of purples and blues that merged with the reflections, but behind me and to either side was nothing.

From my left, I finally saw a figure walking out of the blackness in the distance. It was the most beautiful sight I could ever have hoped to see.

"Lulu," I shouted.

Her long hair floated about her shoulders effortlessly. She arrived in front of me, yet there was no long-lost embrace, so I reached out and hugged her tight. She didn't respond.

"Lucy, what are you doing here?" I asked, releasing her and stepping back.

Then she laughed. This was not my sister.

"Who are you?" I snapped.

"Hello, Laura. I'm you."

"Me?"

"I like meeting identical twins; you don't have such a shocked reaction when looking back at yourself. Living with someone who looks just like you would be good preparation for this moment." She fluffed my long hair with her hands, but I retracted quickly. "Let's take a walk."

At first, I didn't speak. The shock of this person—this *thing*—not being my twin disabled me. Eventually, I said, "Tell me, who are you? And walk where?" I looked into the abyss of blackness.

The other me took a look to her right, behind us, over my shoulder, and finally over the lake. "We can walk wherever you like. What is it that you can see, Laura?"

"A lake of sorts," I said.

She gave a knowing nod. "The lake of reflection, I see. Is that it? You can't see anything else?"

"Why? What is all this? I need to get back to my sister."

The other me smiled at myself kindly, yet not the way Lucy or I would smile—it was a little unsettling.

"Laura, you must go on, or you'll get stuck by the lake of reflection." She placed a warm hand on my shoulder.

"I'm going to level with you," I said. "I have no idea what you're talking about. A moment ago, I was in my house protecting my sister, and then I was pulled here. I know I shouldn't have gotten angry, and if you send me back, I promise it won't happen again. I just need to find a way to connect with my sister. She's in danger. Please, you have to help me—please."

"You're stuck. It happens; some take longer to cross over than others. You have been here twice before."

Remembering the place of nothingness and then the white place I'd visited, I opened my mouth to speak, but she continued over me.

"My name is Astrier. Look." She pointed across the lake. "Do you see?"

"See what?" My gaze followed her finger.

"The answer to everything."

Images shimmered on the silver water, black and white projections from the horizon moving over the lake like a film on canvas. It was a film of my life, memories through my own eyes.

"What is that?" I asked.

"Just watch."

The film didn't appear to run in chronological order—it wasn't playing out from birth to now. Instead, I saw a moment from my teens followed immediately by what I could only imagine was me in a crib. I saw my mum's smiling face and my dad's lips blowing raspberries at me, and then they turned and laughed at each other, presumably at my reaction. Lucy was there in almost all my memories, holding me tight in bed at night when I was scared, braiding my hair as we stood in line at the school canteen—it's as if I could feel the tug from her hand as she crossed the hair. My hand automatically rose, and my fingers fumbled over a neat plait.

"Is this my life? Am I reflecting on my life?"

"Keep watching," Astrier said, and I noticed that she too was wearing a plait in her hair.

The images sped up, and by all accounts, I shouldn't have been able to see them—they were going that fast. Yet somehow I could, and I could feel them, too. The happiness of running along the beach the day we moved to Looe. Sandy water splashing at my calves and Mum calling for us to come back, not to go too far. Then my first day at school. After that, a feeling followed that I could only describe as serene. Wet yet warm, trapped yet free. There were no images, but then, why would there be? I'd realized where I was—I was in my mum's womb, squashed against Lucy with her bony knee pressing against my side. And then I froze. I saw an image of myself looking across a silver lake, watching myself looking across a silver lake.

"What?" I whispered, not taking my eyes off the lake.

"Keep watching."

There was a flash, and I saw images I'd not seen before. These were not my memories, yet I felt like they were. Lucy was shouting at Dad, and he was telling her not to quit counseling. His face was gaunt and browbeaten, and hers was full of rage. Then there were flashes of Lucy being fired from what looked like a job with an estate agent. The man was being very polite, explaining that her attendance was not in line with the company's minimum standard. Lucy was not gracious in her response. There was a similar image from a hairdresser. I couldn't hear what the woman said to her, but I saw Lucy throw down a broom to the salon floor. Then a door slammed, and Lucy stormed across a used car sales lot screaming back over her shoulder at somebody to stick the job.

I turned to the other me. "When did this happen?"

"The car lot incident was last week," she said plainly.

"Last week? I was with her last week—she didn't have a job."

"Look." She pointed back at the lake.

My dad called after Lucy as she stormed out of the house and into Ben's car. They embraced, and my heart gave a silent shudder, reminding me just what was at stake. Then, as if that heartbreaking shudder had just unlocked something, I got it. I understood it all.

"Laura, do you understand?"

"I think I do. Or maybe I feel as if I did for a split second. Now it's gone, like a dream that makes sense when you're asleep then chaos when you wake. Are you me?" I shook my head, already disagreeing with my own question. "No, you're not, but you look like me."

"I've already told you. I am Astrier. You are just seeing me as you—it helps with the understanding process. This is what you are doing here, getting ready for your next destiny."

"Astrier." I said her name as if trying to decode the meaning. "Are you God?" I laughed politely, not wanting to offend.

"Let's just say I am a representative of the universe."

"An angel?"

She smiled back, and it certainly was angelic. "You see, Laura, we are all energy, and you choose whether you want to live as a being or with us on the astral plain. The complication with becoming a being is the transition."

I nod slowly.

Astrier continued. "In transition, you forget us. There are rules on the earthly plane. You cannot travel very fast, for one, and everything has to happen in a set order. But you see, that is just a perception, a rule that beings thought up to help them understand life. Do you understand?"

"Not really, no," I said honestly.

Astrier smiled patiently. "Twenty-two years ago, you chose your mum, and unfortunately for you came the complete loss of astral understanding of the beautiful truth. We are all connected to everything." She stretched her arms wide. "If you want something to happen, then call it into existence, and it will be. It has to be—that's the law. We strive to give what is desired, be it positive or negative."

"But I didn't desire to die."

"No." Astrier hung her head.

"Then why did you kill me?"

"I didn't. You did."

"No—no, I didn't. You say we call our fate into existence, but I didn't ask to die."

"No, but the negative energy that was in your life from other beings was attracting it."

"Why me?"

"To learn," she said.

"Learn? And where are all our loved ones?" I looked about, searching for others, for Grandma Betty.

Astrier laughed animatedly at me. "My dear Laura, she is here." She placed a hand over my chest. "We all are. We can talk to each other anytime, no matter where you are. If Grandma Betty is now a cat, tree, or part of a planet, she can still talk to you. Just let her in. All it takes is one to connect, and the other has no option but to reply, though it might be weak. Try it. Believe it, then call for her."

I wondered what I had to lose. After all, I was dead, so why wouldn't everything Astrier was saying be true? I snatched a breath from the space about me and into my chest.

"Grandma Betty," I called, "are you there?" Within seconds, I felt a light and wonderfully warm feeling of love. There were no words, but I knew it was her. "Where is she?" I asked. "What is she? Can I see her?"

"There is plenty of time for that after you have reflected," Astrier replied. "It is important—you need to choose."

"Choose?"

"Once your reflection is over, it is time for you to move on to your next destiny. Use what you have learned in this life to better your next. I do not tell you what to be and where to go; you do that. You could be a fish, or maybe you'd like to form part of a planet or star. It's your choice."

"I'm not sure if I fully understand yet," I confessed. "When you talk, it makes sense, yet when I think about it, it doesn't."

"That's what reflection is for. You must first learn to receive love before you can share love. Make profound connections until every last particle radiates positivity throughout the universe, be it as a human, a dust mite, a plant, or part of a planet. No regret—only life lessons. Love thy neighbor, Laura."

I still wasn't one hundred percent confident that I understood. However, I was beginning to believe she was talking about reincarnation in some obscure way.

"So now what?"

Astrier pointed toward the lake. "Stay here, and you'll see. Then you must decide."

"Decide? I don't want to decide, though. I want to be wherever Lucy is."

"Oh, Laura." Her laugh was jovial. "Did you not hear me? You are connected forever. Now stay here and reflect."

I didn't want to reflect. Was that really the only option I had?

As if reading my thoughts, Astrier said, "I can see you are still going to jump."

"I don't follow," I replied. "Jump where?"

"Laura, there is really no need. Your sister must learn life lessons herself; this is the easiest way."

"I don't get that bit," I said, slightly more aggressively than I had meant.

"Grandma Betty could hear and see you because she is connected to you, a part of the universe, as are we. When living beings meet people, whether family or others, you entangle. You are a reflection of the people you meet, and you will go on making connections. It's just difficult in the earthly realm because of the funny laws you have. You forget the many times you have reflected before. If you didn't, then you might not be so fast to stomp on the poor spiders in your homes." She gave a little laugh and then said, "But you're still going to jump.

I just hope with this knowledge you can remember it once you jump back."

"Back where, to Lucy?"

And then she was gone.

I thought and thought. If I wanted to stay here, in the space beyond the earthly realm like before, then I could? No, that was never an option. I had to go. Lucy was connecting with me. I'd felt it, and I wasn't going to leave her now.

"Lucy?" I called out.

"I'm sorry, Astrier," I called out to the abyss.

Looking down at the silver lake, I knew how to get back. With that, I jumped into the moving pictures.

CHAPTER 22

THEN–LAURA

Cornwall, three years ago
April (Easter, eleven months later)

Lucy slipped between her sheets. It was nighttime, and I was in her room at our house. I moved to be close to her. Moments before, I had slammed the door on Ben's nose, and now it was nighttime? I stood watching her for a moment before moving to sit at the foot of her bed, perplexed about the time that seemed to be missing.

Odd dreamlike feelings of a memory swelled in my mind—a lake. Silver and purple. I stood and walked in small circles at the foot of Lucy's bed, trying to help myself think better. Then I froze. I'd caught sight of myself in my sister's mirror. I yelped and then stepped closer. Looking back at me was not me, just a cloud of smoke. Where had I gone? Rotating my hands, I looked downward and jumped in shock again when I saw four fingers and a thumb on each hand, all intact. I could see my feet and legs poking out from my floral dress, my chest, everything—I could see me.

Why was I just a mist of air in my reflection? What had happened? Gradually, bit by bit, fragments started to reconnect in my mind. I grasped my head as I saw visions of a silver lake again, and then came memories of a conversation that I couldn't quite hold onto.

Suddenly, I was certain that I'd been there before, wherever "there" was, and breathed a sigh of relief that I'd come back again. However, a niggling feeling that this was the last time seemed to linger, and something in my instincts told me that next time it took me, I'd not be returning.

"One last chance," I said for no good reason. *Odd.* I wondered how long I'd been away this time. The times before had been months.

"Night, Lucy," my dad called through the door, disrupting my thoughts.

"Night, Dad," Lucy called back, and I saw the light that shone through the bottom of the door turn off.

I thought about searching the house for evidence of the date on a newspaper or a calendar somewhere, but I didn't. Instead, I gave in to an overwhelming desire to just lie down next to my sister and hold her tight—everything else could wait.

★   ★   ★

The next morning, as Lucy was listening to music, there was a noise from downstairs. I heard my dad say, "Sure, just go on up, Marie. See you soon."

"Thanks, Robert. Where you off to?" came her reply.

"Church, of course. Happy Easter."

The front door was shut in its normal loud manner, and then the sound of feet on the stairs told me Marie was on her way up.

There was a knock, but Lucy couldn't hear over the music playing out of her headphones, so I opened the door.

"Hey," Marie chimed as the door slowly opened.

For a split second, I forgot. For a second, I felt like I was alive again and greeting my best friend as I used to. Then her brow furrowed and she looked past me, as if checking over my shoulder. What do they call it? Ghosting? My best friend had just ghosted a ghost without even knowing it.

Way to go, Marie, I thought.

"Hey, girl." She pulled an earbud from Lucy's ear.

Lucy jumped a good two inches off the bed. "What? How did you get in?"

"Awe, nice to see you too, bestie … your dad let me in. Sorry, I *did* knock, and the door swung—"

"Whatever, sit." Lucy patted the bed next to her, just like she used to do for me.

I felt a small tingle of longing, and then it hit me. I had just opened a door without any effort at all—I'd just done it; I didn't even know how.

Maybe things will be easier this time, I thought, looking about the room for something meaningful to move, something that would send a clear message. My eyes fell over the open closet. It was a mess as normal, shoes thrown on top of each other, garments half on hangers. I turned to the window, but there was nothing on the window ledge—only mold from condensation. There was nothing anywhere, I realized. No pictures, not even of me. Nothing. Then I saw my old belt buckle on the floor, poking out from the closet. I pulled at it, yet my hand moved effortlessly through the brace buckle. I tried again and again, but it was no good—I couldn't move it. Deflated, I sunk to my knees.

"It's chilly in here." Marie pulled her sweater tighter.

"I know, this damn house is old and falling apart." Lucy laughed. "But it won't matter soon, not when I'm back living with you."

Marie's face morphed into a new expression. "About that …" she said.

"What?" Lucy's tone was sharp. "Oh, don't tell me. Dylan is moving in, and he doesn't want me there? God, I knew he would get between us." Lucy was now on her feet, marching up and down, narrowly missing me with each length of the room. "I told you—I told you something like this would happen."

"Lucy, will you stop this?"

"Stop what? He's pushing me out."

"No one is pushing you out, Lucy."

"Then why can't I live back with you then?" Lucy crashed back onto the bed.

Marie took a breath. "Because we might be—no, we *are*—going traveling."

Lucy didn't react. She just sat there and looked at her feet.

"Thailand," Marie continued.

"When?"

"Next month."

"When?"

"The twenty-fifth."

There was a brief pause. "Three days after my birthday. You know how down I get during May. Happy birthday to me, hey? Boy, was I born on an unlucky day."

"No, Lucy, that's not fair."

"Isn't it? Hang on, let me recap. The day after my twentieth birthday, my sister dies; on my twenty-first, my mum leaves; and now, on my twenty-second, my best friend will leave me too. Great."

They continued their bickering, but I was up on my feet, looking about the room for something to clarify what I'd heard. Twenty-second birthday—had I heard correctly? Nearly a year had passed, and I still didn't remember where I was.

"It's only for six months, maybe even three if we run out of money," Marie was saying. "I've wanted to do this for so long, and I had the money last year but couldn't go—not with all you were going through."

"But you can go now because … ?" Lucy walked over to the window and looked out.

"Because if I don't go now, I might not get another chance. I can't keep putting it off. I'm really sorry the dates are all messed up, but that's the only time Dylan can go. His work agreed to a sabbatical. Lucy, I'm truly sorry. I've been in bits trying to figure out a way to tell you."

"Well you've told me now, so just go," she said, not turning to face her.

"Lucy—"

"It's OK, Marie, really—just leave me. I want to be on my own."

Marie stood up. For a second, I thought she was going to move over to Lucy, and I willed her to do so, to hug her for me and tell her that it was all OK, that I was never going to walk out on her. But she didn't. Instead, she hung her head and left. It wouldn't have mattered what month Marie left; the month of May just gave Lucy an argument to hang on to. In my sister's mind, Marie was leaving her, and that was that.

This was bad. I heard the front door open and close. Standing next to my sister at the window, I watched Marie wave up at Lucy, and I read her thoughts to call our dad. She was going to tell him what had just happened and ask him to come home fast. I stepped slightly off balance at the revelation of the newest addition to my paranormal abilities. Then Marie got into her car and drove off.

Lucy's eyes ever-so-slowly filled with tears, and with a blink, they fell, and so did my sister's world. I hovered inches from the ceiling and watched helplessly as she violently destroyed her room. Below me, she ripped at her bedsheets, screaming at them to die. Shoes from the closest got flung about the room and into the small flat TV with a crack, yet even that didn't stop her rage. I wanted so desperately to sooth her, to wipe her tears away or call for our dad to come home.

After all her clothes were off the hangers and at the foot of her closet, she fell to her knees in the very spot I had fallen earlier. She was sobbing, and I thought her rage had passed. I was wrong. Instead, Lucy clenched her fists tight, so tight I could see the whites of her knuckles. She began to punch the side of her own head over and over and over again.

"I hate you—I hate you," she screamed.

She was talking to herself. In a memory string, I'd seen her do this once before: an hour before she slit her own wrists.

"Stop, Lucy, please stop," I shouted hopelessly from in front of her. *"STOP!"* I grabbed her fist.

She was still. My hand rested half on, half inside her fist, inches away from the side of her head, yet I didn't feel anything. I didn't connect or gain any memories from this touch. Retracting my hand from hers, I watched her collapse into a heap on the floor and sob. Stepping back, I looked again at my sister and realized there were no tiny chains about her. Thinking about it, I'd not seen them on Marie this morning or my dad the night before either.

Why? I asked myself. *Why am I transparent in my reflection, and why have the memory chains disappeared?* I waited for an answer, but nothing came, no voice or feeling. I was addled. I heard the front door and hurried footsteps on the stairs and knew it was Dad.

"Lucy?" Our dad barged through the door, gathering her up into his arms.

I looked on as Lucy's arms flailed. She screamed for him to let her go, kicking the floor with her heels, but Dad just gripped her tighter and tighter, ignoring the blows to his face that came from her frantic hands.

"Shh, honey, shh—I'm here, I'm here," he whispered through his own pain.

When she was exhausted and still, they sobbed together uncontrollably, physically close and yet worlds apart—their lives demolished by heartache.

"I can't let her go, Dad. I can't."

"She's not leaving you, honey. She'll be back."

"No—no, she won't. It won't be the same. Nothing stays the same. I won't let it happen, I won't." Her eyes were red, and as raw as the promise she spoke.

★   ★   ★

May

The weeks that followed were a learning curve, thanks to the past year that I'd missed. Presumably, it was because I had been at the silver lake—an unfamiliar place that had now become poignant in my mind. For some reason that I couldn't comprehend at the time, during the first few weeks of May, I also developed memories of the year on Earth that I'd missed. I focused on staying close to my sister and navigating my new form, which had taken on somewhat of a faded appearance along with a slightly annoying difference: my whole being seemed to trail. If I raised my hand, it left a trail from one point to the next. What really annoyed me about the trails was that I could feel them. When I moved, it was no longer effortless. My mind would be where I'd wanted to go, but the rest of me trailed behind like a slow, petulant dog. It was disconcerting, to say the least, yet I learned to work with it. I just wished I knew what had changed, why things were so difficult. Moving used to come so easy.

Hurt and angry with Marie, Lucy stayed away. I knew my sister, so I knew this must have been extremely difficult for her. I couldn't tell you exactly how she felt about it, though, because her strings were gone, so I had nothing to touch. I hugged her a few times, hoping to feel her, maybe even to take away some of her pain, but I got nothing, zero, nada, zilch. I was frustrated, so I followed and observed.

Occasionally, I was able to move objects, but Lucy was never there to see. I'd pushed Dad's newspaper off the table, but when I tried to pull it out of his hands one morning, nothing happened, not even a light flutter of paper. I'd moved past the table in the hallway and knocked the phone to the floor, but when Lucy came to pick up the mess, I wasn't able to do it again. Frustrated, I moved through the house late at night when Dad and Lucy slept, drifting in and out of rooms trying to practice. Whenever I was about ready to give up, I did it. Standing looking at our old fridge, I wondered if Dad still kept a bar of Cadbury chocolate in the door like he always did, hidden by the red-topped skim milk that Mum drank and no one liked. Without a second thought, I extended my hand and *pop*—the door opened. There was no milk, but there was a bar of unwrapped Cadbury's chocolate all on its own resting against the green-topped semi-skim milk. I closed the fridge, and since then, I'd not been able to move anything. Like I had realized earlier, this time, everything was getting difficult, and I had an unwavering feeling that I wasn't meant to be there anymore. With the strings gone, my abilities, both new and old, came and went with no rhyme or reason. It wasn't fair, but it wasn't going to stop me either.

Lucy spent most of her days with Ben. It wasn't because she needed him, though—she needed Marie. I'd sat in on enough of her therapy sessions to know that Lucy did not crave a man's love. Our dad had showered her in that. No, Lucy craved a woman's love, a woman that would not leave her. You see, I had come to terms with who I was and that I was dead, but my sister had not. Worse, since I had left, so had every other pinnacle woman in her life.

The immediate danger of Ben hurting my sister had subsided, but I still wanted him out of her life. Ben doted on Lucy, and after walking in on them making love, I saw how gentle he was with her. I knew about the monster inside him, though, and knew she was still not safe. The day would come when she would reject him, I was sure. She didn't love him the way he did her, and therein lay the real danger.

"Why not?" Lucy asked irritably into her mobile phone, handing the lady behind the counter a ten-pound note. "I thought we agreed on tonight." She took her change and the bottle of wine and walked back outside.

I hovered above the pavement in front of Tesco Express and listened to Lucy arguing with Marie. This time, however, even I thought it was justified. Marie had agreed to meet with her and was backpedaling because Dylan had messed up their second week's accommodation.

"Well, then let him sort it out—why do you have to be there with him?" Lucy said. "Fuck, it's my birthday tomorrow. Just say it, Marie—you don't want to hang out. I get it." Lucy ended the call before Marie had a chance to reply.

I watched Lucy walk aimlessly through the town, occasionally slipping my hand into hers and pretending she knew I was there. Maybe she did—who knows? Eventually, when the night had cloaked the sky, Lucy walked into Dad's old allotment garden. The familiar smells of freshly turned soil, newly cut grass, and compost mounds tingled in my senses. When we were kids, Dad would take us there every Sunday after church, and Lucy and I would play in the shed with old upside-down flower pots and discarded runner beans, making pots into houses and turning runner beans into people by drawing faces on them. But we'd not been there for years because the allotment didn't belong to our dad anymore.

We must have been about nine or ten when we were inside the dirty old shed one Sunday. I remember screaming and running outside because Lucy had moved a flower pot, and a spider had scuttled out. I saw our mum storming toward Dad's patch, ignoring the neighboring gardeners who said hello as she went.

"Here." She held out a clear plastic bag to Dad.

Lucy had followed me out and was standing next to me. I could see what looked like a jumbled-up Sunday dinner squished together in the bag. My dad took the dangling bag dubiously.

"Every week it's the same," she said. "Well, Robert, if you can't be bothered to come home on time, then you can bloody well eat it here." She turned to us, and we jumped. "Girls, with me—now."

After that, we stopped going, and I soon overheard Dad arranging for Mike next door to take over the plot in his name.

Jimmying the window, Lucy managed to crack it open slightly. Then, after a quick scout, she found a spade and used it to wrench the window open the rest of the way, wide enough for her to squeeze in. She dropped the bag holding the wine lightly onto the floor and hitched herself up and in. The shed was dark inside, and it took a while for her to remember and find the old battery-powered light that Dad had installed on the back of the door. It didn't give off a great deal of light—just enough of a dull yellow glow to see by. Dusty shelves were coated with soil fallen from plant pots. The earthy smell brought back happy memories, and I looked about desperately to see if there was anything left of our childhood games—a flower pot, maybe, one with windows and a door drawn on it—but there wasn't.

I heard a thud and spun to see Lucy had dropped to the floor. She crossed her legs and opened the bottle of wine, taking a long swig. Then she reached for her phone. I read over her shoulder as she read a text from Marie.

YOU'RE RIGHT, I'M SORRY.
IT WAS WRONG OF ME.

Marie sent another text a moment later:

WHERE ARE YOU?
I'LL COME MEET YOU NOW?
Mx

MY DAD'S ALLOTMENT.

DIDN'T KNOW YOUR DAD
HAD AN ALLOTMENT.
Mx

HE SOLD IT TO OUR NEIGHBOR.
COME AND MEET ME, I HAVE WINE.
NEAR ST. MARTIN'S CHURCH.

EAST LOOE?
Mx

YES.

I KNOW THE ONE.
OK, I'LL GET AN UBER.
SEE YOU IN A BIT.
Mx

Feeling better now that Marie had apologized and was on her way, I settled down next to Lucy. Ben had texted a few times, but she ignored him. She was thinking hard about something; I just wished I could get inside her head.

"What are you thinking, sis? I asked. *Talk to me. Say it out loud."*

Forty-five minutes later, I was not feeling so good about this situation. Lucy had all but finished the bottle of wine and had been telling me—well, at least the watering jug she'd been talking to the whole time—but anyway, she had told me her entirely ludicrous plan, a plan that could ruin lives. I had to find a way to stop her, and ideally before Marie got there.

CHAPTER 23

NOW–LUCY

London, present day
April (eleven months later)

Exiting the ladies' toilets, I see Sarah standing at the bar with Simon.

She's early, I think. We've been at the bar by the store since five o'clock when the managers' meeting ended. Sarah was supposed to join me at seven. I check my watch—five past seven. Time has gotten away from me. Smiling brightly, I proceed naturally toward them.

"Hello, Sarah." I greet her with my normal warm smile and then air kiss either side of her face.

From behind her back, Simon raises his brow at me in a sarcastic way that annoys me. "I'll leave you both to it," he says. "Nice bumping into you …"

"Sarah," I help.

"Sarah, yes. See you both soon. Good, right, bye, then." After an awkward wave, he leaves.

"Is he for real?" Sarah asks. "He forgot my name. How long have I worked there? What a twat."

I can't help but laugh at her reaction. "He knows who you are," I say. "It's just a nervous thing. Don't take it personally." I pick up my glass of wine. "Take him out of his suit and work environment, and he is powerless. It's kind of pathetic, really."

She fumbles, trying to sit on the stool next to me, and I laugh. "Having trouble there, Sarah?"

"Bloody stools. Why make them this high? Anyway," she says, eventually gaining the appropriate bottom purchase, "how are things going with you two?"

"Going?" My head drops to one side. "We are fucking, not dating."

"You've been 'fucking' for a long time," she says. "Nearly a year, isn't it?"

"Needs must," I retort and try to change the subject. "How's Dan's new role at work going?"

"Well, he still stays out all night with the boys, if that's what you mean." She sighs. "But isn't that what most twenty-four-year-old men do?"

"I wouldn't know," I say simply, and if I'm honest, a little enviously.

I hanker for a normal relationship like Sarah and Dan. There's a small silence before Sarah shatters it.

"So a little birdy told me it's your birthday next month. The big two-five."

"Who told you that?" I ask, adding bluntly, "I don't do birthdays. You know this."

"You came to *my* birthday," she counters.

"I don't do *my* birthday, I mean."

She drops the topic. We sip our drinks, letting the music from the bar fill the silence. It's been a long year. I got my promotion to floor manager, and with an adequate pay raise. I also started seeing a therapist not long after seeing Ben in the supermarket parking lot, and since then, I've not had any dreams or strange things happen. I think Jean is actually helping me. I'm even wondering if I made the right choice by not calling out to Ben when I saw him that day. I could have asked him what had happened at home after I left. Jean agrees. But it's too late now; I can't find him anymore. I've looked on Facebook, LinkedIn, Google—the lot. Zilch. He's vanished.

"What if we just go for a drink?" Sarah turns to me. "I won't tell anyone it's your birthday; it can be our secret."

"Oh god, don't say that—that's what Simon says to me."

"Yuck! Laura, that's creepy."

"Tell me about it."

"So, secret drinks?" She looks at me with her kind, innocent eyes.

"Who told you?" I ask, still undecided and buying for more time to think.

Her lips twitch, and she leans in. "Simon just did." She winks.

I stay quiet, waiting for her to elaborate.

"He wanted to get you a gift and asked me if you like gold or platinum." Pleased with herself, she continues. "I asked if he could remind me of the date." She clocks my non-smiling face and adds, "Sorry."

Far from impressed yet sufficiently touched by both Simon's snooping and Sarah's seemingly genuine desire to celebrate my birthday, I don't see an alternative but to agree. It's not actually Sarah that would push me on this matter, but I know her well enough to know how she works. This is how it would play out: she would bring it up next time we were out with Beth and Jess, and Beth would sink her teeth into it like a dog with a bone. Since I am the only one out of the four of us that is reluctant to talk about their childhood, I'm sure Beth would seize the opportunity to dig. And so I do what Jean has been asking me to do and let down my guard.

"Fine, we can go for a drink," I say.

She clinks her glass against mine. "Do you think you could sweet talk Mr. Stevenson into giving us the day off on the twenty-third—the day after? We could go out on Thursday night and not worry about work the next day."

I roll my eyes.

"Look, Laura, he is getting you a birthday present, so you're going to have to sleep with him anyway."

I shrug.

There's another long silence, which is interrupted by a group of drunken boys stumbling down Wimbledon High Street dressed in bunny outfits and shouting happy Easter, even though Easter was weeks ago. We have a few more drinks before I make up an acceptable excuse to leave.

"Feels like the start of a migraine," I say, rubbing my temples as I see her suspiciousness. "Don't think I drank enough water in the managers' meeting today."

Sarah's not buying my lie, yet she nods and tells me to get home and hydrate. By now, she is used to my sharp departures and knows that once I say I'm leaving, then I'm leaving. She follows me outside. Opening the door of the Uber, I wait for the driver to say my name and then slide in.

"I'll text when I'm home," Sarah calls through the window.

That's what I love about her—she cares, really cares, about everyone. Unfortunately, I fear she cares about lost souls: me, for instance, and her boyfriend.

My apartment greets me with a harsh bite. Closing the door, I hurry across the newly laid wood floor in the dark and slide down the window that I forgot to shut before leaving for work. I move swiftly over to the free-standing hanging rail which I salvaged—or should I say stole—from the back of a charity shop. I reach for a sweater, pulling it free from the hanger, and then slump on my sofa and drag the orange throw over the top of me. It makes me think of Mr. Clifton, who moved out last month after the rent rose fifteen percent. The raise has basically eaten all of my pay raise.

Life really does suck, I think, lying on my back in the dark. I know what's happening. I'm wallowing in self-pity, yet I can't stop it. I can feel the sadness weighing heavily on my chest as if it has a physical weight. Then the thoughts come—I take a deep breath and stand.

In the kitchen, I boil the kettle and make a cup of black coffee. It's still there—even if I don't think the thoughts, that utter sadness is still there, lurking with me like a bad shadow. I sit back on the sofa, nursing the coffee and warming my hands.

Jean tells me that my mum's illness has made me crave female acceptance, but I disagree. Is that not just a copout for all my bad behavior, a free hall pass to have controlled my sister's friends or to have put Marie in an impossible situation—not to mention how I treat Sarah, how I treat everyone like they owe me something? The thought acts like a self-fulfilling prophecy, and I reach for my phone to text Simon.

PLANS TOMORROW?

I don't wait for a reply, because I know he can't always text back immediately. I send another text.

QUICK COFFEE AT MINE?
<wink face emoji>

Surprisingly, a text comes just a few minutes later.

HOW MUCH WILL THIS
COFFEE COST ME THIS TIME?
NO MORE PROMOTIONS OPEN.
<wink face emoji>
4PM??

I reply without hesitation.

YOU'LL HAVE TO WAIT AND SEE.

X
<wink face emoji>

After rubbing my toothbrush over my teeth in a halfhearted manner, impatient with the chilly apartment, I snuggle down under my duvet and heavy top blanket. At some point between the regrets of agreeing to a birthday drink and not being able to find Ben on Facebook, I drift into another place.

Throwing the bedsheet off, I head for the bathroom. After I shower, I step out and grab a towel from over the door. The rest of the day drags on, so by the time four o'clock comes around, I actually feel excitement when I hear a knock at my door.

Simon is standing on the other side of the threshold, holding the biggest bunch of yellow roses I've ever seen and sporting a cheesy grin.

"Who's the lucky lady?" I ask, reaching for the bunch before he can answer. "Come on in. I would say the place is a mess, but then, you would need to have stuff for it to be a mess. Tea, coffee, beer—no, I don't have beer—vodka, or God's wine—meaning water?" I ask, pulling a vase from the kitchen cupboard. I don't hear a reply. "Simon?" As I turn, he is standing right behind me. It makes me jump. "Wow," I say.

He hands me a bottle of red, then plants a kiss on my forehead.

"I've got ya," he says, trying and failing to sound trendy. I smile politely. It's sweet that he's making an effort.

He takes both of our glasses and sits carefully on my white sofa. One more stain probably would go unnoticed, but I like the way he's always so respectful of my apartment. He waits for me to sit next to him and hands me my glass.

"So what's with the flowers? Feeling guilty about something?"

His reply comes slow and out of character, very much unlike his normal sharp wit that makes me laugh. "You deserve them," is all he says.

I furrow my brow. "We've not even had sex yet." Laughing over the top of my glass, I see him looking intently at me. "What, Simon? What's up with you?"

"Don't do that."

"Do what?" I say.

"That. Make yourself—make *us*—sound like it's just sex."

"It is, we are."

"You know we're not. Just be real for once."

I watch him walk to the window and look down to the street below. After resting my glass on the floor, I follow. I reach my hands around his large midriff, unable to touch my fingers together, and squeeze. His free hand rubs my right arm, and he turns to face me. His eyes look vacant.

"Simon, what's wrong?"

He kisses me, holding one side of my face with his hand like he always does, then holds me. It's tender. It is actually the thing that turns me on the most. I reach my hand up over his broad shoulders and kiss him back passionately. He places his glass on the window ledge, and still kissing me, walks me toward my bed.

I'm deliberately wearing a loose-fitting dress. I know he likes that. He's a big man, yet when he's bearing down on me, it feels gentle—controlled. I grip his arms as they hold his weight, each thrust deeper and deeper. I feel safe beneath him, wanted and safe.

It never takes long, and after, he collapses onto me, and we laugh like we normally do when I gasp for breath. I roll onto my side, up on one elbow, looking at him. He tucks my hair behind my ear, but we don't say anything. I wonder what he thinks when we do this. With my eyes I trace his clammy skin, the darkness under his eyes, and the laughter lines that are aging his pasty face. Then I wonder if his wife looks at him the way I do.

"I've gotten you something," he says.

I smile softly back.

He taps the tip of my nose with his index finger. "Wait here."

Pulling the bedsheet tight around my body, I wait while he makes his way to the sofa, where he fumbles in a coat pocket. I watch his large, naked frame walk back toward me carrying a small black box.

"You can't propose to me, Simon—you are already married," I tease.

"Open it," he says, laughing.

I move over, letting him back into bed. Inside is a delicate gold chain holding a small diamond.

I gasp. "It's beautiful."

He takes it from me. "I wanted to get you something special for your twenty-fifth birthday," he says, fastening it around my neck. "It's nearly as beautiful as you are."

I smile. "It's not my birthday yet. And you didn't have to get me anything ... Are you all right?" I ask. "You seem quiet today."

He doesn't answer immediately, and I'm about to ask again when he responds. "It's Catalina," he says quietly, so quietly I think I've heard wrong.

"Catalina? Your daughter?"

"Yes ... she's going to be two in a few months."

I nod slowly.

"I've agreed to see a marriage counselor." He drops my gaze. "I think I owe it to Catalina to at least try with her mum, you know? To make it work."

I don't say anything. My heart has started to beat a little faster.

"Laura?"

"So we're over, then?" My hand rises to the necklace. This is a goodbye gift, not a birthday present, I realize. That's why it's early. I try to fight an odd urge to cry.

"I don't want to, but—"

"It's fine," I say and smile. "Had to come to an end one day, and let's face it, we were both just using each other."

He looks hurt by my comment but hides it well. "Maybe to start, but—"

I stop him. "I get it. It's fine." It's not, but I'm never going to tell him that. "So," I say brightly, "do I still get to be teacher's pet at work? I promised Sarah I'd get us the day off after my birthday."

He smiles back, though I know it's as fake as mine. "Of course."

I reach out for a cuddle. I don't want him to see my face as it crumples, tears threatening to fall. I'm actually going to miss him. After all we have been through, I'd still not realized I had feelings for him—deeper than I let on. Or maybe it's just the fact that yet another person I've let close is leaving me. Either way, it hurts. He wraps me in his arms, and we stay there holding each other. I don't want to let go. Everything's changing.

CHAPTER 24

THEN—LAURA

Cornwall, three years ago
May

Lucy picked up and threw down pots and other gardening tools, looking for rope. I knew where the rope was and whispered directions away from the location, which worked for a while as she destroyed the wrong part of the shed in her search.

"Found it!" She finally triumphed, holding the reel of thick rope above her head like a trophy. Then she rushed back to the industrial black bin liners she found earlier, ripping one from the roll.

"Lucy, stop," I pleaded. *"Why? Oh, why?"*

"To make her see what a bad friend she is!" she cried. "It's my birthday."

I stiffened. *"Lucy?"* I said. She carried on talking to herself—or me? *"Lucy?"* I repeated louder. Nothing. I finally shouted, *"LUCY?"*

She jumped, clamping her hands over her ears and darting her head about in every direction.

She heard me. Excited, I was about to shout again when there was a noise outside, the sound of an engine in the distance and then a car door.

Marie—she's here. Quickly, I shouted, *"DON'T DO IT!"*

"Where are you?" Lucy replied to the roof of the shed.

"I'm here." Marie stood in the open doorway, looking at the unconventional meeting place. "I see you've started without me." She looked pointedly at the nearly empty wine bottle on the floor. "Lucky I brought another," she said. She stepped inside, being careful not to get any cobwebs on her clothes. "Odd place, but I suppose it's a little like old times down at the park. Do you remember? It looks like I'm playing catch-up." She laughed and cleared a space on the floor to sit.

"That's it?" Lucy's eyes narrowed down on her. "Like nothing happened?"

Marie's head tilted up. "Lucy? You all right?" She didn't seem to notice the bin liner in Lucy's hand.

"No, not really."

I screamed at the top of my lungs for Lucy to stop, but it was too late. With lighting speed, she shoved the liner down over Marie's head and torso, wrapped the rope around and around, encasing her arms and body, and then pulled it tight with a knot. Marie thrashed her head, demanding Lucy get off. All the time, I was shouting as loud as I could, but I stopped when I felt my energy weaken. After tying her feet, Lucy ripped the liner, releasing Marie's head, then quickly stepped back.

"Stay there. Don't say any fucking more; just shut up." Lucy's face was soaked by endless tears as she frantically checked her surroundings.

I wasn't sure if she was talking to me or Marie, but both Marie and I quickly complied with her demands of silence.

"Speak," Lucy said to the roof.

"What do you want me to say?" Marie muttered.

"Shh." Lucy silenced Marie with a finger. "Speak to me again?" Her voice wobbled.

I wanted to, yet I didn't. I had finally connected with Lucy, and who knew how long it would last, yet I couldn't talk to my twin. Not like this. She was drunk and had just tied up our best friend on the floor of our dad's old shed. If I spoke to her again, I'd quite possibly send her over the edge.

"Laura?" she whispered.

I didn't say a word. I considered it—I considered shouting out that Ben was a rapist and a liar, that he could kill her or someone else if he wasn't stopped, yet I didn't. This was not the way. Talking directly to my drunk twin was not the right way at all.

"Lucy?" Marie's small voice interrupted my thoughts. "I'm sorry."

She didn't reply.

"I was out of order to blow you off tonight. You're right to be angry at me. But you're scaring me right now."

Lucy got up and shoved a dirty rag into Marie's mouth.

Marie spat it to the floor. "What the fuck?" she said with venom. "Fuck. Untie me."

Lucy didn't react, but also didn't comply.

"Lucy, un-fucking-tie me—NOW."

"Shh—shut up, Marie, just shut up, will you? Jesus." Lucy paced the room. "Shit, shit, shit." She kicked the wall of the shed hard, and something fell from a shelf and smashed. "What have I done?"

There was nothing I could do. Marie needed to keep her hot head in check and talk my sister down.

"Lucy, it's me. I'm your best mate. Why are you doing this to me?"

Lucy slumped to the ground next to her.

"What's your plan? Kill me?" Silence. "I'm going to level with you, I'm a little frightened."

Lucy looked at her but still didn't say anything.

"Lucy, mate, don't do this. I'm truly sorry, I am. It was a crappy thing to do the day before your birthday; I didn't think. I was being selfish."

Lucy stood and walked outside. I followed. She paced the entrance of the shed, hands on the back of her head, muttering something about my voice being in her head. That went on for at least fifteen minutes. I didn't speak to her, not knowing how clearly she could hear me. Marie didn't move. She called out to my sister a few times, but Lucy just scowled at her before returning to her pacing.

"Who were you talking to?" Marie ventured.

Lucy returned to the shed and plunked herself down on the dirty concrete next to Marie.

"Laura," she said in the smallest voice.

The unfairness of this situation was horrific, and frustration grated at me. I had a chance to tell Lucy the truth, but if I did, I'd run the risk of making her look like a mad woman spouting harmful words. No one would believe her, and she probably wouldn't even believe herself when she sobered up. I bit my lip and just hoped this new ability didn't wear off as fast as the others of late.

Now it was Marie's turn to be silent.

"I heard Laura's voice in my head," Lucy said again.

Both girls looked at each other.

"Untie me, Lucy?" Marie requested.

She shook her head.

Marie nudged her with her shoulder. "Lucy, come on. I won't hit you, I promise. Please, I'm cold sitting on this ground."

Lucy stayed sitting next to her in silence.

What felt like another twenty or so minutes passed before my sister spoke again. "Is this what crazy is?"

Marie shrugged. "Did the voice tell you to tie me up?"

"No, I was going to do that before I heard the voice."

"Oh, thanks." She cracked a smile. "So what did the voice say?"

"My name, then 'Why?' and—" She hesitated. "'Don't do it.'"

"And you didn't want to listen to this voice? Look, Lucy, please untie me."

Lucy scrambled away. "No, I don't want to go to a mental prison." She cowered in the corner.

"What the hell, girl?" Marie looked baffled at her.

"I kidnapped you, I tied you up. And I heard voices in my head." She pulled her legs in close, tucking her head to her knees.

I felt helpless for my sister. I'd made it worse, but there was nothing I could do, so I just watched them.

"Look at me. Lucy, look at me." Marie wriggled toward her on her bottom. "Lucy Whitcombe, you are my best bloody friend. I'm not going to send you off to the loony bin. You're still grieving."

Lucy raised her head. Her bloodshot eyes made me want to cry out, but I didn't. Marie was finally getting through.

"Untie me, please?" she asked again. "Let me be there for you. I'm your best mate, Lucy, and I messed up tonight—I know that. Let me be sorry; I just want to hug you."

After another slight hesitation, Lucy reached for a pair of clippers to cut the rope. She helped Marie to her feet. Once both girls were standing, Marie pulled Lucy into a sharp embrace. The girls stood embracing for a long moment. Lucy agreed to return to Hellen and tell her about the voices, and Marie promised to instant message every day, at least every day that she had Internet connection. Both agreed to never take the other for granted again.

The car ride home was silent, and I wondered if Lucy would still be able to hear me tomorrow. I would explain it all when she had sobered. Although I couldn't touch their thoughts anymore, I did have an uncanny sense of just knowing what people thought or felt. That saddened me, for I could tell that the two people I loved so much in life were about to part forever. Too much had happened between them, and this Thailand trip was exactly what Lucy had feared—a goodbye.

★   ★   ★

May (twenty-second birthday)

"Lucy, you can't just barge in like that."

Lucy was standing in the middle of Hellen's office, still dressed in last night's clothes and smelling of last night's alcohol.

"I didn't know what else to do."

"Sit." Hellen gestured for Lucy to take a seat. "You need to call ahead. You're not my only client, and it wasn't very fair to just storm into someone else's session like that."

Lucy looked like she had changed her mind and wanted to leave, and I knew Hellen was seeing the same thing.

Her tone softened. "It's your birthday today, isn't it?"

Lucy didn't answer right away. "Yes."

"And you're feeling anxious?" Hellen examined my sister's dirty jeans, and I presumed she could smell the stale alcohol. "Where have you been?" she asked. "Your clothes look dirty."

Lucy shrugged.

"Were you out last night? Have you even been home?"

She shrugged again, and silence fell.

"I should go," Lucy finally said.

"Why?"

"It was a mistake."

"What was?"

"Coming here. It was all a mistake—the shed, the messages, the lot. Marie, everyone. Everyone leaves me in the end anyway. I'm just one big mess, and I'm crazy to think you can help."

"Shed? Message? Has Ben been messaging you again? I thought you broke up."

Hellen was so far off the mark it was unreal. I never thought she was any good, but boy, she was surpassing herself.

"No, we are—well, kind of. Oh, I don't know. It's not that.

299

It's just all too much. Too much. Life, what the hell is the point? I think I've gone crazy, Hellen." She looked up.

Either Hellen had dealt with this situation before or she had a very good poker face. "Why do you say that, Lucy?"

"Damn it! Stop with the W questions—why, what, when, who—it's what I learned as a salesperson. Open questions and all that bullshit—just help me." Lucy stood. "Tell me I'm not mad."

"It's not about being mad or crazy, Lucy. It's about talking through what's in your head, what you're feeling. You have to tell me, not me tell you."

Lucy was striding the length of the office. I felt helpless, but I dared not speak to her—she was still drunk. She'd been up all night in the garden drinking the bottle of wine Marie had left in the cab. What if I had pushed her too far by talking to her in the shed, pushed her over the edge? My thoughts pained me.

"She spoke to me—Laura," she said, stopping in front of Hellen. "And no, it wasn't just my own thoughts. It was different from that, you know"—her words were rushed—"audio in my head." She tapped her temple. "Like a radio."

Hellen's poker face was diminishing.

"You do think I'm crazy." Lucy stood abruptly.

"No, Lucy, no, I don't."

"You do, I can see it. There." She pointed in Hellen's face "I see it in your eyes; you think I've gone bloody mad." She backed toward the door ever so slowly. "Now what? Lock me up?"

Helen held up a hand to speak, but Lucy cut her off.

"It was a mistake coming here." She yanked open the door and stumbled through it, down the corridor, and down the stairs to the foyer.

Panicked, I tried to figure out the best way to help my sister. I couldn't talk to her in this state, but I was worried what she might do next. She hailed a cab, and I climbed in behind her. After she told the driver our home address, I relaxed, at least until we got there. In her room, Lucy shoved clothes, makeup, toothpaste, and tampons into a backpack and left the house again. I followed her on foot into town. She looked confused, undecided about where to go and what to do. She made her way to the Union Tavern yet didn't go in; instead, she stood opposite as if she were a tourist admiring the Tudor décor. She couldn't call Marie. Last night had put a stop to that support network. What was she doing?

She pulled her phone from a side pocket on her backpack and typed a message into the notepad application. It read:

> I have to go away for a while; I need to figure things out on my own.
> I will come back someday, but don't come looking for me. Don't know where I'll go.
> London, maybe, see the queen. I'm sorry. I really am.
> Lucy x

She cut and pasted the message, sending it to Dad, Marie, and Ben. Three people. The only three people in her life. If your heart could break when you're already dead, then mine just had. My sister felt as alone as I did, yet I knew what lay ahead for me, and I wasn't scared. But she didn't. My little sister didn't know what life lay ahead.

Turning away from the pub, she walked toward the cash point, dropping her mobile phone into the street gutter. After withdrawing just under the maximum amount, which was all she had in her account, she discarded her cards into a bin, then hailed a cab.

"Exeter St. David's to London Paddington," a guard said, looking at the train ticket Lucy held. "Yep, this is the right platform. Train's coming in now." He pointed, and she followed his finger toward the slow-moving, oncoming train.

"Thank you," she said and shoved the ticket back into her pocket.

It was as if a dark cloud blotted out the light from the sky as the train pulled into the station. A little to her left, the doors slid open. She hesitated, giving a glance back over her shoulder. No one was following her, no one stopping her from leaving. She stepped onto the train and found a seat by the window facing in the correct direction. I sat in the seat opposite her, and then I saw him—Ben. He was on the platform, looking panicked. The doors to the train closed, and I saw him move to a window and look in, then on to the next and the next. Then there was a jolt, and the train started to move. Lucy's face was buried in her hands, and she couldn't see him. He was only a window away.

Thud, thud.

"Lucy."

Her head sprang up, and she looked back at him in shock. Her hands slammed the window. "I'm sorry."

"No!" He looked at her lividly. "I'll find you!" he screamed.

"I'm sorry," she said again as the train began to move.

I had to make sure she didn't go back. She couldn't go back. I knew my dad would be devastated, but it was better than her staying and falling victim to Ben. I just needed to figure out a way to keep her safe until I could get an effective message through to her.

She didn't watch as the train sped around the side of the cliffs, and she didn't look out the window at the sea or its waves crashing against the cliff below, a beautiful sight we had both once loved so much. Neither did she notice the train passing through the tunnel that had been bored through the side of the large, rocky cliff, and she gave no screams of excitement like when we were children. Instead, she cried into her hands until she grew tired and fell asleep.

Though it hurt to see her running away from our family, our dad in particular, and from Marie, this is what I wanted, what I thought Lucy needed. Still, despair weighed heavily on my soul. Our journey had quite literally just begun, and I didn't know what to do next, how to protect or guide her. I rested in the seat next to her and watched her sleep, thinking all the time about my next move, a new plan.

Her head shook softly against the window, which was blackened by the night sky. Eyes closed, she looked peaceful. And then I felt it—stronger this time, like a vortex. I'd not had enough time. Ben knew where Lucy was going, and she didn't know he was a danger. I thought quickly, but there was no point resisting; I knew it was futile. I reached out and placed my hands on my sister's head, closing my eyes. I had to give a clear message, not too long, with just the crucial information. I'd find a way back to deliver the rest—or at least I hoped I would. Then I thought the words into my hand and hopefully into her dream.

"Wait for me—I will find you. Don't go home. Be careful of Ben."

Then it was dark.

Wait. I'll find you. Be careful. Don't go home.

CHAPTER 25

NOW–LUCY

London, present day
May

There's a knock at the door. It's Dan, Sarah's boyfriend. I tuck my white vest into my jeans and go to answer it. He's come to fix a pipe I broke yesterday after a half-assed DIY attempt at fixing my kitchen sink. I should have just asked the management company before I meddled with it, but now I can't. Instead, I called Sarah and asked to borrow her man. I'm hoping he will help me move my old sofa as well. I left out that part when I asked. In my experience, it's harder for people to say no to my face.

"Hey, Dan," I say, swinging open the door. "Thanks for coming over." He steps through, and I close it. "Tea, coffee? Gin?" I joke.

I've met Dan before, but only a few times. He's a nice enough guy, but it's a shame that he's a bit of a dick to Sarah.

"I'm good, thanks," he replies. "Last night's alcohol should see me through today."

I smile. "Glad you could come. I should never have touched it, but the drip was driving me mad."

Dan is already on the floor with his head under the sink, and I have to step away from his large legs that splay out.

"Can you fix it?"

"The problem, or what you broke?"

I tilt my head to look into the sink's cupboard. "Did I break something?"

"Only joking, princess." He slides out, making me scuttle backward. "You just loosened the wrong thing. If you have a wrench, I'll get it sorted in no time."

I blink.

"A wrench—you know, to tighten bolts?"

"Oh," I say and run into the lounge area to fetch my toolbox. "Here." I thrust the small open box at him. "Is there one in there?"

He looks inside and removes a tool. He was right, and it doesn't take long. Minutes later, I feel a little foolish. I hate being a damsel in distress, and I'm still irritated by his earlier reference that I'm a princess—I'm far from that. However, I'm also only one person, and I need help getting this old sofa out of my apartment.

"Dan," I say, "would you mind ever so much helping me lift my sofa downstairs to the bins?"

"Not that one, I hope?" He points to my new, huge, L-shaped, tanned leather sofa that Simon bought me. It was another guilt present for dumping me. I think he's still a little worried that when his daughter's birthday comes around, I'll flip out and want him back. Sad, though I *will* miss him when he actually stops fucking me next month. I asked if I would get an invite to the birthday party, but he didn't find it funny.

"No," I say, shaking my head. "This one. It's not that heavy, just awkward."

He strides toward it with confidence. "No problem. Come on, you grab that end." I comply, and we start to heave and twist it out of my apartment.

Halfway through my door, it jams. "Push it harder," I say.

He laughs on the other side of the sofa. "Any time."

I give it a tug, but it doesn't move.

"Hold on," he says. "Climb over and let me go on that side. Your door frame will get damaged doing this; I'll wriggle it out."

He holds my hand as I climb over, and our eyes lock for longer than appropriate. I look away, and he swaps places with me. He starts calling out directions.

"OK, now lift the leg as I twist," he calls. "That's it—lift, lift." With a *pop*, the sofa is free.

After dropping the old white sofa into the bin room, we make our way back up to my apartment breathless and a little sweatier than I thought. Back inside, I expect Dan to get his things and leave. Instead, he asks for my offer of gin.

"OK, so I was joking about the gin. I have vodka, though." I look at my watch: 4:46 p.m.

"It's not too early for you, is it?" he asks.

I shrug, then pour two neat glasses and hand him one.

He takes it with caution. "No chaser? Are you trying to get me drunk?"

"Are you a lightweight and can't handle your liquor?" I ask and sip on my drink. "Neck it—that is, if you can't handle the taste of good vodka." My smile is deliberately sarcastic.

Not waiting for a reply, I move to the sofa, gathering up the old orange throw and dashing it into the corner. *Out with the old and in with the new,* I think.

I turn to Dan. "Come sit."

He complies. I want to get to know him better, find out what makes him tick. If he makes a move, I'll scream and slap him, like in the movies. I'll call Sarah in floods of tears and tell her everything. She can leave him, move in here with me. The new sofa is big enough to sleep on. I'll take the sofa, and she can have my bed—I'm cool with that.

"So why didn't you go with Sarah to her parents'?" I ask.

"It's complicated."

"What is?"

"Her parents," he says. "Sarah doesn't really like going there, and she doesn't want me talking to her dad. It's madness, I tell her, but she won't listen."

"Why? What's up with her dad?"

At first, he looks reluctant to tell me, but then he gives it up anyway. "She thinks he is cheating on her mum, and she doesn't want him rubbing off on me."

"What?" I'm a little astonished.

"Told you, madness."

"Sarah," I say aloud but really to myself. "Oh, honey, and I thought I was the crazy one." I see Dan smiling. "But no smoke without fire, Danny boy—you are always out late. And if a girl suspects her man, they are normally always right." I tap his glass with mine. "Know what I mean?"

He follows it up with a wink. It's as if I can see him calculating the risk in his head: flirt back or leave before I get him to drop his pants.

"I don't know what you're alluding to there, Laura, but I assure you that I'm nothing like her father." His mouth says one thing, but his eyes say another.

"That's good because I don't like older men." If he stays, I've got him. If he leaves, then I got him wrong. I weight it in my mind. "Another?" I take his glass from his hand.

"Sure."

Got ya. I think.

Three vodkas in, and poor Dan has relaxed enough to tell me how trapped he feels with Sarah—yada, yada, yada. How in the beginning, it felt fun, yet how now that they live together, she's stopped giving him what a man needs. I down my fourth just to deal with the rest of what he has to say, then pour another from the bottle by my feet.

"Sarah talks about you a lot," he says.

"Me? What does she say? That I'm a bitch of a manager?"

He moves to get comfortable, pulling his T-shirt from the pinch of his belly. "Well, that, yes." He laughs. "But aren't you two good friends? She's arranging you a birthday bash next week."

"I don't do birthdays; it's just a drink." His reference irritates me. "And I also don't do good friends," I say and look at him from behind my glass. "We are coworkers, good coworkers—that's all." He's trying to suss me out; I can feel it. His eyes bore into me. "Sarah's a nice girl; you should hold onto her. Now me, I like a simpler life: don't get too attached to people because I don't plan on sticking around that long."

"Really?"

"Yeah, I'll probably travel in the next six months or so—don't tell Sarah, though." I wink, then I jump. "Hey!" Dan's arm has fallen around my waist. I don't move.

"So tell me about you, Laura. You're so easygoing. Why hasn't a nice man snapped you up yet?"

I shrug, then think of Simon at home with his wife. "Don't know. Tell me about you," I quickly add, deflecting. "How do you know about plumbing?"

"My father," he begins.

I listen as he tells me about his upbringing on the Isle of Man; he speaks fondly of his parents and shares how the island hosted a huge motorbike event and how he loved the sound of the engines. It's nice to listen to someone who had a fun childhood.

"I wanted to be a mechanic."

"What changed?" I genuinely want to know the answer. "Did your dad say no?" I ask, half-expecting his perfect childhood to come to an end and his father to halt his desires.

"Me," he says. "I wanted to come to London, get rich. Earn lots of money and meet a girl." He pokes me in the side, and I laugh and wriggle. Then I feel a pang of guilt for Sarah. She is my friend, yet I can feel my primal desires over and above anything.

"And I did," he continues. "I was lucky and landed an awesome job the moment I got here. I'm richer than if I'd stayed on the island, and there's a pretty girl sitting right next to me."

"Dan, are you drunk?"

He shakes his head. "Not at all." He leans in, and I feel his stubble on my cheek. "I want to stay here with you tonight," he whispers, and then his heavy frame is above me, pressing me down.

This is it. This is where I'm supposed to slap his face, call Sarah, and tell her that Dan is a creep like I'd planned. But I don't. Instead, I let his hand slip down the front of my jeans, his body trapping me under his the way Simon used to do—and I like it. I feel wanted again. Love is for other girls, weak girls. This is for me: lust, raw passion, danger. I tug at his belt buckle, eager. I want him too.

At 1 a.m., I wake to a click as the latch on my door closes. The bed is empty. I'm glad because I have to cry. Jean says I'm attracted to men like Dan because they are unattainable and temporary, meaning I don't need to commit any feeling to them. She says I think I'm using them by letting them use me. She's right. But I can't help myself—I can't stop it. I like it and want it at the time, but afterwards, I'm this pathetic, sniveling wreck.

This time, I've really screwed up. Dan is not some random guy from a bar or my boss I'm blackmailing; he's Sarah's boyfriend. And I have to tell her. The whole reason I was doing it was to test him. It just went too far.

Tears still in full flow, I kick off the covers and make my way to the kitchen. I take a glass and turn on the tap. Then I turn it off again and pour myself another vodka instead. What have I become?

★ ★ ★

May, 25th birthday

"Here, Laura, have another one—it's your birthday." Sarah thrusts a glass of wine into my hand.

Jess shouts "Cheers!" and we all repeat it.

Sarah, Jess, Beth, and I are the only ones here, as I limited how many people Sarah was allowed to invite. Why I agreed to let Sarah do this is still beyond me. I do my best to remember the last message from my sister, the exhortation to trust Sarah and be her friend. And then I feel sick. I'm living my life for Laura, and I had to go and mess it up. Laura wanted me to be friends with Sarah, not sleep with her boyfriend. I felt repulsed by myself. Our mum was right—I *am* selfish. First I hurt Marie, and now Sarah. I have to tell her, make it right. That's what Laura would do—the real Laura.

"Laura?" Beth calls. "Hey, Laura?" She taps my shoulder. "You OK there? You look like you're a million miles away. What ya thinking?"

"I'm not feeling too well," I say to the group. "I might bail early, guys."

They all protest at once. "Ah, come on." "No." "No way!"

I shake my head. "Honestly, you'll have more fun without me."

Sarah's icy stare bothers me more than usual.

"Nope, not buying that BS." Beth holds up her index finger. "You, my lovely, are going nowhere." She gives me a knowing look and says, "I know you're flat-out broke. Sarah told us."

"What?" I say.

"It's fine," she says. "We've got you, Laura. It's your birthday, and all your drinks all night are on us. Right, girls?"

They nod at me like woodpeckers, and I can't help but laugh. There's no getting out of this one, not with Beth here. She will sense something is up if I push it.

"Fine, fine." I play along. "But when I get my next paycheck, I'll buy you all a drink."

We stay in the fancy wine bar for a few more drinks. The night is going perfectly, and if I wasn't feeling so guilty about Dan, I'd really be enjoying myself. Beth is now too drunk to rile me with her sarcasms, and her inability to make sense is hilarious.

"Cheers," Sarah says, returning from the bar with a bottle of prosecco, three champagne glasses, and three cocktail umbrellas.

A small vibration distracts me. Freeing my phone from my bag I read,

HAVING FUN?

x

It's Dan. I shove the phone back into my bag and close it before picking up the freshly poured glass. "Cheers."

My phone vibrates again, and I ignore it.

She's my friend, I think, looking across the table at her. She reminds me of her—of Marie. They have the same hair. There are some differences, though. For one thing, Marie would definitely beat me black and blue if I slept with her man. Sarah, on the other hand, would crumble. And that's why I can't tell her—I need to protect her. I remove the phone from my bag again, planning to text Dan and tell him to stay away from me.

I read his second message.

I FEEL SO GUILTY.

x

SO DO I.

L

After I send my reply, I see the speech bubbles. In a moment, he's replied again.

BUT I CAN'T STOP
THINKING ABOUT YOU.
x

I put the phone away again. *That's not what I wanted to happen,* I think.

"Who's that?" Sarah shouts over the music.

I don't know what to say. Normally I'm good at thinking on my feet, but looking into the face of a friend who I'm shafting, I've got nothing in my locker.

"Is it Simon?" Her innocent words give me an out.

I nod.

"I thought it was over?"

Everyone is looking at me now, and I feel my phone vibrate again. "D day is next month." I try a smile. It feels fake.

Beth snorts a sound that resembles a laugh, and Jess pats her on the back like a child. "Getting notice on the end of a relationship?" she says. "Times are changing."

"Something like that," I say. She's right. It *is* the end of a relationship, someone else who chose another over me. My hands are sweaty, and the walls feel claustrophobic. "Just going for a smoke," I say and stand. The others try to follow me. "No," I say. "Stay here. Hold the table, or it will get snapped up with all of us gone."

Then I make my way outside. It's cold—I should have brought my jacket with me. My phone vibrates again.

LAURA, PLEASE DON'T TELL SARAH.
I DON'T WANT HER GETTING HURT.
x

I ALSO DON'T WANT YOU GETTING HURT.
I LIKE YOU, LAURA. I KNOW YOU MIGHT
NOT BELIEVE ME, BUT I'VE NEVER

CHEATED BEFORE. IT'S CRAZY, I KNOW.
BUT I REALLY LIKE YOU.
x

A guy next to me holds out a lighter. I look at him. He nods to the cigarette hanging out of my mouth.

I lean toward the flame. "Thanks." Then I turn my attention back to my phone.

IT'S WRONG.
SHOULD NEVER HAVE HAPPENED.
L

CAN I SEE YOU TONIGHT?
x

NO, I type, then delete it. Should I hear him out? If I care about her this much, I can still save her. I can blackmail him to leave her and get out her life.

MY PLACE. 2 A.M.
L

I shove the phone back in my bag. "*Damn it,*" I whisper to myself. What am I doing?

CHAPTER 26
NOW & THEN—LAURA

The Lake of Reflection

Now and then, I found myself wondering what my life would have been like. I imagined myself as a yoga teacher, working alongside Ed, or maybe in a small studio next door offering meditation. I would have bought my first apartment with Lucy, and Marie would have arranged the best parties. My first car would have been a VW Beetle, the old-fashioned kind. How many hearts would I have broken? And how many heartbreaks of my own would I have gone through before Mr. Right swept me off my feet into a life of babies and white picket fences?

Lucy would have been the best auntie, the coolest, with all the advice that I could never have given. She would have known the best bands to listen to, where all the coolest concerts were, and the best drinking advice—oh and drugs. I could never give that sort of guidance, but Lucy would have handled it like a pro. I pictured my teenaged daughter in her room getting ready to leave for Glastonbury, Wellington boots in hand. Lucy would tell her how uncool it is to give into peer pressure, followed by some inspirational spiel on how to be a strong woman. I thought about this a lot.

Over the span of two life years, I watched Lucy get close to Sarah. For me, it felt like a blink of an eye, yet two years for them saw a friendship become stronger than any other Lucy had had before. The time spent at work and then socializing bonded them tighter than she and Marie had been, even tighter than the countless lonely nights with Priya on the streets. I watched as both girls gained each other's trust as friends, and then I saw Lucy shatter it all when Sarah found out about her and Dan. I'd be lying if I said I wasn't disappointed in my sister—we all judge—but I had one thing the living world did not: perspective.

My time at the silver lake had shown me my past life—*our* past life. I remembered living on a farm of sorts somewhere hot. I felt the arid soil beneath my paws, yellow like sand yet hard like rock. I paced the wire fence protecting my master. He was a good man. He fed me well and made sure I felt safe—that is, until men on horses set our home on fire. Frightened, I escaped and hid down some kind of drainage system, an old sewer, maybe. When darkness fell, I returned.

First, I smelled *burning* paper, and then I saw the charred remains of my master's outhouse, where I was never allowed to go. His arm was heavy and lifeless when I nudged it with my snout. I did not recognize his face—it was not the same, no longer gentle and kind—and his beautiful brown skin was black with flecks of white, charred like our home. In the hot sun, without water, I did not last long.

I chose to become a human, to right the wrongs done to my master. To protect, not harm and kill. Not that I remembered this once I'd made my transition—in my mother's womb, I split. The separation from my sister was too much for my prior being, and rather than being soothed by the womb and coming to a new life peacefully, my sister, who was trapped for three hours, hung onto what she had known before: great love, greater loss, fear, and then separation. This might not have played a major factor in our lives if things had panned out differently. Nurture definitely impacts nature.

I knew I'd see my sister again, and I knew I couldn't leave the lake without her—after all, I was only half there. My other half was still in the living world. Astrier told me that even though Lucy's emotions would have to be cleared at the lake before we moved on to our next life, I didn't have to wait for her. In the meantime, I was free, and I could have gone to find Grandma Betty.

It just didn't feel right. I wanted to protect my sister, and I knew I'd always feel like that until we found my old master. When Lucy was here, we'd heal together. Then we would search the universe until we found our old master again. Some bonds can't be broken. However, Lucy had to live a full life first and gain as much positive understanding from Earth as possible. We did not need any more negativity in our soul. If Lucy could stay out of danger and reconcile with our dad before her death, then all would be right.

By then, Lucy was twenty-seven. Sarah had banished her from her life, and Lucy had left Furniture Forever and found a job working as a medical sales rep in London. I was proud of my sister. She was seeing a new therapist whom she was opening up to a lot more, and he had convinced her to take up meditation.

Lucy was not the only one opening up—I had too. I'd let Astrier show me what the silver lake really looked like. I knew I had a clear choice: stay at the lake and wait for Lucy or move on to my next destination. Astrier explained I'd not learned enough to go to the place she was. I decided to call it heaven as there was no human word for it. One day, when I had truly learned the universal truth, I would meet her there. I understood, and even if she had offered for me to go there now, I'd have said no.

Beyond the lake, colors like an aurora flashed over the black sky. Not just shades of green, though—pinks and yellows too.

Then, in the other direction from the lake, where I had once only seen black, I saw tomorrow. I could see into anyone's future by one day—the most I could view at the time since I was new to this. When I didn't want to see tomorrow, it was a field of vibrant green grass, forget-me-nots, and daisies. I'd listen to beautiful bird songs flooding the blue sky and watch copious amounts of energy radiating from the stars, which shone as brightly in the daylight as at night. When I wasn't looking into Lucy's tomorrow, I would often sit, leaning back on my hands and looking back over the silver lake. The aurora was breathtaking, with sunlight beating down on my brow. I used this time to think of some good dreams, a way to guide my sister into the next correct decision when she meditated or slept, changing her tomorrows in positive ways. I was content.

Then, one day, I finally saw it—the tomorrow I'd started to hope was never going to come.

CHAPTER 27

NOW–LUCY

London, present day
May (two years later)

"Everyone is in here," Ben says and opens the internal door to the garage.

Once we're inside, he locks it. The lights are off. Music from the house is still blaring through the walls, and then loud whoops rattle from outside, just behind a steel garage door. A round table—a poker table—is in the center of the converted garage. I am having trouble standing and am slouched on my stomach. Then I'm on the floor. Ben is kneeling beside me.

I'm watching from a bird's eye view like an out-of-body experience. A fleeting thought, wondering what I'm seeing, chips into my dream.

There's flickering from a broken light filament above us. I try to stand, my hands behind me as I rest on my palms. I try to speak.

Ben is taking a picture of me. I see myself move to stand, but he straddles me. I fall backward like a rag doll.

Ben's jeans are unzipped.

He pulls my dress strap back onto my shoulder. My eyes are shut, and I've stopped moving. I just lie there. Then he reaches for my neck, and I see my silver heart necklace. He slips his hand around my throat and lightly squeezes. I struggle and flap my arms, and he releases his grip. I stop moving. He lays his body down on top of me and uses his knee to move my legs apart. Still watching from above, he replaces one hand around my neck. Confusion seeps into my mind. What's he doing to me?

Squeals from the garden echo through the garage, and then there is a deafening crash as someone—or something—falls into the garage door. I see Ben spring to his feet and flee, leaving me alone on the hard ground.

There is a pen, black with gold writing on the side.
I wake.

Pressing the button on my espresso maker, I wait for its choking noises to finish, listening to the splatter of my caffeine hitting the tiny cup before drinking it back in two swift mouthfuls.

I really need get that down to one, I think and head for my door. Locking my apartment, I take the elevator to the lobby and exit the building. Holland Park Avenue is busy as normal. The London commute is in full swing, and I join the hustle. Entering Notting Hill Gate, I take the central line south. Due to my late start, I manage to snag a seat, so I sit back with a copy of a metro paper. The tube jostles me. The lady opposite me is reading the other side of my paper.

So off-putting, I think.

I exit onto Oxford Street and take the back road to Regent Street, where I have my first appointment of the day. I took a job as a sales rep selling medical software about eighteen months back, after working with Sarah became unbearable. What I did to her was inexcusable, and I've regretted it ever since. Jeffrey, my therapist, is helping me forgive myself. I need to do this before

Sarah can—or so Jeffrey says, not that I'm sure she ever will. Therapy with Jeffrey is going well. I think he's finally the guy to set me on the right path, and for all intents and purposes, things are good. My life goals are to own my own house and be friends with Sarah again before I turn thirty—just three more years.

However, I just can't shirk last night's dream. It was odd. Why was I looking down on myself? My dreams are normally from my own eyes, not like a movie. And I know it was a dream about my twentieth birthday because I was wearing my necklace, and I'm sure I was in Marie's garage. The poker table, the music, my dress—it had to have been. But I never slept with Ben that night.

As I get close to my first appointment, I make a mental note to talk through this dream with Jeffrey when I see him in two days. We meet the same time each week: Wednesday at two o'clock. I have a lot of dreams, and Jeffrey has shown me that my dreams are not messages from my dead sister but rather my subconscious trying to make sense of my own fears and feelings. I enjoy interpreting the strange ones with him, though one about rape and my twentieth will be hard.

I think Jeffrey will tell me it's mixed emotions. You see, Darren has appealed his sentence according to the Looe online paper that I still read now and then, I still can't find Ben anywhere on social media, and my twenty-seventh birthday is tomorrow. Yes, I'm pretty sure I've figured out what this dream means. I just need to get through the next few days. I'm confident my emotions will settle down then, at least until next year. Still, the eerie feeling lingers. Raising my finger, I press the white plastic button on my appointment's intercom and wait for a reply.

My appointments take me from Regent Street to Oxford Circus, Kings Cross, and then, inconveniently, back in the direction I'd come from to Covent Garden. To add insult to injury, my final appointment is all the way over on the other side of town in Borough Market.

Stepping out of the London Bridge underground, I smell the rain before I feel it, and I instantly regret not picking up the umbrella I walked past on the way out my door this morning. I was running late, though, and needed to make my first client meeting on time if I wanted to get the contract.

I walk quickly, watching the pavement morph from dry to wet with each step, large drops increasing in speed. I duck into the London Bridge station for cover and to buy an umbrella. Inside, I navigate down to the lower level of the station where the shops are. I find a shop with small blue and pink umbrellas outside. Not having a lot of time, I grab a blue one and pay at the till.

As the young girl rings up my purchase, I get an email. It's my last client—they cancelled.

"Wait," I say to the girl. I check my phone to make doubly sure and then explain, "I won't need that now, sorry."

The girl looks slightly annoyed, but there's no need for a hideous blue umbrella if I'm getting right back on the underground.

Understanding that this is the nature of my business does not negate how annoying it is that I am on the other side of London during rush hour, now for no reason. With this in mind, I head toward the Shard. One drink won't hurt, and what's the point in rushing home to nobody?

I arrive at the Shard a little wet from the short dash I had to make from the station to here. I take the elevator up to the thirty-first floor and walk confidently into Aqua, a prestigious and sufficiently classy establishment where I often take clients. That's mainly because I can expense the ridiculous price of champagne, which I've quickly become accustomed to given the amount of entertaining I'm allowed to do to win business. I find a seat at the bar, dumping my coat and bag onto the tall chair next to mine.

The bar is fairly empty. However, given the fact that it is six p.m. on a Monday and the bar has just opened, this is hardly surprising. I see Nathan on the other side of the bar. His back is to me, yet I know it's him with his sharp white shirt and smooth black waistcoat making him look adorable as always. I'm glad he's working tonight; I need a friendly face. He is about the closest person to a friend that I have right now, and I know this will weigh heavily on my heart when I'm sitting on the tube home, but for now, I'm pleased.

He turns, and my eye catches his. Without hesitation, he makes for me. "Laura, how the devil are you? Meeting a client?" He leans in, and we air kiss each other's cheeks. He makes a *mwah* sound with each of his.

I can't help but giggle—he has that effect on me. "My client canceled," I explain, "so I thought, why not?"

"'Why not' indeed, and I'm glad you did." He glances over his shoulder to make sure no one is listening. "I went on that date," he says, looking at me with wide eyes as he waits for my reaction.

"Nathan, that's great." I'm genuinely pleased for him. "And was he really a rich oil tycoon like we guessed?"

"Sadly not, my love. Now, don't laugh or judge, because I like this one, OK?"

I nod.

"He's a broker."

"Like a stock broker?" I ask.

"A boat broker!"

I tip my chin, remembering the night I saw him chatting to Nathan. "That would explain the shoes then," I say and laugh.

"Stop it—they were moccasins!"

"Looked like decking shoes to me."

Nathan raises one eyebrow. "Dom Pérignon?"

"God, no—I'm paying. A glass of Veuve will do."

"Veuve Clicquot coming up, madam."

I watch Nathan glide about his bar effortlessly, returning with a chilled glass and pouring my champagne in front of me.

"One glass of bubbly," he says, placing the flute on a napkin and sliding it over. "So other than the shoes, do you approve?"

"Of course," I say in mock horror. "The man was sex on bloody legs."

There's no hiding Nathan's delight in my approval. We're distracted by a blonde sitting down on the other corner of the square bar with a man who is extremely pleasing to the eye, and both Nathan and I grin.

"I'll be right back," he says and moves to take the couple's order.

Sipping my drink and watching Nathan work his friendly magic, I find myself wondering if he is this friendly with other people or just me. As my sips get larger and I feel that warm fuzzy feeling, I consider asking him out—as friends. It's not the first time I've had this thought, nor is it the first time I've talked myself out of it. What if he *is* as friendly with everyone, part of his job? I imagine what his pity face would look like as he gave me some excuse not to go out with me. The rejection is too much to bear. Anyway, it would only be a matter of time before I ruined it, sold him out for a personal gain of some ilk.

Maybe next time, I conclude again as he returns to me.

"Another?" He picks up my empty glass.

I smile.

When he returns, I ask if he thinks the couple is together. Is she paid for or a business meeting? This time, we both agree it's a business meeting.

"I wish my clients looked like him," I say, looking over at the man wishfully.

"Now that would be dangerous—you'd be too busy kissing all the time to get any work done." He laughs and moves on to serve other customers.

The bar is filling up, and I agree with myself to have one more glass after this and then leave.

There's movement next to me. "Is this seat taken?" The voice is oddly familiar.

I reach for my bag and coat. "No," I say, clearing the chair of my belongings. I sneak a glance and immediately freeze.

"Lucy?" he says.

"Ben?"

"Wow." He takes a step back to look at me. "Look at you. The girl who jilted me, in the flesh."

I'm lost for words. All kinds of thoughts rush into my head, and I hone in on Jeffery's advice. Ben is just an ex-boyfriend. The words I thought I heard Laura speak to me were fears and emotions—just dreams, I remind myself.

I try again to speak. "Ben!"

"Yes, I think we have established that." He gives a little laugh and edges onto the chair next to me.

Seeing him has thrown me, and fragmented images from last night's dream pinch in my mind. He looks different. I know the last time I saw him was in the rain, also in a state of sheer panic, but he's changed so much from what I remember. His gaunt face with its sharp chiseled features has plumped and filled out. He must have gained at least fifty pounds—forty in muscle alone by the looks of it. He hangs his suit jacket off the back of the chair and rolls his shirt sleeves halfway up his forearms.

"What are you doing here?" I ask.

"I think I should be asking you that. Spoken to your dad recently?"

"Why? Is he OK?" Suddenly, panic takes over. I move to stand.

"He's fine; sit down."

Speechless, I just stare at him. It's Ben, right here in front of me. For so long, I've had him in my head as some kind of demon, someone who I knew—loved, even—but a person I left behind, and he had remained left behind because of my sister's words. I shake the notion off. My sister is not real; she's dead. I sit.

"So you really haven't been home since?" he asks. "Not even called?"

I shake my head just slightly and whisper, "No."

"Shit. What's it been, four—no, five years or something?"

"Something like that," I say.

"And what can I get you to drink, sir?" Nathan interjects.

Nathan is looking at me, his eyes searching mine to see if I'm OK. I smile and nod.

"I'll take a large scotch, and a glass of champagne for the lady."

"Any particular scotch, sir?" Nathan asks. "May I suggest the Dalmore Cigar Malt Reserve?" He smiles back at Ben with his best smarmy zest.

"Go on, then, why not?"

Nathan nods in approval. "And for the lady?"

"Moet?" Ben glances over, and I nod.

Nathan looks at me just briefly. I know what he's thinking—he knows me well enough by now. I'm always saying how overrated Moet is and that I don't care much for it, yet if truth be told, it's just an act—I'll gladly drink anything. He might also be thinking that I'm being chatted up by a guy I don't particularly like, and I'm not sure if he is right or wrong at the moment. I take a large gulp of my drink while Ben is distracted with ordering. I remind myself that Laura is gone and Ben is just an ex-boyfriend.

Ben turns his attention back to me again. "So all this time you really were visiting the Queen in London."

I remember the text I sent so long ago. "Something like that. And you? What brings you here?"

"Oh, no." Moving his chair to face me, he says, "You're not getting out of it that easy."

"Out of what?" I ask.

"Lucy, you just left. One text and *boom*, you vanished. Your dad, your poor dad."

"Stop," I snap.

"OK. But Lucy, we were all really worried about you. Your dad still is." He runs his hand through his hair, which is slicked to one side, just like he used to. It's Ben, all right. That little hand action takes me back in time, and I feel my stomach twist.

"I had to get away," I tell him. "It was kinder to him. To everyone."

"I'm not sure your dad saw it like that, and I know I didn't."

I down the last part of my champagne. "Just drop it, Ben. I don't need you telling me that."

He holds up a hand in self-defense. "It's all good; don't attack," he says. "I'm glad you're alive and OK. Look, it's nice bumping into you. I can't believe it's really you." He leans back as if to get a better look. "Wow. So much time has passed. Tell me, what have you been up to?" He looks about the bar. "Obviously time's been good to you, drinking in a swish place like this. I'm just here for work, not on my money—I can't afford this joint." He stops. "Oh, wait, you're not waiting for someone, are you? A date?" He looks about awkwardly.

His reaction makes me laugh. "No, I just finished work."

"One Dalmore, and Moet for the lady." Nathan screws up his nose without Ben seeing. "Can I get you anything else?"

"No, thank you." Ben says.

Nathan hesitates but then moves away painfully slowly.

"He's a bit odd, that one," Ben gestures with his eyes at Nathan, and I smile.

Maybe fate is working after all, I think. Only last week, Jeffery and I were working on letting go of the resentment that I hold for people. Perhaps Ben can shed some light on what happened once I left and give me the answers I need to move on, to let go—forgive and be forgiven. If Ben can forgive me, then maybe I can even go home.

I ask how long he has been in London, not giving away that I saw him once in Croydon.

"A few years now," he says. "I was in South London for a while—"

"Where?" I ask. "What part?"

"Everywhere. Came to Brixton, and when I couldn't afford the rent, I moved out further. Clapham, then Croydon—all over

South London. And you?"

"South London too. But why? I mean, why did you leave Cornwall?"

Sipping his drink, he gestures for me to do the same. "To find you."

I take a large sip.

"We waited for you to come home—'we' being your dad, me, and Marie. The police wouldn't look for you because you sent a text, so you weren't a missing person. Marie canceled her Thailand trip and came to London with your dad and me—"

"What?" I placed my glass down. "My dad? You all came looking for me? And Marie didn't go traveling?" I don't mention that I saw pictures on her Facebook page of Thailand.

"She went the following year," Ben says. "She lives in Oz now, down under, but yes, we all looked for you, even Marie's guy at the time—Dylan. They broke up not long after that."

"Because of me?"

"Kind of, but they wouldn't have lasted anyway. He was way too homely for Marie. She's engaged to some surfer type; the wedding is next month in Perth."

"And my dad?"

Ben drops eye contact with me.

"Ben, my dad?" I repeat, then add as an afterthought, "and my mum?"

"He took it bad. Blamed your mum—still does, probably. I wouldn't know. I've been gone so long now."

"How long?" I ask.

He drops eye contact again. "Just over four years, nearly five."

"Why?" I knew Ben had been in South London and even suspected it had been for me, but hearing him say it—I had never prepared for that emotion.

As Ben continued the story of how he took a job as a laborer on a building site so that he could keep looking for me, I felt guilty. I had no clue they had all searched for me like that.

"But how did you know I was in South London?" I interjected.

"We didn't. I worked out what train you took, and we looked in and around Paddington. It was work that took me south of the river."

"And you don't know anything about my dad?"

"I message Marie now and then over Facebook, and she told me last week that—" He hesitates.

"What? Ben, what?"

"He's getting back with your mum."

I roll my eyes. "Of course," I say. "I thought you said he blamed her for my leaving?"

He shrugs. "I don't know. But Lucy, don't be hard on him—you're the one that left, not him."

Hanging my head, I say, "I know."

"Another?" He nods at my glass and waves to Nathan without waiting for a reply.

I'm over my cut-off point. I should leave like I agreed with myself—I'm trying to put boundaries on my drinking. But this is different. It's Ben, my real past, sitting right in front of me here and now—I can't just leave.

"Same again?" Nathan directs the question at me.

Ben answers, "Yes."

I raise my eyebrows, keeping up my pretense. After all, I am Laura to Nathan.

"Excuse me for a second," Ben says to me. "I just need to make a call. My PA was trying to upgrade my room here. I need to see if she has managed to do it or not."

"Here? At the Shard?" I blink and can feel disbelief on my face.

His face wrinkles into a familiar joy, and I see the smile I used to love so much. "Yes, here. I'm not a laborer anymore. I work for Royal Dutch."

I'm silent, trying to process what he is saying.

"Shell? You know—oil, gas, petrol?"

"Doing what?" I ask.

"Sorry, hold on." He looks at his phone, presumably at an email or text. "Damn it." He sighs. "No upgrades," he says, putting his phone on the bar and picking up his glass. "Cheers."

"Cheers," I say and touch his glass with mine. "So what is it you do, exactly?" I'm asking because it's difficult to think of Ben as a high-flying executive type. That was always my dream; he never cared much for the idea of a career. Maybe my leaving was for the best.

"Ah, just sales stuff," he says. "I travel a lot. But enough about me—I want to know about you. I can't believe I found you when I wasn't even looking. All this time, and you were right under my nose."

Something in the way he looks at me makes me feel like he still has feelings for me. His eyes are kind, searching for something—a second chance, maybe. I can't help but gaze back. I know that could never be now, and I don't know what story to make up, what story would be good enough to explain the last five years. I consider slipping off to the toilets and making a run for it.

I'd lose Nathan, I randomly think. I could never come back if I run.

"I'm going to use the ladies' room," I say to buy time. "Excuse me for a second."

"Not doing a runner on me, are you?" He laughs.

Oh, the irony, I think. I leave my coat and take my bag. "Be right back," I say.

I sit on the lid of the toilet with my head in my hands and think. Do I really want to run? Anything I tell him I'd have to remember somehow. Maybe I can just leave out details and keep it vague—very vague. I'm drunk, or getting there. I can feel the lightness that champagne gives me. I stand, deciding I'm going to run, and then sit again. I don't want to. I stand again, this time steadying myself as a rush of lightheadedness hits me. When it passes, I head back to the bar.

"You're back?" Ben smiles.

"I don't want to talk about where I've been or what I'm doing," I tell him, my words firm.

"OK." He nods, but his mouth curls at the corners. "We don't have to talk," he says and winks seductively.

Is he suggesting what I think he is? "Absolutely not!" I don't hide my astonishment.

"Joke—it's a joke. Chill, girl." I can't help but think he feels slightly injured by my rejection. "Drink up," he says. "We can talk about me, or even the price of eggs if you wish." He nudges my drink. "It's just nice being with you again, that's all."

I'm about to reach for my glass when a smash from the table behind us distracts us. A couple is on their feet, and the man is dabbing at the woman's skirt with a white cotton napkin. She snatches the napkin, clearly not impressed. I glance to my left in time to see Nathan there. He winks and swaps my glass. I smile, and he blows me a kiss just before Ben turns back.

Thank goodness. I wouldn't want to offend Ben.

"Well, that was a bit of light entertainment," Ben says, reaching over to pick up my glass and hand it to me. "Now, where were we? Oh, yes—here's to saying nothing." He gestures for me to drink. "Cheers."

"Cheers" I say and swig a large mouthful of Veuve Clicquot. I've never actually compared Veuve and Moet side by side before, but I can definitely taste the difference now. I smile back at Ben, who looks pleased. I take another large gulp and watch his grin grow wider still.

"Easy, tiger." He laughs.

I replace the glass and feel myself sway.

"You OK?" he asks.

"Yes, just a bit lightheaded. I've not eaten yet."

"I've got an idea—let's get room service. No funny business." He leans back in jest. "You have to see this room. It's just their standard suite, and it's still mind-blowing."

I look over at Nathan, who's serving on the other side of the bar.

"Lucy," Ben says, calling my attention back to himself, "I promise. No funny business. You were like my best friend, and I just want to spend time with you. Dinner, that's all. No need to tell me anything you don't want to. I fly out to France tomorrow."

"France?" I ask, "OK, well, how about dinner and you can tell me all about your life? It sounds way more interesting than mine."

"Deal," he says. "Now drink the rest. No waste."

"No, it's fine," I say. "I'll leave it."

"Lucy Whitcombe, are you leaving drink in the glass?"

I nod.

"OK, fine. Just one more sip, then, for old times. For me."

"Are you trying to get me drunk, Ben?" I take one last small sip and look for Nathan, but he's not behind the bar. I pick up my jacket and follow Ben.

In the elevator, we don't talk. Champagne has that effect on me nowadays, and after drinking nearly four glasses without eating, I'm lucky to be this coherent. Since quitting the vodka and limiting myself to one glass with dinner at night, my tolerance for alcohol has somewhat lessened.

Ben is looking at me, I can feel it. I, on the other hand, am focusing my gaze on the marble floor. The elevator is still rising.

"How are you feeling?" he asks.

I don't answer but smile instead.

"I'll fix you some water once we are in the room."

"And the fastest burger they can cook," I mumble as my stomach acids spit. *God, I'm hungry*, I think.

The lights come on as he pushes open the door, and he gestures for me to step in first. The carpet is soft, and I instantly want to remove my shoes and feel my toes squish into its fibers. It's blue, sky blue. Floor to ceiling windows engulf my sight, and the city lights welcome me. I notice four huge building in particular. One I know is the Gherkin, and I can't remember the name of the other. It's the newest out of them all—I think it looks like an old mobile phone or walkie talkie.

I turn. "Wow, Ben. Bloody wow."

He looks slightly confused, but I'm in awe of this room. He's probably in shock that I'm here. I bounce on the bed, making small circles with my hand. The sheets are so soft. There's a dark blue ottoman at the foot of the bed, a couch opposite, and a cute desk with an executive leather chair looking out over the city. I stand to move toward it, then fall back again.

Buzzed, I think. I try again. I stand, and then Ben is right in front of me. He's looking me dead in the eye, and then he reaches out his hand and places it softly on my left breast. Astonishment washes over me.

Wham. Wham. I slap his hand off, then his face. I'm about to shout, but there's no time for words before he slaps me back—hard. I fall to the side, cracking my head on the bedside table.

It's black.

I see Ben pull my dress strap back onto my shoulder. Am I dreaming? My eyes are shut, so I just lie there. I'm having the same dream as last night, but it feels different. He reaches for my neck, and I see it—*I see it!* My silver heart necklace. I move closer. I can't be dreaming because I'm thinking, making responsive decisions. Bending, I look even closer. That's not my necklace—I have the right side of the heart, and this is the left. I jump back. I see her face—I see my sister's face. I'm not in my dream, I realize. This is Laura—this is what happened to her. It wasn't Darren, but rather Ben—Ben did it, Ben!

"Laura?" I can't help but shout out.

He slips his hand around her throat and squeezes.

"Stop it—get off her."

It's black.

We're at the party, in Marie's kitchen. I—Lucy—am playing beer pong, and Ben is standing by the door watching me. I see Laura by the sink. My—her—back is to the door. She is swapping out her vodka for soda. Ben is watching her.

My thoughts are confusing, yet I feel their potency.

It's black.

I'm in a beer garden, or a smoking area, maybe. Everyone is dressed up nice, and I hear the dull thud of music from the wall next to us. Ben and a girl I don't know are sitting at a table. Ben drops his lighter, and the girl bends to retrieve it for him. I see Ben, quick as lightning, empty some kind of powder into her drink.

It's black.

We're in an alleyway. The girl is propped up behind a dumpster, not moving. I feel bilious. I know what's happening now. His hand slips up her skirt. Then he puts her hand down her own panties. He quickly snaps a few pictures on his phone and then moves back to her.

It's black.

Ben reaches up and grips her throat the way I'd seen before, the way he did to my sister.

It's black.

There is a pen. It's fancy, black with two gold bands. There's writing, but I can't make out what it says. The image enlarges. It's the name of the hotel—Shangri-La.

It's black.

I'm awake. I'm in the hotel room. My eyes are closed, and I keep them shut tight. I tell myself not to shake, but it's so hard. The man I once loved and thought I knew had raped and ultimately killed my sister. Frozen by this thought, I lie still. I need to think fast. By the feel of things, Ben has moved me over to the sofa. I'm fully exposed and can feel the room's air-conditioning ever so lightly against my body. One of my hands rests on my breast and the other over my private part below. I hear the recognizable click of a camera phone followed by another, and another.

He moves my hand again. It must feel different—I feel his hesitation. I groan, hoping I can fool him. I get it now; I get what my sister is showing me. When I went to the toilet, he must have dropped something into my drink. He doesn't know that Nathan swapped them out, and I only took a very small sip before that. That explains why I felt giddy but not enough to render me defenseless.

There's a *crack* and what sounds like breaking glass. My eyes spring open—I can't help it. Ben is looking over his shoulder in the direction of the noise. The small piece of decorative mirror that traces above the bed has smashed.

Laura? My senses heightened, I refuse to question myself any longer. Laura is in this room with me. She has shown me what Ben did, what he is capable of. Now I just hope she can show me how to get out of here.

I snap my eyes shut.

The sound of his belt being unbuckled stiffens me, and I remind myself to relax. If he feels that I'm tense, he will know I'm not under the influence of his drug, presumably Rohypnol. That's what was found in Laura's system. I try to think, and quickly. I remember seeing a lamp at the end of the sofa when I looked around the room, but when I opened my eyes, it wasn't at the end of by my feet, which means it must be behind my head.

I hear Ben's zipper, and feel him pushing my legs open with one hand. I groan and wriggle like the girl in the alley did.

He's easing my legs apart, and I try so desperately to lie still, but impulse makes me wriggle up the sofa into a slouched seated position. Ben grabs my face with one hand and squeezes my cheeks slightly. My eyes are now open.

"So long," he says into my face. Our eyes lock. "I've waited so long for you. You left me."

"I didn't." My words are hard to hear through my fear. My mind races as I try to think about my next step. I need to stay calm and not give in to the utter terror that is looming deep within. His fingers squeeze the skin of my cheeks closer together.

"You did. You all do in the end." He's leering over me, one knee on the sofa. "I thought you were different. I thought you weren't like the other one."

"Like Laura?" I struggle. "Fuck you."

His grip tightens, and I squeal in pain.

"I never meant to hurt her," he says. "Practice—all I wanted to do was practice for you. God, I was an idiot for loving you. You never loved me the way I loved you." He hesitates, his gaze intense as if boring into my soul. "I wanted our first time to be right, gentle. I needed to practice. Don't you see? I had to do it—for you."

"Liar." I yank my head to the side, freeing my face. "You didn't love me—how could you do that? She was my sister."

He presses his forehead to mine. "Oh, Lucy, if only you could know how much you meant to me." His breath is laced with whisky, and the stench snakes into my nostrils. "Did you think I was just going to let you go?" He carries on without letting me answer.

"The day you left, I followed you. It took me five years to find you. I didn't rush; you weren't going anywhere. I took my time to plan out how—when and where. Your new job was a godsend for me, and this hotel—oh, you like coming here, don't you? Is it for that dick behind the bar? Maybe I'll teach him a lesson too. But right now, Lucy"—he squeezes my face—"I'm going to have you and then end you. I've been fighting it for so, so long. At first, I was trying to change. I wanted to change for you, be the man you wanted. But then I saw my error. I'm not the man you need—you're the woman *I* need. You have to be my first."

Moving his hand to my neck, he squeezes. I cough and splutter before he lets off his grip again. "You are my first kill. Don't you see? It's always been you, Lucy." He's tenderly stroking my face with the back of his fingers—the entire situation is ludicrous.

I can't move. I just stare at him, letting his words set in. He has planned this whole night—the room, the chance meeting—everything. And my death? He is actually going to kill me. I feel a single tear fall.

He keeps one hand gripping my cheeks, and his other moves to position himself to enter me. When he shifts back slightly, I see my moment. With my right hand, I reach for the lamp, grasp it, and then—*slam*. He falls off balance, and I pull myself to my feet and run. I don't make it far before his hand grabs for my waist. I reach for the office desk—I won't let him drag me to the floor.

This girl is not going down as easy as the others, I tell myself. He tries to bend me over the desk, but I turn. I freeze momentarily. I'm naked, and my fighting spirit is hindered as the realization sets in. How can I fight him off? He's too strong. Blood scales the side of his face, and I scream. He brings the back of his hand across my face so hard I think my neck might break. With one hand over my mouth, he steps inside my parted legs. I turn my head.

"Look at me," he says, gently moving my face back to look at his.

I close my eyes and tug my head away again.

"Don't look, then. Just feel me. Feel us together again, Lucy."

Like a vortex, emotions and thoughts pass me by as if my whole life is flashing before my eyes. Is this it? Is this how I die, being raped and strangled by my childhood ex-love? No—no it's not, I try to convince myself. I try to clamp my legs shut, but it's no good. He's too strong, but I'm managing to keep him out for now. Then I see it: the pen, black with two gold bands, and the Shangri-La written on the side. My hand is stretched as far as it will go, yet I still can't reach. Ben is getting more frustrated, and his grip is tightening around my windpipe. I cough and splutter again. Is this it?

"Oh, please, no!" I can't help but cry out like a wounded animal.

I squeeze my eyes shut as I feel him push into me, and tears fall. I can't believe this is happening. Then, ordering myself to fight, I try one last time to reach for the pen.

"Help me, Laura, help me," I splutter from behind Ben's hand.

I hear an ear-piercing scratch like nails on a chalkboard but louder—so much louder. Ben's head jolts up, his eyes wide with astonishment. I glance back at the pen, and as if by magic—although I know differently—it flies into my grip. Instantly, my hand grasps the pen as hard as I've ever held anything before. Then, with all my strength, I drive it into the side of Ben's neck.

He stumbles, first back, and then to one side and the other. His hand is pressed against his neck, but blood is firing out in short, sharp bursts from between his fingers. I smell it. It's … it's like metal, with a nasty metallic stench. I realize that some of it hit me when he stumbled. He's staring at me in disbelief as he falls to his knees. Blood, so much blood. It's all over me.

I scream, "Help, help!"

Running to the door, I yank at the handle. I don't care that I have no clothes on; I just need to get out. The door opens, and I glance back. I see him face down in a pool of his own blood.

"Oh my god, are you all right?" asks a woman's voice, muffled.

I feel her hands on my shoulders, but I can't move. Then I hear a man's voice, and in a moment, something—a coat, maybe?—is around my shoulders. I can't stop looking back into the room—not at Ben, though. It's the window. The window of the Shard is cracked from top to bottom, though even that is not what I'm looking at. It's Laura, her face. In the reflection of the window, with the glittering city lights as a backdrop, I see my sister. I blink, and the image vanishes.

I hear the man's voice again. "Quickly, come with us."

Riveted to the spot, however, I keep staring at the window, hesitant to leave. My sister's apparition is gone, and I finally glance down. Ben isn't moving, and there's more blood than I thought. It's not like in the movies. It's everywhere—on the ceiling, up the wall, and with a smell that permeates the room. I stumble off balance, and the hands on my shoulder stabilize me.

Slowly, I'm guided out of the doorway, and I let it close behind me on Ben, my sister, and the realization that I was right for all these years. Laura had been telling me—warning me—that Ben was her rapist. I'd been right about her presence all along. Is this what she stayed for all this time, to protect me? And what about now? Is this it?

Will I ever hear or see my sister again?

NOW–LAURA

Tidy endings don't always happen in life, nor are all endings fair.

What about my sister? She did what she did best and retreated into herself like a scared dog, ready to die, waiting for her owner to wake. Sometimes, we just can't let go of the past, even if we don't remember it. Some events are so painful they are ingrained into your very soul. Still, I know she will do the right thing eventually.

In the end, I stopped visiting Lucy in her dreams, as my messages only confused her. She had to work out life for herself. She knew where I was; she just didn't realize it yet. I knew this the first time I felt her profound love for the sun. On an early morning walk to the coffee shop, she stopped dead in her tracks, looked up, breathed in, and then spontaneously burst out laughing. Now, with each deep breath she takes, she feels me shining down on her, just a thought away, waiting by her side.

You see, I too still have lessons to learn before I'm whole. Staying by the lake would not have helped me or my sister, so I chose my next destiny. Of course, it's the sun—Earth's energy. I am happy here, waiting for her to come, to be back as one, and then to find our master. You might think a twin's love runs deep, but never underestimate the love of a dog for his master, especially if that dog's next life is one of twin siblings—double the love.

One day, Lucy will reach her own silver lake, see all her mistakes, and learn from them as I learned from mine. Then we will go on to be one again and reconnect with the one who was taken from us so brutally.

Beautiful, you may think, yet selfish. What of our family? Did they not deserve the same love?

Yes.

If I was not part of Lucy, we would have failed, but Lucy was—is—me and still had her life to live. I had every confidence in her ability to learn that lesson, figure out how to forgive our mum, and feel how deep our dad's love was for us. You see, our dad was like us, the dog, and we were his master, ripped from him too soon. He needed to mend, to be at peace with my death. Otherwise, he, like Lucy and I, would be chasing the universe looking for his master for one last goodbye, one last "I love you."

We all make profound connections in life, and eventually, those connections tighten and integrate until everything feels everything, and everyone knows everyone, loves everyone. So ask questions and learn lessons—both the happiest and the testing ones. Grow and connect, love your neighbor like they are you.

Why? Because they have love to give, and you have love to return. And your love might just teach them, maybe not in this life, but another. It's simple, really—we just need to learn to love unselfishly.

NOW–LUCY

No one is at the bedsit—no one I know, anyway. Not Priya, not Adewale, and even Sadiq has gone. I had to come back to see where it all started and say a proper goodbye because now is the time to move on with my life.

Finding my way back along the main road, I stand opposite a boutique sandwich shop where the off-licence shop once stood. I feel sad that Sadiq has actually sold the place, and I wonder where he is and what he's doing now. A feeling of disquiet sits within me. I see people coming and going, unaware of the memories I hold. They are good memories, memories of friendship. True friendship. Each person taught me a lesson I'll never forget—each person I'll never see again but will remember always.

Before I turn to leave, I send out a wish to the universe to look out for them all. I'm not going to look for them again; that part of my life has passed. Lucy has passed, and her friends gone. I am Laura.

I didn't return to Cornwall. Life isn't that simple, and my life is not what I left behind. How can I go home as Laura? My dad wouldn't understand; no one would. I don't even understand it myself. And Darren? Well, I try not to think about it. He's out of prison, that's all I can tell you. I often consider calling the police, telling them the whole truth. Maybe I will one day, but today is not that day.

After the incident at the Shard, I told the police the truth that Ben tried to rape me, and I was found to have acted in self-defense. The champagne glass that Nathan swapped out had not yet been washed and was found to have the date rape drug Rohypnol on it, confirming my story.

The press was more interested in how one of the Shard's windows had cracked than in the man found murdered in the room, so my story never hit the news in Cornwall. There were no names or details, just a vague mention that a man was found dead. The man and woman who found me were on vacation from China and leaving the next day, which meant the press had little to no information about what happened, so the murder story was buried under information about the window and speculations about how any impact from inside the room could have shattered a window in such a magnificent structure, arguably London's most famous skyscraper.

I'm meeting Sarah for coffee tomorrow. She has no idea what happened at the Shard or what's happened to me over the last two years, and I never plan on telling her—all I know is that I need her back in my life. I can't lose her as well.

I know Laura is gone from this world. I mean truly gone, yet I also feel that we are still somehow connected. I feel her, and more so when I'm outside on a really sunny day. I plan to mend my relationship with Sarah. Maybe then I'll be able to figure out what to do next since Laura has stopped connecting with me. I haven't been back to see Jeffery, or any other therapist for that matter—they know nothing of what I do. It's too confusing.

Was my sister really there? Could I have really made it all up out of guilt? I hope Laura will come back for me and tell me what to do next—I just don't know. What I do know is that I'm alone.

Recently, I've been thinking of my dad. I even thought about sending a letter to say I'm OK and safe. I wrote it, scribbling down how I felt and why I left. I wrote that I missed him, even missed Mum sometimes. I wrote about Laura and what had happened, and about Ben and the hotel room. Then, standing over my sink, I held a lighter beneath the paper and watched it burn.

I will go back one day. I know going home is the right thing to do, both to clear Darren's name and to mend—or at least try to mend—our family. Most nights, I lie in bed fighting an overwhelming desire to just go to London Paddington and catch a train home.

I still can't do it. It's as if I'm searching for something, for someone. I can't help but feel that someday, I'll finally know whom.

The End